QUEER LEGENDS
QUEER WOLF

To Kat,

With Love.

x

Forthcoming at Q̲ueered̲F̲iction̲

Queer Dimensions (SF Anthology)
Blood Fruit (Horror Anthology)

Q̲ueer L̲egends S̲eries

Queer Wolf

Visit www.queeredfiction.com *for further titles in the* Q̲ueer L̲egends *Urban Fantasty series.*

QUEER LEGENDS
QUEER wOlf

Edited by JAMES EM RASMUSSEN

RJ Bradshaw * Naomi Clark
Charlie Cochrane * Laramie Dean
Moondancer Drake * Ginn Hale
Erica Hildebrand * Michael Itig
Lucas Johnson * Andi Lee
Charles Long * Stephen Osborne
Robert Saldarini * Quinn Smythwood
Jerome Stueart * Anel Viz
Cari Z

QueeredFiction, Durban

This Book Is A Work Of Fiction.

Published by QUEEREDFICTION ©2009

QUEER WOLF
Night Swimming ©RJ Bradshaw; Wolf Strap ©Naomi Clark; Wolves of the West ©Charlie Cochrane; Moon Sing ©Laramie Dean; Family Matters ©Moondancer Drake; Shy Hunter ©Ginn Hale; In the Seeonee Hills ©Erica Hildebrand; Wolf Lover ©Michael Itig; Flip City ©Lucas Johnson; Pavlov's Dog ©Andi Lee; War of the Wolves ©Charles Long; Wrong Turn ©Stephen Osborne; Leader of the Pack ©Robert Saldarini; A Wolf's Moon ©Quinn Smythwood; Where the Sled Dogs Run ©Jerome Stueart; The Stray ©Anel Viz; New Beginnings ©Cari Z

All characters in this anthology are a work of fiction and any resemblance to real persons, living or dead, is purely coincidental. All rights are reserved. No part of this work may be used or reproduced in any manner whatsoever without the written permission of the publisher.

QUEEREDFICTION
Gillitts, Durban
Republic of South Africa.
www.queeredfiction.com

Edited by James EM Rasmussen
Design & Layout by James EM Rasmussen
Cover Photograph by Rik Hermans
Cover Design by James EM Rasmussen

ISBN 978-1-920441-01-2 (Electronic Book)
ISBN 978-1-920441-00-5 (Paperback)

First Published March 2009

CONTENTS

Preface by *Dr Phillip Andrew Bernhardt-House*	vii
Wolf Strap by *Naomi Clark*	1
Moon Sing by *Laramie Dean*	27
Wolf Lover by *Michael Itig*	39
Shy Hunter by *Ginn Hale*	51
The Stray by *Anel Viz*	77
New Beginnings by *Cari Z*	89
Where the Sled Dogs Run by *Jerome Stueart*	109
Pavlov's Dog by *Andi Lee*	125
Wolves of the West by *Charlie Cochrane*	133
Family Matters by *Moondancer Drake*	149
Wrong Turn by *Stephen Osborne*	159
Leader of the Pack by *Robert Saldarini*	181
War of the Wolves by *Charles Long*	191
Flip City by *Lucas Johnson*	205
Night Swimming by *RJ Bradshaw*	223
In the Seeonee Hills by *Erica Hildebrand*	235
A Wolf's Moon by *Quinn Smythwood*	259
Contributors Biography	283

THE QUE(ER)ST FOR THE WEREWOLF

Dr Phillip Andrew Berhardt-House

Of the many subjects of supernatural fiction that might arouse the sexual instincts, werewolves have–until quite recently–not generally been among the first choices in twentieth and twenty-first century popular writing. However, a look at the history of lycanthropy reveals that werewolves have always had an erotic association. From the first appearance of a human-turned-wolf known in worldwide literature, in the *Epic of Gilgamesh*, werewolves or lycanthropes (terms deriving from Old English and Greek, both meaning 'human-wolves') had this connection: Gilgamesh briefly relates the tale of an unnamed shepherd who refused the advances of Ishtar, and is turned into a wolf and attacked by his own hounds. Time's passing and cultural differences would not change this situation.

What is not generally known, though, is that the image of werewolves, likewise, also often had a specifically homoerotic dimension. In early Indo-European societies, young men (and women to a lesser extent) were often turned out of their settled communities to live as hunters and raiders in the wilderness, feared as outlaws and as menaces to society in times of peace, but as first-line warriors and defenders of their tribes in times of conflict. These youthful groups were often identified with particular animals, but dogs and wolves were the most common identification. It was their unrestrained fury in battle that was the root of stories of berserk rages, which over time became tales of dog, wolf, bear, and other transformations. Until their youthful age grade phase had run its course, they were without status or citizenship; but when their adolescent urges had subsided and they had proved to be fit for society after trial in combat and from survival in the harsh realities of life outside the tribe, they would be re-admitted. During these times in the wilderness, sexual relationships that could result in procreation were off-limits, or sometimes simply not allowable by the laws of their respective societies. To attempt marriage or procreation in such a state was considered a 'marriage by rape' or a 'demon wedding,' and in Hittite legal texts, such practices were decried with the judgment that those who did them had 'become a wolf.' We find early medieval Irish laws also speaking of the devastations caused by female werewolves specifically; and indeed, Ireland and Insular Celtic literatures generally are overabundant in werewolves generally, and in female werewolves in particular. Homoerotic relationships amongst these outsider, outlaw societies were not uncommon, though, and were even encouraged.

But, to paraphrase *Monty Python and the Holy Grail*, strange men living in packs in the woods acting like wolves is not a basis for a system of civil defense! Warrior homoeroticism, nonetheless, persisted in certain cultures well into the time of more organized military activities–the examples of Spartan culture, as well as the classical accounts of Gaulish warrior homoeroticism, are particularly outstanding samples of this. The image of the rapturous male lover salivating over youths like a wolf persisted in the dialogues of Plato, while the idea of a 'big bad wolf' as a looming sexual predator and deflowerer of unsuspecting virgins also proliferated, particularly in later folklore well past the Enlightenment.

It may seem strange, therefore, to imagine a time when all werewolves were potentially 'queerwolves' ever having existed, and yet this is the origin of most ideas about lycanthropy that many cultures have. As pagan practices were replaced by Christianity, and a more permissive sexual range of possibilities was stigmatized, even the werewolf image was considerably cleaned up and 'domesticated,' in a sense; if in no other way, its gradual desexualization and its erasure of homoeroticism were certainly identifiable results. We live in different times now, though, and the outsider and outcast figure as werewolf and the often rejected, reviled and so-called 'unnatural' people who are queer seems to be an image that can not only be rehabilitated, but one that is in fact necessary to a fuller integration of queer-positive approaches and acceptance in modern society. Outsiders and even outlaws need not be seen as undesirable, and by accounting for this difference, and the recognition of its necessity for many people, it can in fact become beneficial. Like the werewolf societies of old, they can be a vanguard for the wider human tribe, a safety outlet, a place of connection, and a way to keep overpopulation in check (peacefully, of course!).

Many of the characteristics of werewolves which are familiar from Hollywood films do not apply to the historical-literary situation. What was originally a metaphorical identification with dogs and wolves, and use of wolf skins and such as adornments, eventually became understood as actual physical transformation. Some populations were thought to all have a werewolf phase at some stage in their lives, or for a certain time of the year; for certain people, in other words, it was simply *in their nature* to be such. Other werewolves only transformed in a sort of spiritual body that traveled abroad while the human was asleep in a deep trance, rather than actually involving physical metamorphosis. Curses to bring about lycanthropy did not generally become common until the post-medieval period, and wicked wives and stepmothers were often the cause of these. The shedding of clothing before transformation was not merely a practical measure to save on wardrobe wear-and-tear; it is essential that the clothes be protected for the werewolf in question to become human again. This is the case from the ancient Greek accounts of Arcadian werewolves, to Petronius' *Satyricon*, to the medieval Old French lays of *Bisclavret* and *Melion*. The moon did not play a role in inducing werewolf transformations until the late twelfth and early thirteenth centuries, in the hagiographies of St. Ronan and St. Rumon, and the *Otia Imperialia* of Gervase of Tilbury–and there, it was not the full moon, but the new moon, which brought on the transformation. The hybrid humanoid-wolf form found in so much werewolf imagery of the twentieth century, while not unheard of previously (but usually assigned to cynocephali–'dog-heads'–rather than werewolves), was generally not the case; instead, full transformation from human to lupine form was envisioned as the norm. Werewolf life and death were matters not often dealt with, so no prohibitions on vulnerability to silver or apparent rapid healing and immortality were generally present in much premodern werewolf literature.

However, the only constant with werewolves, as with many other matters, is indeed the reality and necessity of change, of transformation, of adaptation. The new tales of werewolves have taken directions of their own, and will no doubt continue to do so in the future.

It is with great pleasure, therefore, that I commend the present collection of queer werewolf fiction to the reader fortunate enough to be clenching it in their claws at present. Herein you will find something to cater to many different desires and delectations. There are tales of general societal decline as well as nascent lycanthropic utopias; there are stories of intercultural cooperation and utter rejection of a culture's own individuals; there are yarns of yearning to be understood and making tentative first contacts, and of utter chance encounters and making the best of one's mistakes. We can laugh at the narratives of learned and cultured werewolf clubs and a werewolf who has no idea into what lifestyle he's strayed, we can sigh at the burgeoning of new romances and the making do with fetishes gone not-quite-as-planned, and we can weep at young lives destroyed and at the ravages of homophobia despite all efforts to protect people from it. Like the werewolf societies of old, we can see young people setting off into hostile and uncertain worlds–domesticated or wild, or on some border in between–knowing the only loyalties they can count on are the loves they find along the way.

If you love werewolves, no matter in what sense 'love' and 'werewolves' happen to be meant, and if you love men who love men and women who love women, then there will be something to arouse you intellectually, humorously, or erotically within these covers.

You've been searching, questing for the queerest of werewolf stories. You've run a long and hard journey to get to this destination. You've been bitten by the wolf, and can feel the stories of queerwolves from millennia long passed pulsing in your every vein, alive in every panting breath. So, stop salivating and start wolfing down this feast of fiction!

WOLF STRAP

Naomi Clark

The boy was cold by the time the police found him. His blood dried to a tacky rust-red stain on his clothes and face. His limbs bent at cruel angles. He lay in the alley in a mound of fetid rubbish, the scent of death lingering in the cold air, mixing with the reek of rotting food. On the wall behind the teenager, a single word was scrawled in huge letters, the paint the same dark red as the boy's blood.

"Oh Jesus," one of the cops whispered. "A kid? What kind of sick fuck would do this?"

Swallowing bile, his werewolf partner moved closer to the corpse and identified another scent underlying the others, a clean, musky smell that triggered a fresh wave of nausea in him. "Not just any kid, Hesketh," he said. "A Pack kid."

Hesketh wet his lips. "A dead Pack kid."

The silence weighed heavily between them. Neither spoke again.

My wolf snarled and whined at the thought of being trapped on a plane for three hours. I struggled to tamp down my inner beast's fear of containment and focus on happier thoughts. Like Shannon's jasmine and sandalwood fragrance or the soft feel of my favorite hoodie against my skin, or the fact that any minute now I'd be thousands of feet up in the air with absolutely no control over this great winged death trap...

"Damn." I chewed my sleeve, working hard not to hyperventilate as the wolf scratched at the doors of my mind, demanding release.

"Ayla?" Shannon brushed my knee lightly. "Are you okay?"

I dredged up a tight smile for my lover. "Airplanes." I

shrugged and spread my hands in a helpless gesture.

Shannon laughed and her light caress became a squeeze. "My fearless werewolf," she teased.

"Wolves aren't meant to fly," I grumbled, clutching the armrests of my seat. "Wolves belong on the ground."

"Poor baby. I'll have to think of something to distract you." She leaned in, the silky locks of her hair falling over her shoulder to brush my arm in a sensuous sweep. "Do wolves ever join the mile high club?"

I caught the scent of Shannon's arousal, a musky, sweet perfume that never failed to turn both me and the wolf on. For a second the tightness in my chest was nothing to do with fear of flying. Then the engines roared and the plane lurched forwards, breaking the spell. I closed my eyes and tried not to whimper. "Not this one."

Shannon settled back in her seat with a sigh. "You don't have to do this."

"Adam was my nephew. I remember playing with him when he was just a cub, teaching him how to stalk rabbits..." I smiled, hot tears pricking at my eyelids. I fought them back. "I want to say goodbye, you know?"

"Of course you do. But your parents–"

"I might not even see them. Pack funerals...it'll be crowded." I wondered who I was trying to convince, since I certainly hadn't convinced myself. My wolf bristled at the thought of my parents, hackles rising. I opened my eyes enough to see Shannon frowning at me, concern marring her delicate features. "Thanks for coming with me," I said. "You didn't have to. It's going to be... difficult."

Shannon wrapped her hand around mine and opened her mouth, but her words were lost in the roar of the plane's engines as we rose off the runway. I squeaked, a very non-werewolf sound, and scrunched my eyes shut once more.
Shannon's fingers stroked my knuckles, a tender touch that calmed me a little.

"Think happy thoughts."

I was on my way to a city I'd left eight years ago, home to a family who didn't want me, to the funeral of a nephew I barely knew. There weren't enough happy thoughts on the planet.

The death of a child is a tragedy under any circumstances. For Pack it's even worse, given the low birth rates amongst werewolf bitches. Adam's death would affect the whole community, not just his immediate family. There was no way I could stay away from the funeral, no matter how hard it might be for me personally.

It wasn't that my parents had a problem with homosexuality. They just had a problem with my homosexuality. Pack women had babies, it was our duty. No excuses accepted. Mum and Dad had freaked when I came out to them, Mum especially. She was a throwback, my mother. A Stepford Wolf. It was incomprehensible to her that I might not want to get married and start pumping out pups.

For a couple of tense years they tried to persuade me I was just going through a phase, and I tried to convince them I wasn't. The first time I brought a girl home, for my seventeenth birthday party, all hell broke loose. I'd hopped on the first plane out of the city the next morning and never been back. Now, watching the ground dwindle away beneath the rising plane, the clouds drifting in to mask the earth below, my stomach churned with more than just travel sickness.

My wolf raised its hackles, the beast within feeding on my gnawing tension. I wanted my parents to be happy to see me. I wanted them to accept Shannon. I wanted this to be happening under different circumstances.

Despite everything, I felt a little flush of excitement as the captain told us to buckle up for landing. The city looked just as I remembered. A sprawling glitter of high-rise glass buildings, interspersed with lush green parks. Clean and modern, it was a testimony to the partnership between Pack and humans. In other parts of the country relationships were less cordial, and Pack members were treated like freaks, monsters, something I'd experienced firsthand when I first struck out on my own. They lived in ghettos, cut off from the pure humans and existing in an uneasy balance between superior strength and superior numbers. But here the humans had been quick to seize upon the advantages offered by a Pack alliance. Why not use the wolves' strength and heightened senses to benefit everyone? The Pack controlled the construction industry in the city, as well as a lot of the 'green' businesses, taking care of all those beautiful parks. The humans held most of the power in terms of politics and legislation, whereas in law enforcement it was pretty even. The humans liked the security that a werewolf police officer brought to their neighborhood. Not many people were stupid enough to take on a wolf in uniform. I smiled wryly.

My smile faded as I thought of Adam. He'd been eight when I last saw him and pretty into cops and robbers. He'd had a toy gun and plastic badge, the works. I wondered if he'd wanted to become a police officer, if he'd harbored ambitions of protecting this city and its people. I chewed my lip, twisting the hoop piercing my lower lip into my mouth to suck on the cool metal.

Shannon nudged me. "You look pale. Need the sick bag?" she asked lightly, trying to rouse me from my mopey silence.

I shook her off with an irritable snarl and turned back to the window, watching the city grow steadily larger as we landed.

Whatever apprehension I had about seeing my parents again was swept away when I caught sight of Vince in the airport car park. Losing all sense of dignity, I dropped my suitcase and flung myself into his arms with a squeal. He laughed and swung me up easily, his warm, earthy scent enveloping me. Beneath that was a baser, sharper musk that was pure Pack. It had been years since I'd smelled it and it brought tears to my eyes now.

"Oh Vince," I muttered into his hair.

"Ayla, God, it's good to see you." He set me down, held me at arm's length to study me with a crooked smile. "Loving the hair, girlfriend." He ran his hand over my shaggy black spikes. "Makes you look so cute."

I glowered. I was short for a wolf, with an angelic countenance I'd desperately tried to combat with piercings and a punky haircut. Apparently it hadn't worked. "You look exactly the same," I told him. "Still lanky and skinny."

He opened his mouth to retort but Shannon interrupted him by dumping my abandoned suitcase between us. "Nice, Ayla. Just leave the weak and feeble human to carry the luggage." She flicked her honey-blonde hair from her eyes and offered Vince a hand.

"I'm Shannon Ryan."

"Vince Taylor." He shook her hand carefully, avoiding the crushing grip he might have offered me. "Nice to finally meet you, Shannon." Then, gentleman to the last, he picked up both our bags and carried them to his car. "Come on, ladies. Let's get you home."

Vince lived on Larkspur, an estate bordering one of the larger parks in the city. Designed specifically for the Pack, it was a luxury estate catering to the wealthier Pack members, the kind that wanted indoor pools and two-car garages at their disposal. Vince was a sous-chef. I raised an eyebrow as we pulled into his drive.

Catching my expression he grinned.

"It's Joel's place."

"You didn't tell me he was rich." I stared up at the elegant house, suddenly burningly conscious of my clomping boots and battered leather jacket.

"He's an architect. Let's get inside." He paused, pinching the bridge of his nose, a nervous habit that set me on edge instantly. A faint smell of fear, like rotting fruit, touched my nostrils and my inner wolf went on alert. "We need to talk," he said.

"Murdered?" I echoed for perhaps the fifth time. "Adam?" I clutched Shannon's hand tight enough to make her wince. "Murdered?"

Vince pushed a mug of hot chocolate, heavily laced with brandy, towards me. "I didn't want to tell you over the phone."

I wrapped my numb fingers around the mug, letting the too-hot ceramic warm me. "What happened?"

He shifted uncomfortably on the teak kitchen chair. For a werewolf, Vince had always been pretty squeamish. "He was beaten to death."

I closed my eyes against the image that sprang to vivid, bloody life before them. "He was sixteen," I whispered.

"Do the police have any leads?" Shannon asked, sounding far calmer than I thought she ought to. I guess she was used to this kind of talk, more so than me. Shannon was a private investigator, although admittedly the majority of her cases involved cheating spouses and tax evasion, not dead werewolves.

"Not really. Nothing solid. Except–" Vince hesitated, heaved a huge sigh. "There was some graffiti on the alley where they found him. The papers are speculating it was Alpha Humans, but the police aren't saying anything."

I grimaced. I'd seen a couple of reports on Alpha Human attacks in the past few years. The signature was always the same, the legend 'abomination' scrawled near the body. They were a militant group and three or four of them armed with lead pipes would be more than a match for a teenage werewolf. Even an adult wolf, caught unaware, might be taken down. If this was another city, I wouldn't have been surprised, but here, with relations between humans and Pack as good as they were…

"Any similar attacks in the area recently?" I asked, sipping my hot chocolate and trying to sound as detached and professional as Shannon.

"Nothing in the papers. This kind of thing just doesn't happen round here, Ayla, you know that." Vince rubbed the back of his neck, looking equal parts dismayed and baffled.

It did now. I stared at the smooth granite surface of the breakfast bar and once again tried to block the image of Adam, bloodied and battered, from my mind. I couldn't force it away though, and I was infinitely grateful when Vince's other half got home.

I'd heard about Joel, but none of Vince's rapturous emails did the other wolf justice. Lean and blond, sharp-eyed and strong-bodied, the kind of wolf my mum would have loved me to bring home.

"So me and Vince were planning a run tonight," he told me once all the introductions were done. "We'd love you to come with us, Ayla." He glanced at Shannon. "And I guess you…"

"Could run along behind?" Shannon smiled and shook her head. "Don't worry about me. I know I can't compete with you guys in that respect. I'll get an early night, thanks."

I was touched that Joel had thought to invite Shannon along even knowing there was no way a human could join in a wolf run. And I was touched he'd invited me, given my outcast status.

Wolves who left the Pack tended to lead solitary lives because there was always a good reason they'd left in the first place. The kind of reason that stopped them joining another Pack.

The night air was cool and crisp, carrying the scents of city and park to me. Petrol and cherry blossom, fast food and pond water. I inhaled deeply, letting it all wash over me and call to my wolf. New aromas, new places to explore, I promised her. High overhead, skirting through iron-grey clouds, a crescent moon bathed the park in thin, pale rays. In another week or so she would be full and every wolf in the country would be baying their respects to her bone white face.

Beside me, Vince and Joel were stripping off. Moonlight painted them ivory, lending a fey cast to their faces. I inhaled once more, taking in their mingled scents. My wolf stirred, excited by their presence. My runs had been solitary ever since I left home, but my wolf remembered too clearly running through the streets with Vince, chasing rats and snapping playfully at each others' tails.

Feeling the change approach, I quickly shed my clothes too, tossing them over the fence into Joel's garden. The night breeze kissed my bare skin, teasing and inviting. The park stretched out before me, a maze of slender trees and shadowed pathways. As the wolf grew stronger, so did my senses and I picked up the enticing musk of rabbit and deer. Shivering with anticipation, I dropped to all fours and let the change take me.

Shannon once asked me to describe the change to her. She's seen it happen once or twice, but she wanted to know how it felt, what it was like to have your body remake itself so swiftly and completely. The best way to describe it is like your body is eating itself. Everything feels like it's shrinking down, tearing apart because your mind has decided it doesn't need this shape anymore. It needs something different and it burns through your current shape to make it. It's crunching pain, followed by such wicked relief you just want to weep.

It's over very quickly. A few seconds after dropping to the ground, I shook out my ruff and flicked my ears, taking in the myriad new sounds. Car engines stalling, doors slamming, cats yowling. Turning my head, I saw Vince and Joel complete their own changes. Two men became two wolves, one rusty blonde, the other dusty black. The black wolf, Vince, yapped happily at me and darted over to nip at my tail. I snarled and snapped back, my wolf self briefly forgetting he wasn't a threat.

He flattened his ears and licked my muzzle. I whined an apology and returned the gesture. Then I jumped and whirled round to snap at Joel, who'd snuck up behind me to sniff my backside. He growled back, a challenge in his amber eyes. My hackles rose and for a second we stood in deadlock, sizing each other up. The rules and etiquette of wolf shape are very different to those of human shape. Joel was assessing me as a wolf, not as the woman he'd met a couple of hours ago. And I was doing the same, the wolf asking questions the woman wouldn't: friend or foe?

Vince broke the tension by throwing himself at Joel with a playful yip, and the two went tumbling tail over head, an impromptu game of chase breaking out. I shook myself and loped after them, experiencing a spike of envy that my own mate couldn't run with me. I soon forgot that though, when Vince tore away from Joel to come wrestle with me. Then all the old instincts took over and I lost myself to the wolf completely.

I could have run for days. The ground was soft but solid underfoot, the park a wonderland of game and hiding places. The moon grew brighter as the clouds drifted on, illuminating every hidden treasure. I didn't catch any deer, but I found a couple of rabbits. Vince and Joel brought down a few of their own, snapping the little necks with practised bites and tussling over the warm flesh in faux-aggression. I sought out a large pond after my snack, wanting to wash the blood from my muzzle. I hadn't been swimming in my wolf body for a long time and the rush of water over my fur was delicious. It struck me, as it always did, that I could stay wolf forever, give up my human half and abandon myself completely to the wilderness.

But I always banished that thought as quickly as it came, chased it away with an image of honey-blonde hair and sparkling blue eyes, a scent-memory of jasmine and sandalwood. Splashing out of the pond, I found my fellow wolves and let them guide me back to Joel's house. The wolf world was a wonderland but without Shannon it was a lonely one.

I changed shape in the garden, whispering my goodnights to the two men before creeping into the guest room where Shannon slept. My night vision, exceptional as a wolf, was well beyond average for a human, and I stood for a moment admiring the play of moonlight on her face. It brushed her with silver, transforming her into something too ethereal and tantalizing for mere humanity.

Perhaps she sensed my presence. She opened her eyes and beckoned me silently to join her. I slipped under the duvet, sliding my arms around her. She stroked my hair, pulling out a few stray twigs with a sleepy smile. "You smell like wet dog," she mumbled.

I ran my hands down her back, over the soft curve of her hips. "You love it."

"I love you." She kissed me, her lips warm and dry, the last vestiges of sleep falling away from her. She twisted in my arms until we were inextricably tangled, limbs twined together, her hair brushing my throat and shoulders as we kissed. A need hotter than the burn of change consumed me as I nipped and bit tenderly at her throat and she dragged her nails down my sides and pushed her breasts against mine. The sensation left me breathless, helpless in her arms.

She dictated the pace, as always. I had to be careful, so careful not to hurt her. So Shannon took control, kissing and caressing her way down my body while I writhed and moaned in pleasure. She rose up to lick my nipples, sucking them into taut peaks and pulling frantic whimpers from me. The animal part of me wanted to take her, assert my dominance, but I held that part back, clamping down the instincts that roared inside me whenever we made love.

She whispered my name lovingly as she explored and aroused my body, teasing me into a mindless frenzy in the thick half-dark. Silvery shadows slipped around us, illuminating Shannon's sensuous curves as she moved over me. My skin tingled as if all my nerve endings were exposed to her touch. I sought her lips, my hands trailing down between her thighs, fingers seeking out the heat of her to make her cry out with the same passion I was.

And afterwards, sated and shivering with the aftershocks, we lay together and mumbled sweet nonsense to each other, and I was reminded once again why I always came back to humanity.

The funeral was as funerals are. Our Lady of Mercy church was packed–pun intended–and although I did look for my parents, I didn't see them amongst the black-clad throng. Vince gripped my hand throughout the service as I struggled not to cry. It felt odd, hearing the vicar talk about Adam when I'd known so little about him. The little cub I'd taught to chase rabbits was long gone and the young man he'd become was a stranger to me.

A few pews ahead my aunt Vivian, Adam's mother, shook with silent sobs and my uncle Chris pulled her hard against his side, as if he could shield her from her son's death. That moved me more than anything, the solidarity between them, the palpable aura of grief and love around them. The wake was held in a Pack-owned pub a few streets from the church. When I was a kid the Moon in the Water had been called the Prince Regent and it had been a dive, a hangout for human junkies and drunks. Now it was a flourishing business, attracting Pack and humans alike. Today it was closed to humans, however, as the church had been. I sat at the bar nursing half a pint and wondered what Shannon was doing.

A light touch on my shoulder and a waft of rose perfume was all the warning I had that my mother had found me. I stiffened as I turned to face her, part of me automatically assessing myself for flaws. My shirt hadn't been ironed, my shoes needed polishing, my leather jacket didn't go with my linen trousers...

"Ayla," Mum whispered. "Oh, Ayla, I'm so glad you're here." She flung her arms around me before I could respond and, unsure what else to do, I returned her crushing embrace. When we broke apart she held onto my arms, looking me over with moist eyes. "You dyed your hair," she said.

I couldn't help but laugh. How like my mum. "I never liked being blonde."

She smiled tremulously. "Vince said he'd invited you. I didn't know... Your dad and I hoped you'd come. We–" She stopped, reaching into her suit pocket for a tissue to wipe her eyes. "You'll come for dinner tonight, won't you? You are staying in town, aren't you?"

I hesitated. I wanted to, God knew I wanted to, but I was unsure of Shannon's welcome. "I'd love to," I said honestly. "If I can bring my partner."

Surprise and concern flickered over Mum's face. "You're seeing someone? A wolf? A man?"

I struggled to suppress the flare of rage that sparked inside me. "A woman." I held back 'a human.' It didn't seem like the right time.

Mum swallowed whatever she wanted to say with a visible effort. "We'd love to meet her," she said determinedly. We shared strained smiles but were saved from further tension by the appearance of Chris. He was my maternal uncle, so it was little surprise when he turned to Mum with anguish raw on his face.

"Anna, Ayla–" He stopped and shook his head. "God, will this day never end?"

Mum hugged him as fiercely as she had me, but said nothing. I guess there was nothing to say. I sipped at my drink, searching for something myself. All that came to mind was Shannon's question from yesterday. "Do the police have any leads?"

Chris shook his head again. "We all know it was Alpha Humans, but nobody's bloody doing anything. My boy, beaten, mutilated–"

"Mutilated?" I cut in, louder than I'd intended. "Mutilated how?" I'd followed Alpha Humans' activities closely since as a lone wolf I was maybe more vulnerable than most. I'd never heard of them mutilating their victims.

Chris nodded, pressing his hand to his temple. "They skinned him. Took–" He broke down, great sobs shaking his big frame. Mum slipped her arm round his waist and steered him away from the bar, casting a glance back at me and mouthing 'call me.'

Shannon greeted me back at Joel and Vince's with a tight hug and a soft kiss. "How was it?"

"Funeral." I shrugged out of my coat and kicked off my boots. "My uncle Chris said Adam had been mutilated–skinned. Did you ever hear of an Alpha Human attack like that?"

"Not Alpha Humans, no." She sat down on the leather couch with me. "There was a case back in the sixties where some supposed Satanists skinned a wolf though, saying it would give them special powers. We covered it in History one year." She shook her head as if shaking away the thought. "Any word from the police?"

I snorted. "If they know anything, they're not sharing it."

I toyed with a loose thread on the couch throw, thinking of Adam, pale and still in his coffin, beaten to death and then... skinned. Why? Who would do that?

Vince and Joel returned then, both red-eyed and quiet. We sat for a few minutes in somber silence before Vince's natural personality reasserted itself. "We shouldn't just sit here wallowing. Ayla, you wanna visit an old haunt?"

I eyed him suspiciously. "Where did you have in mind?"

"Silks." He laughed as my expression moved from suspicion to disgust. "It's changed a lot since we were kids. Come on, I think we've earned a real drink."

Silks had been a nightmare of Dayglo paint and eighties pop when I was last there. Now it was an edgy, chilled-out bar complete with long leather couches and jazz music. Not exactly my idea of a good time, but an improvement on the old look, I mused as Joel handed me a vodka and coke. And then I noticed the singer on stage.

It was the smell I noticed first, the smell of Pack. Then I noticed the enormous red beehive wig, the towering glittery emerald heels, and the improbably large breasts stuffed into the glittery green spandex dress. I choked on my drink, bewildered laughter bubbling to my lips. "It's a gay bar? A gay Pack bar?"

Vince clapped me on the shoulder. "Times change, Ayla. After you left town, a lot of Pack members came out, you know? We're still not exactly popular, but we're making progress."

I reflected on that as the drag queen on stage sang her way through Fever, husky voice conjuring images of silk sheets and hot kisses. When I'd left home my parents had made me feel I was betraying the Pack. Like I'd made a deliberate choice to prefer women and thus scorn my duty to have children. But at Adam's funeral, Mum had seemed different. Softer. *We'd love to meet her.* I watched the drag queen sashay around the stage, watched the mixed audience of Pack and humans cheer her on.

And of course there was Vince, living openly with Joel in opulent luxury. He'd come out after I left town, telling me later that it was my decision to leave that had given him the courage. Things had changed, I acknowledged. Maybe my self-imposed exile was over.

Once the act came to a close, the audience burst into rapturous applause and the singer slinked off stage to the bar. I had to envy her poise, given the height of her heels. I'd have been flat on my face. To my surprise she came to sit with us, greeting Joel with a flurry of air kisses.

"Sweetie, it's been too long." She lit up a cigarette with elegant fingers. Up close it was easier to see the masculine features, disguised by artful makeup. Slightly square jaw, hands a little too large, but strangely beautiful for her blurring of genders.

"Ayla, Shannon, this is Gloriana," Joel introduced us. "Gloriana, this is an old friend of Vince's and her partner. They're in town for the–for Adam.'

"Oh God." Gloriana took a deep drag on her cigarette. "Awful business. In this town, too, I couldn't believe it. Call me Glory, darlings," she added to me and Shannon. Her voice captivated me, low and rich. "Do you know, Joel, I was in here the night it happened? I saw all the police swarming around."

"Was it near here?" Shannon asked.

"Oh yes, practically on our doorstep." Glory tapped cigarette ash onto the table top. "The smell was horrific. Like nothing I've smelled before. It haunts me." She shivered theatrically. "Sour. Rotten."

The bar seemed to shrink around me as Glory spoke. Too dark, too hot. I ran my hands through my hair and toyed with my lip ring, trying to distract myself from the image of Adam lying battered and beaten in some stinking alleyway. My wolf whined and pawed inside me, roused by my dread.

"Ayla?" Shannon rested her hand on my knee. "You need

some fresh air?"

I nodded gratefully and we made our excuses, hurrying out into the fading afternoon sunshine. I leaned against a wall and closed my eyes, breathing deeply to fight off the sense of vertigo. My wolf still prowled at the edge of my mind, beating against my human self. It was an instinct as old as the moon: feel threatened, out comes the wolf.

Shannon rubbed my fingers, saying nothing but offering comfort nonetheless. We'd been together long enough that words were sometimes superfluous.

As we stood there I became aware a strange odor in the air, a tang that put me in mind of poisoned meat. I inhaled deeply, trying to pinpoint the source of the smell. What had Glory said before I'd flaked out? *Sour. Rotten.*

I pushed myself away from the wall, breaking free of Shannon's hold to track the smell. Where exactly had Adam died? How far from Silks was the scene of the crime?

"Ayla?" Shannon hurried along beside me. "Is everything okay?"

"It's this smell..." I trailed off, veering to the right to head down a side passage next to Silks. Shannon picked up her pace to keep up with me, but didn't ask any more questions. I wasn't officially involved in her PI business, but I'd helped her with enough cases that she knew when to trust my werewolf instincts. And right now they were afire, screaming that something was wrong here. That stench...that open grave stench set my wolf on edge. It was unnatural. Anathema.

The passage twisted and wound away from the club, taking us down a dingy alley littered with broken bottles and dried puke. The sun was disappearing behind the high rise buildings in a blur of hot orange light, casting long shadows across dumpsters and rusted fire escapes. I noticed it all without seeing any of it. The smell pulled me on like a magnet, scratching at my senses and pricking at my inner wolf. The quick staccato click of our heels was the only sounds, echoing off the graffiti-tagged bricks.

And now, here, still sealed off with yellow police tape, was the site of Adam's murder. That wicked word, abomination, scrawled across the wall in dripping red paint. The pavement was still stained with blood, and the overwhelming reek hung over it all.

I swallowed hard, my stomach churning. This was where my cousin had died. Maybe he'd been at Silks or some nearby bar. Maybe he'd come back here for a cigarette or a drink when Alpha Humans had found him.

"What is that smell?" Shannon asked. She ducked under the police tape to examine the scene. "Smells like rotting meat or something." She knelt down, tucking her skirt under her knees carefully and swiped a finger along the ground, then sniffed it. "I can't tell where it's coming from."

"Would it be something the crime scene investigators used? Some chemical, maybe?" I guessed.

She shook her head. "Nothing they use stinks like that." She stood to peer into a nearby trash can. "Nothing in here."

Approaching footsteps resounded off the narrow walls, male voices laughing and muttering followed. Under that rotten meat smell I could detect alcohol mixed with the warm, clean scent of pure humans. I tensed, not sure why, a shiver of stress running down my spine as I realized they were coming our way. "Shannon, let's go."

She ducked back under the tape. "Trouble?" She reached into her handbag where she always carried a small pistol. She'd never had occasion to use it in her PI work, but a couple of nasty threats from the ex-husband of a former client had persuaded her it was better safe than sorry. The thing made me nervous. If you carried a gun, eventually you used it.

"Let's just go," I repeated, taking her hand. As we headed out of the alley, we walked into them, a group of four, big, mean-looking guys. One carried a six-pack of beer; another swung a baseball bat casually. A shot of adrenaline fired through me as my eyes locked with the beer-carrier. I couldn't stop myself; I snarled, prompted by an immediate, instinctive hatred.

"What's this then?" he asked. "Couple of ladies out looking for fun?" He grabbed his crotch suggestively and leered at Shannon.

"One lady, one bitch," one of his friends, a rangy redhead, corrected. "Hear her growling? She's a wolf." He spat at my feet.

"A butch bitch," the ringleader said, looking me over. "Probably just needs a good fuck to bring her round though. Not that bestiality's my thing." He turned his attention to Shannon. "Blondie, though..."

I stepped in front of her. "You touch her, I'll bite your balls off," I growled.

He rolled up his shirt sleeves to reveal a distinctive tattoo on his forearm: the bold insignia of Alpha Humans. Coincidence, to encounter them so close to the site of Adam's murder? Or had they come to gloat?

"You wanna dance, bitch, let's do it," the ringleader challenged me. "One less freak like you in this city is all good."

They closed around us, the redhead raising his baseball bat. Battle rage sang in my blood, the urge to fight and protect my mate burning inside me. Shannon drew her gun, aiming it at the ringleader with shaking hands.

"Back off," she ordered, voice shaking far less than her hands. Good actress, my girl. They didn't buy it though.

"Fuck, a furry lover," the redhead sneered. "We should kill you both."

She opened her mouth to retort. She should have just shot him. He moved before she could, swinging his bat with smooth ease to crash into her ribs with a sick crack. Shannon gasped and dropped to the floor, winded, the gun falling from her hands. A red mist descended on me, conscious thought stopping as primal fury took over.

I launched myself at Redhead with a shriek, fingers flexed into claws. We went down in a tangle as I swiped at his eyes and cheeks, desperate to draw blood. He slammed the bat hard into my leg. I howled in pain and grappled for it, squeezing his wrist until I heard bones grind together. He dropped the bat with a cry.

Shouts erupted from his companions; kicks and punches rained down on me, but I barely noticed. I was too intent on ripping Redhead's throat out, tasting his blood, avenging my mate.

I might have done it if a gun hadn't gone off over my head. Suddenly the blows stopped and Redhead froze beneath me. The mist cleared a little as I heard a new voice.

"Everybody back off. Put down your weapons."

I sensed my attackers retreating and looked up from my victim. Two cops, one smelling strongly of Pack, stood over Shannon. The Pack cop held a smoking gun, angled upwards and away from us. The human cop was reaching down to help Shannon to her feet. I snarled softly, warning him off. He got the hint and stepped away.

"Ayla..." Shannon rolled to her knees, clutching her side. "Are you okay?"

It seemed ridiculous that she should be asking me, until I realized blood was dripping down my nose. I wiped it away with my sleeve and glanced down at Redhead. His face was a bleeding mess, long scratches testimony to my attack.

"Shit," the human cop murmured. "What a fucking mess."

It was a mess, mostly because it took so long to sort out the bullshit from the truth down at the police station. The Alpha Human assholes claimed I'd started it. Four against two are bad odds, but it helped, in a sick way, that Shannon had two broken ribs as a result of Redhead's attack. Me and the men were charged with affray and released on bail. Shannon went straight to A&E. I was desperate to go with her, but as I was hurrying out of the station, something pulled me back.

The smell again; the same bitter stench that hovered over the alley. My stress and concern for Shannon had distracted me briefly, but I couldn't ignore it now. I spun and inhaled deeply, letting my wolf rise inside me enough to sharpen my senses. I got an odd look from the duty sergeant, but nobody stopped me as I pushed through the doors leading from the reception area to the forbidding 'Authorized Personnel Only' Area. Maybe she figured arguing with a werewolf was a bad idea.

I quickly found myself loitering outside the custody suite where the smell seemed strongest. The Pack cop who'd stepped in to save us in the alley, Kinsey from his badge, emerged after a few seconds and did a double take when he saw me there. "Ms Hammond, can I help you?"

"Can't you smell that?" I demanded, too on edge to mind my manners. "How can you not smell that?"

He shifted his weight, a nervous light in his eyes. "Smell what?"

"That stink! It was all over the alley too–you're kidding, right?

You have to smell it!"

Nerves became anger and he grabbed my arm, wrestled me into the custody suite. It was dimly lit, silent, the cells empty. Suddenly I felt nervous. He had about a foot on me, built like a brick shithouse, and undeniably alpha. My wolf cowered a little as he bared his teeth.

"Word of advice, lady. You're not going to be in town long, so keep your snout out of what doesn't concern you. Got it?"

I was so taken aback I nearly submitted meekly until I remembered I was a lone wolf and bared my own teeth in response. "Did you investigate Adam Thatcher's death?"

I thought the change of subject might disarm him, but if anything it made him tenser. "Yeah. My partner and I found him, as it happens. So what?"

"You think those guys who beat up my girlfriend had anything to do with it?"

He released my arm and stepped back, assessing me warily in the half-light. "I'll say it again, don't mess with it. It's none of your business." He flipped the switch to open the door and shoved me out into the hall. "Just keep your pretty nose out of other people's business." He let the door slam shut.

Scowling, I stomped back to the reception and slammed my fist down on the desk, startling the duty sergeant out of her inertia. "Who is Officer Kinsey's partner?"

She blinked at me slowly, as if assessing how crazy I was. "Why?"

"I want to make a complaint."

"You should–"

"What's his name?" I dragged my nails along the desktop, leaving smears of blood–mine and Redhead's–in my wake.

She wet her lips and thought fast. "Graham Hesketh."

I stormed out. Hesketh. I was going to find him and beat Kinsey's secret out of him.

Because Kinsey was Pack, and Hesketh was his partner, it was easy to find Hesketh. A quick call to Vince gave me everything I needed to know.

"Don't do anything stupid, Ayla," he warned me. "You're not thinking straight."

He was right.

Adam and Shannon were mixed up in my head, battered and hurt and I *couldn't* be logical about it. I could only follow my gut and my gut told me Kinsey and Hesketh were involved. So I channeled my anger and raced across town to Hesketh's house. He'd left the station before I made bail. I was optimistically assuming he'd be in, but the house was deserted.

It was a small place, a million miles from the opulence of Joel's house at Larkspur. A rusted bicycle was chained to the fence, looking like it had been there, and would be there, forever. The garden was overgrown with weeds, dandelions flourishing in the long grass. The house itself didn't look neglected, just tired. I stood on the doorstep, shifting my weight from foot to foot as I contemplated my next move. Hesketh was out. I had nothing but fury and instinct fuelling me and, standing outside his silent house, that didn't feel like enough.

The wind shifted, bringing that terrible smell with it. I wrinkled my nose, wishing I could persuade myself it meant nothing. But Glory had said she'd smelled it the night of Adam's death, and it lingered everywhere like a contagion. The alley, the police station, now here.

I cursed under my breath and charged the front door.

The wood cracked sharply, driving splinters into my shoulder. A dog barked in the next garden, probably worried by the scent of a larger, stronger predator in its territory. Dogs and werewolves didn't really mix. I guess we confused them, being neither human enough nor canine enough for them.

The inside of the house was no better than the outside; worn and uncared for. I smelled whiskey hanging in the air, competing with the rotting meat stench. The carpets were soiled with mud, the walls stained with cigarette smoke. An overall atmosphere of despair pervaded the place. If I was into amateur psychology, I might have said Hesketh had some issues.

I tracked the scent through the house, heading up the narrow staircase. Straight ahead of me was a small bathroom, to my left, a bedroom. The smell was strong enough now to make my eyes water, my heart pounding frantically. What would I find? Shannon and Adam flitted through my mind, bloodied and bruised. What had Hesketh done?

I pushed open the door to the bathroom, rubbing my eyes on my sleeve. The off-white porcelain was spattered with flecks of rusty red, streaks of the stuff dripping down the walls into the bathtub. A small furry form lay curled in the tub; grey fur drizzled with blood. The rabbit's neck was broken, its glassy eyes staring up at me sightlessly. I stared back, stomach churning. It wasn't the dead animal itself that upset me. I'd killed too many myself to feel sentimental about them. It was what the rabbit represented that got to me. Some twisted version of nature was at work here, something I couldn't fathom.

There were no dead rabbits in the bedroom, but the smell was thickest here, almost tangible. My wolf clawed at the doors of my mind, telling me this was a situation better suited to her skills than mine. I gritted my teeth and ignored her.

Desperate to find the source of the smell, I tore the room apart: heaved the mattress off the bed, ripped through the wardrobe, tore up the rugs. Maybe my wolf was more in control than I realized, filling me with an animal's blind, instinctive fear and anger. I couldn't stop until I'd found *it*. I didn't even really care anymore what it was.

I was so consumed by my search I didn't hear the steps behind me until it was too late. I whirled with a snarl as a heavy hand clapped down on my shoulder. Hesketh stood behind me, face pale, eyes shrunken with anger.

"What the fuck are you doing, you bitch?" he spat at me.

He hit me before I could answer, smacking me hard across the face and sending me staggering backwards. I collided with the end of his bed and sat down hard, shocked at the strength in his blow, that it was wolf-hard, not human-hard. I sat dazed for a second while Hesketh loomed over me.

"You Pack bastards think you own this fucking town! Think you can just walk all over us!" He slapped me again. "What the fuck are you doing in here?"

He went for a third blow but I caught his wrist, holding him with a crushing grip. "Don't you touch me," I snarled, rising and pushing him back. "What have you done, Hesketh? What's with the rabbit? You think you're one of us? Think you can be Pack by shredding up a few pet bunnies?"

He laughed and pulled free of my grip. "I'm better than you, bitch. You have no idea." There was a mad light in his eyes that unnerved me despite my anger. He glanced around the room as if noticing the destruction I'd caused for the first time. The mad light faded briefly, replaced by sharp panic. "Kinsey said someone would find out. Shit. Oh shit." He scraped his hands over his face. He spun from me, reaching for the chest of drawers against the far wall. I hadn't got round to ripping that apart yet.

Something in his desperate motions fired me too. As he darted for the drawers, so did I, determined to get to whatever he was reaching for before he could. The human part of my brain whispered it could be a gun. The wolf part didn't give a damn.

Hesketh was a fraction quicker than me. He pulled open a drawer and tugged something from it, holding it away from me with a savage grin. I stopped, sickened, when I saw what it was. A long strip of wolf skin, soft and plush with thick smoke-grey fur, tipped with white. Adam's wolf colorings, doused with Adam's scent.

Mutilated. Skinned.

It would give them special powers.

"You evil bastard," I whispered, my heart in my throat, blood boiling in my veins. "You sick fucker."

"He was already dead!" Hesketh shouted. "He was dead, dammit. Those Alpha Human thugs killed him! I didn't do anything wrong!"

I reached for the wolf strap, burning with rage. "You *skinned* my cousin, you monster, you–"

He lashed out, kicking me hard in the stomach. I gasped and bent double, stars dancing in my eyes and blurring the sight of Hesketh dangling Adam's skin before me. "You're calling me a monster? You and your fucking Pack, lording it over us pathetic humans, you're the monsters! This is justice. This is leveling the playing field, bitch. We can be just as good as you, just as strong and fast and that's not sick, that's fair."

I sucked in a deep breath and threw myself at him. We crashed into the wall in a knot of flying fists and savage snarls. I snapped and scratched at him, trying to wrestle the wolf strap from him. He fought back just as fiercely, trying to throw me off him.

We rolled around in the chaos I'd made of his room until he got a handful of my hair and slammed my head against the wall.

Blistering pain shot through my skull and I blanked out for a precious second. Hesketh used that second to shove me off him and scramble to his feet.

When my vision cleared, he'd torn his shirt off and was wrapping the wolf strap around his bare torso.

"No, no, nononono." I barely recognized my own voice. My wolf was rising up inside me, abject horror coursing through us both as Hesketh began to change. This was anathema, this was against everything I knew, everything I believed right down to my bones.

Adam's thick strip of fur spread across Hesketh's body, covering him in rippling grey wolf hair. As it flowed up his chest and along his arms, he began to convulse and shake, gasping as a change his body wasn't made for took him over. His legs buckled, his arms twisted as the wolf strap forced a new shape upon him. His face stretched as the fur covered his neck and cheeks, remaking him, pulling and tugging and dragging at his human form until he was something else.

He wasn't a wolf. It wasn't a Pack wolf that stood before me when the change was done. It was a Hollywood wolfman, tottering upright on two long feet. Long arms hung at his sides, yellowed claws swiping at the air. The muzzle was too long, over crammed with fangs. The eyes were a sickly amber color, filled with rage and madness. This was a monster.

I was frozen. That foul smell filled me, emanating from the wolf strap and now roiling in the air around Hesketh. I wanted to run. Wanted to fight. Wanted to kill him just to get rid of that smell. The change had taken seconds–did I have time to make my own before he struck?

"See this, bitch?" he growled around all those teeth, voice rough and awkward. "We can be just the same as you."

I scrabbled away from him, summoning my wolf, trying to force my own change. The time it would take me was plenty time for Hesketh to eviscerate me, but I had to try.

There was a clatter on the stairs, breaking the spell between us. Shoes! Someone was running up the stairs, calling my name. Glory and Vince burst into the room, both stopping dead when they saw Hesketh.

"Jesus wept," Vince breathed, eyes locked on the wolfman.

"Ayla!"

Hesketh turned on Vince. "More Pack bastards—you think I can't take you all? You think I won't?" He lashed out at Vince, claws slashing through his shirt and tearing at his skin. Vince growled and lunged for Hesketh in response. He knocked him to the floor, grappling with him. Barks and yaps filled the air as they wrestled, and a new wave of panic flooded me. Vince! Had to help Vince, had to stop this creature, this...abomination.

Glory kicked off her shoes and grabbed one up, holding the sparkly stiletto like a weapon.

"Do something!" she roared at me.

I striped, closed my eyes and let the wolf take me. The world became a painful blur for a few long seconds, then I shook myself off and focused on Hesketh and Vince.

Hesketh had Vince pinned to the carpet, misshapen muzzle snapping at Vince's vulnerable throat. Vince had his hands braced against the wolfman's bony shoulders, keeping him barely out of reach. The strain was palpable as Vince fought to shift his weight and throw off Hesketh.

I launched myself at Hesketh, barreling into him and shoving him off Vince, into the wall. Hesketh howled and swiped at me, catching a glancing blow across my chest. I snapped at his hand, clamping my teeth down on his forearm. With a roar, he drove his free hand into my flank, winding me. I released him with a yelp and scuttled away. There was no room to maneuver, no space to fight properly.

I was backed into a corner while Hesketh clambered to his feet, clutching his bleeding forearm to his chest. To Adam's fur. "Fucking animals," he growled.

Vince was on his knees, struggling out of his jacket. I could smell the change taking him, the hot, musky scent that wrapped around him as he summoned his own wolf. Too slow, I thought desperately as Hesketh stalked towards me. Too damn slow against this creature.

I gathered myself up, preparing to dive at his throat. One quick bite, well-aimed, that was all I needed. For Adam.

I sprang as Hesketh prepared his own strike. We clashed with a flurry of snarls and snaps, claws digging into each other, drawing blood, slicing flesh. My world narrowed to Hesketh's yellow eyes and too-long fangs. I could hear voices shouting around me, but they meant nothing. I'd kill him. I'd kill him before I stopped and that was all that mattered.

And then suddenly, Hesketh wasn't fighting me. There was a dull thump and he fell away from me. I fell to the ground with a yowl, hitting the corner of the bed and almost knocking myself out. I shook my head and looked up to see Glory standing over the fallen wolfman brandishing her stiletto.

"You think these things are just for show?" she asked, catching my eye. Her voice shook, but her cherry red lips managed a smile.

I whined and flattened my ears against my skull, eyes swinging back to Hesketh. He was breathing shallowly. A thick trickle of blood seeped down between his eyes, thanks to Glory's designer shoes. He was changing back, body rapidly reverting to human form, wiping away all traces of the monster.

Vince fully changed and late to the party, nuzzled me, checking for injuries. I snapped at him half-heartedly, then licked his face. I was on the verge of changing back when once again there was a thunder of feet on the stairs.

Kinsey appeared, gun in hand, face red with exertion. "Graham!" he yelled. "Hesketh, what–" He stopped short when he saw the scene in Hesketh's bedroom. Two wolves baring their teeth at him in a clear warning, one drag queen waving a shoe threateningly. One monster out cold on the floor.

"Shit," Kinsey said eloquently. He sagged against the door, dropping his gun. "I knew this would happen."

"You knew?" Glory shrieked. "You treacherous bastard! How could you help *this*?" She gestured to Hesketh. "How could you allow this?"

All the fight I'd seen in Kinsey earlier, all the bluster and strength, seemed to be dying before my eyes. "He's my friend," he whispered helplessly. "He wanted to be one of us. I wanted him to know what it was like... The boy was already dead."

If I'd had human vocal chords, I would have told Kinsey there was no excuse, no justification for what they'd done, what they'd made of themselves. I would have screamed at him until my throat bled and my voice died. But I was a wolf, and my wolf had nothing to say.

Pack law is harsh and swift. Kinsey and Hesketh would discover that when it all came out, as would the Alpha Human faction that had enabled them to take Adam's skin. By the time I'd changed back to my human shape, I was too tired and depressed to want revenge anymore. I just wanted Shannon.

They let her out of the hospital a couple of hours after Hesketh and Kinsey were arrested, and I had to be more careful than ever when I hugged her. Even restrained wolf-strength was a threat to those cracked ribs.

"If you were a wolf, you'd be healed already," I murmured to her, kissing her throat. For a perilous second, I almost understood Kinsey's motives. I dismissed the thought as soon as it came.

Shannon brushed my hair from my face, examining the cuts and bruises I'd picked up in my fight with Hesketh.

"You're wolf enough for both of us, I think."

Knowing what had happened didn't help Chris and Vivian. It didn't help me.

I gave the wolf strap to them and they burnt it. Nothing more was said. I suppose there wasn't anything to say.

I took Shannon to meet my parents.

I also took Vince, Joel, and Glory as backup. There were a few awkward silences as my parents took in Glory's hot-pink mini-dress, then Mum asked her where she got her gorgeous gold shoes from, and suddenly it was like we'd been doing this for years.

Tension eased out of me second by second as Shannon and Dad chatted about her work, and Glory and Mum discussed boutiques and costume jewelry over roast beef and vegetables. It was homely. Comfortable.

Next to me, Vince patted my knee and winked at me.

I smiled back, a warm glow settling over me. Shannon caught my eye and blew me a kiss that wafted to me on the scent of jasmine and sandalwood. For the first time since the plane had touched down, my wolf and I felt just fine.

MOON SING

Laramie Dean

I don't call it Hunting like Doll does, you know, with reverence or whatever. She says it's *spiritual* for her and Stephanie, when they take down a rabbit or a deer and bring it back for the house. But that's the thing, see. I'm not going to take anything down, not in that way. This is a person, dude.

"Stalking," Brucie smirked when I tried to tell him, fumbling and fucking up all the words like I do, and he smacked me upside the back of my head. But that seems pretty creepy too, like I'm obsessing.

Maybe I'm obsessing.

I wanted to tell Doll what was happening, how I was feeling at least, but she's so busy these days, doing the newlywed thing. And she teaches classes at the U and that's gotta be uber-stressful too, ya know? And Stephanie usually just smiles at me and pushes that really fine blonde hair back over one ear all nervous like she does and tells me something stupid, like I'm too young for an earring. Probably a good thing I didn't tell no one in the house about the Prince Albert, huh?

Brucie's the oldest one in the house, still thinks he's the alpha male or whatever, and he's always pissed off 'cause he's been single for over a year. I guess you could call us a pack if you wanted to, but it's Doll's rule that we behave like people.

"We're Breed," Brucie growled at dinner one night and threw his plate of spaghetti at the wall. It smeared crimson against the pretty pink paper Stephanie put up in this wide gooey streak. Pretty gross. And he slammed his hands on the table and stood up. Brucie's a pretty big guy, all six and a half feet two hundred fifty pounds of him and he don't take shit and he stood up and just glared at Doll. "We're Breed, don't you get that, we do what we want, take what we want, we don't act like humans 'cause we ain't *human*."

And Doll, she's sitting there just calmly spooling spaghetti around her fork and smiling up at him, this little smile that's driving him crazy.

"This is my house," she told him finally, spooling and spooling. "Door's always open, Brucie. You know that. The door never closes either."

Doll's real name ain't Doll–duh–but that's what she told me to call her when she found me when I was just a kid. I mean, younger than now kinda kid. She was smiling that same calm smile that she uses on Brucie when he gets like that and I guess I loved her right then.

And Brucie, his nostrils are flaring and his eyes are starting to go emerald, and Stephanie is chewing on one fingernail, eyes flicking back and forth, back and forth, and Maggie's the youngest, just a little kid, and she starts to cry. But no one moves and she starts to suck on her thumb.

"We Hunt," Doll finally says and that little smile is gone. She's got flint eyes now and they're a hint emerald too. "Of course we do. We're Breed, you're right. But being Breed means we are animal and human both."

Brucie don't say nothing to that. He came to Doll when he was shot in the gut, thought he was dying, and she fixed him up. Gave him a place to stay, just like she did for me and for Maggie, got him a job at a gas station. Maybe that's what he hates so much, real responsibility for once in his life, or maybe it just chafes him knowing that he ruled the streets one time and that he could live in the woods and run with a pack and be strong and be a leader.

But there ain't no woods nowhere no more.

That's what he tells me.

"We live in *their* world," Doll says to him. "We have to play by their rules."

Brucie keeps on not saying nothing. His hands stay flat on the table. The nails have grown long and blackened, but then they start to melt away and he slides back into his chair, this big hulking Wolfman with his arms folded across his barrel chest. Sulking. I have to hide a smile, pretend to wipe my mouth with my napkin.

"That's bullshit," Brucie says finally and picks up his fork.

Doll is nodding. "It might be," she says. "It might be. But for now there's nothing we can do, but blend."

I thought about that a lot and I guess I'm still thinking about it. Obsessing, like Brucie says I do. Because there's a part of me that wants to run free just like Brucie says we used to do, to dance under the moon wearing only my silver-tinged fur, singing the ancient songs I don't know how I know but I do. That's how things were before man covered this continent in a swarm, Brucie told me one night. We were free. We did what we wanted. Breed, we're older than man. We're of the old, Brucie told me, we're of magic, Drewbaby.

I been thinking about magic a lot too, 'specially now.

Stephanie's got a bunch of these old books, witchcraft and stuff, 'cause she wants to know the why of us, why we are what we are, I guess.

Doll doesn't like words like 'werewolf', says it's Creature Feature stuff, but I always liked those old movies. They're kinda funny. Harmless. Only Doll says they're not. They give us a bad image, or whatever. I wanted to tell her maybe if we were just open about everything we'd have a better image, but she told us we have to wait.

I hate waiting.

So in the meantime I'm reading all these old books about magic and witches and warlocks, wicked cool shit like that. It's 'cause of those books that I met Jason. I wasn't Hunting at all. Or stalking neither.

I was s'posed to be doing the school thing, but I cut out after lunch and headed down to the park so I could read some more.

'Werewolves are traditionally inclined towards the darker elements of the world,' this book tells me, and I'm smirking, 'cause what does 'darker elements' mean anyway? Fuck that shit. But then it says, 'Once the werewolf has found a witch with whom he can hunt, they consummate their relationship in an unholy ritual that mates them for the rest of their unnatural lives.'

My eyebrows shot up when I read that. I thought about mating plenty, I'll tell you what. I wanted to mate with Brandon Edwards and Connor O'Rourke and probably half the football team, but they just called me punk and faggot and boring shit like that. I didn't dye my hair every color of the rainbow to impress those assholes. I pretend they're dead or were never born. I pretend like I couldn't just gut them like deer if I wanted to. I let 'em talk their shit and promise myself that I'll do something about it someday.

Doesn't stop me from fantasizing about 'em when I jerk off, of course.

Werewolves mate with witches. Huh, I thought. That was kinda interesting. And witches didn't have to be women either, did they? Weren't there boy-witches? Warlocks or whatever?

Then someone says, "Good book?" and I jump right the hell outta my skin. And cover it up right away. Stephanie would kick my ass if she knew that I took it out of the house.

"Yeah, I guess," I say, all hostile. I'm seventeen; I'm s'posed to be surly, right? And I'm trying to check out this guy suddenly in front of me, all inconspicuous, which is tough, 'cause he's quite the hottie. Looks familiar, my age I guess, short blonde hair, green eyes, little snub nose, taller than me, which isn't hard since I barely make five foot five, got his hands crammed into the pockets of his jeans. Expensive looking jeans. Some cutsie little t-shirt with a cartoon tiger that makes his eyes look even greener.

"What's it about?" he says.

"Fuck if I know," I says, and he blinks but he doesn't go away and he smiles, and it's kinda like Doll's smile, small and sorta secretive. Gives him these little dimples that I think could drive me crazy for the rest of my life.

I scowl even deeper, feel the lines sinking into my face.

"My name's Jason," he says after too long. "We go to school together. I've seen you around."

"Cool," I say and I'm still cautious. Who's the wolf now, I think, 'cause I wanna bolt like a scared rabbit.

"I'm cutting too," he says. "It's a pretty day, you know? Makes me want to run and not stop running. All over the city if I could." He looks up at the sun and it's painting his face warm colors, like rose. He looks like a big tawny cat basking like that. He has muscles under his t-shirt and I can't take my eyes off 'em. He opens one eye, catches me staring–*dammit*–but he smiles that sphinx-smile and says, "You're Drew, huh."

I swallow my entire body 'cause it's crept into my throat and there aren't words anyway. "Yeah," I say finally, after six billion years have crawled by.

We look at each other. He's still smiling and he says, "Nice to meet you," and puts his hand on my shoulder and I feel this *jolt*, you know? This electricity from him to me, sinking through my skin and veins and blood and into my bones. I freeze, I can't move. And I start to get hard. Thank god for baggy jeans, I remember thinking, but then he's already on his way, walking down the path that curves around into this little copse of trees, and he looks back over his shoulder and he says, "Enjoy the book, Drew" and then he's gone and I'm left gasping like a fish on this park bench and my jeans aren't baggy enough.

And since then he's all I can think about. We see each other at school and he smiles that damned sexy pixie smile and sometimes he waves. I find myself following him after lunch, a safe distance back, so he doesn't know I'm there; I know his scent. I start to dream about him. He comes into my room through the window, eyes glowing like gems, floats right down onto my bed and of course we start kissing.

Nothing more than that–and these are my dreams, goddamn it! Shouldn't I be more in control?

I want to *Hunt*. This city is too small. There are too many people. I want to get *out* but I don't know where.

Doll and Stephanie are busy being married lesbians, and Doll's got lesson plans and papers to write, and Stephanie is still looking for a job, Maggie's only a kid, and Brucie just makes fun of me. "You don't know nothing about this guy," isn't exactly what I wanna hear, but he's right, which only pisses me off more.

"Listen up kid," Brucie tells me. "It don't ever work out if they're not Breed. We're meant for each other, Breed to Breed, Animal to Animal, and that's how it's always been. You can't change shit like that." He pauses. "I'm sorry." And I think he means it. Weird. For a second Brucie actually sounds like a person. Then he cuffs me upside the head and grins and says, "Now fuck off. I gotta get some sleep before work." The way he says 'work' it's like there's rotten meat in his mouth, spoiled fish sitting out in the sun.

I feel this pang for him, but I scoot out of his room anyway.

I don't know what to do. I want to sneak out at night, which is one of Doll's biggest no-no's, but I can't help myself! I can feel something building in me, building up crazy in my head and in my body, and finally I can't take it no more.

So last night I shucked all my clothes and let the shift happen, *finally*, the release I need, let the fur slide easy from every pore, let my nose press out and out and out some more until it's a snout filled with beautiful sharp teeth. The moonlight fills my room like silver water, and all I want to do is swim in it.

So that's what I do. Swimming in the moonlight, dancing under it, dancing in and out of the trees in the park, and singing singing singing up to the sky, where I can almost see the stars.

When I sneak back into my room someone's there. I can feel them–I can *smell* them–before I even drop onto the floor on all fours, because my hands and feet are still paws, and my eyes are emeralds that glow in the dark. Is it Brucie? Maggie? Doll? Did they notice that I was gone? Fuck, I think, I'm in deep shit now.

They're sitting on my bed, hands folded, just waiting for me and suddenly I knew it isn't Brucie or Doll or anyone else.

I recognize the scent.

And something else. Can't put my finger on it, but it's like a tug, or a pull. Some indefinable *else*.

"You're beautiful like that, you know," Jason says from the dark.

The shock makes the shift happen and suddenly I'm just a naked high school kid. I'm trying to cover myself up and he's smiling that little smile. "The fuck are you doing in my room?" I snarl, which is probably the least important question, considering he just saw me turn from a wolf to a person and isn't batting an eye. That's pretty f'in weird.

"I had to come," Jason says. "You know. You feel it too, right? I can't stay away from you."

I'm shrugging on my jeans and trying to cover myself while I do it. "I don't know what you're talking about," I say.

"Yes you do." His voice is soft, but there's this note of something–iron, maybe, command. Or just certainty. Like he knows what he's talking about. And I think he does.

"Okay," I say and turn to face him. "Maybe I do. So what? You just break and enter? And how'd you know where I live?"

"I have my little tricks," he says. He stands up. "You're all I think about, Drew. Ever since that day in the park. Maybe before. And you've been thinking about me too. Haven't you."

It's not a question.

We stare at each other. I'm hyper-aware of how thin I am, how bony my chest must be.

"Yeah," I say in a voice barely above a whisper, more of a growl, like the sound I'd make when I'm Animal. "I do."

He stands up and walks across my room to me. He's very close, and his smell is all around me now: his cologne, the conditioner in his hair, the musky smell of his sweat...and his fear. And excitement. They're mixed together. My forehead wrinkles. What is he afraid of? Me? Is he afraid of *me*? "Do you know what I am?" he whispers, very close to me. Very very.

"Um...a queer?"

"Well, yeah," he says and smiles. "But...do you know what I *am*?"

I think my eyes are flickering emerald. I close my eyes suddenly and just let my mind go, let it out, let the Animal part of me go. "You're not like everyone else," I say and it sounds wicked stupid, but when I open my eyes, he's nodding.

And he's different suddenly.

There's this crackling noise in the air and I look down at his hands and there's sparkage between them, dancing veins and shivers of black electricity.

I look back up to his eyes and they're *black*, like big punched holes, no whites at all. Like droplets of black oil. They're creepy... but fascinating. I can't look away. Don't even want to.

He's smiling a little. "I'm not like everyone else," he says, black-eyed and crackling, "but neither are you."

Then I know. I know what he is and maybe I knew it all along.

"We're meant," Jason says and the black fades out of his eyes and he's just a boy again. Like me. "We're *meant*," he says again, and our mouths press up against each other, and our hands come together and lock. I can taste him, I'm tasting him, he's tasting me, and we're on my bed, and there go my jeans and his shirt and his jeans, I'm making this growling sound, we're twined, I'm growling against him, and that energy begins to crackle again, but it isn't black now, it's blue, all around us, over us, pressing, thrusting, it hurts but it hurts *good*, sweet, like singing, like running free with him, like being in the moon with him.

He's still there in the morning, blinking at me, green-eyed. "I feel like I've been waiting for you all my life," he says, kisses me again.

"You're a warlock," I say.

He shakes his head. "I don't like that word," he says. "It means liar in Romanian or something. I'm not a liar. I've never been good at lying."

"I have to lie," I say shyly. "People would run screaming if they knew what I was."

"I didn't."

"You're different," I say and put my hand on him. He shivers and smiles and moves under my hand. "They'd put me somewhere, wouldn't they? Breed can't be out like that."

His forehead creases. "Breed? That's the word?"

"I like Breed," I say. "But 'werewolf' is okay too."

"I don't have a word for me," Jason says. "I don't feel like a witch or a warlock or a shaman or a mage. Or anything. I do magic. I make things happen. I call storms, I read thoughts, I stick pins in dolls and I can float three feet above the floor. I sing to the moon. And so do you."

I give him my best sexy wolf face. "Read my thoughts now," I say and we're off again.

We miss school. We walk in the park and I tell him about how I don't remember my parents and how Doll found me in an alley, naked and snarling with animal blood on my mouth. And he tells me about his spells and conjures a rose from the earth and gives it to me. I inhale its scent. It smells like him.

"I wish you weren't afraid," he says.

"I'm not afraid of nothin'," I say, but of course I am. I don't want him to know.

"Of people finding out," he says.

I shrug. "I don't care about the queer thing," I say. "I'm cool with that."

"That's not what I mean," he says. "You're beautiful. People should know."

"Doll doesn't think it's a good idea."

He's frowning and for a moment his eyes flash that night-shot black again. "I hate that," he says.

"Hate what?"

"That she's right," he says. "It isn't fair."

"Lots of shit isn't fair," I say. We're holding hands and they spark together. "That's how the world is."

"The world needs to change," he says.

I can't argue with that.

Doll is waiting for me when I get home, sitting on the same spot on my bed where Jason was last night. I try to keep my face from moving, but I'm kicking myself inside.

They're Breed too, with keener noses than mine. Fuck!

"I'm not angry," Doll tells me before I can say anything. "I'm just concerned, Drewbaby."

"You shouldn't be," I say and the words sound cruel and then I feel bad. Doll's been good to me. Better than most people.

"You're young," she says. "Too young. You don't know what you want and you don't know the world."

"I don't care," I say and I'm trying so hard not follow the script for some Afterschool Special, but I can't help it. The words just come.

"This boy...he knows what you are."

I nod slowly. I try to ignore the flash of pain that crosses her face and the brief odor of fear that makes my nose wrinkle. It smells like tin, like tomato sauce going bad. "But it's okay," I say. "No, really. Jason is cool."

She's nodding sympathetically now. I hate that look. I hate that nod. I want to back into the corner and snarl. "Humans never understand us," she says after a moment. "Brucie is right about that, Drew. Baby. Please don't misunderstand me. I want us to exist in the human world so that they know us before they judge us. We'll come out eventually. But there are only so many steps we can take at once. And your friend...he probably doesn't understand that."

"You don't even know him."

That sympathetic look won't leave her face. "I don't have to," she says. "I know this world. More than you do. I know how beautiful it can be and I know how it can hurt. How it can cut. And you're too young to know that for yourself."

"You think I don't know what it's like to be cut?" I can feel the Animal inside me, rising, rising up, teeth and claws bared. "You think I don't know how it feels when they call me faggot? What's one more word, Doll?"

"The world is not ready for us," she says. She's trembling. "And they may never be."

We don't say anything. We stare. Our eyes are matching green.

"Stay with us," she says at last. "We love you. We're your home. We're safe."

I don't know what to say. She's right. This is the only home I've ever known. My head is spinning. When did it come to this? I wonder. I'm not going anywhere, am I? I live here!

But it has come to this.

I'm trembling too. I'm about to break.

"There will be other boys," she whispers, and I back away from her, and I'm a wolf, and goddamnit, that was my favorite t-shirt, but I'm out the window before she can say another word. Lithe and loping away into the darkness of the night, avoiding the streetlights, avoiding people, bigger than a regular dog, bigger than a regular wolf, people scream when they see me. So I slip through alleys and back streets and it isn't dark enough, it's never dark *enough.*

I don't even have to think and it isn't just his scent that I'm following; I can feel Jason and I know he's thinking about me. That helps. I find him easily. I'm outside his window and there he is, a flicker, a flame behind the shades and the shades go up and he's looking down at me. I step out of the safety of the shadow of the oak in his yard and I stand there, a wolf in the open.

He disappears from the window then, and I back away, and after a moment he's out the door.

"Drew?" he calls, his voice half-hushed and I can smell his excitement. "Drew?"

Then I'm human again, naked before him. He looks grateful and he reaches out for me, but I won't let him touch me. Not yet.

"I have to leave," I say and I hate how brusque I sound, like I hated how cruel I sounded talking to Doll. Like I hate what I'm about to do. Fear crawls and claws inside me. I don't want to say this. I have to say this.

"Jason," I say. "Do you love me?"

It's a stupid question. I know it the moment it leaves my lips. Of course he doesn't love me; how can he love me? We just met; we don't really know each other at all–but we're different than other people.

I have to hold on to that.

He's looking at me and his face is pale in all that dark.

I lick my lips.

Do you love me?

"Yes," he says at last.

I don't have words at first. Then he looks up and I look up and there's the moon, not quite full, hanging over us, watching us.

"It's crazy," I say. "This...it's all crazy."

"Yes," he says.

"But I have to leave," I say. "Get out of the city. School, other people...I don't know. I can't be here anymore, do you get that? I can't do it. Not right now. It's too...close. And if I can't be Breed, if I can't be open about it, I don't want to be here."

"You're leaving," he says slowly.

"Yes." And I know it's true. For the first time, I know it's true. "I have to. Jason, I can't *breathe*."

He's looking at me. More than that. He's looking *into* me.

I lick my lips again. I'm so afraid.

"Come," I say, but the word doesn't come out right, so I cough and I look into him too and I say, "Come with me. Jason. Tonight. Please."

It's too soon, I think, it's crazy, I think, we have lives, we have–

"Yes," he says for the third time. His eyes are swallowed by night-shot black, open galaxies. His hand on my hand. His mouth on mine.

"You mean it?" I whisper.

"We are meant," he tells me. "Those books, they're wrong about a lot of things. Darkness and unnatural things, they're *wrong.*

But not about this. I feel it, you feel it. *We* feel it. We are meant."

We don't talk anymore, but he doesn't go back to his house and I don't go back to mine. I feel a pang about that, but I can't see them again.

That'll just make it harder. I want them to understand–god–but even if they don't, it doesn't–can't–matter to me.

Because I have to do this.

We have to.

We have to love each other, and we have to run with each other, and we have to sing.

He's lying beside me now. Snoring a little. I'm awake. We're under the stars, somewhere dark and quiet, somewhere where there are trees and no people. They're close, though, so we have to go further.

Maybe someday we'll come back.

Maybe someday the world will be ready.

Maybe I'll *make* it be ready.

He opens his eyes now and he smiles. He traces my chin with one finger. I put it in my mouth, so I can taste him. He doesn't have to say anything. We're both afraid. And we're both so excited.

And there's the moon, above us.

We look up.

And we begin to sing.

WOLF LOVER

Michael Itig

The ropes were hidden under the pillow. In the drawer were some handcuffs in case things got out of control. Taking a slug of beer from a bottle, I knew I was going to be in for a good night.

The doorbell rang. Eight o'clock. Punctual. Nice. Too early maybe too eager, but fashionably late has become a bore. I don't know how many hours, days, weeks of my life I've wasted waiting for a bit of rough trade to make the appointed time. A bit of housetraining doesn't do any harm.

Before I answered I poured a beer, the glass chilled from the freezer. Into it went a shot of vodka–just a small one, not enough to be detectable.

As soon as I pulled open the door he stepped in. "Nigel?" His breath frosted in the blast of November air.

"Yeah."

"Tom." He held out his hand and I thrust in the beer glass.

He was tall, nearer seven foot than six, thin face and a widow's peak. A fair bit older than the photos I'd seen of him–but aren't they all?–I placed him about forty-but-fit. To sum up: a good foot taller and a decade-plus older than myself.

"Come into my boudoir," I said, dripping with irony.

He eyed up the studio. "Nice place you got here." He sounded sincere, but he shouldn't. It was a matchbox: single bed, a sink in one corner and a cooker in the other. Dirty washing shoved under the bed. I shrugged, "Bachelor pad, I'm afraid."

"Good area. Nice and central."

"All I could afford." I took another swig and he did the same. Had he noticed the vodka? To encourage him, I finished the dregs of my bottle, eyes on him all the time. He took another sip. A second flashed by and we were touching, hands exploring bodies beneath shirts. I pulled him close. His mouth wet and cool from drink, but his tongue was rough. He tasted of cigarettes: dull, musky, masculine. A buzz went through me, the thrill of the chase.

Fast forward: he was undressing me, pulling off my shirt and I dropped my pants. He was still clothed, not an item removed, but his hands and mouth were all over me, eager to explore. I could hardly suppress a smile: he was hungry for me.

Fast forward again: lights off, candles lit. He pushed me onto the bed, a bottle of lube in his hand. Undressed now, his body thin, wiry and smooth. "How do you want it?"

"Doggy style."

Flipping onto my knees, I reached for a bottle of poppers. I felt him enter me as blood rushed through my head. On all fours, my hands slid up the bed towards the pillow. I could feel him against me; his chest, all muscle and ribs, against my back. I pushed up, face down. He balanced hands either side of me, his long arms outstretched. Soon a good rhythm had begun.

There was a grunt behind me, a breath on my neck. I slid my hand under the pillow, the movement slow and unseen. I clenched with each stroke, pulling him in, hoping to hold him there. Deeper, further, harder. Fingers wrapped around the rope.

I let out a cry. Just a faint one–couldn't help it.

He was away, immersed in the moment. I tugged the rope and, with a huge relief, it worked. The door to the bathroom opened, the bulb switched on, a strand of light illuminating us on the bed. An ultraviolet glow cast across our flesh.

I felt his body clench: I had him now.

His breath became heavier: big exhalations, a grunt, then definitely a snarl. I could see his hands tighten either side of me, fists clenching. Against my back I could feel the muscles ripple in his chest, the fur across it. I found I couldn't move, held in place too tightly, his movements now rapid and violent. Again I looked at his hands but they were no longer human, now paws. He growled, definitely a growl.

A shudder went through me. It was exquisite.

His body convulsed two, three times before he let out a full howl. Then several ever-smaller spasms followed. I tugged the rope again to kill the light and quickly brought myself off as he whimpered behind me.

The final moments were a disappointment. I couldn't help but lament that it was always the bark but never the bite, as I splattered across the pillow.

"That was a cheap trick," he said, his face still distorted by the receding muzzle.

"A bit of a luxury."

"Sorry?"

"Cheap joke. It's a point-two lux light, the same wavelength of moonlight."

He nodded, not really understanding. "Yeah. Knew it would be something like that." He was buttoning up his shirt, then lacing up his shoes. All I'd put on was a pair of boots and a necklace and was lounging legs wide open, hoping to tempt him back. I swigged another beer. He shook his head. "You shouldn't have done it. You should just let things happen naturally."

"You'd never have let it happen. You'd have locked yourself up at full moon."

"They used to lock up people like me, you know."

"People like me, too." I did my best cheeky-boy smirk.

He looked angry for a moment, not wolf-angry, but pleading, like a little boy. "You were in danger. I could've killed you."

"The orgasm holds you in place; the coming's the kill you need."

"One day, you're going to fall for the wrong person and going to get hurt." He sighed, then shrugged, pulling a pen and paper from his pocket. "Here, there's a place for people like you." He handed it to me, gave me a kiss, then made it to the door.

"See you around sometime?"

"Maybe," he said and then was gone. I knew he was lying. Always the bark, never the bite...

I unfolded the piece of paper. It said:

Rabid Babes, Tuesdays, Basement Bar, Central Station.

Central Station was a bar, near a railway station, but not as central as I would've liked. It took a good twenty minutes to get to and I wasn't dressed for the winter. Getting into the warmth felt good. Upstairs was a slightly older crowd downing plenty of bottled beer, but it was the basement that was the main attraction. Downstairs was a locker room and entrance stall; not too pricey.

The main room, however, was crowded. There must have been a hundred men packed into the tiny rooms. Black walls dripped with sweat and condensation, a heady mix of breath and beer. The clientele were of all shapes and sizes. Some decked in leather, some in suits, some younger guys in trackies and trainers. But it wasn't anything unusual, in that there was nothing wolf-like about it.

Then I noticed the lights. Someone had rigged up some point-two lux bulbs–like the ones in my bathroom–up by the speakers. I bit my lip. There was going be a party and it wasn't even full moon.

A tall guy brushed past me, for a moment I thought it was Tom until I realized his hair was silver. What kind of fur was he going to have? I scanned, guessing who'd make the best wolf.

Then I saw him. In the corner, a little lost boy. Blond hair was flopping over his forehead, shirt half off, hung over a tight white vest. Could have been an image from a porn mag, but he looked so sad. Nervous even, scanning the room as if he'd lost someone.

My target found, I homed in.

I tried to speak to him, but the rumble of the music and crowd drowned me out. He just looked and smiled and nodded. Some miming helped me offer to buy him a drink, and two bottles later we were both swigging in a quiet corner. His name was Luke and at twenty-five he was younger than me but older than he looked. His eyes kept wandering though, as if he couldn't fix on me.

"You looking for someone in particular?"

"Nah," he said.

It was then I caught a glint from the chain that hung around his neck and on it, what looked like a memento, something silver. A bullet.

I grabbed it. "Hey...does that hurt you?"

He seemed stunned that I'd been forward and asked outright. It was as if he wanted to say something but couldn't. He nodded. "Yeah. It's a painful memory."

A delicious adrenaline buzz hit me; already I was falling for the masochistic lure of the werewolf who wore his own bullet. I imagined him topless, smooth chest, the necklace hanging down between his nipples, leaving a small red burn where it touched. Maybe a hiss of smoke too, but that might be just too fanciful.

I couldn't help it. I kissed him. But he kissed back. I could feel him relax, a tangible sense of relief. He didn't wander after that and we kissed for some time.

Suddenly, the music and lights fell. The barman spoke into a microphone behind the bar. "Okay guys, brace yourself. It's show time."

My hand tightened around his. This was it: the money shot. I couldn't wait for my first glimpse of my new-found blond wolf. But I felt him tugging. The trick lights came up. Shirts and teeth glowed with UV and I was being pulled through the heaving crowd, some already beginning to growl. Luke let go, was lost in transformation. I caught sight of the silver guy from before, falling on all fours, snout and teeth showing, silver streaks all over his body. I saw Luke in the exit, silhouette only, and in the corner nearby a pair of wolves were entwined, rutting like, well, animals. I followed Luke, running up the stairs.

"Hey, hey, what's wrong? You turn into a pumpkin or something?"

"No, no, I've got to go, that's all." Something was wrong. Maybe the change has agitated him? He was clutching the silver bullet. Realizing that all this was a bit obvious, he turned by way of explanation. "It's the wolf stuff, I've been there, seen that, it's too soon for me to go through it again. I thought I was ready, but I'm not." He looked at me with puppy-dog eyes.

Wolf lover I may be, but I'm human after all. I took his hand. "It's okay. I understand." He was young and I started to wonder how long it had been since the first bite.

"See you again?"

This hit me, the biggest thrill of the night. "Sure, I mean, yeah. You got a number?"

I gave him some paper–the same Tom had given me–and he wrote it down.

There was a sudden howl from within and we both turned for a moment. I felt caught between what was going on inside and the young man beside me. I turned back but he was gone. I ran up the stairs, but he'd made a quick getaway: he was running down the street. I went back in, heading for the basement, but the ticket guy stopped me.

"Oi! The sign says no readmission after the moonlight hour."

It didn't matter. I'd had my money's worth.

Seeing Luke was different. He *was* different. Yet there was something wonderfully normal about him. He worked in a bookshop. Ate mostly in a vegan café, even though he wasn't vegan. He still lived with his parents, but fortunately had a large attic room that gave us plenty of privacy, snug beneath the eaves.

Two weeks can be a hugely long time when you're in the first flush of a relationship–what is it they say about gay years? Or is that dog years? It's as if every day, every hour is important. Like your life has begun again, because this is a new start, full of potential.

The great thing was we were taking it slowly. I'd never done that before, usually getting my legs–or arse–in the air before shaking hands. But our first few nights were different. Kissing and caressing, savoring the moment. Holding back before the full-blown fuck. He was very gentle, a little bit needy to tell the truth, and I wondered what kind of wolf he would make.

Even in our sensuous chastity, there was a dynamic there; a tension always present in man-wolf sex, like active versus passive, or positive and negative poles that ensures that there's always electricity flowing from one to the other. Guess that was why I was hooked.

He liked to doodle, drawings all over the walls.

I browsed his books, hundreds of them–I never had been much of a reader myself, but he talked passionately about them. And he seemed interested in me.

He wanted to see my pad-he hadn't yet, his own place seeming more comfortable and glamorous.

"And what about previous guys?" he asked.

"Not much to say, really. Thought I had the pick of the kennels, but mostly they turned out already to have name tags. What

about you?"
"Just one guy. Seth. But it was a deep thing, a sad thing."
"What happened?"
He shrugged.
"Another time, perhaps. Hey, when do I get to see your place?"
"Oh, I dunno. It's a bit of a dump really."
"I'd still like to see it. Besides, maybe we'd get a bit more privacy."
I eyed the calendar on the wall, on which was marked not just days of the month but phases of the moon. I was in luck: "How about tomorrow?"
His eyes went to the calendar; he'd caught scent of my plans. Typical wolf.
"Not tomorrow. I hate full moon."
Just hearing those words made me slightly hard in anticipation.
He continued, "Besides, I've got to be somewhere. The night after?"
I agreed; but had missed the target.

I lay on my bed, the window open. No lights on, instead I was bathing in the bright moonshine, pining for the effect it would have on Luke. I imagined him as a wolf: blond hair resulting in a golden hound, more a labrador than a wolf, but young and strong. Damn, damn, damn. Sod the bite, this time I wouldn't even get the bark. I swigged some beer and smoked a cigarette, taking a heavy drag. The idea was formulating in my head. It would be another twenty-eight days before I got the opportunity. It was true: it was an age in both doggy and gay years. But he was coming over tomorrow.

I got off the bed and began to set things up. Time to show Luke the ropes...

Candles were lit. Luke was a drinker fortunately; I'd have no problem plying him with beer or vodka. The ropes were under pillow again, running in a pulley system under the bed to the bathroom to the switch for the bulb. There was a knock at the door. All was ready.

"How are you?" I said, grinning and handing him a spiked beer.

"All the better for seeing you." He said sweet things like that.

"Missed me?" I egged him on.

"Not half."

We kissed, but this time I deliberately punctuated the kiss with little breaks for alcohol. Best to keep him sweet.

We moved to the bed. There was a bottle of lube prominently on the table nearby. I nodded that way, "Do you think it's time that we...y'know?"

He broke out in a blushing grin. "Was wondering if you'd ever ask..."

I began to work him up with a bit of spit, then some lube.

Sex is the easiest thing in the world when you're in love. It really is. Within no time we were slip-sliding all over each others' bodies, inside and out. But soon I'd manipulated him into position, he was riding me face down on the bed and we were loving it.

I could feel him become more intense, more drawn into the moment. I knew it would be difficult for him to pull out now. So I put my hand forward under the pillow and pulled the rope.

The bathroom door opened silently and the gentle glow of the light cut across him.

I could feel him. His movements became stronger, fiercer. Muscles tensed on his stomach, as if in spasm. I closed my eyes and revelled in it.

But then I opened them. Something was wrong. The light was shining across us, true, but his hands either side of me...they were human. Still normal. A man's hands, not paws.

He let out a groan, his body taut as he climaxed.

I rolled him off me and he flopped on the bed, regaining his breath, sleepy, sated.

He opened his eyes. "Nige, what's wrong?"

"Nothing. I'm okay. Sorry, I left the bathroom light on. Better switch it off..."

"Okay."

After the light I blew out the candles and we slipped into

darkness. I returned to bed and, with some awkward shuffling, plumping up the pillow to disguise what I was doing, I let the ropes fall under the bed.

"Are you okay?" he asked.

"Yeah, it's nothing."

"Something's wrong. Did I hurt you? Are you okay?"

What could I tell him? That I was sulking being a disappointed fetishist?

"I was just wondering about that necklace you wear... Where did you get it?"

"It's a reminder. A keepsake. You remember we met at Rabid Babes, right?"

I nodded and leaned into him, eager for him to go on.

"Well, it's where I'd met him before. He was one of them, you know, a werewolf. We were together before he got bitten. He really wasn't used to it, didn't have the knack of control... We used to keep him caged for full moon, he'd spend the night howling... He was a nice person, he really was. But...but..." his voice began to crack. "One night he found a weak spot and broke out... You know how the police are with wolves... I'm sure he wouldn't have hurt anyone...but the neighbors called them out, and when they caught him, he'd cornered a family, terrorizing their children. Just a new wolf, all instinct, didn't know what he was doing... And so they shot him."

"Did they kill him?"

"No, he got away. As he was a young wolf, he was very fast too. He came back and I dug the bullet out...he was bleeding a fair bit...whimpering badly..."

He put his arms around me.

"When he turned back again, he said he didn't want to see me any more... Said he couldn't control himself... That he felt ashamed of it...of being a wolf. His parents weren't happy about it; they didn't help at all. So he went away. Gave me the bullet as a reminder, but upped and left. That was over a year ago."

He snuggled into me.

"That was why I went to Rabid Babes. I think I was still looking for him...sorry, I don't mean to...I met you. That's what's important now."

He put his head on my lap, and I began to stroke his hair.

"You okay with all this?"

"Yeah," I said. "I'm okay."

Outside, the moon, though still quite full, showed the first signs of beginning to wane.

So this was how it came about that I was in strange and new territory: a relationship. It really was a foreign land to me. I still saw Luke. He spent a number of nights at my pad. We made meals together. We did things, like–oh I don't know–make breakfast. I found myself buying things such as skimmed milk and tofu because he liked them. I no longer put vodka in beer.

The sex was still quite regular, but not the same. The dynamic had gone, the spark jumping from pole to pole. I thought about the wolf in him, what he would've been like...

This went on for several weeks. Then, by accident or by design, I found myself at Central Station. And it was a Tuesday. I thought about it for a long time. It was nearly the moonshine hour. No re-admittance, no going back now. Slowly, I descended the stairs...

Luke came round one afternoon. I hadn't been expecting him, but this was fine. After all, he was my boyfriend, surely it was reasonable that he come and go.

"Hi. Just calling by. Just fancied a drink, that's all."

"Sure. Come in."

More beer. He slunk onto the sofa in the corner, fiddling with the laptop in front of him, browsing my movie collection. *An American Werewolf in London. The Howling. Dog Soldiers.* I must have seemed very predictable. Hell, I was predictable. He seemed nervous.

"Nige, I wanted to ask you... Is everything okay?"

"Okay?"

"You know...between us. Something hasn't been right. Well, since the night I told you about Seth, to be precise."

I thought about Central Station, about what I'd got up at Rabid Babes. I found myself swirling my bottle around, creating a whirlpool within.

He looked at me with puppy-dog eyes. I can never resist puppy-dog eyes.

We knocked over a bottle, spilling it all over clothes as we tore them off. He pulled back from me and looked at me for a moment. He really was a handsome man. I unbuckled my belt, trousers falling loose as I maneuvered him to the bed. He wanted me all right, offering no resistance, his body supple and yielding.

It was getting late. I knew what was coming. I was inside him, pushing him back and taking in the sight of him. I felt strong. I felt in control. And he wanted it.

Outside the moon began to rise.

If all my blood had been flowing to my cock, now it was flowing back from it, surging up me, carrying the orgasm throughout. The hairs on the back of my neck stood on end, the hairs on my back itself stood on end. I was powerful, I was being reborn. A fit of ecstasy surged through me, as I realized the bite I'd taken had been successful. I looked down at my hands, now paws. My teeth large, I felt hungry and heard myself growl as I came. Then afterwards I let out a howl of triumph, finding my new voice.

Luke finished himself off as the signs began to recede. I'd had the kill I wanted and that had been enough. His necklace glinted on his come-spattered neck though afterwards he took the thing off. "First full moon for a year that I haven't been pining; time to put this away," he said, dropped it beside the bed.

But I took the bullet for him. It hung on my chest, giving a tingle of heat as it touched my skin.

"Then I'll wear it for you."

That night we slept huddled together, curled up, safe in our pack. From now on I knew it was always going to be there, the dynamic that I'd always been looking for. True, there was going to be a lot to learn, but now the bite was within me, it was part of me, the hunt didn't matter anymore.

Luke slept sound into the night, well after the moonlight faded.

SHY HUNTER

Ginn Hale

David didn't like doing rescue work up on Mount Kierly. The rough shale slipped beneath his feet. Dark pines cut black silhouettes against the cloud-filled night sky and yellow eyes shone down on him from the branches.

Every rescue up here felt like a trap. This one even smelled like a trap, though the lost hiker was real enough. Her boyfriend and mother were down at the base camp, both too distraught to sleep. For all David knew, Calvin had already devoured the hiker and left this trail to lure dessert to him. Calvin's musk drifted down from high branches and wafted off bare stones, ever-present and yet oddly stale.

Then David heard a distant but distinct noise: a high-pitched sneeze followed by a second, a third, and an exhausted obscenity. David swung back to fetch Lisa and the team, wanting to tell them that he thought he'd found their errant hiker.

Unfortunately, his present form didn't allow for conversation. He gave two sharp barks. Lisa grinned patting his thick hide.

"David's got her scent," Lisa called out, then looked at him. "Get to her and keep her safe, okay?"

David nodded. He could tell Lisa was worried about Calvin as well. She didn't need to be, though; Calvin never kept his victims alive. He didn't have that kind of self-control. If the hiker was alive then Calvin hadn't found her.

David charged ahead and the rest of the wilderness rescue team followed quickly behind.

A week later, his photo was in the paper, along with an article praising working dogs. He was pictured sitting beside Lisa, wearing an orange rescue pack and a bandana that made him look a complete fool. Lisa, on the other hand, looked cool, with her sunglasses pushed up and the Red Cross tattoo on her forearm prominently displayed.

After the article ran, Lisa had a new girlfriend every night. David received a basket of designer dog biscuits and several squeaky toys.

He tossed one of the toys–a red one shaped remotely like a hedgehog–at the wall and caught it.

"That's getting annoying," Lisa commented from the bathroom. She was preparing for another night out.

"I'm bored," David replied. He tossed the toy again and it emitted a satisfying squeal on impact with the wall.

Lisa leaned out of the bathroom door, still threading a stud earring through an earlobe, and studied David. "Well, get changed and I'll take you for another walk. But it will have to be fast. I'm supposed to pick Lilly up at seven."

David hefted the toy back and forth between his hands, feeling the dexterity of his human fingers, the tenderness of his human palm. It was strange that the body he'd been born with could seem so foreign.

"I don't need another walk," David said at last. "I'm bored with walks."

"Well, maybe you need to go out. You know, as a person." Lisa slid the earring backing into place. "You might meet someone."

"And bring him back to my kennel?" David asked.

"You have your own room and your own real-person bed. You can be as human as you want to be." Lisa gave him a hard, serious look. "We both know that you've been hiding in that dog skin of yours because Robert dumped you. It's time you got over it. Not all men are Robert."

"No, some of them are Calvin," David replied and he felt a sick twisting in his gut. Lisa's delicate mouth flattened into a hard line.

"Granted, you've had some shitty luck, but you're not going to meet anyone here. And if you don't try to meet someone, then sooner or later you're going to get desperate and before you know it, you'll be waking up next to that poodle from down the block."

"Dickie?" Davis scowled. "That's just sick."

"Yeah and it might be asking a little much of your family.

Gay, they don't care about. Werewolf, they seem to be dealing with. But if you turned into a dog-fucker too?" Lisa shook her head. "No way would you get invited home for Christmas."

David laughed. His parents had been amazingly accepting. After he came out they had joined PFLAG, marched in rallies, and had taken part in more protests than David himself. They were old hippies, so political activism came easily.

The results of Calvin's assault had been different, harder for them to accept. At first they had been happy just to have David back with them and alive. But then the changes had started. His skin split as his bones went soft and shifted. Stiff hair jutted from his wounds. His screams had come out low and animalistic.

For the first three months David had had no control over his body. Changes came without warning, prompted by strong scents, exciting television programs, even–humiliatingly–perusal of the old porn magazine he'd stashed years before.

David's mom had cried almost daily. His father had spent hours researching werewolves, trying to track down cures. His little sister had told him he looked gross, but then curled up with him on his bed and hugged him.

Slowly, David had learned to control his condition. It was excruciating when his body twisted between forms, so he learned to change quickly, like tearing off a band-aid. After a change, his muscles ached and a ravenous hunger filled him. If he gave into the craving he would glut himself like an animal. But if he waited, the hunger receded. Even so, David remained wary of the bestial voracity that haunted his flesh.

There were other limits, as well. He couldn't get drunk and expect to remain in human form. He couldn't be out in the wild, with the tempting scents of rabbits and birds, deer and squirrels saturating the air. There were places that he could go as a man and others that were only safe for him in his canine form.

He'd also learned a great deal about werewolf myths; particularly that they were created by people who weren't werewolves themselves and had no idea what they were talking about. The full moon was nothing to him. He could wear sterling silver and attend church with impunity. He was inclined to ignore most of the myths, though from time to time he did catch himself glancing in the mirror to check if his eyebrows had grown together.

"You know, being human isn't just a matter of the shape you take," Lisa said. "It has to do with interacting with people. Getting out there and mixing it up."

"Yeah, I know," David admitted.

"So, are you going to go out tonight or not?"

"Yeah, I am," David said. "What have I got to lose at this point?"

"Exactly." Lisa looked relieved and David could tell that she'd been expecting him to put up more of an argument. "Good. So go put on some pants and take off that dog collar. You're starting to creep me out."

Whispers wasn't the kind of club that David normally went to. Then again, he didn't normally go to any kind of club, unless the dog daycare Lisa ran counted, and he doubted that it did.

The dance floor was packed with men. The smell of sweat and cologne carried on waves of body heat. Swirling light and music pounded through the tight space in synchronized throbs. The DJ scratched out sharp lines of static.

Dancing felt good. It reacquainted David with his human body. His physical awareness shifted. Acute hearing and smell gave way to the exquisite sensitivity of delicate, exposed skin. His eyes took in the shapes and colors of the men around him. His mind filled with half-forgotten words, while his long limbs stretched and flexed.

Hands brushed his back and men met his eyes and smiled at him, but David still felt a little shy. There was an awkwardness to his conversations. He hadn't spoken more than a few simple sentences in months. He watched the men around him and nodded when it seemed appropriate.

He hoped he looked like a good listener and not just a man resisting the urge to sniff a crotch.

A fit man in his mid-thirties leaned close to David. He smelled like beer and David found it pleasantly masculine. He asked David if he was with anyone and David said no. Then something at the edge of David's sight caught his attention. His gaze slid to the other side of the dance floor.

He met the stare of a pale young man, whose shaggy black hair and drab clothes seemed less a fashion statement than a matter of insecurity. He wasn't dancing, but was instead standing at the edge of the dance floor. David remembered looking like that once himself, desperate to meet someone, but too nervous to do more than watch. That kind of vulnerability attracted men like Calvin.

Protective concern sparked up in David's consciousness. He remembered how easily he had accepted Calvin's offer for a ride and how eager he had been for Calvin's attention. How completely he had misinterpreted the hunger in Calvin's expression and how deeply Calvin's teeth had torn into his body. There was an instant of quiet as the DJ switched from thumping dance tunes to a slow love song.

"Sorry, but I think I see someone I know," David said to the man beside him.

He wove through the knots of dancers. The young man watched as David drew nearer, but didn't withdraw or move closer himself. When David reached him, he smiled.

Now beside him, David felt at a loss. A deep feeling of protectiveness had drawn him; the same feeling that surged through him when he searched for lost hikers and skiers. But now that he had reached the young man, he found that he had no rescue team to back him up.

"I'm Edgar," the pale young man said. He extended his hand.

"David."

They shook hands, an oddly formal exchange in the midst of so many half-naked, embracing men. Edgar's fingers felt cool against David's warm grip.

"David?" The young man looked puzzled. "I thought...I mean... You're NightStalker from gothdate.com, aren't you?"

"NightStalker?" David raised his brows at the name. "No, sorry. I'm just David from Chestnut Avenue."

Edgar looked him over, taking in his height and build. His eyes lingered on the white scar on David's shoulder, then lifted back to his face. David offered his best smile. Edgar seemed to relax, his forced, nervous grin fading to a simple curve of his lips.

"David from Chestnut Avenue seems all right," Edgar said. "To be honest, I was a little nervous about meeting a guy from online. I've never done it before."

"Neither have I," David said. He didn't bother to explain that he was rarely able to turn on a computer, much less surf the net. His paws were simply too large and inflexible.

The slow love song that had washed over the dance floor ended and a pounding dance rhythm burst through the air. The lights flashed and spun, illuminating expanses of skin and casting strange, jerking shadows.

"You look kind of cold," David raised his voice to carry over the music. Edgar nodded, but David wasn't sure he'd really heard the comment.

"So, what do you do?" Edgar asked.

"I work at the Bow-House. Take care of dogs," David said. "You?"

"I'm a freelance illustrator." He frowned as a stocky man with a thick beard and a leather vest pushed between them. "It's pretty loud and crowded in here."

David nodded.

"Maybe we could go somewhere else?"

"Aren't you going to miss your date?" David asked.

"His loss, your gain," Edgar replied. He pushed the hair back from his bright green eyes and gave David a very inviting smile. A tight pulse of arousal shot through David. He hesitated for only a moment and then allowed desire to envelope the concern that had initially drawn him to Edgar.

"Where would you like to go?" he asked.

They ended up at Edgar's basement apartment. Several muted paintings were hung on the walls. The slightly sweet, chemical smell of lemon perfumed the small space. David couldn't pull anything else out of the air, but he didn't try either.

He watched Edgar steal shy, desiring glances at his chest and abdomen. Edgar's white skin turned rosy and David knew he was looking at the hard bulge in David's tight jeans. Edgar's fingers trembled when he took David's hand.

Edgar led them through the spartan living room and into a spotless kitchen. They stopped in front of a door. David guessed that Edgar's bedroom was behind it. Edgar stared at the door, but didn't move to open it. He seemed suddenly nervous.

"You want something to drink?" Edgar asked abruptly.

"No. I'm fine," David replied. "Do you want something?"

"A shower," Edgar said. He gave a nervous laugh. "I'm kind of sweaty from the club. I probably stink like a pig right now."

"You smell just fine to me," David told him and it was true. Only a very faint, woody scent clung to Edgar's body. David liked it. He wished he could smell more of it.

"You could come with me." Edgar made the offer hesitantly. "Not that you're dirty, but it might be nice." His pale face flushed red and he looked down.

"Sure," David said.

They stripped each other in the bathroom. Edgar ran his hands over David's hard, animal muscles. He touched the jagged white scars that cut across David's shoulder, chest, and stomach, but didn't ask what had caused them.

David tenderly exposed Edgar's delicate skin and marveled at the perfection. He caressed Edgar's tight pink nipples and then ran his hands down to Edgar's hips. Edgar closed his eyes and leaned closer into the touch. David traced the length of Edgar's erection, admiring both the stiff line and Edgar's beautifully rapt expression. Edgar timidly brushed his hands over David's thighs and allowed his fingers to stroke David's penis.

It seemed like such a delicate moment that David was loathe to break it. But he had to. He had no idea of how his condition could be transmitted. Calvin had passed it to him through the mingled blood of savage wounds and a desperate defense. But for all David knew, it could be transmitted in an innocent spill of semen as well.

He kissed Edgar's soft lips gently and pulled back just a little.

"Do you have a condom?" he asked. He had worried that the question would fluster Edgar, but instead Edgar looked a little relieved.

"In my bedroom," Edgar said. "I'll get them if you want."

"Yeah, you probably should," David said.

When Edgar returned he proved to be skilled at sliding them on and then making David forget that he was even wearing one. They kissed and fucked in the shower until the hot water ran out; then retired to Edgar's bedroom.

For all his earlier hesitation, Edgar was a voracious lover once the lights were out. He was not as delicate as David had first imagined. His lean body was strong and supple. He kissed, licked and sucked every inch of David's flesh. But he took an exceptional relish in riding David's thick cock, arching and bucking, urging David deeper into him with each thrust.

When exhaustion finally over came them both, the sheets were sweat soaked and tangled into a ball in a corner of the bed. The blankets lay on the floor. Edgar curled up against David. David's arms wrapped around him and they slept.

David woke later than he normally would have. The darkness of the basement apartment and the previous night's exertions had made him both unaware of the bright sunlight outside and unwilling to consider it. It was the obnoxious refrain of his cell phone that finally woke him. He staggered into the bathroom, found his pants, and answered Lisa's call.

It pleased her that he'd spent the night out and that he'd met someone, even if he didn't know the guy's last name. But she wondered if he was aware that he was three hours late for work?

David apologized and promised he'd be in right away. He cleaned himself up then peeked into the bedroom where Edgar lay sound asleep. He kissed him and Edgar smiled, but didn't wake up.

David left a note on the bedside, thanking Edgar for the great night and asking him to call. He left his phone number and signed his full name.

On his way out, he stopped in the kitchen and checked the fridge for something to eat. He found two full catsup bottles, an egg, and a couple cans of Guinness stout. The cupboards offered him several black teas, half a jar of honey, and a plastic container of protein powder. No wonder Edgar was so skinny. David guessed that Edgar ate out a lot. He spent his walk to work wondering what Edgar's favorite restaurants were.

When David arrived at the Bow-House, he found the dogs playing in the open run and Lisa on the phone. She frowned and beckoned David over.

"You know that kid who went missing in town three days

ago?" Lisa asked.

David nodded.

"The police want to know if they can borrow David to try and track him down," Lisa said.

David just nodded again.

"All right, but I want to be very clear here." Lisa used her coolest tone. "David is a tracker, not an attack dog. He's sensitive and he needs to be treated respectfully. No leash when he's tracking... Yes, I'm serious!" Lisa rolled her eyes at David, then returned her attention to the phone. "And I'll have to charge you... I know, but this isn't wilderness rescue. This is city work."

David left Lisa to argue out the payment. In his room he stripped off his clothes, noting that the tang of lemons still lingered on them. He took in a deep breath, preparing himself and then changed. His throat strained against a cry of pain as his bones and muscles burned molten and skin tore away. He dropped to all fours, feeling as if he were melting inside. His own blood dribbled down his face and soaked through his rough hide.

All color drained from his vision and suddenly he could smell the rich, woody scent of Edgar's sweat still clinging to his skin. He could hear Lisa in the kitchen, pulling on a pair of rubber gloves. He recognized each individual call of every dog outside. They all smelled like hot meat. David closed his eyes and lay on the floor. Slowly, the familiar hunger passed.

He padded out of his room and Lisa sprayed the traces of skin and blood off him. She dried his dark coat with a blow-dryer and tied a ridiculous pink bandana around his neck.

"I know you don't like it, but it makes you look less like a wild animal." Lisa patted his head.

Two police officers arrived a few minutes later. They were both part of the K-9 unit, but their dogs were attack animals, not trackers. David didn't like the fact that their car smelled like another animal's territory, but he got in anyway.

He spent the remainder of the morning and most of the afternoon picking out the scent of a runaway teenage boy. He followed the trail from a sprawling middle class house, down through the Capitol Hill district and into a reeking alley behind a strip club. When he caught a whiff of Calvin's musk, he knew he wouldn't find the boy alive. He knew he would find bloody scraps and stripped bones. Dread gripped him and for a few moments, he couldn't make himself move. Then, he pushed himself ahead the same way he forced himself through the pain of transformation. He made it fast, knocking the dumpster lid open and howling over the broken remains inside.

While three other police officers removed the pieces of the boy's body, a detective searched the blood soaked pockets of the boy's pants. He discovered twenty dollars and a list of bands written on the back of a print out of an email. An email from a man called NightStalker.

David ran towards Edgar's apartment, dodging traffic and jumping fences. The police tried to follow for a few blocks, but he was far too fast for them.

He didn't think about what he would say to Edgar or how annoyed Lisa would be. All he could concentrate on was the fact that Calvin had targeted Edgar. The afternoon was growing late and David's shadow stretched out as if racing ahead of him.

When he reached the brick apartment building he was panting hard. An old woman frowned at him from her yard, then picked up her cat and went inside. David scratched at the security door and then collapsed on the apartment steps.

He took in a slow breath of air. There was no hint of Calvin's presence here. Above a little brown bird chirped from its perch in a tree. David took in another deep breath to reassure himself.

Then the terrible thought came to him that Calvin didn't need to be physically close. All he needed to do was make a date online and his prey would come tottering to him. Edgar could be making the arrangements right now. David's exquisitely sensitive nose wouldn't tell him a thing about it.

He cursed himself for being an idiot and not getting Edgar's phone number. He glared at the security door and the small intercom beside it.

He needed pants.

He found a pair, as well as a t-shirt, on a nearby clothesline. The pants were yellow plaid and loose, but David was glad to have them. After he changed, he wiped his body down using the bandanna Lisa had given him, then dressed.

He pushed the button to Edgar's apartment and after a brief greeting, Edgar buzzed him in. David hurried down the stairs to the basement level and to Edgar's apartment.

Edgar glanced up at him from where he sat at his drafting table. He held a cup of steaming tea in one hand and a pen in the other. A small ink drawing lay on the table in front of him.

"You have to stay away from that NightStalker guy," David blurted out.

Edgar smiled and David realized that the demand made him sound like a jealous idiot.

"He's a murderer," David explained. "We–the police–just found the body of a boy he killed."

Edgar's smile dropped. "When?" he asked.

"An hour ago, maybe," David replied. "I mean, that's when they found him. They used one of our dogs to track the boy. He was probably killed two or three days ago."

Edgar capped his pen and set it aside very deliberately. Then he stood, went to David, and hugged him. David didn't know what prompted the embrace, but his entire body responded. He clung to Edgar, filling with relief as he felt Edgar's slim body.

"I was so worried," David whispered.

Edgar closed his eyes and pressed closer to David.

"You know, I really thought you were him last night," Edgar said. "I thought you were pretending not to be because you were embarrassed."

"No, I'm not him. I'm nothing like him."

"Obviously." Edgar gently pulled back from David's embrace. "Do you want a cup of tea? Or would a beer be better?"

"Tea's fine," David said. He would have asked for the beer, but didn't trust himself to hold his form. He sat down on Edgar's clean, beige couch and listened as Edgar heated up the water in the microwave, then tossed in a tea bag.

"Honey?" Edgar offered from the kitchen.

"No thanks. Could I use your phone?"

"Of course," Edgar brought him the tea and then fished a sleek cell phone from his pocket. "I have to get this drawing finished. It shouldn't take me more than an hour. Do you think you'll want to get some dinner then, or something?"

David nodded and Edgar returned to his drafting table. David took the phone into the bathroom and called Lisa.

"Do you think he's resorting to this because of us?" Lisa asked, once David had explained everything. "We've rescued a lot of people who would otherwise have ended up as his dinner."

"Maybe," David said. "But it's just as likely that we've gotten so many people down the mountain alive because Calvin wasn't there anymore."

"You think he's moved into town?"

David's stomach knotted.

"Yeah. He'll have staked out a lair somewhere isolated, like the old warehouse district or by the tracks. It'll be somewhere he can enjoy himself without the screams attracting attention."

There was a long silence on the other end of the phone.

"Are you going to be okay?" Lisa asked.

"Yeah, I'll be fine. I just don't want to leave Edgar right now."

He gave Lisa Edgar's address and she agreed to bring him clothes.

Edgar took David out to an Ethiopian restaurant called *Axum*. It occupied an old brick building only five blocks from the apartment. The moment David stepped inside the warmly lit space he was overwhelmed with heady, rich and foreign scents. The waiter recognized Edgar and inquired cordially about his latest commission. Edgar said he'd just finished it and introduced David as a good friend.

The menu was incomprehensible to David. He didn't recognize a single dish on it and when he read the descriptions, he found that he couldn't even identify most of the basic ingredients.

"What are you having?" David asked Edgar.

"Either the kitfo or the gored gored," Edgar replied. David nodded as if he knew what either was. The menu described them both as rare meat, ground or cubed and seasoned with strong spices—cardamom, garlic, ginger and chilies. The thought of ground meat brought the memory of the runaway boy's savaged face rushing back. He turned the menu over and read about the restaurant's traditional Ethiopian coffee, which was served with copal incense. "I think I'll just have the vegetarian platter," David said.

Edgar looked surprised. "You're a vegetarian?"

"No. I just don't feel like being a carnivore today."

Edgar smiled and David noticed that the soft amber light of the lamps lent his pale skin a golden luster, making him look less boyish.

They ordered. Edgar settled on the kitfo and promised David a traditional coffee service after the meal.

"I noticed you reading about it," Edgar commented.

"It sounds interesting. Coffee and incense."

When the dishes came, David was relieved to find that his own food was plentiful and richly flavored. He even enjoyed the spongy bread it was served on. Edgar's meal looked disturbingly raw, but it smelled of butter and the same woody, warm spices that David associated with Edgar's skin and sweat.

"Do you like your dinner?" Edgar asked.

"Yeah. I wasn't sure that I would, but this is all really tasty. How's yours?"

"Perfect," Edgar replied, though he seemed somehow embarrassed by the admission.

"So, are you originally from around here?" David carefully scooped up a spicy assortment of lentils with his bread.

"No. I moved here from the east coast about a month ago."

"Do you have family out here?"

Edgar paused for a few moments before answering.

"I might, but I haven't concerned myself with my family for a long time." He shrugged and took another bite of his vivid red kitfo. "What about you?"

"My parents own a small organic farm out in the county. I visit them pretty often," David said.

"Sounds nice."

"It is." David wondered if Edgar's family had rejected him because he was gay. The way Edgar had dismissed them made him think so.

"You're lucky," Edgar said.

"I know," David admitted. "I'm luckier than I deserve to be."

"I hope that was a subtle declaration of how fortunate you feel to have met me." Edgar smiled.

David had no idea how Edgar could be so relaxed after coming so close to being Calvin's next meal. But then, Edgar hadn't seen the body in the dumpster. He probably hadn't really considered how easily the same thing could have happened to him.

"I think we were both lucky to have left that dance club when we did last night. If we had stayed much longer–" David wanted to believe that if Calvin had walked in he would have tried to stop him from taking Edgar; but a sick uncertainty haunted him. His entire body ached with the memory of Calvin's jaws. He had fought for his own life, but he didn't know if he was brave enough to fight for someone else's.

Either way, David suspected that Calvin would have taken Edgar if he'd wanted him and there was little doubt that Calvin would have wanted him.

The moment David had first seen Edgar, he'd been aware of how he'd stir Calvin's appetite. David had sensed the same attraction in himself. He'd felt hunger and fascination when he'd seen Edgar and it had drawn him. The thought made David sick.

"Is something bothering you?" Edgar asked.

David looked up and realized that he'd been staring at his plate in silence.

"I just don't have much of an appetite, I guess," David said.

"Were you there?" Edgar asked. "When the police found the body?"

David nodded.

Edgar considered this quietly for a moment. David could almost see him trying to imagine what the scene must have been like: the gutted death that he had so narrowly missed himself.

"Was it...bad?"

"Yeah, it was," David said. He pushed his food aside. It didn't matter how hungry he was. He couldn't eat.

"The police will catch him," Edgar said.

"Sure," David said, but he didn't believe it. He'd outrun a squad car himself just this afternoon. They wouldn't stop Calvin. David had driven a hunting knife into his stomach and Calvin had pulled it out and tossed it aside with a laugh.

"You don't want to be out right now, do you?" Edgar asked.

David thought of lying, but he knew he wasn't good at it. "Not really," he admitted.

"Why don't we take a rain check on the coffee?" Edgar suggested. "You want to go back to my place?"

David did. They paid and Edgar left an extravagant tip. He smiled, seeing David trying to work out the percentage.

"I just finished a commission and I'm working on another. I can afford to be generous. Anyway I've heard flashing your wallet is a good way to impress a date."

In the quiet of the basement apartment, Edgar drew David in with the scent of him, the delicate pink blush of his pale skin. David pulled him into his arms, kissed him.

Edgar showed him his drawings and paintings. Most were minutely detailed diagrams of animals, plants, and machines. There was a cool perfection to them that David couldn't imagine achieving.

"What's this one?" David glanced at a sketch. It was unlike any of the other pictures, full of rough lines and hard eraser marks. Gray, ghostly masses seemed to float up between wild black strokes and the paper's white surface. David thought he could make out a face–contorted and half-animal.

The longer he stared at the page, the more solid the faint image seemed to become. It disturbed him, because he suspected that what he saw wasn't what Edgar had drawn, but an image that lurked in his own thoughts.

"That's an ongoing project. I'm trying to build a better mousetrap."

"Mousetrap?" David asked.

"It's a figure of speech. You know, find a better way to do something," Edgar replied. He put a CD into his computer and the wireless speakers hummed to life with classical music. Edgar caught David's hand.

"Would you care to dance?" he asked. David smiled at the formality.

"Yeah," he said and then added, "it would be a pleasure."

They danced; the closeness of their bodies stirring a deep, slow arousal in David. He let go of his worry, holding Edgar against him. Before the CD ended they were on the couch, entwined, pressing and kissing. Edgar had two condoms left and they used both. It wasn't the exhausting sex of the night before, but something more comforting and caring.

Edgar seemed to sense that David didn't want animal lust, nor to feel his own strength. Edgar held him in his arms and stroked his hair. He kissed David's shoulders and they lay quietly together. The apartment was warm and it was easy to lie across the couch only half-dressed, drifting in and out of sleep.

Edgar's cell phone chirped quietly and he answered it. He patted David's shoulder gently and rose from the couch. David closed his eyes, half-listening.

"Yes. You were right. It's difficult," Edgar said. He sounded a little more clipped than usual. "Two or three months." He listened to the person on the other end of the line. "No, difficult doesn't mean I'm giving up. You can tell Linda that I'll have it done before her birthday."

There was another pause, or perhaps David drifted off. The next thing he heard was Edgar saying, "Goodbye," and snapping his phone closed.

He cracked his eyes open. Edgar was standing in the kitchen, heating a cup of water in the microwave.

"Pushy customer?" David asked.

"It's a private commission, so the work is pretty personal to the man who's hired me."

"Still, it's almost ten. A little late for business calls."

"He's not in the country," Edgar replied. "But I'd expect as much even if he were. People get worried when they care about something." Edgar smiled at David through the doorway, then turned back to the microwave and removed the cup. "When there's so much emotion involved, people can be demanding. At the same time, it feels good to know that I'm doing something that's important to someone." Edgar dunked a tea bag in his water, added two spoonfuls of honey, and stirred it. He glanced back over his shoulder at David. "You want that beer now?"

"Sure," David said.

Edgar brought it to him. David only drank a little before laying his head down on Edgar's lap, Edgar stroking his hair. David thought he ought to get up, but before he could, he drifted to sleep.

Over the next two months David spent more and more of his time with Edgar. He grew accustomed to Edgar's largely nocturnal lifestyle. He discovered that he enjoyed the quiet afternoons spent reading while Edgar painted. He spent days on end in his human form rediscovering its limits and pleasures.

Edgar always seemed a little surprised and flattered when David asked him out. They went to see two of the bands that Lisa's new girlfriend played bass for. They took in midnight movies and made out in the velvet seats of the old Pickford Theatre. Edgar delighted in the activities as if they were new discoveries and his reserve steadily faded. David even managed to cajole him into drag for Lisa's birthday party.

The nights he slept alone, David was restless, so he found excuses to do it as little as possible. He began to keep spare clothes at Edgar's apartment, as well as a razor and shampoo. He was touched when he dropped by one late afternoon to find that Edgar had bought cereal and milk for him. After that, Edgar's bare kitchen shelves and empty refrigerator quickly filled.

The sterile quality of the apartment faded in the face of David's habitation. One of his dropped socks lay beside the bedroom door. A tangled blanket remained on the couch after a late night of watching television together. The sharp smell of lemon cleaners vanished beneath the warm, mingled scents of their bodies. A deep happiness pervaded David when he was with Edgar and he sensed that Edgar, as quiet and reticent as he was, felt the same.

At the same time, David's awareness of Calvin's presence grew. At first he caught only a hint of Calvin's musk and it was miles from Edgar's apartment. But as weeks passed, Calvin moved closer. David smelled him in the aisles of grocery stores and in coffee shops. More than once, David caught sight of a tall blonde man and a sick terror gripped him.

Just before summer break, a twelve year old girl from Edgar's apartment went missing. The police contacted Lisa and this time, David wore a leash.

He found the little girl's body behind Edgar's favorite

restaurant, her neck crushed and her limbs broken. The contents of her school bag lay crushed and strewn in wild arcs around her body. David imagined Calvin hurling her, like a rag doll, again and again against the concrete wall. The flesh of her face and chest had been chewed and spat out in sticky globs, as if she were somehow unworthy even of eating. She had not been the prey Calvin hungered for, only flesh he had vented his frustration against.

David knew exactly who Calvin wanted. His voice shook when he called Edgar. He begged him not to leave his apartment, not to allow anyone in. He could hear the sleepy confusion in Edgar's agreement and it made him even more afraid.

"I have to go," David told Lisa.

"Go," she said, then caught his hand. "Be careful."

When David reached Edgar's apartment, he failed to answer when David called to him over the intercom. In a panic, David hurled himself at the door. The metal bit into his shoulder and groaned under the force of his body. David stepped back for a second try, but Edgar's sleepy voice greeted him from the small speaker. A moment later, David was in the building and sprinting down the stairs.

"What's happened?" Edgar asked. His black hair hung around his face in disarray.

"He killed another kid," David said. "The girl from Jefferson Elementary, her family lives on the third floor of this building. We found her body under the dumpster behind *Axum*."

Edgar frowned and sat down on the couch.

"Do the police have any suspects?" Edgar asked.

"They have shit," David replied. "He walks right past them and eats people's kids! He was probably the guy who crapped in the police station parking lot. The cops don't even know how to look for a guy like Calvin! They keep thinking he has to fit a profile, have a mother complex, walk on two legs, die when he gets shot–"

Edgar gazed at David with a look of quiet concern and David realized that he wasn't making much sense.

"I know him," David said at last. "He's a monster. Really, a monster–" A tremor broke David's voice. He hated to think of what Calvin was and what he become because of Calvin. He looked away from Edgar, trying to hide the self-loathing that roiled through him. He didn't want Edgar to know.

"He's the man who left those scars on you, isn't he?" Edgar asked softly.

David nodded.

"Come here. Sit down with me," Edgar said. David came to him. "Do you think he's trying to find you again?" Edgar asked.

"No." David's throat tightened and he had to wait a moment before he could speak again. "He wants you. That's why he came down from the mountain. There's something about you that he's drawn to. That's why he's hunting in this neighborhood. He's at your coffee shop and behind your favorite restaurant. I keep seeing him in shop windows and I smell him everywhere. He's here and he won't give up until he finds you."

Edgar was quiet for several moments. David listened to his slow, even breathing.

"Have you told any of this to the police?" Edgar asked.

"I called in an anonymous description of him," David said, then shook his head. "But I know I sound crazy. I know. And Lisa thinks that if I went to the police they would end up suspecting me."

"Probably," Edgar said.

He sounded so sure that it frightened David.

"It isn't me," David said.

"I know," Edgar assured and smiled slightly. "I've known a few rotten men in my life, David and you aren't even close to being one. You're certainly not a murderer." Edgar squeezed David's thigh in an almost paternal manner. He stood, but didn't step away from David.

"I need a cup of tea. You want something?"

"I want to get out of here," David gripped Edgar's leg, hard. "I want you to come with me."

Edgar sighed heavily. "Where do you want to go?" he asked.

"My parents farm, maybe, or somewhere farther away. Somewhere Calvin will never look for us," David said.

"He really hurt you, didn't he?" Edgar asked. He stroked David's hair.

"It's not just me–"

"I know," Edgar cut in. His voice was soft but very firm. "I'm not going to move to Borneo, but if it makes you feel better, we can spend the night at your place."

"You don't understand!" David glared up at Edgar. "He's a fucking monster!"

"I do understand." Edgar stared into David's eyes. There was a hardness in Edgar's expression that David had never seen before. "I've had my own encounters with monsters. The one thing I've learned is that you can't outrun them. Sooner or later they find you and you have to face them."

David shook his head. "Calvin isn't some metaphor or life lesson—"

"I believe you and I've already agreed to leave for the night," Edgar said. "Let's leave it at that for now, all right?"

David didn't want to, but he also knew he was too upset to offer any kind of intelligent argument. At least Edgar had agreed to come away with him tonight.

"All right," David agreed. Edgar looked relieved.

"I guess I'd better get an overnight bag packed," Edgar said. He frowned at his drafting table and then looked at David. "While I'm getting dressed and packed, do you think you could run to the mail drop and get that illustration mailed for me?"

David picked up the padded manila envelope. The nearest mailbox was two blocks away. He didn't want to go, but he also knew that he had to get a grip on himself. He couldn't start acting like a paranoid, possessive madman and expect Edgar to take anything he said seriously.

"Promise you won't let anyone in," David said.

Edgar nodded. He wandered into the bathroom, then laughed. "My God, my hair looks like a bird's nest." He leaned out of the bathroom door. "Has it been this bad all this time?"

David smiled weakly and nodded.

"Great," Edgar sighed. "I guess I'll wash my hair at your house. We're taking my car. Hopefully the tinted windows will hide my shame."

"Sure," David agreed. "I'll be right back."

"I'll be here," Edgar said. "I promise."

David ran all the way to the mailbox. He dropped the slim envelope in and turned back. A few feet away from him a man was talking loudly on his cell phone, inquiring fearfully about a little girl.

David hurried down the street. A mother gripped her daughter's hand tightly as David came up beside them at the crosswalk. David kept his gaze pointedly averted. He studied the chestnut trees across the street. When the walk signal flashed he let the mother and child go ahead. As they reached the other side of the street, David glanced past them to Edgar's apartment building. Calvin stood in front of the thick glass security door, running his tanned hand over the intercom keys.

Then he lifted a silver key with a tattered bit of red yarn hanging from it. He unlocked the door and easily pulled it open.

An animalistic roar burst up from David's throat and he sprinted forward. His muscles screamed and his bones felt like fire, but he didn't care. He tore past the woman and her child, hardly noticing the woman's surprised squeal.

Hearing David, Calvin held the door open and turned back. For an instant, surprise registered on his handsome face; then he smiled.

Fury surged through David and he sprang, slamming into Calvin and pitching them both into the building. Calvin's back cracked against the handrail of the staircase. David fell on top of him, sinking his lengthening teeth deep into the meat of Calvin's shoulder.

He felt Calvin's muscles flex and twist and suddenly, Calvin's huge haunches were under him. Calvin kicked into David's chest with a brutal strength and David was launched into the air, flipping like a piece of rag. He crashed against the stairs and tumbled down, the cement steps hammering both muscle and bone.

Dizzy sickness welled in him as he hit the basement floor. Calvin bounded past him.

David forced himself up, his body shifting and twisting into any shape that would allow him to follow Calvin. Twice he caught Calvin and tore into his thick flesh. The first time, Calvin pounded David's face with large human fists and threw David against the concrete floor.

David tasted his own blood and felt his ribs spearing into his lung. He growled Calvin's name and lurched forward. He sank his clawed fingers into Calvin's right calf and ripped the muscle from the bone.

At last Calvin gasped in pain, but almost instantly the muscle writhed back up his leg. Calvin spun and kicked David against the wall, again and again. Shocks of blinding pain ripped through David. He felt his hip bones split, his vertebra crack. His vision blurred and all he could smell was his own blood. A keening, involuntary whimper escaped him and to his utter horror, Edgar's door opened.

"David?" Edgar leaned out and his curious expression instantly melted into horror. "Oh god, David," he whispered.

Calvin drew in a deep breath, filling his lungs with Edgar's scent. His entire body rippled with excitement. He grinned and David glimpsed his blood red tongue dart over the tips of his long teeth. Calvin turned on Edgar.

Edgar stepped back into his apartment. Calvin surged after him. David dragged himself forward on all fours.

The door fell open under his weight, but he didn't have the strength to do more than lay there, bleeding on the white tile floor, and watch Calvin slowly stalk closer to where Edgar stood beside the couch. Edgar gripped a pitifully small penknife in his hand.

"You." Calvin's voice was husky and on the edge of arousal. He leaned closer to Edgar. "You are going to die slow, Baby."

Edgar looked past Calvin to David. His eyes shone as if he were on the verge of tears. Every fiber of David's being wanted to stand, to go to Edgar. He felt his muscles tugging at his bones, but couldn't rise.

Calvin glanced over his shoulder, saw David, and snorted.

"You think that piece of shit pup is gonna save you?" Calvin demanded. He sounded both angry and amused. "Ain't nothing gonna save you, Baby. I'm gonna eat you alive and then I'm gonna finish what I started with your boyfriend."

"No, you won't. You won't touch him." Edgar raised his gaze to meet Calvin's. His expression was so calm that it seemed to unsettle Calvin.

David prayed that somehow Edgar could keep Calvin talking. He just needed a little more time. A furious heat poured through the marrow of his bones and David felt them melting back together. It was agony and yet he welcomed it. His ribs slowly rose from their collapsed splinters. He drew in a full breath. He pushed himself up to his knees.

"I'm gonna do a lot more than touch him, Baby." Calvin growled at Edgar. "And I'm gonna eat you both." He reached for Edgar, and Edgar lifted his hand, catching Calvin's thick wrist between his fingers.

"No," Edgar said softly and a ripple of darkness pulsed through the room. The table lamp and the overhead light went black. David's pupils dilated, drinking in the faint light from the hallway. The black air surrounding him suddenly felt too thick. A single breath seemed to extend for minutes. His heartbeat was a leaden throb.

In the weird darkness, Calvin stood strangely still, his mouth open, his arm extended. Edgar lifted his hand to Calvin's jaw as if stroking his cheek.

David saw the silver flash of the fine blade.

Edgar's hand dropped fluidly to Calvin's shoulder, then his elbow and wrist. Edgar traced the blade through ligaments and tendons, cutting with cool precision. And, very slowly, David saw blood begin to rise across Calvin's skin. Calvin's jaw drooped and then fell from his skull like a stone sinking through water. His arms went limp. His fingers dropped, one after another, to the tiles. A look of utter terror came into Calvin's eyes, but he remained motionlessly suspended in the darkness.

Edgar circled him. Calvin's knees gave out and he fell to the floor in a slow spill. Lazy, dark rivulets of blood poured from his body. Shadows within the surrounding darkness seemed to lap up the pooling blood.

Edgar knelt beside Calvin.

"Before I kill you," Edgar's voice was low and soft, "I've been hired to tell you that Annie Mueller's family loved her and they miss her and they will never forgive you for taking her from them." Edgar placed the edge of his small blade against Calvin's neck. "I also want you to know that I'm doing this for David. You will never touch him again."

Edgar leaned forward and the blade sank through Calvin's throat. Calvin started to make a sound, but only dark bubbles rose from the deep wound in his throat. Then his head rolled from his body.

Edgar turned and gazed at David. He looked exhausted and hollow. David tried to speak, but his throat felt like it was full of water.

"Don't look at me, David," Edgar said. "Close your eyes. You need to rest."

Then another wave of darkness engulfed the room and David saw nothing more.

David woke feeling like he'd lost a wrestling match with a bus. He rolled over and discovered that he was alone in Edgar's bed. The sharp smell of lemon wafted over him, blotting out all other scents. He tried to call Edgar's name, but it came as a whisper. Still, that was enough.

Edgar stepped into the doorway. The uncertainty in his face seemed strange to David after witnessing him kill so coldly. Edgar cupped a mug of tea in his pale hands.

"This is for you." Edgar brought it to him and David accepted it, though his fingers felt weak and clumsy. He drank slowly.

Edgar sat on the edge of the bed. He gazed down at his own bare, white feet and then at the wall.

"Your friend Lisa called," he said. "I told her you'd come down with the stomach flu. She didn't seem to believe me."

"I don't get sick." David was pleased that his voice came a little more firmly now.

"No, you wouldn't," Edgar said. "It would take something extraordinary to injure a body like yours. Not that you didn't manage it anyway." Edgar looked at David, both tenderness and annoyance playing in his features. "You are the single stupidest, bravest man I've even known. That Calvin could have killed you."

"But he didn't." David let the memory come back to him. "You killed him." He searched Edgar's delicate face, wishing he could find better words for the question he needed to ask. "What are you?"

Edgar flinched.

"I'm like you," he said. "Someone who fell prey to a monster, fought him, and survived. Your monster was a werewolf. Mine was a Creature of Darkness." Edgar frowned. "I suppose you would have called him a vampire."

"A vampire?" David couldn't help the disbelief in his voice. "You're a vampire?"

"Yes, more or less." Edgar's pale cheeks flushed.

"You love garlic," David protested. "You have a reflection and–"

"I can't endure sunlight," Edgar broke in. "I can drink the life from a man and live on nothing but a little protein for months if I have to. And I'm...old."

"Old?" David asked.

"I'm a little over ninety." Edgar looked incredibly embarrassed, but somehow it reassured David. For all the cold composure Edgar had displayed when he had killed Calvin, sitting here now, he was exactly the same man David had fallen in love with.

"You cradle robber," David teased. "I'm only twenty-five, you know."

"Yes, I know." Edgar reached out and shyly placed his hand against David's thigh. "I didn't mean to seduce you. I just set a lure to draw a werewolf to me. I thought it would be Calvin, but then you came–"

"And you came, as well," David said just to see Edgar flush pink. David drained the last of his tea. He studied Edgar, knowing there was more he should ask. "So, you're what? A bounty hunter?"

"Not so much now," Edgar said. "I really do make most of my living as an illustrator. But the Muellers are friends of mine, so I took their offer." Edgar cocked his head slightly and studied David. "Do you actually work at a dog kennel?"

"Yes, I really spend my days exercising and grooming dogs, though I also volunteer for the Wilderness Search and Rescue."

"But in your other form?"

"Yeah," David admitted and this time it was him feeling a little shy. "Did you know all along? I mean, about my condition?"

Edgar nodded.

"I knew, but you weren't anything like what I expected," Edgar said. "You are so...good. That may not sound like much of a compliment, but among our kind–creatures with so much darkness in them–you shine like a star. I should have told you what I was, what I was doing. But compared to you, I felt so cruel and so ugly." Edgar sighed heavily. "I didn't want you to see me for what I really am. But, of course, you did."

"I did," David said. Edgar looked away. David caught his hand. Edgar looked up at him and David could see that he was both surprised and relieved.

"You aren't cruel and you aren't ugly. You did what had to be done. And honestly, I'm glad you were there. I'm even happier that you're here now." David squeezed Edgar's hand. "You did what I could never do." As David spoke, he felt the truth of his words. He hadn't killed Calvin and not because he lacked strength or courage, but because killing was not in his nature. He had fought to bring Calvin down, but not to kill him. Strangely, that knowledge reassured David. He'd spent so much time being afraid of the creature within, thinking that he could so easily become another Calvin. But now he knew that wasn't true and his fear seemed to melt away.

"You know," David leaned closer to Edgar and kissed his ear, "I need someone like you in my life."

"I need you, too," Edgar replied.

David grinned. "Well, luckily, I happen to be right here."

"I know." Edgar looked at him and David could see the desire in his eyes. Edgar glanced down at his own hands. "I shouldn't take advantage of you while you're weak."

"When is there a better time to take advantage of me?" David teased.

"After you've got a condom on," Edgar replied slyly.

David laughed and quickly found them in the night stand drawer. He pulled Edgar close and Edgar relaxed into his arms. David drew him back into the warmth of the bed and they remained there until well after nightfall.

THE STRAY

Anel Viz

A couple of days after the first incident with the stray, Farkas suddenly changed his mind and agreed to move in with me. It had taken me months to convince him.

It is an unusual name, Farkas. Unlike mine–I'm just John. I'd assumed it was his last name, but it isn't. It's Hungarian and pronounced 'Farkash'.

To me living together seemed reasonable and natural. Our relationship had lasted over three years–closer to four by the time he moved in–and not once had we had a serious disagreement. My place was also large enough for the both of us. Yet he resisted.

"Is there someone else?" I asked.

"You know there isn't."

"Are you afraid we'll end up fighting if we live together?"

"Not really."

"That it'll mean giving up your independence? It won't, you know."

"It's not that either."

"Then what?"

We didn't go through this every day, of course; I didn't nag. The one thing he couldn't stand was nagging and he was the alpha male in the relationship.

But I didn't let the matter drop either. And it was always no. His explanation never varied. He was used to having his own place. Every so often he just wanted to be alone. He needed his space.

Then one morning over breakfast he says out of nowhere, "I've made up my mind. I'm ready."

"Ready for what?" How was I supposed to know?

Once I understood and my excitement had died down, I said, "Should we get a dog while we are at it?"

THE STRAY

"Whatever for? We both work all day. It wouldn't be fair to the poor animal."

Dogs had been more on my mind that day than our living together. The evening before I'd heard some whining and scratching at the front door and found an enormous stray dog standing on the doorstep, so big that at first I thought it was a wolf. But it couldn't have been; it was too tame, downright sociable.

"Hello there, big guy," I said. "Are you lost?"

He wagged his tail in response. Reassured by his friendly manner, I bent down to pet him. He was an unneutered male and he had no collar.

He responded by sniffing my crotch. He was as bold as he was trusting.

"Would you like some water? Wait here. I'll get you some."

He didn't wait. He followed me into the house.

I tried 'stay' on him and he stopped in the living room and didn't move till I'd given the command 'come'.

He probably knew a few tricks as well, like 'roll over' and 'play dead', but I never cared for that sort of thing. It seems demeaning to the dog. I did ask–that is, tell–him to 'shake' and when he gave me his paw I asked, "So what's your name, pooch?" I wasn't expecting an answer and of course he didn't give one.

Farkas hadn't come over that night, but knowing he still might come I thought I'd better call to warn him about the dog. He wasn't at home, so I left a message.

I didn't have any dog food, so I fed him table scraps. Right before bed I took out the garbage. I saw a squad car cruising the street, not a common sight in my neighborhood. It pulled up and the policeman rolled down his window.

"You should be careful going out tonight," he said. "A few people have reported seeing a wolf roaming around the neighborhood."

"I don't think it was a wolf, just a big dog. I found a stray out on the lawn a while back and took him in. He's a real friendly mutt. No license, no collar. I'm going to look for the owner in the morning."

"Does it look like a wolf?"

"Sort of...from a distance it would. I really think you're wasting your time."

He thanked me and drove on.

The dog looked a lot more like a wolf than I had admitted–charcoal grey, pointed muzzle, curved tail that hung down like a German shepherd's–but he definitely wasn't one. I could tell by his fur, which was too silky. He was also perfectly behaved. I let him out in the back yard to do his business.

Only one area of his training had been neglected. He didn't know that furniture was for people only and tried to get in bed with me.

"No you don't," I told him. "No one sleeps in this bed except myself and Farkas."

He looked puzzled.

"Off!" I ordered, and he obeyed.

I woke up the next morning with Farkas next to me. "So he let you in," I said.

"Who?"

"The dog."

"What dog?"

"You didn't notice him?"

I called for him. I whistled. I got up and searched the house. No dog. The bowls were still on the kitchen floor. How on earth had he managed to get out? I ought to have called him Houdini.

That explains why I was thinking dogs rather than live-in-lover when Farkas broke the news that he wanted to move in with me.

A month later I came back one night from a trip to the drugstore and found the dog curled up on the living room rug.

"So you've come back," I said. "Long time no see. Where's Farkas?"

He wagged his tail.

"Not telling, huh? You didn't scare him away, did you?"

Farkas hadn't left a note. When two hours later he still wasn't home I began to worry. I stayed up till after midnight, then dragged myself to bed. The dog followed and got in with me.

"Don't you remember the rules?" I asked sleepily. "No dogs in bed."

I woke up cradled in Farkas's arms. "When did you get back?" I asked.

THE STRAY

"Back from where?"

"From wherever you went. Dog still here?"

"What dog?"

The more awake I became, the more I recognized that familiar comforting warmth down below and the feeling of having been stretched. I forgot about the dog.

"You fucked me in my sleep, didn't you?"

He grinned sheepishly.

"What the hell did you go and do that for? Why didn't you wake me first?"

"Believe me, I tried, but you were dead to the world."

I believed him. If you can sleep through your lover sticking his dick up your butt, nothing will wake you.

"Just don't do it again," I said. "Wait till morning."

"It is morning."

The dog slipped quietly out of my mind until the next time he showed up.

I didn't feel angry, just annoyed. It's impossible for me to stay mad at Farkas. I'm head over heels in love with the guy. He's so beautiful, with his shaggy black mane and exotic features–swarthy complexion and a slightly Oriental cast to his brown eyes with orange-gold highlights; gleaming white teeth and bright pink tongue; long, lanky, very muscular body, large hands and feet, and hairy all over. He always takes the initiative in bed and is active from start to finish. He's very oral and loves to give me tongue baths, bury his nose in my most intimate crevices and nuzzle me all over. It drives me crazy.

He is also very athletic. He loves the outdoors, especially hiking in the woods, and he jogs five miles every day. I tried jogging with him a couple of times, but there was no way I could keep up. What Farkas calls jogging is more like a sprint that goes on and on and he won't slow down to my pace. When we play sports it's most often frisbee. He adores frisbee. In fact, the first time I saw him he was playing with some of his buddies in the park.

He was so gorgeous, running barefoot on the grass, wearing just a pair of hiking shorts, leaping for the frisbee, smiling and glistening with sweat. All I could do was stare and think "Woof!" He waved to me and called, "Come and play!" And play we did, all night in his room.

The dog continued to come by once every few weeks. He'd scratch at my door, stay the night and disappear by morning. Somehow, against all odds, he and Farkas never crossed paths. Farkas always had a good explanation for his absence. Of course I could get nothing from the dog.

"It almost seems like you're avoiding each other," I told Farkas. "As if there was some mutual antipathy between you."

"It's not that way at all. I'd love to meet this stray of yours. I'm sorry I missed him again."

"Then it's the dog who prefers to keep away when he knows you're here. Well, at least between you and the dog I'm never alone in the evening."

That was true. I started counting on a visit from the dog on nights Farkas was out. One night he called me from a gay and lesbian bar, The Black Poodle. He'd stopped off for a beer on the way home and found that they'd be showing the all-night werewolf film festival on their giant screen. Did I want to come and join him?

"Non-stop werewolf movies?"

"From dusk to dawn."

"Don't bars have to close at two?"

"The bars do, not the premises. They'll be selling while it's still legal and filling the pitchers at two. Are you coming?"

"No thanks. One werewolf movie at a time is about all I can take. I didn't know you were that much of a fan."

"I love them. Not that I could watch them every day. Why don't you come? Maybe you'll get hooked too."

"It's tempting, but I don't want to miss the dog."

"What makes you think he'll come?"

"You're not here."

I was right. Not half an hour after I hung up, the stray scratched at the door.

Another time Farkas said he was going to visit a cousin.

"You have a cousin?"

"Of course I have a cousin. I have lots of cousins."

"Does this one also have a funny name?"

"Lorenz. But we call him Larry or Lon."

"Lorenz sounds like a common enough name."

"He's about my only cousin who *does* have a standard name.

Farkas is uncommon enough, but some of the others–Pecsét, Mázlis, Lány, Hû–they're downright bizarre. We even have an Öregcserkész, but we just call him Cserk."

When he got back early the next afternoon I asked if he'd had fun.

"I had a great visit. I'm thinking of going back next month."

"Why don't you invite him here instead?"

"I'm not sure you'd like him."

"Why shouldn't I like him?"

"He can be a bit surly till he gets to know you. I don't mean he sulks, just sort of grumpy. He's very frisky. And he's a slob. His table manners are abominable."

"In other words, not entirely housebroken."

"It's an odd way of putting it, but yes, I guess you could say that."

"I'd like to meet him anyway."

I kept at him till he called and Larry had agreed to come for the weekend, but not that month. We set it up for the month after.

I had to work late that night and with stopping off at the stores I didn't get home until after dark. There was an unfamiliar car in the driveway, which I assumed was Larry's.

They weren't in the house, but the dog was. In fact, there were two.

"I see you've brought a friend," I said. "Did Farkas let you in? Have you two finally met? Where's he gone to anyway? Out for a walk?"

The other stray was nowhere near as friendly. He didn't know how to play, either. He got a bit rough and actually bit me on the arm, not viciously, but hard enough to draw blood.

My old friend didn't like that. He must have felt protective and went for the other. To break up the dogfight I threw the new mutt bodily out the front door. I heard a car pull away while I was in the bathroom bandaging my arm. Larry must have chickened out about meeting me and left, taking Farkas with him. I didn't care one way or the other about Larry, but I was pissed at Farkas.

I turned my attention to the dog. "Look what I got you," I said, holding up the leash and collar.

He eyed them suspiciously.

"How about a walk in the park? I'll bring the frisbee."

He wagged his tail and barked once, the first time I'd heard him bark.

He was obviously used to the leash. I tested him on the way to the park and he heeled on command, sitting when I came to a stop. I slipped it off him when we got to the park and we played frisbee for hours.

Farkas still hadn't come home when we got back. He stayed out all night. I waited up for him, getting more annoyed by the minute.

The dog started getting antsy a little before dawn and I let him out in the back yard.

Farkas arrived a little while later, feeling very guilty and apologized profusely. His cousin had been in a foul mood and wanted to talk it out. Larry drove them way out of town and rambled on for hours, complaining about nothing in particular and refusing to drive him back. He wished he'd thought to take his cell phone.

"Fine, I forgive you. Come and meet Houdini. He's in the back yard."

"Houdini?"

"My faithful stray. I just let him out a few minutes ago."

"It'll take more than a chain-link fence to keep a Houdini from escaping."

Sure enough, the dog was gone.

Then Farkas noticed my arm. "He bit you!"

"Not him, another dog he brought with him. I don't think he meant to, but I'd better get rabies shots."

"Why bother?"

"So I don't turn rabid and die. Maybe you should too."

"What for? I've never seen either dog."

"Just in case. We do exchange gallons of bodily fluids."

"That's not how it works. Besides, I get a booster every two or three years."

"For rabies?" I was surprised. "And you asked me why I should bother? I never heard of people getting rabies boosters."

"Vets do. I've been getting them since I was a teenager. I used to have an afternoon job helping out at a veterinary clinic. I formed a lot of habits then. I'd say that vet probably had a greater influence on my life than anyone."

"I hear they hurt."

"Rabies shots? They may have long ago, but they don't anymore."

I got the first of a series of six shots, one scheduled every five days. Farkas was right–they weren't particularly painful. I asked at the hospital about regular boosters. They told me I was nuts.

In the meantime Farkas had started acting strangely. For one, he became more protective. Always watching me, as if he was genuinely concerned there was something wrong, which made no sense since I had more energy and felt stronger than I ever had before. I even started jogging with him and found I could keep up. Also he became less dominant and our relationship changed. I initiated foreplay more often and topped him as often as he topped me. Just the smell of him made me horny.

The weekend before I was due for my last shot, I started feeling restless. The house felt like a cage. I paced back and forth all day and kept going to the window. Farkas told me to stay away from it.

"Why?" I asked.

"Because there's a full moon tonight."

"What has that got to do with anything?"

"You'll see. Or maybe you won't. I'm not sure yet."

I ignored him. He wasn't making any sense. I was by the window when the moon began to rise. I felt a howl rise in my throat.

Farkas jumped up and in no time flat had pulled down the blinds.

"What's happening?" I asked.

He took me in his arms. "Hush. It's nothing to worry about."

That's all I remember about that night, except making love and even that seemed to take place in a dream. We went at it for hours. I felt as if all my senses were heightened. The urge was stronger, overpowering. We were insatiable, driven, like animals in season.

We woke the next morning in a tangle of arms, legs and crumpled, semen-stained sheets. I felt washed out and could tell he did too.

"What happened?" I asked.

"Don't you know?"
"No."
"Then I'll let you figure it out for yourself."
That evening he dragged me to the Black Poodle, though the last thing I felt like doing was going out. "It's about time you met the others," he said.
"What others?"
"You'll see."
The bar was fairly crowded and everyone there seemed to know Farkas. Not one of them was drinking anything stronger than coffee. They all looked as if they'd overindulged the night before. I told Farkas it looked like we fit right in.
"Yeah, the full moon is a big party night for everyone here. Hey, there's my cousin Lány. I'll introduce you."
"Is she as surly as Larry?"
"Far from it."
"What's she doing hooked up with a dude? Here, of all places!"
I thought I'd whispered my question, but he heard me from halfway across the room and turned his head.
"Well, I'll be! It's Mázlis. They're not partners; they're relatives. Come meet the family!"
Lány gave me a big hug and said, "So this is John! It looks like he'll fit right in. Was it Larry?
"Who else?"
I was puzzled. "I haven't met Larry," I said.
Mázlis gave me a friendly punch in the arm and winked. "What gives, Farkas? Doesn't he know?"
"No. For the time being I mean to keep him guessing. It's more exciting that way."
I had no idea what they were talking about.
The bartender, Barney, a burly, bearish man with bushy brown eyebrows, massive forearms and paw-like hands, came up to us and asked, "What'll it be? Coffee? Good to see you, Farkas. It's been ages since you've come for first waning. This your new beau?"
"Yes. John. But I'd hardly call him new. We've been together for about five years."
"Welcome to the Poodle, John. You're lucky dogs, the pair of

THE STRAY

you." And he gave me a friendly growl.

I would discover that they were a jolly crew, but that evening they were anything but, a subdued lot who moved sluggishly and spoke in hushed voices. The giant flat-screen TV was tuned to what might have been the Nature channel, the sound turned down. Someone called out, "Hey, Barney, can you turn up the volume a wee bit? They're about to start a program on the phases of the moon." A number of the people milling around winced at the raised voice, but most gathered around the TV. Farkas made a move to join them.

"You never tire of that program, do you?" Lány teased.

"You forget it's been a while since I've seen it," he pointed out, his eyes already on the screen.

"It's been on before?" I asked.

"Often," Barney said. "You see they're only half paying attention to it. They're waiting for the good part."

I remained at the bar with Barney, Mázlis and Lány. "I can't begin to tell you how happy I am that you and Farkas are a couple," she said. "I used to worry about him, he was such a lone wolf. That's not to say he doesn't have lots of friends–everyone likes Farkas–but there were times when he'd just go off quietly by himself. You could tell that he needed a special somebody."

I glanced around the bar. There wasn't much to see–a vast, dimly lit room much like any other tavern, with posters and autographed photos of celebrities on the oak paneled walls. Most of the posters were from the Sierra Club's "Save the Wolves" campaign.

A stirring among the people below the television attracted our attention. We turned to look. A full moon, pale white and glowing, filled the entire screen. The same thrill I had felt the night before traveled up from the bottom of my spine to a tight bundle of nerves at the base of my brain. I thought for a moment that I was getting an erection and glanced down to see if I was showing, but despite the tingling in my loins I wasn't hard.

Lány was staring at the screen. We all were. "Isn't it beautiful?" she said.

The picture changed; the group below the screen broke up. Farkas came up to me and gave me a warm hug, then took me by the hand to introduce me to his other friends.

We started going to the Poodle regularly every Friday night and for first waning, the come-down party after the full moon. When spring came round Farkas and I got together with a group of guys from the Poodle for a frisbee game on Sunday afternoons. We played for hours on the grass, barefoot and wearing just our shorts. It gradually dawned on me that they were the same people I'd seen playing in the park with Farkas on the day we met.

There were many other activities, such as volleyball and beach parties and movie nights. Horror films were especially popular. Classic horror films, not gory modern chainsaw flicks. The highlight of the summer was a camping trip in August that went on for four days and three nights, the last timed to coincide with the full moon. We reserved a rustic campground and we had all two hundred acres to ourselves–woods, trails, lake and playing fields. Some couples brought their dogs. I hadn't seen my stray for a long time. I was sorry he wasn't there. He would have had the time of his life.

The first two nights we all sat together under the stars around a bonfire, toasted marshmallows, drank beer, told stories, and watched the moon growing fuller, but the night of the full moon we stayed at our individual campsites.

As soon as the sky started to darken, Farkas and I brought our sleeping bags out to our little campfire. The campsites were far apart; I saw the faint light of the other fires glowing bright amber between the trees. Everywhere was silence. We spoke in whispers, thinking of the wild intimacies to come.

Then the moon rose and worked its magic. As it climbed, isolated howls rose from around the campgrounds, gradually melding into a chorus. Then an eerie stillness descended and we made love passionately. Through the dreamlike haze that always enveloped us on nights like this I heard the grunts and yelps of countless couples rutting like animals. I suppose we must have sounded the same.

I remember the exhilaration of running naked through the woods with Farkas and glimpsing other shadowy couples, darting naked among the trees. I remember seeing a silhouetted pack of greyhounds racing while we stood on the summit of a hill. And I remember our laughter when we rushed with the others headlong into the lake, breaking the reflected moon into a thousand glittering splinters.

I woke at the first light of dawn, slipped into a pair of shorts, and walked to the outhouses. Most couples had retired into their tents, but a small handful remained lying outside on top of sleeping bags in a state of exhaustion and oblivious to my passing. Only one or two raised their heads, smiled at me and nuzzled back into the warmth of their partners.

After the camping trip I asked Farkas how he could have given up such good friends for so long. He said, "I had you."

"Couldn't you have had me and them?"

"I wanted them to like you and you to like them. I wasn't sure you'd fit in, at least not at first."

Apart from a marked increase in social activities, our personal lives haven't changed much since Farkas moved in.

I can think of only two exceptions. First, the stray dog that made himself a part of my life for a few brief months. I often wonder if he still comes around sometimes when we're out partying at the Black Poodle or when the moon is full and Farkas and I are too involved with each other to hear him scratching at the door. The other is the mystery of our lovemaking on full-moon nights. I get the impression that our friends share a joke that I'm not in on–maybe I'm a bit dense–because sometimes they tease me.

"You'll catch on eventually," they say.

NEW BEGINNINGS

Cari Z

Michael loped around the perimeter of the compound, searching for new scents. There had been nothing fresh; a few vanilla humans around the edges of the barricade and here the telltales of a drug dealer. Had he been caught during a patrol, Michael would have had more than a warning growl. Drugs weren't tolerated. They weakened the human half and the wolf became too strong.

He ran on, long strides eating up the ground and stopped at the front gate; sniffing an old scent. It had been strong a few days ago. Overpowering. The scent of blood and pain and desperation and underneath it all...Tori.

Tori was a young werewolf, which came with a built-in set of difficulties made worse because he was also gay. Werewolves could smell attraction. In a social structure that was already fiercely regimented and male dominant, homosexuality threw a wrench into the works that few Alphas wanted to deal with. Gay wolves were turned out of packs or forbidden entrance. Some were simply killed outright.

You couldn't live without a pack; you couldn't bury the wolf and live with humans. Michael's was the only pack for a thousand miles whose members were all homosexual, negating many of the challenges of a regular pack. They were a small group and they kept their borders tight. The city was a dangerous place for man and wolf alike. There were all sorts of creatures to take advantage of a lone boy.

Michael realized he was growling. Tori had been hurt, weak from fear and hunger when Michael had found him during a patrol. They had immediately recognized each other for what they were, even though Michael was in wolf form and Tori human. He had helped the boy focus enough to change and had brought him, limping and afraid, to see the Alpha.

Terrell was a tall black man with shoulders like a linebacker who ruled his pack as a benevolent Alpha. As long as the rules were followed he was easy to get along with. As soon as someone broke them he became frightening in his dominance. He had been Alpha for over twenty years, unchallenged for fifteen. He kept them safe and all of his wolves knew it.

Michael was Terrell's second, the enforcer. Terrell protected the pack from threats inside and out and Michael was the one who brought them to his attention. Not all wolves were looking for sanctuary. Some were looking for trouble.

Michael panted. He was tired. Completing his circuit, he headed back to the center of the compound, a large apartment building that Terrell owned. Apartments had been combined to make larger family units, and the bottom floor was an open space dedicated as meeting hall, combat arena, lounging area and kitchen. There were only two ground floor rooms set aside as private quarters. The pack numbered nearly thirty wolves, twice what there had been a decade ago when Michael had joined. For the most part their interactions were seamless.

Michael padded silently up to the building, changing from wolf to human in a small space beside the entrance; he pulled on the t-shirt and sweat pants he'd been wearing before his patrol.

Inside, he headed to where Terrell, and his mate Phillip, were seated in a corner. The pack's number three, Anthony, sat with them. They were talking, but Anthony–seeing him approach–stood, respectfully taking his leave.

Michael slumped into a chair, his languorous pose belying the tension that crawled inside.

"Report," Terrell said, getting to business.

"Clean. Nothing likely to cause us a problem."

"Good." His Alpha nodded, pleased. "Phillip and I are running a trade tonight and I don't need any unpermitted causing us any issues."

"Anything good?"

"A few new computers," Phillip said. "We could really use them."

"Nice." *As long as the internet service is reliable.* He didn't voice his thoughts. Terrell was indulgent of his mate. Michael wouldn't do himself any favors by raining on Phillip's parade. "What's the new kid up to?"

"Tori's settling in okay." Terrell shrugged. "It's not easy adjusting to a new pack; he's gotten in a few fights. At least he's off the streets."

"Yeah." Michael frowned. "How old is he, anyway?"

"He says he's twenty."

"He looks younger."

Phillip interjected, "Looks can be deceiving among wolves." He grinned at Michael, "Case in point." Phillip was one of the few people who knew just how old Michael really was.

"Smart ass," Michael mock-growled; the lovers smiled. Phillip glanced at the time before rising gracefully.

"I'll go check on the trade goods," he said. Terrell watched him go before he turned back to his second.

"I actually wanted to talk to you about Tori."

"Go ahead."

"I want you to mentor him."

Michael sat up straight. "What?" Mentoring was pretty common for newcomers, but it wasn't Michael's thing. "Why not ask Anthony?"

"I did. He talked to Tori and told me that he thinks you'd be better for him."

Michael, taken aback, arched a brow. "I just found him and brought him here, I haven't spoken with him since."

"Well, that was enough for him to form a bond...or so Anthony tells me."

"You honestly think I'll be good for him?" Michael asked. "I'm not...I'm kind of–"

"A mean son-of-a-bitch," Terrell softened the words with a smile. "Yes, but this kid comes from worse. He shares your room, your job and your life until he's integrated." He forestalled the rebellion he glimpsed in Michael's face, "No arguments. I don't want to have to turn him away after everything he's been through, but the pack comes first."

Michael nodded. Cohesion was key to pack functioning. He sighed. "Fine. Does Tori know?"

"Anthony mentioned it to him. He's not sure you'll take him, though, and the kid's wound as tight as a spring. Help him. Just be yourself."

"If he doesn't leave after a few days of me being myself, he'll be as integrated as he can be," Michael said.

"I know."

Michael stood. The young wolves usually hung out in a group near the combat arena, but Tori wasn't among them. Michael kept searching. He was moving in the direction of the kitchen before catching sight of the boy. Tori was sitting in a corner, pressed tight against the wall, hugging his knees, staring vacantly out into the room. His eyes were large in his face, bright blue, contrasting with his delicate Asian features and build.

Michael crossed to him. There was an undercurrent of interest as pack members watched him go. As soon as he got within ten feet of Tori, the boy unfolded and made a brief obeisance. "Sir."

There was no accent, but his manners were odd. "No need to bow," Michael told him. "Gather your things and move them to my quarters. You're going to be learning from me for a while."

The ghost of a smile flickered over Tori's face, he half bent before he caught himself. "Yes, sir." He moved away from the wall, eyes downcast as he passed. Michael watched him with mixed emotions. There was no doubt the kid needed help. He didn't feel like the right person to be giving it, but Michael would sooner die than disobey his Alpha.

He stifled a yawn. He pushed himself too hard, but didn't trust the safety of the pack to anyone else. Passing by the kitchen he grabbed two plates, filling them with fried chicken and basted ribs before heading back to his room. His living quarters were the closest to the main entrance, fitting given his position. It was small and simple, spartan. Michael set the boy's plate on a couch and sat on the bed, looking out the window at the darkening sky.

Tori's soft knock at the door came shortly after.

"Enter."

He did, quiet as a mouse, his worldly possessions held under one arm.

"You can have the couch until we get a bed carried down for you." *If your stay lasts that long.* "Eat."

The boy set his things down beside the couch, then sat, folding his legs into a lotus position. Only once Michael was well into his plate did Tori start hungrily at his own. *A traditionalist. Where did he come from?*

"How did you get here, Tori?" he asked.

"I ran." Tori's voice was flat, the life seemed to have drained from him.

"Why were you running?"

"Because I didn't dare walk."

Michael arched a brow, "Where were you running from?"

Tori responded slowly, "Home."

"Where is home?"

Tori froze, his face a mask of distress. Michael chose not to force an answer. "Don't worry about it."

"I want to tell you," Tori whispered. He raised his eyes and they were startling, filled with emotion. "I do, but–"

"Later." Michael couldn't make his voice reassuring, but he could make it commanding. It eased the pain in the boy's face.

Michael finished eating in silence. Tori immediately reached for his empty plate as he set it aside.

"I'll take it back for you."

"You don't have to wait on me," Michael said.

"It's appropriate for me to serve you. You're my superior."

"I'm also trying to be your friend."

Tori smiled. It disappeared as fast as it had come. "You'll be that too. That doesn't change my duty or my honor." He inclined his head slightly. "I'm pleased to take it."

"Well…" Michael was nonplussed. "At least wait until you've finished your own meal."

"Thank you." He started in on his ribs. The mood in the room had changed from fearful to content in the space of a heartbeat. Frowning, Michael sat back against the wall and closed his eyes. Meditation was a regular part of a well-adjusted werewolf's life. It helped calm the wolf and relax the mind and body. Pushing aside the mystery that was Tori, Michael focused on his breathing and relaxing his body. He worked down from the top, tongue pressed lightly to the roof of his mouth, eyes shut but lifted towards a distant horizon. He absently noted the faint clack of plates as Tori carried them out. Tuned the exterior world out and relaxed his shoulders, releasing tension in his chest. By the time he got down to his toes, he felt loose and calm. Most werewolves meditated daily, Michael twice a day.

Finally opening his eyes he found Tori, in the same lotus position he'd taken earlier, completely still. Michael barely saw his chest move.

Suddenly his eyes opened, and Michael was momentarily transfixed.

Tori grinned shyly. "I hope I didn't disturb you?"

"You didn't." Michael passed a hand over his face. "I need to sleep. You don't have to bed down yet, you can go to the common room."

"I want to stay with you."

Michael shrugged. "You can pick a book and read if you want." He crossed to the bathroom, making fast use of it. Tori was looking through Michael's small library but stopped when Michael reentered.

"You won't keep me up," he said, waving him to continue.

"Thank you, sir."

"Tori, you can call me Michael."

"Yes, Michael."

He didn't know whether the kid read or not. As soon as his head hit the pillow Michael was asleep.

He woke to strange smells, whimpering and an awful choking sound. The wolf raised its hackles but Michael calmed it. *Tori.* The kid was screaming in his sleep...or trying to.

Michael rolled out of bed and over to the couch in one fast motion. Gripping Tori's shoulder, he shook him.

A hand lashed out, fingers curled like claws. Tucking his head, Michael took the blow against his scalp, then caught the flailing hand. "Tori!" The kid woke still panicking. "Tori!" He put more dominance into his voice, more command. "It's all right." For emphasis, he leaned in and soundly bit the side of Tori's neck. The boy stilled. Michael held him a moment, then relaxed his grip gently. He pulled his head away, resisting a sudden urge to nuzzle.

"I'm sorry," Tori said, "I'm sorry, I'm sorry–"

"I know," he silenced the small voiced mantra. "You had a nightmare." He ran his callused palm over Tori's cheek, wiping away tears. He couldn't resist adding, "Don't be afraid."

"I'm not afraid when I can see you."

Michael felt the stirrings of attraction. It wasn't right, Tori was so young. He gave him a final, gentle shake, then let go and returned to bed. He could feel Tori's eyes on his back, even as he fell asleep.

He woke half an hour before dawn. Michael varied the patrol times, but liked the early morning best. The quiet peace before anything stirred. He checked on Tori. The air was free of the scent of fear and he was sleeping soundly. Michael slipped quietly out the room.

The first floor was abandoned, the pack having dispersed to their rooms. Only Anthony was still up, taking his turn at the electronic monitors that covered the compound. "How is Tori?" he asked.

Michael grunted. "He had a nightmare. Pretty bad."

"Strange. He didn't have any nightmares before."

"Maybe I frightened him."

"Or maybe he felt comfortable enough with you to relax."

"Maybe." Michael stretched, pulling off his t-shirt. "I'm going on patrol. I should be about an hour."

"You might consider taking company." Anthony's tone was deferent, but Michael didn't like the words.

"You think I can't do the job alone?"

"Not at all."

The air was cool and inviting. Michael let himself run, stretching his legs and enjoying the freedom. He made three circles of the compound, scenting the residues of last night's trade, but nothing new. His mood was light when he returned. He changed quickly, then entered the main chamber.

Tori was waiting for him, sitting across from Anthony. He came to his feet at the sight of Michael.

"What are you doing up?"

"May I go with you next time?" Tori asked, ignoring the question. Michael glared at Anthony, who shrugged and spread his hands. Tori, watching the exchange, lowered his gaze, "I'm sorry, I spoke out of place."

"It's fine." *Terrell did say the kid should share my job.* "You'll go with me next time."

"Thank you, Michael."

Michael ignored Anthony's obvious interest.

"Get yourself some breakfast and I'll go over the routes with you."

Tori was at Michael's side almost constantly for the next two weeks; Michael showing him the extent of the compound, the gates, guard points and camera locations. Tori was intelligent and attentive, and he enjoyed Michael's company.

He enjoyed it a little too much.

Michael, a loner even inside the pack, noticed Tori's regard with a growing discomfort. Tori wasn't obvious, but he also wasn't experienced, not having sufficient control over himself to hide the scent of his interest. Michael had determined to ignore it. It wouldn't be right to take advantage of Tori's infatuation. When a wolf took a mate, it was for life. Casual encounters were almost nonexistent. Michael steeled his own instinctive reaction and treated him with kindness, but maintained the distance.

Tori was also finally opening up to the other members of the pack. He was a practiced judoka and started a trend in the combat arena. His slender size didn't seem to be much of a disadvantage even when it came to larger opponents. He became popular, even dominant, among his peers.

"He's doing much better," Terrell noted.

"I know."

"Have you found out anything about him?" Phillip asked, cozying up against his mate's shoulder.

"Not really. He doesn't like to talk about the past. He's had a few more nightmares, but nothing like that first night."

"Interesting," Phillip said with a grin.

"God, you sound like Anthony," Michael said. "He thinks everything about me and this kid is 'interesting'."

"Have you noticed how he only lets himself relax when you're in the room?" Phillip said. "When you leave, he stops whatever he's doing and watches for your return. I think he's getting attached."

"That's no good." Michael grimaced.

"Why not?" Terrell asked. "It is a sign of integration."

"Good. Then you can put him back with the other pups and he'll be fine."

"Anthony doesn't think so."

"What does he know?"

"Oh, the man's only got a PhD in clinical psychology." Terrell frowned. "Why is it so damn difficult for you, Michael? No one thinks you'd be taking advantage of him but you, he's old enough to know his own mind."

"Maybe he thinks he does," Michael retorted, "but knowing your head and knowing your heart are two different things." He kept his voice low. No one would eavesdrop on the Alpha, but wolves had excellent hearing.

"You must think Tori exceptionally immature. He doesn't strike me as such. He's bright, he's quick, he's willing–"

"He has a cute ass," Phillip interjected.

"Exactly. What's not to like?"

Michael swallowed, realizing he wasn't going to get out of this interrogation without some uncomfortable honesty. "I was abandoned by my last mate." The declaration was abrupt, but the buried pain unfolded like a fresh wound.

Phillip blinked. "What?"

"Rejected...scorned...after ten years together." He echoed Tori now, lowered his gaze. "And he was also young and cute and willing, and seemed as devoted to me as I was to him...up until the day he left."

"What happened?"

"He found someone new." The words came clipped, raw. "Someone he decided was more to his taste. Someone young, beautiful..." The wound had not healed, time had not done its job. "...and female."

"Ouch," Phillip murmured.

"The past doesn't predict the future," Terrell argued. "Tori cares about you, Michael, it's as plain as day."

"Caring is fine. The pack should be caring. Singling me out as the object of his affections is something else entirely." Michael looked up, pushing away the past. "Will you take him off my watch?"

"Not yet," Terrell said, despite the sympathy in his tone.

"Maybe in another two weeks. Let him run with the pack beneath the full moon, and he'll either be one of us or he never will be."

"Fine. May I be excused?" Terrell nodded and Michael strode off to his room. He locked the door for the first time since Tori had taken up residence and sat down on his bed to meditate. It hadn't been so difficult in years. Images of the past flashed through his mind, distracting him, angering him, causing him pain. He heard a hand tentatively try the door. Feeling guilty, Michael grew angry at himself. His hands clenched into fists and he felt the change come unbidden. His jaw lengthened and fangs began to sprout, his growing claws puncturing his palms.

A soothing, wordless crooning passed through the door. It gave him something beyond himself to focus on. Taking deep steadying breaths, Michael felt his body receding back into its human state. The wolf quieted and when he finally opened his eyes, the rage that had spurred the transformation on was gone.

Opening the door he found Tori kneeling there, looking up at him, eyes filled with worry and need.

"Are you all right?" he asked softly.

"Well enough. Stand up." He held out a hand to Tori.

"You're hurt." Tori studied Michael's palms as he stood, fingers tracing around the jagged red talon crescents

"I did it to myself." Michael shook his head tiredly. "It'll heal by morning."

"Can I get you anything? Do you need to eat?"

"No." Michael removed his hand from Tori's, ignored the sudden surge of longing he felt coming from the boy. Stepping towards his bed, he sat down. Closing his eyes, he found himself unable to relax.

"May I help you with your meditation?" Tori asked. "We often performed guided meditations back–" he broke off. "It can help when the mind is unsettled."

Michael kept his eyes closed. "We can try it if you like."

Tori sat across from Michael on a bed that had taken the place of the couch. It left them with very little space between. Their knees were gently touching. "I'll have to touch you...is that all right?"

Michael hesitated. The dark behind his eyelids made it easier to say, "Do whatever you need to."

A brief silence as Tori weighed his words then he began. "Right now, you're a river moving too swiftly. We need to slow this down." He very lightly touched Michael's temples. "We need to slow this down." He laid a hand over his heart. "We need to focus your energies here." He pressed a finger briefly to a spot just below Michael's belly button. "We start with the source, start with the head. Thoughts are meaningless, flashes of nothing. They appear, but they don't affect you. We note them and then we let them go."

Tori's voice was as smooth as a gentle stream; calm but lively enough to keep Michael's attention. His touch was light and brief, grounding and guiding Michael, reducing all the frustrations and anger. They must have spent over an hour at it, because by the time Michael opened his eyes again, the sky was black and Tori's voice was becoming hoarse.

"How do you feel?"

"Better." Michael stretched his stiff shoulders, popping the right one. He felt completely in control. "Much better," he couldn't conceal his surprise. "That was very well done, you should consider group sessions."

"Do you think the Alpha would mind?"

"Terrell wouldn't mind at all. There's nothing more dangerous than a wolf on edge." He looked away; suddenly ashamed. "I haven't been like that in a long time."

"Sleep will help. It sorts through what the conscious mind can't deal with."

Michael drew his eyes back to study Tori curiously. "Do you remember what you were sorting through in your nightmares?"

Tori's cheeks flushed. "Yes."

Back to monosyllables again, not good. "Will you tell me?"

Tori's breath grew rapid.

"You don't have to tell me–" Michael began before he was cut short.

"My father was Alpha of our pack." Tori spoke quickly, words running together like a flood forced through a narrow break in a dam wall. "He was challenged by my uncle and…lost." Instinctively Michael knew that the fight had been to the death. He folded his hands together, preventing them from reaching out to Tori. "My uncle believes that no true wolf should stray from the natural order. He banished me from the pack. They chased me away. Two of my cousins tried to kill me." Tori's voice grew smaller as he ran out of air, fading to murmurs and then whispers. "I ran for three days without rest. I knew about your pack. My father had considered sending me since this is the only place I could be free." He shuddered, drew in a breath; lungs greedy for air. "I know they're still looking for me. I can feel them."

Now it was Michael's turn to soothe. He forced himself to take both of Tori's hands in his own.

"You don't need to be afraid here. What happened to you was wrong and terrible," he said. "And you'll never forget it, but it will never happen again." More emotion than he had intended slipped into his voice, his eyes locked with Tori's. "You're part of our pack now. We're family, and we won't let you go." He squeezed Tori's hands, a simple showing of strength. "I won't let you go. Got it?"

"Yes," Tori whispered. The look on his face moved Michael to pull him close. He collapsed against Michael, clutching at him and sobbing soundlessly, riding the storm of emotions that overwhelmed him until he had cried himself out. Easing the young werewolf down onto the bed, Michael was surprised when Tori pulled him down.

"Please don't go yet," he begged. "Not yet."

"I'll stay until you fall asleep," Michael told him, disturbed and aroused by the young man's desperation. Ruled by impulse for a moment, he bent to Tori and kissed each closed eyelid, tasting the salt of his tears. Then licked the tracks that flowed down each cheek; pausing to kiss each trail's end. *What the fuck are you doing?* He couldn't allow himself do this, couldn't encourage the kid. Michael drew back and Tori slowly opened his eyes. The iris' blue was nearly drowned by the dark pupils, dilated and full of desire.

"Don't stop."

Michael was dominant. There was nothing Tori could do to make him comply. Nevertheless he obeyed. He ran the tip of his tongue along Tori's jaw, down his neck, into the hollow of his throat. He first kissed then nuzzled into the soft flesh. Tori's response was a quick intake of breath, a brief tightening of his hands on Michael's shoulders.

Sliding one hand beneath Tori's shirt, Michael stroked fingers up the tight abdomen to the chest, caressing the hard, pointed nubs of Tori's nipples even as he ripped at the collar with his teeth. He drew the fabric apart to reveal beautiful honey-tinted skin and laved Tori's chest with his rough tongue, sliding his questing hand down to his lover's hips making Tori moan.

Michael slipped his hand beneath the waistband of Tori's sweat pants down his thigh, brushing quickly past the erection. Tori raised his hips in invitation, need making him bold. Michael ignored it, stroking further downward, then after a teasing handful of seconds, inched back up tantalizingly slow, until he had his lover panting for a more intimate touch. When his fingers finally curled around Tori's cock, it was straining against the fabric of his pants. He was larger than Michael had anticipated. Tori held his breath, frozen until the first firm stroke made him shudder beneath Michael.

He gasped. Michael kissed his way down the firm planes of Tori's abdomen, following the treasure trail of fine dark hairs towards his goal. Using his free hand, he pulled down Tori's pants with the younger man eager to help, kicking them off.

Uncovered, he revealed more beauty, uncut and hard. Michael finished his path with rapid kisses then engulfed Tori's erection to the root, fingers passing through sparse pubic hairs to cup his lover's sac. It was too much for Tori and he suddenly screamed Michael's name, arching his hips and stiffening like a board under the force of his orgasm. Drinking his seed, Michael relished the half forgotten flavor of it; memories of his mate tore at the edges of his consciousness. He forced them down.

Tori's member stopped spurting, softening but Michael wasn't ready to release him. A hunger had been woken and it demanded satisfaction. Pulling his own clothing off, Michael sank back onto Tori's body, covering the panting mouth with a kiss. He shared the remnants of release with his lover's eager tongue, and Tori's arms curled around his shoulders like vines, pulling tight. Michael's hardness rubbed against Tori's lingering erection in an intimate frottage. It didn't take long for Tori to stiffen.

Reaching down Michael held their cocks tightly together, pumping his hand as they kissed. They held each other, all sweat and friction and burning need. Stroking furiously, alternating from one to the other to both until they fell together over the edge. Michael gritted his teeth against a yell, forcing it into a groan as he came hard his ejaculate covering their bodies. Tori came less forcefully but just as long.

Through the haze of pleasure, Michael felt a tenuous mated bond and groaned again, this time in remorse. He had never thought to feel that bond a second time, and it wasn't welcome. He didn't want it but his heart decried him as a liar when he looked into Tori's eyes. Keeping the bond was wrong, but severing it now would be cruel. He couldn't do it. *Later.* When they weren't so close. When he didn't feel so good. It would be best... *for Tori.* It was a promise easier made than kept.

The next morning Michael acted as if nothing had happened and while Tori was obviously curious, he wasn't hurt. They presented themselves as if nothing had changed to the rest of the pack but a few people realized the truth. Terrell of course, the Alpha knew everything that went on in his pack and therefore Phillip knew. Anthony was no less keen in his awareness. Tori was brighter than before, and even if the rest of the pack didn't know for sure, they began to treat him with the same unconscious deference that they showed Phillip.

Days it was easy to be aloof. Nights were another story. Tori was in his bedroom, his scent and need filling the air, but he never asked outright. Michael ignored him for nearly a week and neither of them slept well. On the seventh night, once the door was shut, he drew Tori immediately to his bed, stripped him down and kissed him hard, his body moving in a sensuous apology. Tori understood. He gave himself fully to Michael. Unable to commit to the bond, Michael took his young lover, reveling in the tightness of his ass and Tori's passionate response. In the afterglow of sex he began to wonder why he was resisting so hard, but they still slept in separate beds.

A week after they had consummated their relationship, Tori had another bad nightmare. The muted screams woke Michael and he moved quickly, sliding into the smaller bed, embracing Tori, waking him gently. Kissing the back of his neck, he waited patiently for the young man to get control of his shuddering body.

"Same nightmare?" he asked gently once it was over.

"No, different. Worse." Tori's voice sounded hollow. "It's like my cousins are with me. I saw them in my mind calling to me." Michael wondered if Tori was still sensitive to his familial bond, and for some reason unable to fully sever that relationship.

"You think they're here in the city?" he asked.

"I...don't know." Tori shivered suddenly.

"You're not going to get back to sleep any time soon." Michael pulled back the blanket. "C'mon, we'll run a sweep of the perimeter."

"I don't want to keep you up."

"Not your fault. I needed to do an early check anyway." *Maybe we'll catch that drug dealer this time.* "I'll let Mick know we're going." He spoke of the werewolf assigned watch duty on the rosters, but when Michael emerged from his room he found Mick playing a computer game on one of the monitors.

"That's not the way to guard the compound," Michael chided him.

Mick hung his head. "Sorry."

"See anything?"

"All clear," he responded, flashing through cameras as Michael stood beside him.

"Good. Tori and I are going to run a patrol; we should be back in forty-five minutes."

"Got it."

Tori joined him and they changed, setting out into the early-morning darkness. Tori blended perfectly with the misty surroundings, his coat black fringed with grey at the ears and paws. As Michael had learned, Tori's wolf was small and agile and fast. Michael's coloring by comparison was a dark gray with a smattering of white across his muzzle and tracing various scars. His wolf form was larger and heavier, but he could still move swiftly. They roamed the perimeter together, as they had for the past month. It was the end of the last night before the full moon, and they were edgy with energy.

They caught the new scent almost simultaneously and were drawn to where something fluttered on a wall. A metal bolt had been stuck into the wall, probably shot there, and a perforated piece of thick white paper clung to it. Michael raised his head and sniffed, searching for any threat. Beside him Tori, anxious, was whining softly. Michael briefly licked his face, then shifted into human form. Naked, he grabbed at the paper. The writing wasn't English.

Instinct overwhelmed him and he threw himself at Tori even as shots rang out. One clipped Tori's left ear, and the next slammed into Michael's thigh. A third bullet took a chunk out of the brick wall close to his head, and Michael pulled back from the edge. Through the wave of pain he tried to detect the sniper's location.

Tori yelped in shock, then smelling Michael's blood growled. He began to shift.

"No," Michael said through gritted teeth. "Stay wolf. They're trying to kill you, you're faster this way. Stay wolf!" Tori obeyed with a whine. Another bullet smacked into their protective wall, closer this time. "Fuck."

Michael was aware that by the time Mick noticed and sent help, the sniper would have them in his sights and they'd both be dead. None of the monitors would reveal their predicament. The sniper had been smart.

"Tori, you're going to have to run. Get help," he said. "Don't follow a straight line. They'll be waiting for you."

Through their bond he felt Tori's reluctance to leave him, also anger and guilt. "On three." He brushed a reassuring hand through Tori's fur. "One, two, three." Michael stuck his head briefly around the corner, then yanked it back as a shower of bullets tore into the brick, sending shards flying. Tori took off in the opposite direction, running low, his path zigzagging between wall and field. The sniper spotted him quickly, switching targets and Michael's chest tightened as dust spat up around Tori but the wolf ran on and vanished from view.

Michael wasted no time changing into his wolf form. It was harder, injured. The wolf wanted to snap and snarl, but Michael fought its instincts and slunk out from behind the wall. He had to find the sniper before reinforcements arrived, or anyone coming out of the compound would be vulnerable. He scaled a chain link fence with difficulty, his injury hampering him. Outside of the compound, he felt his restraint slip away. He had prey to find, to hunt and kill. He moved into the surrounding terrain, breathing in scents old and new.

Tori's hunters were skilled and smart, but no longer invisible. Michael had caught their scent. There was enough of a hint of Tori to tell that they were kin. He counted two of them.

The tall building they had chosen to snipe from was abandoned. It was easy to find a way in through the broken walls.

Inside he could tell more; one–the sniper–was in human form and the other in wolf form, waiting, guarding. Michael would have to pass the wolf to reach the sniper. Exaggerating his wound, the blood already staining the air, he limped heavily through the derelict structure.

His feint was successful and he lured the waiting wolf from the shadows. The slender, coal black wolf lunged at Michael, jaws snapping triumphantly.

Jaws that Michael deftly evaded; the wolf's teeth closed on nothing but air. He raked claws down his enemy's face and lunged for his throat. He caught more skin than muscle, but held on regardless. The black wolf twisted and snapped his fangs; unable to reach Michael his desperation turned extreme. He tore himself free of Michael's jaws, bleeding heavily. Michael gave him no chance to recover. He lunged again for the throat and was thwarted as the black wolf managed a sudden spurt of speed, twisted away and sank his teeth into Michael's injured hindquarter.

Pain…searing and white hot bled through Michael. He couldn't ignore it this time. He whimpered, but it did not hold him back from making another attack. This time he found the windpipe; clamped his jaws tight, driving teeth deep into the flesh. The black wolf struggled, wildly at first then gradually growing weaker until his body went limp and Michael heard the heart whisper to a stop. He dropped the corpse; muscles trembling under the strain. Collapsing on the cooling black fur; he felt spent.

In the distance he heard Terrell howl. Knowing his Alpha was coming galvanized him to action. It was Michael's duty to protect the pack. To do that he had to reach the sniper. He forced himself to his feet and stumbled towards the shadowed stairs from which the scent of the sniper trailed.

It led him to the top of the building and he was quivering with exhaustion by the time he got there.

He spotted the sniper leaning against an empty frame where a window had once nested, the rifle pointed down into the compound. He turned as soon as Michael entered the room, werewolf senses difficult to fool. His features were similar to Tori's, but he was larger, more muscular. The shock held him frozen only a moment, then he swung the gun around even as Michael jumped. A shot rang out, Michael locked his teeth around the sniper's right arm, and the gun dropped. From the corner of his eye, Michael glimpsed the flash of a knife before his vision faded into grey. He kept his jaws locked, oblivious to further pain and to the screams of his prey. Familiar scents washed over him, familiar wolves and the enemy died in moments, falling to his Alpha's wrath. Michael could finally let go. He could let everything go...but something held him back.

Time passed. The world was a blur of sleep and pain with brief periods of consciousness that reassured him that his pack was with him; his pack, his Alpha and most of all, his mate. At some point in this sorry business the mated bond had become undeniable. Tori was with him, a soothing presence at the edge of his mind.

Werewolves healed much faster than men or wolves, but Michael's injuries were extensive. He stayed on his back in the pack's infirmary for nearly a week, tended to by a human veterinarian who was mated to a pack member. When he'd healed enough to shift back into his human form he exhausted himself and blacked out with the effort.

When he came to Tori was lying beside him, holding him carefully. The shot to his leg had broken his femur and that would take more time to heal. His mate's breathing was soft and even, but his scent betrayed his distress.

Tori uncapped a bottle of water and brought it to Michael's dry lips. It was difficult and slow but Michael managed to drink half the contents.

"Enough," he croaked and focused his eyes on the young

man. Tori looked tired and drawn. "You okay?"

Tori gave him a small smile. "Fine. They never touched me." Michael snorted. "Liar."

"The shot just grazed me. You were shot…twice…stabbed a few times." His voice was unsteady. "It's my fault, I knew they would hunt me down. I should never have come."

"You did the right thing."

"They almost killed you." His voice was filled with pain. "I could never have lived with that."

"No need." Michael tried a smile. It hurt, but was worth it to see Tori's mood lighten. "I'm alive. You're alive. They're dead. Happy ending."

"I love you."

"I know." Michael couldn't say what was in his heart, so he settled for "I'm yours."

"Good." Tori bent forward and kissed Michael, lips lingering. "I don't think I could stand it any other way."

"Then we're lucky you don't have to." Sleep pulled at him. Tori settled in next to him, his scent serene. What they had together was enough, and more than Michael had ever hoped to have again. Tori was his second chance, his new beginning. For the first time in years Michael was able to let all his tension go and he slept peacefully.

QUEER WOLF

WHERE THE SLED DOGS RUN

Jerome Stueart

You start having secrets in fourth grade. You have codes, cliques and clubs you can't get into unless you know the handshake or the password. In fourth grade, we learn about being exclusive, and about belonging, and about the joy of secret notes. It was in fourth grade that I got my first secret note. Only, I was the teacher.

I teach at the Horwood Mather Elementary School, named after polar explorer Horwood Mather. Every fall I get to take twenty-two students to the Mather House on the other side of the city. He ran for office but died soon after he was elected, one of the big tragedies of his story. The walls of the Mather House are paneled in dark wood and trophy animals line the hallways–mostly deer–and they give you blank stares. My imaginative students all think they're being watched and they scream, or wave, or get disgusted, or pet them.

One special room though always catches their attention. I call it the Sled Dog room, but it used to be the West Library. Now it has memorabilia from Mather's Arctic trips, mostly concerning the sled dogs he brought back. A team of seven dogs. Each dog has its portrait on the wall like a family gallery. In very nice photos, black and silver and grey, the dogs, huskies and malamutes, stand majestic and strong, most of them named for cities. Kids love them, write stories about them when they get back to class, and tape souvenir postcards of them to their desks.

It was on this trip that I got to bring home a souvenir, too.

Someone slipped a note in my jacket pocket, scribbled on the back of a business card. It read: *I can tell you where the sled dogs ran in the city.* It was a Mather House business card, Chief Archivist, C. Girard Forte. He'd scribbled a phone number.

I looked around the room, hoping to catch sight of Mr Forte, as I thought I remembered him as part of the tour–a nice looking burly guy. But my kids, clutching their new "Polar Explorers" certificates were filing out to the bus and I didn't have time to follow up on the question. I was kind of intrigued though, in a fourth-grade way.

The information on Mather's sled dogs was anecdotal, at best. The guides all knew a couple of stories about the dogs, like which ones were Mr Mather's favorites–Kansas City and Uruk–but when kids asked, did they run in the city, the answer had always been: "Mr Mather walked the dogs regularly, but we don't know if they ever ran as a team again." Kids hated that answer. They liked to believe the dogs ran in the city. That Mather teamed them up and mushed them down the streets when the snow came, yelling *gee* and *haw* through the parked cabs.

At home, over canned Beef Barley soup, I tried to remember Mr Forte's face. I pictured a round face with a brown beard. Small rectangular glasses. I cut up some cheese slices and opened a new box of Ritz, laughing at myself. This was the fantasy of unattached and lonely gay men who teach fourth grade. We cruise museums.

I thumbtacked the card to a corkboard. I didn't really think there was anything more than a simple exchange of information at the end of that offer. I turned my attention to cueing up some Monster movies for tomorrow's math lesson.

My students participate in Monster Math, a curriculum that included clips of old black and white monster movies to go along with some word problems and multiplication tables. *Dracula's throwing a party. He invites twenty-one guests and their partners. How many people might show up at Dracula's Castle?* For a few months, my students become monster experts!

They talk Monsters all day long. They talk about what Monsters eat–or *who* they eat–and what the rules are, when they can bite, when they can't, how often they have to eat. It's gory and they laugh a lot, which is good for a Math class.

"When he's not a werewolf, what is he?" someone asks.

"He's a fireman," someone else answers.

"But they only go out when there's a fire. What is he when he's not a werewolf or a fireman?"

"He's a person who has a house and a dog," someone says.

That seems to satisfy them for a few minutes until someone asks:

"Does the dog think of him as a person or another dog?"

About twice a year, students will ask me about my personal life. Someone gets married or pregnant and they wonder about me.

"Where's your wife, Mr Halliard?" someone asks.

"Where's yours?" I always ask.

"No, I mean. Why aren't you married?"

"I haven't found the right person."

"Where do you find the right person?" someone asks.

I love kids. "That's a very good question. Let's talk about cryptoriums, which monsters live in crypts?"

It's not that I'm not ready to talk about it, I just don't want to. Inherent in their questions is not the stigma of being gay, but of being alone. Sometimes that's harder to talk about.

Or maybe this is my excuse. Either way, I deflect.

"Mummies want coins," I say.

"Mummies want kids!" they say to a lot of laughter.

"Mummies want four coins from every kid here or they'll eat you. How many coins do the mummies get?"

They scream, count out coins and try to multiply by twenty-two as I count down the minutes till disaster!

Desperate, they ask suddenly, "Will mummies take an I owe you?"

"Mummies," I say, "have to pay the bills too."

"They should get a better job," someone says. "Or marry daddies!"

My life is not fourth grade. I have friends to go to movies with, friends to invite over. I go to a gay friendly church, to a coffee house for live music. Still, I called the number anyway.

I got the Mather House. No one answered, just a recording saying that all archival material would be accepted at the West door of the Mather Archives. Just ring the doorbell. So, naturally, on Saturday, I went over to the Mather House to see what I could find out about sled dogs, or Mr Forte.

The West Door of the Mather Archives was shrouded by bushes and two large spruce trees. I rang the bell and waited. It was October, but the temperatures were nice. The leaves were beginning to turn. The spruces, though, would stay full and green all winter.

The door opened and a woman smiled at me. "Hello, come in." She was of native descent. "What can I do for you?" The room was dark and cramped and crowded with shelves stuffed with paper and old books. Boots sat on the floor on a small rug. It wasn't meant for the public. A lit hallway lay behind her, probably to offices. No reception desk. Maybe I had the wrong door.

"Is Mr Forte in? He left me a note to get back in touch with him."

She shook her head. "He's not in on Saturdays."

I paused, feeling a bit dumb. Then, thinking back to every thriller and mystery I'd ever watched, I decided to go for the password phrase. "He mentioned he might know where the sled dogs ran in the city," I said, feeling clandestine in an Orson Welles kind of way.

And that felt really stupid. She didn't react like she knew what I was talking about. She stood there quietly, so I pulled out the card.

She took it. "You're the teacher at Mather Elementary," she said, smiling.

"Yes," I said. "I have this note." I felt like a kid late for class.

She looked at it and I saw her eyebrow rise and then fall. She looked at me. "I'm not sure what Mr Forte wanted you to know. We know Mather took the dogs to play in the park, but not as a team. And there were safety issues, too."

"Safety issues?"

"Well, the dogs were part wolf." She didn't smile. She let that linger for a few seconds.

"Well," I laughed uncomfortably. "That's not on the tour."

She handed back the card. "There's a lot we don't put on the tour. It's a big, complicated story. But it's all in the books. Have you read any of the books on Horwood Mather that we offer in the gift shop?" With that, she walked toward the door. "It was very nice talking with you, Mr Halliard. I'll tell Mr Forte you came by."

As I turned from the house, the door didn't shut right away, as if she were watching me leave. I turned around and saw the door pressed closed with a thump.

I took the card from my pocket to read the note again, but it wasn't the same card.

Try being less obvious, it read. It had a different number on it. I flipped it over. C. Girard Forte. Did she switch cards with me? It was the same handwriting though–presumably Mr Forte's. I walked down the street past restaurants and stores, whipped around a corner, opened my cell phone and called the new number.

"So," the voice said, with a slight French accent. "Do you want to know from me or do you want to go back to the museum and get the standard answer?"

"Who is this?" I asked.

"Fourth and Gillium, the corner next to the Paper Café."

"I'm sorry. I really don't want to play games–" I started.

"What? You're not up for a mystery–a mystery no other human being in this city knows?" He laughed. "It's a coffee shop. Go have coffee." I started to say that I would have to call later. I didn't want to be embarrassed again. "Be nice to whatever comes up to you."

"What?"

He hung up.

The Paper Café demands interpretation from its patrons. On the walls are the framed front pages of important newspapers in world history. The papers change and regulars debate their relevance. I'd been here three or four times with friends.

I ordered a caramel latté and sat outside. It was sunny on the sidewalks of the University district and everyone was out today. I watched couples holding hands–straight couples, gay couples–people with strollers, people with dogs. I sat there making excuses for myself and got so distracted that I completely missed when the dog came up and started lapping up my latté. Someone's malamute. He was huge and his head easily came up and over table height to make latté lapping an easy crime.

"Hey," I swatted at him and he ducked. Of course, I wasn't going to finish the coffee now. He looked at me and sat, licked the caramel foam off his black lips. A leash draped from his collar. He'd run from someone. I looked around to see who. No one even noticed him.

"Was it good?" I asked him.

He stood up, walked over to me and licked my hand.

"Yeah, you're welcome. You should find your folks."

The dog lay down under the table on one of my feet.

I laughed a little to myself, wondering if I should go get another drink when I noticed something was different about the street. All the people had disappeared. The familiar stores were gone, replaced by others with residences above them. It was night. The sidewalks were not bright with sunshine anymore, but lamp-glow on snow. There was snow on the street. I wanted to stand up but I didn't. I didn't feel any colder. I couldn't see the table in front of me anymore and for that matter I couldn't see myself. But suddenly, from the top of the street came a cry of a man and I turned to the sound of huffing dogs, malamutes and huskies harnessed to a sled, moving through the snow, kicking it up behind them, silent except for their breathing and the sliding of the sled. It scraped by me and I was the only one who saw it. The windows of all the other buildings were dark. As he passed me, I got scared–as if he would veer into me–this phantom, or hallucination. I pulled back–into the sunshine of a crowded street and the dog under the table.

The dog stretched and stood up and looked at me.

"What?" I said. I must have been daydreaming about the sled dogs.

The dog, his wide face mischievous just watched me. I realized that he could have been one of those sled dogs. Not surprising that I dreamed of him, since he'd been at my feet.

I wondered where Mr Forte was. I took out my cell phone, trying to brush away the dream and pulled out the card to call his number. The message on the card had changed.

What did you think? Impressive, yes? I dropped the card.

It landed on the ground. The dog came over and nuzzled it. I didn't know what to think. The dog lay down and stared at the card.

I looked around. I thought if I could see someone else looking at me or watching then they could explain what the hell was going on. Everyone else was minding their own business.

I pointed at the dog. "You. What's going on?"

The dog didn't move, just kept staring at the card. I kneeled and I saw the words on its tags. Blue etched into the silver. *Chicago*, it read, and it looked like there was a number to call. Chicago was the name of one of the seven dogs. This was coincidence, I decided.

The dog blinked, but stared at the card on the ground. I picked it up. The message read: *Don't be scared. You love mysteries.*

This time I held onto it–but I thought something was alive in the card itself. I flipped it over and it still had the Mather House logo on it, and C. Girard Forte. I flipped it back again. *Follow the dog, okay?* It read. I flipped it over again and it read, *Stop flipping the card and follow the dog.*

I remember breathing at that point, like I'd stopped.

The dog stood up and walked past me and then looked back to see if I was following.

The dog turned the corner, following the sidewalk.

I followed, cautiously, very far behind and praying the whole time that God would not let me get hurt for following something supernatural. It was irrational, but nothing had prepared me for this moment. I tapped a man on the arm as he passed me. "Do you see the dog?" I asked.

"The husky?" he asked back.

"Well, yeah, the malamute. They're similar."

"Yeah, he's nice. But he's getting away from you."

So I followed the dog, always keeping half a block between us. The dog would stop and look back to make sure I was following. I flipped over the card, but nothing changed on the card.

Finally the dog led me to a big stone building about three blocks away and then down an alley to a red door. The dog sat. Clearly it wanted me to knock on the door.

The card was right. I did love mysteries, and puzzles, and games. I loved math and monsters and the unknown, but I also valued safety. Now I was being asked to go and knock on a stranger's door by a dog and a business card.

I didn't know what universe I was in anymore but I walked down the alley. The dog watched me with an air of approval.

I watched the door. It didn't open. I had to knock.

I heard unlatching, three bolts, and then the red door opened. A short Native American man came out. "Hey, you must be the teacher."

I didn't know how to answer. "Yeah."

He smiled. "Cool. Come on in." The dog went in by itself, behind the man's legs and disappeared.

I walked up to the door slowly and when I got to the threshold, I stopped and held out the card. "Do you know about the card?" I asked.

"Yeah. We know about the card."

Beyond him, the living room was inviting. It was a big wooden floored space holding a blue couch, two floor lamps, and a stereo playing classical music. A woman turned down the music.

"He's scared," she said.

The man said, "Yeah. It isn't easy, is it?"

I didn't know what to say. "What's happening? Is this the end of the world?"

The man smiled. "No. But if you like, we'll show you another one."

"Another world?"

The woman said, "Let's get him some tea first."

Another man came out of a back room. This one I recognized. "Mr Forte?" I asked.

He was about my height, wore a khaki button down shirt over big shoulders, with slightly curly brown hair both on his head and between the buttons of his shirt. He smiled when he leaned in for a handshake. He had friendly eyes. No glasses. "Girard," he said, with that faint French accent. He gestured towards the other man, "Jimmy." Jimmy walked towards me and I shook his hand. "And Roberta in the kitchen."

"I can make coffee. Anyone want coffee?" she called out.

"We don't want coffee," Girard said.

"I'll take some," Jimmy said.

If this had not been so weird, I would have laughed. I wanted to laugh.

"So you guys own the dog?" I asked Jimmy and Girard.

They looked at each other. Girard turned to me, sympathy on his face, a little guilt. "It's a bit complicated, really. But, sort of." He walked towards the sofa. "Come, sit down. You're having a weird day."

I laughed then.

Roberta walked in with tea.

Jimmy said, "You probably won't trust the tea we're gonna serve you. And I wouldn't blame you. The last time you had something to drink, you saw things."

Roberta snapped, "Jimmy!" She turned to me, "There's nothing in this tea."

I stared at them. "Am I on drugs?"

Girard said, "Are you?"

"No, am I on drugs? Was there a drug in the coffee?" I wouldn't sit. Jimmy was right.

"You are not on drugs," Girard told me. "There was nothing in the coffee. Everything you saw I can explain."

Roberta set the tray down on the table. "And there's nothing wrong with this tea. It's decaf Earl Grey," Roberta said. "You don't have to sit, Mr Halliard"

"Drew, call me Drew. I'm really not used to this," I told them.

"We know. If you sit, we can explain. Or you can leave if you want."

I looked at the door. It was still slightly ajar. No one would blame me for leaving. I could grade math papers.

I still had the card in my hand.

It read: *You don't want to grade math papers.* I dropped the card again, "Can you read my mind?"

"Not exactly," Girard said.

Roberta turned to him, "Stop it. Okay. We don't need to scare him anymore. Can we just be normal for a while?"

Girard said firmly, "I'm being myself. I want him to know us as ourselves. We talked about this." I liked his authority, the way he spoke.

"Yeah, but we talked about going slowly," she said. "Tea first. Let the man get comfortable. He's not used to this."

For the first time I noticed the cross on the wall. Girard

followed my gaze. "Catholic," he said.

"Practicing?" I asked.

"Well, I'm there once a month at least." He caught on. "We're not devils."

Jimmy swiveled in the easy chair. "We're not angels either." He laughed.

"Then what are you?"

They looked at each other.

Girard said. "Shamans." Then he asked me to sit again.

Shamans, I felt strangely reassured by this knowledge.

"What's going to happen to me after I sit and talk with you? Will I leave?"

Jimmy said, "I hope so." Jimmy turned to Girard, "Is he staying the night?"

"We're gonna talk," Girard said to me, ignoring Jimmy. "And tell you some history and you're gonna drink tea and then, whenever you're ready, you can leave all by yourself. Promise."

Everything here was balancing on whether I was brave enough–or stupid enough–to sit down on a stranger's couch. Girard's voice and face and body were a good reason to stay. I could really like sitting on that couch about a knee's-length away from Girard.

"Why didn't you just all meet me at the Paper Café?"

Girard leaned back in his chair; spread his arms onto the armrests, which opened his shirt more. "When you didn't call right away, I thought I'd been too forward. I didn't know you'd go to the Mather House and meet up with Janelle and Erica. It's not your fault. I just would have met you at Mather House if I'd known you were coming. I left you my office number, but it gets transferred back to the main switchboard on the weekends and that just plays a message."

Roberta interrupted. "The tea is getting cold. And I'd like you to enjoy it while it's hot."

"Drew, we could have jumped you by now," Jimmy said, dangling a leg over the arm of his chair.

I walked over to the couch and sat down. It wasn't a firm couch, but I didn't sink in, either. As a death-trap, it was nice. "I'm sorry I didn't call earlier," I said to Girard, who was better up close than from across the room. "You wouldn't believe what

I was thinking."

Jimmy raised an eyebrow. "Then again..."

"You *know* what I'm thinking?" I asked Girard, afraid he might really know.

He glanced at Roberta and Jimmy and then back at me. "We can talk about that at another time." He smiled. I wasn't sure what I was more nervous about; Girard knowing I found him attractive, or him having freaky powers?

He went on. "Anyway, when you went to the Mather House, I couldn't tell you anything on the card–'cause you weren't looking at it. We didn't want to talk about this in public–we weren't sure how you'd react. And I wanted to show you something on that street."

He looked at me like I should know what he was talking about, but I was caught up in his eyes, one blue, one brown. He looked sincere and concerned. "The sled dogs," I said.

"Yeah," he said, smiling.

"Where the sled dogs ran in the city," I said. "That wasn't a dream?"

"Have you ever had a dream like that?" Jimmy asked.

All the years I had taken those students to the Mather house, I'd never dreamed of sled dogs. We talked about them. I knew their names. "Chicago, Jericho, Uruk, Mari, Yinxsu, Kansas City..." I trailed off.

"Dawson," Jimmy said. "Don't forget Dawson." He leaned forward.

"Right. Dawson, the rambunctious trickster."

Jimmy grinned. "That's Dawson."

I looked at Girard. "So, what was it that you wanted to tell me that you couldn't say in public? That you feared I might overreact too–besides–*hey*, I have the power to read your mind and write messages on cards."

Girard looked at Roberta and Jimmy. They nodded.

"I'm not sure how to say this," he started. It almost felt like he was coming out. I remember moments like this, when it came time to say it I got tongue-tied.

Roberta blurted, "That's Dawson." She looked at Jimmy.

I looked around the room for a dog.

"No," Roberta said. "Jimmy's Dawson."

I looked at Jimmy. He looked very proud. "That's me."

"What?" I said, not getting it.

"Okay," Girard stopped us. "This isn't working."

"It was your idea," Roberta said.

"Yeah, but he's not gonna make the leap."

Jimmy argued, "He's almost cool with mind-reading and trick cards. He can handle werewolves."

"Werewolves!" I stood up.

They stood up with me. Jimmy said, "Werewolves!"

I started babbling. "You mean the people who turn into monsters by the light of the moon, eat human flesh, are afraid of silver?"

Girard said, "Nope."

"Oh."

He smiled. I was either the biggest sucker in the world, or he had a genuine calming effect on me.

Jimmy said, "We're talking about people who can turn back and forth into wolf-dogs, live forever, and can sort of read people's minds, and if you touch them, you can read their minds."

I looked at Jimmy and then Girard and then Roberta, who were all looking at me.

"What do they eat?"

"Corn on the cob, potatoes, steak," Jimmy said. "That's what I want, at least." He looked at Roberta. "But we're having soup tonight, I think."

Roberta didn't answer. She concentrated on me. "We're not here to eat you, Drew."

"Okay, what are you here for?"

"We just wanted someone to tell," Girard said.

He half smiled and winked. We were all standing awkwardly around the coffee table.

"You wanted to tell me that you were werewolves."

"And that we were famous sled dogs," Jimmy said.

"We thought with your experience in the Mather House and we know you teach about werewolves—sort of—you'd be able to understand."

"My math curriculum."

Girard put his big hand on my shoulder. It was warm. I could feel the heat from the rest of his body. "It's lonely," he said.

"We haven't told anyone. We have to turn once a day and that makes it awkward to have other friends."

I looked at them all quickly, tried to meet their eyes. They all wanted to know that I wasn't going to freak out. I didn't know what to say.

"I'm gay," I told them.

Girard smiled. "So are we."

"You're gay *too*..."

"Werewolves don't breed."

He was gay? His hand was on my shoulder. He was looking at me with those blue and brown eyes and smiling through that beard and I forgot about everything else. All I saw was a damn cute guy who had the same kind of baggage anyone else had. I kept thinking, He's gay and he's cute.

Jimmy sat down. "You're *gay*, man. I don't know. This is gonna take awhile to sink in."

We all sat down. Girard let go of my shoulder. "Okay," he said. "That's all the big news. The rest is just history and stuff. Can you handle the werewolf stuff, Drew?"

He was the dog I'd followed, with the wide face and the mischievous smile. Okay, that put a twist on things. "So you have a dog phase and a people phase."

"And a half-in, half out phase too," Jimmy said. "Wanna see?"

Roberta slapped his leg. "No. He does not want to see. It's all talk today."

"I can't say how this is going to change the way I see the whole world," I said. "But I'm okay right now."

I looked at them all. Roberta drank her tea. Jimmy grinned like he'd won the lottery and Girard looked very proud of me.

"So the sled dogs run the museum?" I asked.

"Yeah," Girard said. "For the most part. There are a couple of people who aren't, you know, werewolves. We used to live there too."

They told me about how they'd split up thirty years ago into two groups; three of them wanted to tell people, four of them wanted to stay silent. "So what does it matter if people know that the sled dogs ran in the city?"

Girard put his hand on my knee, a very affirming friendly gesture. "Horwood Mather brought us all back from the Arctic.

He wanted to bring us down here to help him with the *other* werewolves in town. They were a bit unpredictable. Mather had a plan to bring us down to teach them teamwork. Give them a social structure. He was one too."

"Horwood Mather was a werewolf? But he *died*," I said. "I thought you lived forever."

"We can be killed by another werewolf. They got to him after the election." He was silent a moment. "We were wolves that were part sled dog that's why he valued us. But some of our group," he looked at the others, "found they liked being more independent, being human and resented getting harnessed up. They wanted to live as people, blend in. The mushing only lasted the first few years. The ones he'd brought down to teach teamwork started breaking apart as a team. We took on human names–we all did–but eventually, the mushing stopped. We haven't run as a team in the city for eighty years."

Jimmy said, "You can't force them to run. We tried. It's in our blood–at least I thought it was." He looked sad. "I miss it. I miss running as a team."

Girard said, "The others don't talk about the running in the city because they don't want to remember. They hide in that house."

Roberta put down her tea. "And we hide in this one."

We were silent for a moment. I reached out and put my hand on Roberta's arm and met her eyes. I wanted her to know that she wasn't alone. I kept my right hand on her arm. Then I looked at Girard and put my left hand on his arm. That felt wonderful. He smiled. Jimmy held out his hands.

I said, "What was it like to run in the city free, full out speed down the streets in the snow?"

And they showed me a collective memory, this time from the perspective of Mather himself. I was on the sled, balanced. I could see my gloved hands on the brake bar. The dogs ran ahead of me, pulling me, fast through the night streets. Around the blind corners, through a world that slept while they slid through. I could feel the cold wind on my face, hear them huffing. I could see their breaths, see Mather's breath. We blinked through the lamplights and the dogs ran for miles.

I was in that moment for a long time, down ten or fifteen streets, all somewhere in the 1920s.

When we separated, I told them, "I have an idea."

The fourth grade class is ready for my surprise. Two weeks after I met Girard, two weeks after we started dating–tentatively at first, more boldly later–I thought my class might be ready to talk about the Mather House again. This time to get their question answered. Where *did* the sled dogs run in the city? Maybe even to see it for themselves.

"Now, remember. Everyone? Remember that we are friendly to these dogs and they won't hurt us. And they're gonna tell you a story about being sled dogs. A story you'll believe when they show you."

I hear them scratch at the fourth grade door.

I know what you're thinking. How could I let three werewolves into my fourth grade class? But let me tell you, everything we knew about them was wrong. If my students never see the real thing–they're gonna believe all those movies and all those stories. But if they can see it firsthand, from the werewolves themselves, see their stories, they'll believe. Then they won't be afraid.

"This is Chicago, Dawson and Mari," I say, opening the door. The kids squeal and clap and smile and laugh and yell out the dogs' names. They leap out of their seats, even when I try to tell them to sit back down. They can barely restrain themselves from wanting to touch these dogs.

Three malamutes sit waiting in that doorway, in the hallway light. I know they are still uncertain if they want to risk it all by coming in and exposing themselves. I can tell that.

It's written on the card I have in front of me.

Tell them to be gentle.

QUEER WOLF

PAVLOV'S DOG

Andi Lee

The Pavlov's Dog Public House was a tired looking hodgepodge of a building that backed onto sprawling woodlands, yet was only fifteen minutes from the local high street. Far enough out for privacy but close enough for its clientele to get there and stumble back home without much trouble. It was covered in faded posters and fliers advertising bands, with brighter, newer posters pasted haphazardly over others. The pub's sign bore a white wolf with a severed arm in its mouth.

The Canidae's Omega scowled at it, but pushed the door open; grimacing as rock music blasted out of cheap speakers. His briefcase was a dead weight and he found it difficult to maneuver his way through the crowd. He was uncomfortable in the presence of so many humans, even if he was one himself. Although Omegas were part of every werewolf pack, they were not werewolves themselves. They looked after pack business when wolves could not. He pushed through to the bar. A girl with green hair leaned across shouting over the music, "What can I get ya?"

"I'm looking for Josh Deverell. Can you tell him Peter Canidae is here?" Her eyes widened and Peter knew she was Pack. She probably hadn't been fully initiated, but he suspected that it would happen soon. Josh would need people like her. All packs needed some kind of human cover.

"You better come round back." He followed her through a narrow corridor to the foot of a staircase. She yelled up the stairs and Peter cringed. She wasn't refined enough to be an Omega, but it was really none of his business. Josh appeared at the top of the stairs and beckoned him up. He was led him into a room where another werewolf sat at a kitchen table. It was so ordinary, so human. Peter barely remembered ordinary. He placed his briefcase on the table and took his time removing documents.

"I'm the Canidae Council's First Omega," he finally began.

"The Council has reviewed your application for your own pack. You have your own business and a regular income that won't be disrupted by the full moon. You back onto enough woodland and you aren't near another pack. Your only issue is the proximity to the human population." He paused and watched both men tense, try not to protest. It was petty, but experience had taught him that a firm hierarchy needed to be maintained. "The Council has, however, concluded that as long as you take the proper precautions and have an Omega to help your pack blend into the community, then your request is approved."

Josh's mouth opened and closed. He looked towards the other werewolf before trying again. "We've got the go ahead?"

Peter nodded, opening the documents "I need you and," he glanced at Josh's companion recalling the second name on the application, "Caleb Ellory, to sign here and here. I don't need to tell you that you have to abide by the Canidae Council's rules. A feral pack will be...exterminated." He watched Josh for a reaction knowing the alpha's history. It was all in the Council file on him. He was rewarded with a flinch, a paling of Josh's skin. "Blend in, don't create havoc. Bite anyone—they're your responsibility. You know the rest."

They signed the forms. Keeping their own copies they slid the document over the table to Peter.

"We've another request for the council. It's an application to allow a friend of mine to transfer from his current pack." Caleb handed him more forms and Peter took a moment to study them before placing them neatly within his briefcase.

"I can give you no guarantees," he said. The hierarchy had to be maintained.

Two large grey wolves raced one another out of the trees; transforming into their human forms mid lope. Fur rippled and limbs stretched out, naked skin expanding like elastic. They stopped only to cover their naked bodies with the discarded clothes they'd left behind when the full moon had called them, before making their way towards the closed and dark, Pavlov's Dog.

Josh fumbled with his keys, cursing his inability to get his newly reformed fingers to work. For a building that seemed so run down, Pavlov's Dog was like Fort Knox. It didn't help that Caleb's lips were soon attached to the pulse just behind his ear, sucking gently; tongue teasing his skin. He finally managed to open the back door and Caleb detached himself long enough to jab in the security code.

They didn't bother turning on the lights–their eyesight better in the dark. Josh pulled Caleb to him, his whole body rejoicing as Caleb melted against him, backing out of the narrow corridor. Between kisses, fondles and the occasional curse they reached the lounge where the floor was slightly less sticky than in the bar; preferable as neither wore shoes. It was eerie without the hum of people or the beat of live music, but neither of them noticed.

Tonight was a full moon and electricity crackled around them like wildfire. The moon drew them closer, made their senses sharper, their needs more urgent. Josh thought he would go mad if he didn't satisfy them.

Caleb tasted like the hunt. Like evergreen; fresh grass overlaid with the thick metallic tang of their kill–a wild hare, not a serious hunt, but playful. They had run, then stalked their prey together, neither needing more. They had been celebrating.

The moon was still high, full above the cold winter mist, but being alpha werewolves had advantages. One of which was being able to change back into human form early on a full moon–because Josh did not want to do this in wolf form. There was something to be said for being human. Opposable thumbs.

Oh yeah.

Caleb's hands were large and callused from a lifetime of playing guitar. He had toured seedy clubs and bars similar to Pavlov's Dog in a small time rock band. It was how they met–instant werewolf attraction. Although Josh had tried to deny it, hesitant to get involved with another wolf, frightened of where it might lead.

He'd watched his own pack turn on itself, give in to animal hunger, animal instincts and slowly lose their humanity. They had gone feral. He'd thought all wolves were like that, until Caleb and his band, Dead End, had come to Pavlov's Dog. He'd heard them from upstairs and come down to watch them play before he even realized Caleb was a werewolf. Even once he had he couldn't leave, couldn't turn away, couldn't help but be drawn to Caleb.

It hadn't been easy for either of them to admit that what they had was any more than lust and circumstance. Not long after that gig, Caleb had suddenly found himself in need of a safe place to bring his newly changed friend and Josh couldn't turn them out. The idea of Pack had started to seem like a good idea then. A pack put together under his rules; by human humanity and animal bonds.

Caleb shoved his hand down the front of the jeans Josh had hastily pulled on. Caleb's hand found Josh's erection, his thumb brushing over the head and his long talented fingers grasping the root. He did this thing where he twisted his wrist and tightened his grasp. It never failed to make Josh see stars. He forgot what he was thinking about. All that remained was Caleb.

Caleb's wrist twisted, fingers tightening; he jacked Josh slowly, like sweet torture. All the while his mouth was working against Josh's; lips firmly attached, tongues exploring and caressing. The night of a full moon made them so much more sensitive. Josh closed his eyes, but he felt the air around them shift, knew the exact moment Caleb opened his eyes and stared at him.

The hunt wasn't just about blood lust–or lust in general–it was the way everything felt, like he'd been reborn, like he was finally free. It was a werewolf thing, a Pack feeling that came from being more than human. With the wolf's heightened senses and a human's ability to feel, to love, it made fireworks go off inside Josh's skull.

Caleb ripped his mouth from Josh's, took gulps of air then dropped to his knees. Josh opening his eyes, saw Caleb's pupils bleed outwards, saw him lick his lips and pull Josh's jeans further down his hips. Josh steadied himself with one hand on Caleb's shoulder, moaning, unable to be silent. Caleb's touch was electric. Caleb sucked Josh's cock into his mouth, no gentle teasing, no playful nips, just sucked him right down. The heat of his mouth was intense, the graze of teeth sensual and thrilling. He grabbed handfuls of Caleb's hair, wrapping the long ash blond locks around his fingers.

"You do that again, and I'm gonna hit the fucking moon, man," Josh said, his voice breathless and raspy.

Caleb's eyes were laughing.

"Bedroom–no fucking in the bar, even when it's closed. Your rules, remember?" Josh drew Caleb up, embracing him. It scared him to think of his life before. He had been the sole landlord of Pavlov's Dog for more years than he wanted to remember. It had been a lonely existence for someone who by his very nature was a social animal. He'd avoided the wolves and kept himself at a distance, never able to trust himself around humans who didn't know what he was. Josh wasn't sure how he'd survived without Caleb–without the pack they were building together. He couldn't remember how the sign above the door looked without Caleb's name next to his own.

The Pavlov's Dog was not only a great divey rock bar, but it was the best place to hide a pack. With the woodlands sprawling behind, it was the perfect place to create a safe haven. Maybe Josh had known that all along, maybe that was why he'd chosen it. He'd just been waiting for the right person to come along. Now, they were creating a good place for their people. He pulled Caleb up the back stairs to their private quarters, shoved open the door to their bedroom as Caleb tackled him to the floor, stripping Josh of his t-shirt.

The bed was close, but Josh wanted to feel this fuck in every bone, wanted rug burns on his elbows and knees, wanted something rough and lasting.

"I can't believe we're doing this." Caleb said as he sat over Josh; his hair framing a chiseled face and sea-green eyes. Josh knew Caleb didn't mean sex. What he meant was the pack; becoming Alpha and Beta, becoming responsible for other people. Neither had thought that they'd get permission.

"Believe it. We have paperwork and everything. We're officially a pack."

"A family." Caleb rolled the words in his mouth as if he couldn't quite believe it, and maybe he couldn't. Josh hadn't considered himself part of a family for a very long time. This time...it would last. This time it would be different.

"Well come on, daddy, let's fuck before the kids get home." Josh winked and rolled his hips upwards, his erection rubbing against Caleb's denim clad ass.

Caleb moved with the speed given him by his wolf blood,

quickly stripping naked, then pushing Josh's jeans over his hips, flinging them across the room. The cool air made Josh shiver; goose bumps covering his arms for a few moments until Caleb's hot kisses and lingering touches warmed him.

Caleb licked at Josh's lips–wolfish kisses–down his chin and nuzzled his neck. It was as if he was trying to mark him, but Josh didn't mind. He wanted to roll in Caleb, to smell of him. He wanted their scents to mingle until no one could distinguish one from the other. He wanted their pack to know what they were to each other, not just because they said it, but because they could scent it. He wanted other packs to know…wanted to mark his territory and snarl a warning at anyone who came near him and his. Josh had never thought of himself as dominant, but that was changing. Caleb nipped his way down to Josh's nipples, biting at them with his pearly teeth and chuckling when Josh bucked into him.

Excitement crackled around them like a second skin; Josh could feel his energy wrap around Caleb's; feel his animal instincts call out. The energy was loud. It was white noise in his ears; overlaid by the rhythm of his heart, music composed by Caleb, carefully crafted by his hands, his mouth and his lust.

Josh wished he could shape lyrics to it. He wished he could make music as sweet, as rocking as Caleb, briefly he was aware that once they'd passed out from sheer exhaustion Caleb would wake again, a heavy rock riff waiting to be written.

Josh wanted to be like that but then someone needed to be the practical one, and he was practical–but right now he was practically insane for Caleb.

"Get. Up. Here." Caleb laid his body flush over Josh's. Josh found Caleb's lips, demanded entrance and tasted him deeply. The hunt was there again, still fresh, along with something else, something faint, earthy–Pack. It was their scent; the pack's collective scent. Faint, but present and soon it would be strong, it would be within them all and Josh didn't dread it, couldn't wait for it to happen.

Josh flipped them over, ground his hips against Caleb, feeling Caleb's erection slide wet against his hip.

Fuck.

It was a feeling Josh never wanted to end. He never wanted

any of this to end and for once in his life he actually believed that it wouldn't. He felt as though he was on fire. His blood raced through his veins, his heart pumped faster and his cock was hard and straining against Caleb's belly. He wanted to be inside Caleb, to be surrounded by him, attached in the most intimate of ways.

Josh spat into his hand and reached between their bodies, fingers trailing down the swirl of hair beneath his bellybutton before fisting his cock quickly, slicking it up. Then he followed the crease of Caleb's ass until he felt the tight knot of muscle. It quivered under his touch. He pushed a finger inside; loosening him. His finger deliberately dug deep, but missed the prostate teasingly. Caleb cursed him and tried to change the angle himself.

Josh laughed and shook his head.

"Naughty boy." He stood, looking down at his lover. "Turn over."

Caleb did as he asked without question. Josh felt his breath catch in his throat at the sight. Caleb's back was firm and smooth, his ass was perfectly shaped. Josh groaned as Caleb teased him, clenching his butt cheeks together. Josh knelt and clutched a cheek with one hand, gently prying it apart. He ran his tongue down the crease, reaching Caleb's balls before he dragged it back. He stiffened his tongue and plunged it into Caleb's clenching hole.

Caleb gave a strangled cry, arms and legs flailed as Josh plunged his tongue as deep as it would go. His ass opened up wide and welcoming; his inner walls hot and pulsing against his tongue. Josh pried his ass cheeks apart further. He slipped a finger in next to his tongue, going directly for Caleb's prostate. Caleb cried out.

"Get your tongue out of my ass and fuck me!" Caleb groaned craning his neck to glare at him.

Josh swirled his tongue around Caleb's opening one last time then moved away. His lips glistening as Josh pulled Caleb's hips to him, making him move onto all fours before he thrust inside. Sparks flared behind Josh's eyelids. He reached for Caleb's erection and jacked him in time to his thrusts. He fucked Caleb hard, his cock forcing its way deeper, sensation by delicious sensation. Caleb reached back, callused fingers urging Josh on.

"More, you fucker. What are you? Not strong enough to be Alpha?" His voice was choppy and full of teasing desire.

Josh growled. His free hand grabbed hold of Caleb's hair, pushing it to the side, exposing the length of his neck. His thrusts became harder, his hold on Caleb's dick more erratic and Caleb howled when Josh's human teeth bit into his neck. Caleb came hard, his come spilling over the carpet beneath them. It gave Josh renewed energy and his thrusts became deep and fast as he angled his cock, overloading Caleb with sensation. When Josh came it was explosive. His balls tightened and his stomach convulsed and before he knew it, he was emptying himself into Caleb. They fell in a heap on the floor, neither having the energy to move to the bed.

"Was this like…our honeymoon or something?" Caleb asked, sweat dripping off his forehead. Josh wanted to lick it away, but had lost all ability to move.

"Nah…wouldn't this be our wedding night?"

They turned their heads to look at each other; both burst out laughing.

"I kinda love you, you dumb shit," Caleb said.

"It's a damned good job, 'cause I love you too." Despite their lethargy, they both managed to move until they were in each others arms. Being leader of the pack wouldn't be easy, but for once in Josh's life he saw a brighter future for himself and for others. The certainty settled over him like a blanket and he fell asleep listening to the riff of Caleb's heart.

WOLVES OF THE WEST

Charlie Cochrane

"Heathens." George O'Driscoll leaned on the balcony rail, observing with barely disguised disdain the tourist masses, their heads bent over cases or faces staring up at tiny dinosaur skulls on huge dinosaur necks.

"They pay your salary." Rory Carter's chirpy voice–perpetually chirpy except at times of high passion or drama–sounded over his shoulder.

"Not any more since we've waived the admission fee. It's all grants and such nonsense now, or so I understand." O'Driscoll's face indicated that he might not really know what he was talking about. "And I suspect the people who dole out the funding are as heathen as this mob. Wouldn't know a plesiosaur from a plasmid."

"But they're here to learn, George." The voice of reason spoke again. "Perhaps they'll have more of an idea when they go home; grant them that." Rory surreptitiously drew his finger along the back of O'Driscoll's hand. "Still smooth. The crowds you so despise will be long gone, all at home loading the microwave with Sainsbury's meals, by the time the fun begins."

The chairman rapped the table with his gavel. "I bring this meeting of the Western Lycanthropes to order." Anyone observing the handsome, studious faces around the table would have felt there was no apparent disorder to deal with. The only indications that this wasn't some dry, departmental meeting came from the occasional, anxious glances which the participants cast over to the windows, where a bank of cloud obscured the night sky. That and the fact that their clothes were neatly piled behind their chairs, ready to be claimed the next day, should it prove necessary.

"Gentlemen, we begin with a paper on the Red wolf, *Canis lupus rufus*."

Rory's mind began to wander. He'd heard many a paper–scientific, historical, literary–over the years, as they'd waited for the leaden English skies to clear. This one didn't enthuse him. Not like the occasion when someone had presented a cogent–if only in their eyes–case that Esau had indeed been one of their brethren, which would explain the hairiness. A thesis countered by another member who'd sworn blind that Esau had been a Neanderthal. Harsh words and blows had ensued, turning to snarls and bites as the moon had broached the clouds. Things rarely got that exciting.

Well, Rory reflected, casting a surreptitious glance around the room, *we're hardly an exciting bunch.* Most of his associates worked in museums or universities, although one particularly enterprising lad had secured a job behind the meat counter at Harrod's. That was one way of mixing business and pleasure. Given that those present shared more than just the tendency to be influenced by the full moon, it might have seemed surprising that none of them were employed in the entertainment industry. Yet, while it would be easy to hide your sexual inclinations in a profession awash with the gay and eccentric, how could you take the stage as Romeo if the lunar calendar didn't work out? You might find yourself appearing more like Chewbacca.

"Long term analysis of mitochondrial DNA..." the speaker droned on.

Rory looked out at the dark, lowering sky; not even the brightest moon could penetrate that yet. There'd be plenty of wet commuters, scurrying home under hats and umbrellas. Still, a community of like minded–or like skinned–people could find worse places to live or work. If only the little patisserie sold *pain au pate de fois gras* or the French ice cream shop produced a monthly batch of chicken and raspberry ripple, it might be well nigh ideal. There was also the positive advantage that when the full moon coincided with a football match, you could travel home and no-one noticed the difference.

Whether local house prices would be quite so buoyant if anyone realized how many of the flats off the high road were occupied by those of a lycanthropic inclination, was unlikely. There would always be the worry that, no matter how well bred these creatures were, they might frighten the au pair, who'd head back to Croatia, or wherever, leaving no-one to look after little Georgina.

At least their sexual orientation would be less of an issue, its significance reducing as you got further west, where the rainbow flags flew proudly. There was another community of similarly inclined–in both senses–gentlemen down South, who benefited from the same open-mindedness of their neighbors, although no-one was sure what the reaction would be should these men take to the beach in all their hirsute glory. Maybe the little old ladies would just think someone was exercising a pack of particularly shaggy greyhounds. Anyway, the Wolves of the West mob regarded their southern brethren with disdain, convinced they were common, plebeian and too fond of fish and chips.

"The mitochondrial DNA indicates…"

Rory had heard a number of papers that droned on about this seemingly fascinating stuff. One had been in the long list–and it was a very long list, every full moon for over one hundred and fifty seven years–of scientific theories for their condition. Somehow certain individuals had absorbed–by process unspecified, perhaps it was the biological equivalent of a tea bag–wolf mitochondria, which reacted under the rays of the full moon to initiate a process of metamorphosis. As a rationale it had something to be said for it, better than the theory that aliens had spliced wolf DNA into his genome when he was a baby. Or that his dear mama had been frightened by wolves when he was in utero.

Something made it happen, though. Night of the full moon, even when the photons couldn't fully penetrate, the changes began. Rory's skin was downy now, had been since the sun neared the horizon–his teeth ached, his bones were coiled as if to leap into action. Like a sprinter awaiting the 'B' of the bang. George was tense, too; he sat, unmoving, face drawn, eyes straying to the window every few minutes.

"Gentlemen," the chairman's voice interrupted the speaker, much to everyone's relief. "It begins."

Every face turned to watch the tattering clouds allow the first rays through. The downy hair thickened, altered its structure, losing human traits and adopting lupine; Rory recalled, with pain, a boring talk about the microscopic changes that could be observed at each point–much more interesting to watch those same changes as they affected his lover. O'Driscoll's handsome face was metamorphosing now, the fine-looking nose lengthening, the jaw thrusting forward to join it and make a muzzle.

Please let it go all the way tonight.

They'd both wanted that. It was a hope they articulated each month, a hope so often thwarted by the vagaries of the English climate. Weather that, no sooner had they begun the great change, swathed the moon in cloud again to leave them half-formed, mongrel. Fit only to haunt the museum deploring–half in human tones, half in wolf speak–the general ignorance of those who trod its hallowed halls. To bay politely at the hidden moon, raising only a disdainful reply from the local dogs and to walk home in shadows, hugging the darkness.

Tonight they wished to experience the rare ecstasy of a full transformation, to race through the museum's corridors on all fours, horrifying the security men. Or at least letting them pretend to be horrified. To wander home through the streets, cocking a leg at lamp posts and scaring the hell out of the urban foxes. Stopping off at The Taj Mahal restaurant, owned by Mr Khan who knew all about werewolves–and werebears and weretigers–to feast on chicken carcasses, snuggling up to the bag lady at West Brompton who tickled behind their ears and said that they were such lovely Alsatians.

"Ah-oooooooooooh." George threw back his head, muscles straining and moving, the well-bred baying turning to a deeper, wilder note. As the rays of the moon breasted the curtains, illuminating him in quicksilver light, the great change took effect. O'Driscoll, now *Frost,* leapt onto the table, transforming as he sprang to land on all fours–a magnificent, bright eyed, sleek pelted beast. If wolves truly had alpha males, which had been a topic of at least three papers, then Frost was the dominant member of this group. He was taller by a handbreadth than any other individual. Stronger, wilder and more daring.

Rory felt the wolf-blood course, the dozens of changes begin as the rays of the moon hit him, too. Soon he'd be at George's side and they'd bound off together, Frost and Ice, side by side as always. Two legged or four legged. First floor flat or hall of the Earth Sciences department. Elegant pine bed or marble floor. Making love gently to the music of Vaughn Williams or mating roughly to the sound of howling filtering through from the Science Museum. Wolves were said to be monogamous and even some possessors of the pink pound achieved the same fidelity, shape shifters or not. Rory Carter and George O'Driscoll did not break the mould.

A huge, rough tongue drew itself over Ice's cheek–a wolf kiss, a symbolic gesture of love that was constant in spirit whatever corporeal shape the soul wore. Ice reciprocated the gesture, long and lovingly, before the pair sprang off through the door.

"Does it never tire you?" Rory sprawled on the sofa, a huge mug of Starbuck's coffee in his hand. Coffee, which George–turned out like a bandbox even if it was Saturday–had been out to buy, while his lover had dragged his protesting pyjamaed frame from bedroom to lounge.

"Never," O'Driscoll cradled his own mug, picking a grey hair from his immaculate trousers. They'd have to vacuum carefully today; they always did the day after the moon had waxed to its largest, most powerful point. "I feel as if I've enough energy to…" he searched for the appropriate challenge, "…climb Everest."

"You hate heights." Rory smiled affectionately. "Or you will in an hour or two. When all trace of Frost is gone."

"Then I'd better settle for running a marathon." If George had ever resented the transformation back from magnificent animal to rather staid, if handsome, man, he had grown out of it. When he'd been young, the first few changes had left him bitter, aggrieved that he reached such heights of passion and power only once a month, if that. He'd made the most of those fleeting hours, mating with any other wolf that would accept him, settling for Newfoundlands if none of his grey brothers could be found. Wild, insatiable under the full moon, he'd been quiet, reserved at all other times, no human mate found or even required. Until Rory had come along.

"Are you thinking about the Zoo?"

Strange how Rory had always known what George was thinking, from the moment they'd met until now, well over a century of physical and mental communion. "I was. Such an unseasonably warm May..."

"It was June. Still remarkably warm, though." Rory looked towards the picture that graced the chimney breast. A very old watercolor, showing the Zoological gardens as they'd been in the 1870's. "Happy days."

"They were. They still are." Though there had been plenty of sad times in between. They'd both cried like children when the old queen died. Even now Rory draped a black ribbon over the mantelpiece come January twenty second. Then the desperate waste over in France and Belgium, *the flower of a generation*-some people called those poor lads-sacrificed on a martial altar to appease some deity of empire or patriotism. He and Rory had driven ambulances, borne the dead and dying on stretchers, prayed-for once-that the clouds would keep the moon well hidden. Just as well no-one had checked their birth certificates, or even realized the significance of the fact that neither possessed one, both men predating the time when such things were obligatory.

"You've put on a bit of weight around the waistline," Rory dug a finger into the little roll of fat hidden beneath George's shirt. "Although all Frost seems to have gained is muscle. Such haunches."

O'Driscoll knew he'd been a trimmer beast when they'd first met, that night of snarling and circling, weighing each other up. He'd been young and lean, yet to develop the strength of a fully grown lycanthrope, which naturally took years. Those muscles only got exercised a dozen or so times a year and only if the weather played fair. Ice had hardly changed at all; pretty strapping in his human form, as lithe as a willow wand when the moon changed him. George had almost ignored him, that first night, thinking him too lacking in physique to be a rival, too wary and unreceptive to be a mate. A single clash of teeth and they'd split apart as if struck by a blow. They'd not met again for two months, a heavy July thunderstorm having ruined everyone's chance of transformation. August they'd been in the zoo together, again, less wary now, more a case of a cagey tolerance; roaming the pathways and shrubbery of Regent's Park in unison if not exactly cheek by jowl.

"September...it was that September." Rory's face bore a dreamy look, his thoughts away north and east, a couple of miles and a century of time away.

"It was." They'd met again under clear skies, accepted each other as pack members, ruled the environs of the Zoo once more. Frost had followed Ice home, rested under the pergola with him, drunk in the heady scent of musk roses in the sheltered garden. Waited until he knew.

You couldn't just assume. There'd been an occasion when a presupposed member of the brotherhood had turned out to be nothing more than an escapee from one of the cages. Feral animals were not unknown, even in this refined part of the city. Some eccentric explorer might have populated a menagerie with the acquisitions of his travels and be none too fussy about where they took themselves off to at night.

They'd sat together, still wary, eyeing one another as the night passed, the eventual lightening of the sky leading to the other great transformation, the return to the human race. Would O'Driscoll be the only one to undergo it? As the hair of the creature beside him receded, the animal shape changed and a naked, beautiful man emerged from the wolf's guise, George had known–blindingly, as sure as he'd known the first time the moon worked on him–that his life had changed forever. They'd gone to Rory's room, made love as the world around them woke.

"The best September of my life," O'Driscoll gently slapped his lover's thigh. "Now, I apologise for my pragmatism, but we're out of shallots and parsley, so we must leave the Zoo, even if it is only in our mind's eye, and get ourselves down to Waitrose."

"Gentlemen, I thank you for coming to this extraordinary meeting." The chairman looked grave. Extraordinary it was, in more ways than one, to be gathered together when the moon was a week into its waning. All eyes were fixed on the head of the table–ostensibly fixed, although there was a lot of looking out of their corners going on, people trying to see if any of their colleagues knew what was happening. Rory didn't; nor his lover. He was as perplexed as the rest of those present if bemused faces were anything to go by.

"We have received a complaint." A gasp ran around the table, as clear in its progress as one of those dreadful Mexican waves.

A complaint. Rory could only remember two of those in all the years he'd been a member of this select gathering. There'd been a nasty little affair back in the 1950's when one of their number had gone wandering over Green Park, scaring the wildfowl and then attempting to mount an off duty guardsmen. It had all been a bit galling for the lycanthrope involved, especially as the very same guardsman had been more than receptive to his amatory overtures the week before, when his paramour was in non-hirsute form. They'd had to oil the guardsman's palms with pound notes and dispatch his devotee to Australia. Punishment enough for anyone, even though the cricket would be more entertaining.

Then there'd been the case of Frederick, one of the leading lights at University college–who was a bit out of their usual patch but he rode a fast bike. He'd become overexcited one full moon, back in the 1920's, not been able to control his hunger and satisfied himself with a supper of poodle. It had taken a visit from the chairman himself to mollify Lady Lavington about her beloved pet. He'd explained that the misdemeanor had to be laid fairly at the feet of one of the dogs that guarded the dinosaur fossils. He pleaded that the circumstances had been mitigating, the poodle having been found allegedly gnawing on a stegosaur's metatarsal at the time, the Alsatian acting as jury, judge and hangman in one fell swoop. A generous contribution to an animal charity had brought the case to a conclusion, filthy lucre once more proving the salve to many a complaint.

The chairman had reported Lord Lavington as secretly delighted at the loss of the verminous pest, although possibly not the sort of man they'd want to have taking too close an interest in their business. 'Congo' Lavington had taken his gun in search of mkole-mbembe and other strange, apocryphal creatures—the date of the attack might have suggested to him another explanation, closer to the truth.

"One of you has been indiscreet. Horribly so." The chairman took a long, steady look at each of the assembled members. Rory racked his brains, but apart from having to relieve himself in the bushes at Wentworth he could bring no transgression to mind. He took a glance at his colleagues, all of whom looked equally perplexed.

"I refer to this." The chairman held up a copy of The Sun, making another shudder of distaste fly around the table. He opened the paper gingerly, as if he feared catching mange from it. "The headline reads *Wolf eats Sabrina's Chihuahua*. I quote," the chairman shivered slightly, "the lady in question. *I'd just stepped out of the shower when I saw this brute eating my little Destiny*."

Perhaps, of all those present, Rory was the only one who didn't have to have it explained who Sabrina was. He followed all the England sports teams, was well aware, even before the chairman began his explanation, that the lady–euphemistic term–was the girlfriend of a premiership footballer.

The tabloids must have loved this story. It contained all the elements–scantily clad girl, pets, football–that meant so much to them. If only the wolf in question had been governed by some absurd EC rule they'd have had a full house.

"Surely," O'Driscoll's clear tones cut across discussions of whether 'WAG' referred to Wives and Girlfriends or what one did with a tail, "this is just a case of the Lavington's poodle again? I mean, we didn't even end up out of pocket then, his Lordship being so grateful for the little beast's removal. Perhaps this footballer will give us an equally hefty donation straight into the committee's coffers. It bought an awful lot of corner cuts of Aberdeen Angus beef..." George's eyes had a faraway, dreamy look–one Rory always associated with either amorous encounters or Yorkshire pudding.

"Ah. There's more to it than that." The chairman sat down, looking suddenly weary beyond his years, all three hundred of them. "You will notice that Mr Harper is not present." Everyone looked around rather theatrically, as if the said Harper had secreted himself behind the wastepaper basket. "I have asked him to wait outside until we've had time to take in the full situation. You will remember he wasn't here the night of the great change."

He wasn't, that's right. Rory was cross that he hadn't already sussed it out.

"He was, in fact, in a bar, picking up a young man." A murmur of approval, tinged with jealously from some quarters, arose from around the table. "This young man. Paul Remington." The chairman pointed to the footballer named in the story, the picture in The Sun showing him looking extremely concerned at his fiancée's plight.

"But..." George had lost the dreamy look and now seemed simply puzzled, "...he's got this girlfriend."

"Dr. O'Driscoll, she is what is known as a moustache–"

"Beard, Mr Chairman." Rory wondered if he was the only one of them in touch with the modern world. "A woman who is worn on the arm as a disguise. Beard."

"But why...?"

"The world at large is not as enlightened as we would hope it to be." The chairman stared at the article, shaking his head. "Harper tells me that this case is particularly sad. It would be almost impossible for this young man to divulge his true nature."

It was true. It would be suicide, both figuratively and maybe literally, to come out when you're the darling of the terraces. The assembled lycanthropes murmured sympathetically.

"Why pick someone up on the night of the great change?" George, as usual, kept hitting the crux of the matter.

The chairman shrugged his shoulders, eloquently.

"Harper is young; he has yet to learn the appropriate amount of discretion. He assures me that he intended to keep out of the moonlight, indeed had managed very well until he was overcome in the night by the urge to *use the facilities*. He passed under a skylight on the way back from the bathroom, then decided his only option was to hide in the kitchen until dawn when he could gather his clothes and–in imitation of the strategy employed by the same tabloid reporters who have written about him–make his excuses then leave. He didn't realize that the house is shared, although the main bedroom isn't. Miss Sabrina's dog woke her early, so she let him out of her bedroom so he could go and use *his* facilities. Plucky little creature; when he found Harper in occupancy of the kitchen he immediately tried to claim his territory."

"So they got into a fight and brute strength won?" Rory could imagine one great movement of Harper's maw dispatching the nasty little thing. Chihuahuas were worse than pineapples for getting stuck in your teeth.

"No. Recognizing the need for discretion, he went off tail between legs to sleep in the utility room. It was the young lady's screams that woke him. The dog was already dead, but Harper–the first shoots of the change back only just budding in his bones–was spotted and got the blame. By the time Miss Sabrina's mother, her agent, her tame newshound and the local bobby arrived, Harper was human, dressed and out through the garden gate."

"And he didn't kill the dog?" Rory felt just as confused as when he'd tried to read Finnegan's Wake.

"He swears he didn't. Says the ghastly little thing was lying like a rag on the floor, as if its neck had been snapped. Yet Sabrina's agent has complained to us, demanding compensation."

"Why to us?"

"Unfortunately gentleman, he is Lord Lavington's grandson. He knew where to come..."

"You knock."

"It's a bell."

"Then you ring." Rory took a step back from the door, hands firmly in pockets. Five minutes they'd spent on the intercom at the gate, explaining to some numbskull of a minder that they *did* have an appointment, that their business *was* entirely legitimate. Neither was going to ring that bell in case they got a second grilling.

"For goodness sake..." George pressed the button, then stepped back a good yard, probably afraid that Miss Sabrina might answer, in all her peroxide glory.

The thick, oaken door opened and a disembodied voice from the other side of the timbers said, "Come in."

"Thank you." The hall was spacious, the décor and furnishings showing a degree of taste that surprised the visitors. "We're so pleased you agreed to see us."

"I won't say it's my pleasure. Bad business. Wish the papers hadn't got involved." Paul Remington was well spoken, pleasantly mannered, not at all what Rory had expected. "That bloody agent. Should be keelhauled, the lot of them." He turned, gestured politely. "Coffee's ready, please come through."

The conservatory, although obviously a recent addition, was in keeping with the rest of the house. 1930's art deco, lovingly restored, no signs of nouveau riche bad taste on display. "Is your fiancée at home?" Rory accepted a cup of coffee, the aroma of which was promising.

"No, she's out shopping. She does a lot of that." Remington shrugged. "I suppose it's one of the few things she has to keep her occupied. That and the gym."

"Mr Remington," O'Driscoll spoke softly, kindly, "does she know?" The question needed no elaboration. When the appointment had been made, they'd been frank with their host; he knew that Harper had told all.

"She does. We have a financial arrangement, which gives her a home, an allowance and enough publicity so that she can make her way afterwards as a pop singer or TV celebrity or," Remington shuddered, "a novelist. With a ghost writer, I hasten to add."

"Not the sort of books you'd read?" Rory, always alert to what could be gathered from the contents of a bookshelf, had noticed the titles. Forster, Austen, a Proust in the original French with a bookmark half way through it.

"No. I'm not sure what would be more of a death knell to my career–coming out or admitting I'm struggling through 'A la recherché du temps perdu'."

"Mr Remington, you're wasted in the Premiership." O'Driscoll spoke as if that settled the matter. "So what do we do now? I'm instructed by my society to offer a remunerative package–"

"Not required, despite what Sabrina's friend said. I'll buy her another little mutt, then another WAG will be in the tabloids tomorrow. It'll all blow over."

"Wasn't she upset, though? The paper said…" George's words trailed off.

"Do you really believe what the papers say? Sabrina's agent may have told me all about your society, but *she* believes that Stephen was really just an escapee from the house up the road–they maintain quite a menagerie. She knows which side her bread is buttered–she'll keep mum *and* the status quo for as long as required."

"What then?" Rory had noted the word 'afterwards' in relation to the Remington domestic set-up. "Are you intending to turn your purported fiancée into a purported wife?"

The footballer smiled ruefully. "Not a chance. We will split up, amicably, Sabrina will get a settlement–which she'll lose if she tries the old kiss and tell, I'm not that daft–and I'll be left, ostensibly heartbroken."

"It's no way to live. All these lies." O'Driscoll stood up, went over to the window. Frost, who knew all about skulking in the shadows, brought almost to the verge of tears by another man's need to hide his true nature.

"That's the life I've chosen. Lying to my club, lying to my fans, to the press, everyone. Even my mother thinks she's getting to cry at a posh wedding down at The Chewton Glen."

"Why did you lie about the dog?" Rory had his own theory, wondered if he was putting two and two together only to reach thirteen. "Harper said he found it already dead and he isn't an habitual liar. We've arranged our lives so we keep subterfuge to a minimum."

"Then you're very fortunate." Remington finished his coffee, laid down the cup. "Can I get you a top-up? I've had my caffeine for the day; even when it's my day off from training, the approved diet still applies."

"No, thank you. You can tell me how the dog died."

The footballer was silent, merely shrugging and spreading his hands in an empty gesture.

"Forget the dog. Tell me about your family." The question, launched over O'Driscoll's shoulder as he still contemplated the garden, took his listeners by surprise.

"Why do you want to be told about them? They don't even *know*."

"I find that unlikely. Mothers always know, even when they pretend they don't." O'Driscoll turned, eyes bright with tears. "I'm not sure you can ever hide your true nature from those who love you the most."

Remington studied his feet. His fortune was founded on them; two nimble pins, an excellent eye on the pitch and the unerring habit of being in the right part of the box when a cross came in. It all added up to the house, the cars, the well-provided for 'beard'. "I hope that's true. They've not disowned me. Not even when I've put the marriage off twice."

"What did they think the first time you *changed*? Or have they never seen it happen?"

Somewhere in the house the minder was whistling. It was some chirpy pop song that Rory vaguely recognized. He had plenty of opportunity to try to put a name to it, the length of time it took Remington to answer George's question.

"Change? I don't know–"

"Yes, you do." O'Driscoll spoke slowly and calmly, as if addressing a child. "Sabrina may have seen Stephen Harper, but he wasn't the man who killed *'little Destiny'*. That would have been you. Harper picked you up not just because you're handsome, and clever; I suspect he was drawn by more than one thing you have in common."

"Dr O'Driscoll." The footballer suddenly smiled, the broad grin enhancing his handsome features. "If I can't admit I read Proust, if I can't admit I'm gay, how could I even contemplate telling the world what happens on the night of a full moon?"

"You could–" O'Driscoll began, but Rory interrupted him.

"What on earth do you do if it clashes with a big match? I mean if it's the Champions' League or something? Do the floodlights cancel out the effect or do your colleagues just think you don't shave out of superstition..." Rory's voice trailed off, drowned by the others' laughter.

"You will excuse my friend, he has the annoying habit of never keeping to the point."

"Are you all like that? You sound a lot more fun than my fellow players. They're only interested in card schools and Playboy." Remington smiled ruefully, appearing much more like some bookish research student than a man who earned a living knocking the ball past unsuspecting goalies. "One day, when I've made enough to set me up for life, I'll bribe the team doctor into saying that I can't play again and then..." he made a pair of fangs with his fingers, "the world's my oyster. Or chicken carcass."

"Mr Remington, have you ever thought of moving out west? You'd find yourself at home..."

"Nice bloke."

"Indeed. Stephen Harper may be a bit daft, but he has taste. How awful," Rory looked out at the passing cars, "to have to hide all that you are from those you work with."

"It's not unusual. We're luckier than most. I understand our brothers in Midwestern America daren't come out on neither front. Still, at least they can blame any of their misdemeanors on those wretched *Canis lupus rufus* things."

"Ah well, no Waitrose beef this time, but the Wolves of the West may consider this complaint resolved. Stephen Harper might even have found himself a more lasting partner than the ones he usually picks up." Rory ran his finger along George's hand. "It worked for me. If only the Lavington situation could have been buried with his Lordship; maybe we need to send Harper and Remington round to see his grandson next 'great change', put the wind up him. Sadly we've the best part of another three weeks before that happens." He renewed his caressing of George's hand. "Before we get the chance to play again."

"Only as wolves." O'Driscoll's face was a picture of lasciviousness, quite unlike Frost's fierce visage. "Plenty of other fun to be had in the interim. I bet you didn't know that both the basement and first floor flats are empty the next few days? I suspect the owners have gone off together for a dirty weekend."

"It isn't the weekend."

"Don't be pernickety. They're away, so if you felt the desire to let rip a bit there's only next door to worry about and that's being gutted." O'Driscoll lightly touched his lover's hand. "It'd be like that first September, the whole house to ourselves. Remember?"

"Couldn't ever forget, George. I think you make love even better as a human than as a wolf and that's saying something. Put the foot down on the old accelerator, then. Home's a-calling."

QUEER WOLF

FAMILY MATTERS

Moondancer Drake

Tala walked the perimeter of the metal fencing, her gaze intent through the diamond weave. The shape of the African wolf kept her true nature from prying eyes. Brittle leaves crackled under Tala's wide paws and her candle-flame fur rippled under the chilly wind, protecting her from the cold. She'd been certain there was someone prowling around the side yard when she got home, but she'd circled their property twice without even the scent of anything unfamiliar.

The little girl next door waved as Tala passed. Like most of their neighbors the five year old assumed that the creature was nothing more than an exotic watch dog owned by the family. For the sake of her mate and her children Tala intended to keep them believing it. She liked her neighbors well enough, but like most humans, the knowledge that they lived next to a family of weres would be far from comforting.

Still nothing. Tala wondered if the person she thought she'd sensed earlier was nothing more than her stress-affected imagination. With two emergency deliveries and four hours in surgery fighting to save an infant, she was beyond exhausted and desperately needed to unwind. Satisfied there was no intruder, Tala made her way back to the house and slipped inside.

Once passed the swinging pet door, she released her hold on her primal form. Her muscles stretched as paws became hands and fingers. Still on all fours she arched her shoulders and bent her neck, bracing for the pressure. The change rippled through her body and soon fur gave way to ebon skin and a sharply tailored suit. Tala got to her feet and brushed the wrinkles out of her linen pants.

From the front hall she caught a pungent whiff from deeper in the house. Making her way down the hall toward the kitchen, the scent became overpowering. By the time she reached the archway the stench was so strong it nearly knocked her off her feet.

"Bella, my love, what's died in here?"

The familiar small frame of Tala's mate stood leaning over the secondary stove set into the kitchen island. Mirabella pushed a cluster of blond curls out of her eyes and looked up. One hand continued stirring the contents of a copper pot, using a wooden spoon from the set she used for spell work only. "Nothing died." Her Spanish accented purr held an impatient edge to it. "Lynn and Zhen are still having trouble with some of those *pendejos* stealing from their orchard. I'm making them some charms to try to convince the little *mierdas* to go scavenge someplace else."

Tala strolled to the sink and undid the latch of the double set windows, opening them to let the cool air in. "The smell of it alone should keep people away. Hell, it would me." She took a ceramic mug from the dish drainer and poured tea from the pot on the stove.

"Ha. Ha." Mirabella said sarcastically. She stirred the dark brown contents with one hand, while she sprinkled dried bright green leaves over the top with the other. "If you're going to freeze me to death, you can at least fetch me the cheesecloth from the hall. Make yourself useful instead of poking fun at my cooking."

Tala crossed to Mirabella and kissed her cheek. "If your cooking tasted as bad as your spell work, I'd have died from starvation in the first year we were together. You'd not have to worry about my teasing you then."

Mirabella smacked Tala hard on the hand with the wooden spoon. "Alright, you. Out of my kitchen. And don't forget my cheesecloth."

Tala chuckled and walked out of the kitchen sucking her sore knuckles. Seconds later she pulled her hand away and grimaced at the foul taste of the brown liquid covering her skin.

It took a few moments to find the proper drawer Mirabella was talking about in the hutch, before she found the cloth wrapped in paper on top a pile of beeswax bricks. It wasn't surprising. Her mate kept her supplies like she kept her desk at the law firm downtown–perfectly organized. Mirabella avoided Tala's office for the same reason. Whereas she liked everything in its place, Tala preferred what she called her comfortable clutter.

The phone rang, punctuated by a thud as the back door opened and the sound of their sons' voices filtered though the kitchen archway into the hall. Tala thought to warn the teens not to comment on their mother's labors, but the voice on the other end of the receiver drew her attention.

"Tala?" Greer asked shakily.

Tala attempted to ignore the colorful Spanish phrases seeping through the doorway to the hall. It was a sure sign the warning would have come far too late. "Tala here, what do you need?"

"I'm glad to catch you at home, lass. I need you and Bella to take your pack up to Cherokee Marsh. Brett called a few moments ago and said somethin' about trouble, but before he could tell me more the connection died. I tried Rune, but there wasn't any answer at her place. Your pack's the next closest."

"The pack's spread thinner in the city than I'd like, but it shouldn't take more than twenty minutes to gather a few of them at least. In the meantime, keep trying to get a hold of Brett."

Silence fell in the kitchen, which made Tala nervous. She looked up as Mirabella peeked her head though the archway, wiping her hands on a dishtowel. Tala covered the phone and dropped her voice to a whisper. "What's up?"

"I was about to ask you the same thing, *amante.*" Mirabella motioned toward the kitchen with a thumb. "I put the boys to work filling the bottles. I'll finish later after they clean up in there."

Tala nodded. "It's Greer. She says there's trouble at the nature reserve. No idea what kind of trouble though. Can you call Margo and Ellen? Tell them to call whoever they can and meet us at the south parking lot, near the Information building."

Mirabella glanced toward the kitchen. "What about the boys. If there's trouble we shouldn't leave them alone tonight."

"I agree. I'll call their dads as soon as I get off the phone with Greer. They're not going to be happy being told they need a sitter." Tala fumbled in the inside pocket of her jacket for her iPhone. Normally Mirabella would stay with the boys, but Tala wasn't prepared to go into the unknown shorthanded. Mark and Donald wouldn't mind. Donald had been the donor for both Mirabella's pregnancies and the men loved the teens as much as their mothers did.

"The boys will cope." Miribella grinned. "Mark and Donald

don't get much time with them since they started back at school anyways."

Tala waited until Mirabella returned to the kitchen to get her cell phone before removing her palm from the receiver. "Bella's making the call now. We'll handle it. You've got enough to worry about up there anyway. If you hear anything else from Brett, call Bella's cell."

"Thanks." Greer hung up.

Tala replaced the phone and took off her jacket. She'd call the boys' fathers from upstairs. There was still time to change out of her work clothes before Mirabella was ready to leave. On the way up the stairs she tossed her jacket over one arm and unbuttoned the top two buttons of her blouse.

So much for her quiet evening.

It was just three minutes shy of the twenty minute mark when the last car pulled into the front parking lot of Cherokee Marsh. The sun had dipped low, but once shifted there'd be little worry about the lack of light. Tonight they were hunting, but Tala wished she knew what it was they would be hunting for.

With a nod she signaled for the pack to move. All five slipped past a line of Hawthorn bushes and in an instant a motley group of creatures spread out through tall grasses. A lynx that was Mirabella slunk at Tala's right. A salt and pepper furred wolverine squeezed through a pair of saplings ahead of them, following the two shapes of Kelly and Ellen. The black and grey wolf sisters continued to scout ahead and Tala held back, studying the dark underbrush for any sign of movement. The park was closed. Besides Brett, who watched over the place as a full time ranger, there was no reason for anyone to be here. If there was the pack would deal with them.

The trip to the ranger's ranch house was quiet, far too quiet for Tala's taste. The park's animals were scared of something. Brett's gold colored van was in the drive, mud spattered as usual. There was a light on upstairs and two on the lower floor.

"Check around the house to see if you can catch scent of anything unusual." Tala growled to her co-leader, Margo. "Bella and I will see if Brett's inside."

Margo nuzzled Ellen's sleek black muzzle with her own and Tala watched as the wolverine and the two wolf sisters split off to search. Tala moved herself protectively closer to Mirabella as they walked toward the back of the house. Her mate was a capable woman, but far less combat experienced than the rest of the Clan women here tonight. Without knowing what to expect, she'd have to be especially cautious to keep Mirabella safe.

The back door was open when they got there and the screen door hung precariously on its hinges. "Let me go in first." Tala said and pushed past the screen. Mirabella entered slowly behind her.

Inside she could hear movement ahead. Tala identified two distinct voices and neither sounded anything like Brett's southern drawl. She moved forward slowly and breathed in the scent of the place. There was the familiar sandalwood incense that Brett loved to burn and the tang of the hot sauce he put on everything he ate. Mixed among the stronger scents was something else, a sweet metallic scent like a brand new penny.

Blood.

Her medical background overriding her instinct for caution, Tala ran down the hall. She followed the new scent until she reached a bedroom door that stood open half a fingers width. Tala pushed the edge with her nose and the door swung open an inch.

The first thing she saw was Brett against the far wall between a wide dresser and the TV. His head rested on his bent knees and a hand lay limp upon the grey carpet. Relief mixed with anger as her keen gaze swept over him. The scent of blood was stronger, but she saw no obvious sign of injury and could hear his soft breathing. At least he was still alive.

She inched the door open further and noticed three figures that stood in a cluster on the other side of a bed from the open door. They wore black military fatigues and each had a wide-bladed bowie strapped on a belt.

Keeping herself low Tala crept into the room, her attention never wavering from the strangers. Their skin was such a dark green it was almost black, none of the three had a scrap of hair on their heads. Their features were androgynous and they had no scent to them at all, making it impossible to tell if they were male or female. It all meant something to Tala. They were dealing with rogue Fae.

One of the figures turned in her direction and its companions followed its gaze. Black eyes without a touch of white to soften their harsh intensity, met her brown.

"Where is it," the first demanded. The voice had a deep tone to it, more masculine than feminine. "You will give it to us, shifter."

Tala took a step forward. In the time it took to breath in and out, her body had shifted from that of the African red wolf, to her hybrid battle form. So what if the Fae took it as a challenge. Brett was hurt and she didn't have time for games.

"Just being here you're in violation of the treaty. You have no right to demand anything." Out of the corner of her eye Tala watched Mirabella cross the room to kneel beside Brett. She'd shifted as well, but to her human form.

"Where is it?" The Fae said in unison. "It belongs to us."

Tala moved so she was between the Fae and Mirabella. "I don't know what *it* is. Still, you'll get nothing from us through violence. Give yourselves up and you'll not be harmed."

"No." The first Fae said. There was no anger in his tone or any emotion at all. "If you do not give it to us, you all will die."

"I doubt that." She held back a laugh. Fae were tough, this was true, but against a pack of weres, they didn't stand a chance. Tala refrained from mentioning this. No point in revealing their advantage. "Stay where you are. One move and I'll be sending you home in pieces."

There was a moan from behind her and Tala heard Mirabella whisper a response. At least Brett was coming around. The Fae continued to stare at her with their blank expressions. She prided herself on being able to tell what moves her opponents were going to make, but with this bunch that would prove difficult.

Finally the Fae who Tala guessed to be the leader stepped forward and motioned with a hand for his companions to stay back. "You are the master of your pack?"

"You could say that." Tala scowled, keeping her attention on all three Fae. This change was unexpected and she never trusted it when someone changed manner so quickly. "I don't appreciate when one of our own is manhandled, especially not by supposed allies.

The Fae shrugged, his black expression melting into a look of aloof boredom. "You and I both know we are not of the weak Fae folk that pander to your people and the witches. We have seen the evil brought upon the earth by the humans the Tri-council chooses to protect."

Tala glanced back at Mirabella and Brett. "What is it you three want? I tire of hearing the same old propaganda from outcasts."

"You can't let them get the orb." Brett whispered so softly that even with her acute hearing Tala barely heard him. "They plan to use it to poison the city."

"Poison?" Mirabella whispered. "How?"

"The water tower." Brett said. The Faes' eyes widened and Tala turned to see Brett pull something from under a patch of carpet that touched the wall and press it into Mirabella's hands. "Run, Miss Bella. Run."

Mirabella stuffed the object into the pocket of her jeans. In a split second transformation, the lynx was sprinting out the room, down the hallway and toward the broken screen door. The Fae scrambled over the top of the bed and Tala moved to block the door with her bulk. Sure she couldn't get out of the room easily the size she was now, but then with her in the way neither could the Fae.

They skidded to a halt in front of her but before she could reach out for the leader, all three had turned, running for the closed windows. The leader leapt over Brett with the grace of a gymnast, his bowie knife in his hand and flashing in one smooth movement, he broke through the thin curtain and glass like paper. The other Fae followed him without hesitation.

Tala ran to the window and caught sight of the black furred form of Ellen pushing her way though the grass, with Kelly close behind her. The Fae were already turning the corner of the house in pursuit of Mirabella. "Rogue Fae. Three of them. I want them alive."

The two wolves sprung forward in perfect unison, their time as battle sisters giving them a connection that few outside the Clan would understand or experience. Tala pushed herself through what was left of the shattered window, taking a chunk of the frame and wall as she went. They were after her mate and she'd be damned if she'd let them get her.

By the time she'd made it around the house the Fae were way ahead of her, followed by two wolves and a wolverine. Tala howled as she tore off after the group and the responding howl assured her that the rest of the pack were on their way.

The runners slowed as Mirabella led them through the marsh itself and they were caught up in the reeds and muck. By the way they struggled through it, it was obvious Cherokee Marsh was not a place they called home. *Good.* With her love of nature photography Mirabella visited the park often and that familiarity gave her an advantage over her pursuers.

A Fae stumbled and went down to one knee in the muck, only to be beset by two wolves. The leader and the remaining Fae didn't so much as glance back at their downed comrade as they continued on after the lynx. Just over a patch of cattails the second Fae got tangled in the reeds only to find himself on the wrong end of a fired up wolverine.

One left. Tala pushed herself hard, but the Fae leader was faster. Best she could dare hope was for him to stumble, but he appeared far more familiar with wetland terrain than his companions had been. He pulled something from his waist and silver flashed across the moonlit marsh grasses. Mirabella cried out and Tala's thought went to the bowie knives.

No. Tala dug deep for the strength she need and her muscles screamed as she ran faster. As the Fae slowed to look for the lynx Tala leapt upon him. They tumbled to the ground, a tangle of fur and fists. Few creatures could take a well trained were like herself head on, but for a while the Fae was holding his own. Mud mixed with blood as they wrestled in the dank water.

When her foe finally stilled Tala pulled herself to her feet and looked down at him. His arm was bent at an odd angle and black blood stained the edges of his lips and under an eye. Her own shoulder was dislocated and her side ached. She took only long enough to allow Kelly–the first to reach her–to help her get her shoulder back in place before she was running forward to search for Mirabella.

She found her mate–still in lynx form–hiding beneath a clump of browning loosestrife flowers. There was blood on her shoulder, but when Tala looked closely she was relieved to find the cut was not deep.

After she shifted to human, Tala helped Mirabella to her feet and hugged her. "You took us on quite a run there, love."

Mirabella chuckled, the breathiness of her voice showing she was still out of breath. "Good thing I spend far too much time here after all, isn't it?"

"Fine. No more teasing about you moving out to live in a stilt house" Tala grinned and held Mirabella tight against her. "At least not for a few days."

The grass rustled as Ellen and Margo approached. "The prisoners are restrained and we've called Greer to arrange for someone from the Tri-council to pick them up," Margo said. "You want to tell us what these guys wanted?"

"I'll explain later." Tala led Mirabella back toward the rest of the pack, thankful that her family was safe once again. Soon the orb would be in the hands of their leaders and life could go back to normal.

Tala laughed at herself and kissed the top of Mirabella's curls as they walked. Or as normal as their life could ever be.

WRONG TURN

Stephen Osborne

I wasn't entirely sure I was still in the same city. The buildings suddenly had a different look to them, an indefinable shift in architecture and age. I couldn't really place my finger on it, but I felt like I was now on foreign territory.

One of the worst qualities I inherited from my father was the absolute inability to pull over and ask for directions. I suppose to do so would be to admit defeat and that the unerring Thomas sense of direction could go haywire. All I knew was that I had been driving for the better part of an hour without the slightest idea of where I was.

The clock on the dashboard read just after midnight, so it was actually a few minutes before the witching hour–I've never known a car clock that kept good time. I made another turn for no other reason than instinct and the street where I now found myself was even darker. The pavement was slick with rain, and the few people on the sidewalks moved quickly, bundled up against the cold drizzle.

Ahead, I saw several young men heading towards a doorway. A neon sign in the window advertised some brand of beer. The men moved with the grace of dancers, jostling against each other playfully. I imagined that they were stage gypsies, fresh from a performance of a musical, going in to the bar for a few drinks and to dance the rest of the night away. The easy way they groped at each other told me that it was a gay bar.

I pulled the car to the curb. I hadn't planned on going to a bar, but I certainly wasn't going to be finding my way to the hotel anytime soon and something about the young men, one in particular, fascinated me.

I had only caught a glimpse of him before he and his friends disappeared inside, but he'd seemed uncommonly sexy. He'd been shorter than his companions and not quite as thin. He moved with a confidence that I found particularly attractive. The quick look I'd caught of his face showed him to be quite handsome, with dark hair and a few days' worth of stubble on his cheeks.

It wouldn't hurt to check out the bar. I could even use asking for directions as an excuse to talk to him.

When I entered, it seemed to me that the noise level suddenly dropped. It wasn't a large establishment, but there were several dozen people, mostly young men, seated at the small tables or standing near the walls. I'm sure it was my imagination, but I felt like every eye in the place was on me as I strode slowly to the bar. The place was dimly lit, as gay bars invariably are, and I didn't really get a good look at the bartender until I sat down and she approached.

She was young, but her eyes had that weary look that said she'd seen and done it all. Her hair was long and wild. She looked at me questioningly and I swear she sniffed the air, although what she could smell besides the smoky atmosphere was beyond me. The smile she'd had ready disappeared and she spoke somewhat sternly. "What will you have?"

"Gin and tonic," I replied.

As she made the drink she arched an eyebrow at me. "Not from around here, are you?"

"Is it that obvious?"

She placed a paper napkin down on the bar and set my drink on it. "I know everyone here."

"I'm a bit lost," I admitted.

"More than a little." She rested her elbows on the bar and leaned her face towards mine. "Want a little advice?"

I knew I'd get it whatever my reply, so I said, "Sure."

"Finish your drink and find your road quickly."

I chuckled uneasily. "Are you always so welcoming of strangers?"

She managed a weak smile. "You seem like a nice guy and I'm just a little bit psychic. Bad things could happen to you here. I wouldn't want you to get hurt."

I sipped my drink. "I really wasn't planning on sticking around. I just thought I'd ask for directions, and..."

Suddenly the dark-haired young man came up and stood at my side. He had a friendly grin on his somewhat round face as he nodded to the bartender. "You're not scaring off the customers again, are you, Carol?"

She cocked her head slightly and favored him with a genuine smile. "Now, I wouldn't do that, now would I, Shawn?" I could see they were used to bantering with each other. There was no stool beside me, so he stood at the bar. The stools were tall enough that I still had to look down slightly at him.

"I'm Shawn Jameson," he said, offering me his hand.

It wasn't one of those clammy hands where you want to wipe yours off after shaking. It was more like a cozy fire on a wintry day. "I'm Kevin Thomas," I told him. "I was just saying that I'm horribly lost."

"I guessed as much," he said, settling his back against the bar. He was scrutinizing my face and I must have blushed for he apologized. "I'm sorry. It's just that you remind me of someone I used to know."

"Isn't that an old line?" I asked, using the opportunity to examine him in turn. The scruff on his face gave him that bad boy look I'm attracted to, but there was a youthfulness to his cheeks that made me realize he was younger than I'd thought. Now that I was over thirty, everyone seemed younger than me.

He laughed softly. "It may be an old line, but it's the first time I've used it. Can I buy you a drink?"

The drink turned into two. The conversation went easily, and we found we had many things in common. Eventually a stool was vacated and he pulled it over to sit next to me. I noticed he moved the stool *very* close to mine. As we sat and chatted, it was impossible for our knees not to brush together.

After our second drink he smiled at me. "Would I be too forward if I asked you to dance?"

I hadn't even noticed when I'd entered, but now I saw that there was a tiny dance floor tucked away at the back. There were only four couples presently dancing to the country tune playing. "I'm not much of a dancer," I admitted. Remembering the ease with which he and his friends had moved I assumed Shawn would be an excellent dancer.

He stood and extended a hand, exuding old world charm. "Just follow my lead. Besides, it's country music night. If you can stomp your foot, you can dance."

I let him lead me to the dance floor. It seemed to me that several of the couples there gave us odd looks, but I put this down to them wondering who he was dancing with. As we began to sway to the music, the song switched to a slow, torch song. I think it was Barbara Mandrell singing, but I'm not sure. With a sly grin Shawn pulled me close to him. I put my head on his shoulder and enjoyed the feel of his body as we moved to the music. I was feeling a bit drunk, although normally three gin and tonics don't have that effect on me. I can only assume that holding Shawn was intoxicating in itself.

As we swayed I closed my eyes, enjoying the warmth of his body but I opened them quickly when I heard a hiss coming from beside us. There were two young men dancing next to us and the blond one actually had his lip curled as he looked at me. Had he *hissed* at me? Was he Shawn's ex, angered that his old boyfriend had found someone new? Shawn, if he heard the sound, paid it no attention.

I rested my head on his shoulder and tried my best to ignore everyone around us. I heard him chuckle. "You smell really nice. Just the right hint of cologne."

"Thanks," I said, not sure of what else to say. When words failed me, I settled for clutching him tighter. I felt his warm hands on my back and just for a second it felt like his fingernails dug into my flesh. I took a sharp intake of breath and immediately he pulled away.

"I'm sorry," he said. Even in the dim lighting I could tell he was blushing. "That was clumsy of me. Are you hurt?"

I couldn't tell if his nails had torn through my shirt or not. I actually felt like I might be bleeding slightly, but I couldn't quite reach around to feel. The pain wasn't bad, though, so I assured him I was fine. Truth be told, though, the air seemed to be getting thick in the bar and my intoxication was only increasing. I staggered slightly. "I probably should be getting back on the road," I told him.

He didn't bother trying to hide his disappointment. "Are you sure? Let's have just one more drink."

"No, really. It's getting very late."

It took the better part of ten minutes to convince Shawn that I wasn't leaving because of anything he had done. He gave me very explicit directions on how to get to my hotel, making sure I knew that if I didn't cross the bridge on 10th Street I was going to remain hopelessly lost. I gave him my cell phone number and he promised to call. Usually when I meet someone at a bar and give them my number, I give ten to one odds that they'll call. Somehow I knew Shawn would.

Before I could start for the door, he leaned in and kissed me. It was a soft, tender kiss and I must admit something about it–and him–aroused me. "I'll call tomorrow," he promised.

As soon as I hit the fresh air I felt somewhat better. The atmosphere of the bar had been so thick and cloying that stepping outside felt like entering a different world. I walked slowly to my car, running through my mind every word, every movement he'd made all night. It had been years since I'd met anyone who affected me like Shawn Jameson.

I was so lost in thought that I didn't see the man step between two parked cars and move in front of me. I looked up to see the young blond man from the dance floor glaring at me. I began to step around him, but again he blocked my way.

He put a hand on my shoulder and growled, "Your type's not welcome around here."

I had no idea what he meant but I didn't like him or his manner. I smacked his hand away. "I'm leaving, so you don't have anything to worry about."

"Leave Shawn alone, as well," he said.

"I'm sure that's something for Shawn to decide, not you," I said, attempting to pass again. Once more he moved into my path. He was wearing a thin muscle t-shirt. I could see how athletic he was and I didn't want to get into a fight with him. "Look, I'm not even from around here. I'm just in town visiting my uncle. I'll be gone in a few days. I doubt I'll even see Shawn again."

To my surprise this brought a smile to his face. His grin revealed abnormally long, sharp teeth. "I know you won't," he said.

And then he began to transform.

It happened in seconds, yet I don't think I missed any detail. First his fingernails grew into gnarled claws and a thick fur sprouted onto the backs of his hands. His face contorted impossibly, with the nose becoming a snout and his mouth turning into that of a wild animal, with sharp fangs and a strong, dangerous looking jaw. Hair seemed to grow out of every pore. His chest expanded, straining even further the fabric of the shirt.

I was too shocked to move. My brain seemed only to be able to focus on the fact that I'd just witnessed the transformation of a werewolf.

Then he sprang.

In mid-air the shift from human to wolf was complete. His clothes shredded, falling off him. I was still frozen in place, but managed to raise my arms up in a feeble attempt to protect myself.

A swift movement came from behind me and suddenly something flew up into the air and collided with the creature. Howls of anger filled the air as I realized that another wolf, this one with dark fur, had saved me. The two animals hit the pavement with a furious crash and were fighting, teeth and claws snapping at each other. The wolf with the lighter colored fur realized it was over-matched and rolled quickly away from the other. With a snarl on its lips it slunk away, tail literally between its legs.

The wolf that had saved me looked back, staring right into my eyes before bounding off and disappearing down an alley. I knew those eyes. I'd been gazing into them all night. The wolf, I knew, was Shawn Jameson.

I slept little that night.

When I got up a little before noon I showered and dressed, moving like an automaton. I knew—despite the craziness of it all—that what I'd seen had been real. I got into my rental car and headed for my uncle's small apartment, intending to tell him all about it. I was nearly there when my cell phone buzzed. I knew that it would be Shawn on the other end.

"Hello," I said, realizing that my heart was racing with the anticipation of hearing his voice again. I told myself that was stupid. He was a werewolf. Hell, I was certain that everyone in the bar last night had been a werewolf. I recalled how odd the whole neighborhood had seemed. It wouldn't surprise me to find that the whole area was populated with werewolves.

"How are you?" he asked.

"That's a loaded question. Do you mean how am I generally, or how am I after being attacked by a werewolf only to be saved by another wolf, who just happened to have your eyes."

He laughed uneasily. "I was sort of hoping that you'd have convinced yourself that you'd just had too much to drink and hallucinated the whole thing. Most people would."

"I guess I'm not most people."

"You shouldn't have been there, of course. Humans aren't supposed to be able to cross the bridge into our little city. You shouldn't have even been able to see it."

"You're telling me there's a magic bridge that separates Wolf Town from Human Town?" I replied, trying not to sound too amused by the concept.

"Hey, you already accept the existence of werewolves. What's a little bridge with a perception filter compared to that?"

"Point taken." I could see him plainly, as if he were in the car with me. I could still feel his lips, his warm body pressed against me. "I want to see you again," I said suddenly.

"I was hoping you'd say that."

My uncle greeted me at the door and asked if I'd had lunch yet. Uncle Larry was one of my few remaining relatives and I enjoyed spending time with him. His cramped apartment was filled with bookshelves and seemed more like a library than a home. Larry was a retired professor and one of the wisest men I knew. He was the perfect person to discuss the events of the previous night with.

I opened my mouth, but only said, "I'd love some lunch."

Somehow I wasn't ready to discuss werewolves with anyone. Not when I was falling for one.

I met Shawn on the Magic Bridge. Walking up to it, I began to see that he wasn't joking about it. My eyes told me that I was moving towards a dead end, but as I came closer the overhanging leaves of a huge oak seemed to part and reveal the bridge. I knew that it had been there all the time, but it wasn't until the last moment that I registered it. I don't know that I believed in a perception field, but the bridge certainly was hidden. As I approached, I saw that he was already at our meeting point. He was standing midway, looking out over the waters below. He was dressed casually in jeans and a flannel shirt. My first thought was that he was the hottest looking guy I'd seen in ages. Then I reminded myself that he wasn't entirely human.

He turned when he heard me approach.

"I wasn't sure that you'd show," he said, grinning. He gave me a short kiss that made my heart race. What was it about this guy that drove me so crazy? He was dangerous. He was, literally, an animal.

"I had to come," I said honestly. "I haven't been able to think about anything else. I've got so many questions."

Shawn chuckled. "I'm sure you do."

"First of all, who is Blondie?"

"Levon. He's in my clan. He's a bit of a fanatic and doesn't believe in mixing with humans. It's an old world school of thought, but there are still a fair number who think that way. To Levon and people like him, humans aren't to be trusted."

"He would have killed me if you hadn't been there."

Shawn's face darkened. "I'd like to think he was just trying to scare you off, but...honestly, I don't know."

I had a dozen more questions, but he stopped me with a smile. "I'm hungry. Let's get some food."

"Your side of the bridge or mine?"

He shrugged. "Yours."

Uncle Larry moved slowly, having both a bad back and arthritis in both knees. He settled into his favorite chair, falling back with the air of a man who intends to stay there for an extended period. "Now, my young man, what have you been up to for the last several days?"

I tried to be offhand. "Just sightseeing."

"Pshaw," he said, waving a hand. "There's not enough sights in this city to take up more than a few hours of your time. You've met someone."

There didn't seem to be any reason to deny it, so I nodded. "His name is Shawn."

"I knew it. I can always tell. Last few times you've been here you've been grinning like a fool. Only one thing makes a man grin like that. So what's he like? What's he do?"

I almost laughed. Shawn and I had talked quite a lot, but with learning about werewolves and clans and moon cycles and transformations I never thought to inquire about something as mundane as what he did for a living. "You know," I admitted, "I haven't the foggiest idea."

Uncle Larry's eyebrows danced a bit.

"I see. Like that, is it?"

"No, it's not what you're thinking. We've just talked a lot."

"He's not Catholic, is he?" Larry had some set ideas in his head, and never hesitated to give you his opinion, no matter how politically incorrect or insensitive it might be. "I've told you about those gay Catholics. They've got the double guilt. They can be trouble."

According to Larry, Catholics all suffer from guilt programmed into them by their religion. He thinks all homosexuals also have some sense of guilt, brought on by their sense of somehow having let down their parents or other family members. I've tried to tell him he's wrong about this, but he insists that it is true.

"Religion hasn't come up, either," I told him.

He grimaced. "Yet you say you've talked a lot. What have you been discussing, the latest single from Madonna? You've got to thresh out the important things when you start to date."

I laughed. Talking about Shawn's being a werewolf, to my way of thinking, definitely fell into the category of important things.

I sat and watched television with Uncle Larry for most of the evening. True to form, he budged from his chair only once for a restroom break. Any running to the kitchen for snacks or drinks was done by me, and I wondered how long it would be before he was unable to live by himself.

Leaving Larry's apartment building, I began to make my way down to where my rental car was parked. The night was fairly quiet, the sounds of the city seeming far off and somehow separate from the street I was on. A cool breeze was blowing, and the moon cast a spectral glow. A cat, sitting on a fence post, paused from his grooming ritual to watch me as I came closer. Deciding I was no threat, he continued to lick his paw but some sound caused his ears to twitch and he suddenly bolted across the lawn.

A low growl came from somewhere ahead, possibly a repeat of the sound that had alarmed the cat. I stopped, scanning my surroundings. I could see nothing out of the ordinary. My car was still a half-block away. Maybe I'd imagined the sound? After all the talk about wolves it wouldn't be unlikely to mistake some common sound for Levon ready to pounce.

A shadow by a tree several yards ahead moved and the growl sounded again. Not my imagination, then. I suddenly wished I had a gun loaded with silver bullets, although where I'd get silver bullets–or even if they worked–was beyond me. The shadow moved again and the pale wolf stepped forward, fangs glistening.

I spun around and ran. I could hear the wolf's paws scrabbling on the sidewalk after me. I knew I couldn't outrun it. Any second now I'd feel the creature leap onto my back and feel its teeth sink into my flesh; its claws shred my clothes and skin.

"Holy shit! What is that?"

I was barely aware of the young couple until I barreled into them. The speaker, a young man not yet out of his teens, grabbed hold of me to keep the two of us from crashing to the ground. He wasn't looking at me, though. His astonished gaze was fixed on some point behind me. I turned my head, expecting to see the animal ready to spring. Instead I saw that the wolf had turned and was disappearing back into the shadows. It took a moment for my heart to stop racing. I had been saved again, this time by two teenagers. Maybe killing me was one thing, but Levon wasn't willing to take out innocent bystanders. Whatever the reason, I was glad the young couple had wandered by.

The girl, a blond with over-sized glasses, stared off into the bushes where the wolf had gone. "I think that was some dog. A really big one!"

"Dude," the boy said, finally releasing me so that I could stand on my own. "Are you okay?"

I tried to catch my breath. "I think so. Thanks." I tried to say more, but my heart still felt like it was going to burst.

"What the hell was that?" the boy repeated. "That was bigger than any dog I've ever seen."

"I don't know," I lied. "It just started chasing me. I–"

The girl interrupted me. "We should call the police."

The young man was visibly shaken. He asked me again if I was all right.

"I'm fine. My uncle's apartment is just down here. I can sit there for a while and recover."

He nodded. "We'll walk with you. That thing is still around somewhere. Jennie, have you got your cell phone?"

The girl already had it out and was pressing buttons. "I've never called 911 before," she said with a nervous laugh.

I nearly laughed myself, thinking of how the cops would deal with Levon in his wolf form. Not well, I thought.

I'm sure Larry was shocked to see me again, but he merely raised his eyebrows and deadpanned, "Did you miss me?"

I had finally calmed down but I still didn't want to try to get to my car again, not with old Levon prowling around somewhere out there. How did he find me? He must have followed me to Uncle Larry's, which was a disquieting thought. Attacking me outside of the bar in the heat of the moment was one thing, but stalking me showed that Levon was indeed dangerous.

I looked at my uncle and tried to smile. I had to tell him something resembling the truth. "I was attacked," I said, "on the way to my car. Some kids came along, though, and scared the guy off. I'm fine. Just a little shaken."

"You were mugged? In this neighborhood?"

I didn't want Larry to think he wasn't safe going down the street to get his groceries, so I went on. "It was someone I know. He seems to have something against me."

We sat down. I chose a spot on the couch and Larry lowered himself into his favorite chair. He was frowning. "You seem to have made an enemy in a relatively short time. Does this have something to do with this guy you've met?"

I hesitated. Maybe I could get some advice from Larry without going into the whole story. "His name is Levon. He's not really an ex-boyfriend of Shawn's, but he certainly has an attachment. He's not playing with a full deck, so reason doesn't really enter into the picture. It's hard to explain."

Uncle Larry nodded. "Apparently. I don't pretend to understand all the nuances of the gay lifestyle, but in my years I've learned that reason doesn't often come into play where love is concerned. Shouldn't you call the police? You say this Levon attacked you–"

"I don't want to bring the police into it."

"But you say this young man is unbalanced..."

"I'll find a way to take care of him," I said, although I couldn't find any conviction in my own words. I'd have to talk with Shawn and see if he could deal with Levon. It was the only way. After all, I stood no chance in a battle with a werewolf, unless, of course, I could find a weapon. "Do you have any silver in the house?" I asked suddenly.

My request took Larry aback. He thought a moment before shaking his head. "Nothing pure silver that I can think of. Why? What do you need silver for?"

I bit my lip. I would have to let my uncle in on a little more. I just hoped he didn't laugh it off. "I told you this Levon character isn't all there. He believes that he's a werewolf."

Larry repeated my last sentence, incredulous. "And you want silver to do what, exactly? Make silver bullets? Shooting a crazy person is still murder."

"No, but aren't werewolves supposed to be repelled by silver?"

Nodding, Larry said, "But as this person can't really *be* a werewolf, that won't work, will it?"

"If he truly believes himself to be a werewolf, his mind will tell him that the sight of silver is abhorrent to him, right? I'm clutching at straws here, but this guy must have followed me. I can't walk around looking over my shoulder all the time."

"I still think you need to go to the police with this. Some idiot believing himself to be a werewolf and–"

I interrupted him, wanting to steer away from talk of the police. "You must know something about werewolves and legends like that. You taught classes in folklore, didn't you?"

Uncle Larry smiled grimly. "That was a hell of a long time ago. We didn't study werewolves, though."

"Still, you must have done some reading on them."

"A little. You know me, always interested in the arcane and unknown." Larry cleared his throat. "You wouldn't mind grabbing me a beer, would you?"

Smiling I got up and went to the kitchen. Knowing he could still hear me, I opened his ancient refrigerator and asked, "Are there any werewolf legends that concern this area? Any stories you know of?"

"Oddly," he answered, raising his voice, "there are. I remember a story from years ago. There was supposed to be a werewolf that terrorized this very neighborhood. It was well over a hundred years ago, but I recall reading that a child had disappeared. The parents insisted they saw a huge animal taking away their baby. For quite a while after that, werewolf stories were pretty common around campfires and at Halloween parties. When I researched the story I was sure that I'd find that it was all an urban legend, but I did find newspaper accounts of the event. The parents really did believe that a werewolf had snatched their child. Ridiculous, of course, but it certainly provided for some good tall tales."

I returned with a bottle which I'd already opened and handed it to Larry. He took it with a nod of thanks.

"According to the legends, werewolves are repelled by silver, right?" I asked.

My uncle drank deeply before replying. "There are many versions of the werewolf story. Most people's knowledge of werewolves comes from Hollywood, although in folklore werewolf tales are as varied as those of vampires. In some versions, men actually become wolves while in others they turn into a sort of hybrid, sprouting hair and fangs but still walking upright. Some tales tell of cursed men who became lycanthropes through no fault of their own, but that's not always the case. I remember reading about a way to become a werewolf by killing a coyote in a cemetery during a full moon. Supposedly then you skin the animal and put the carcass over your shoulders and recite an incantation. Instant werewolf!"

"Are there other ways to become a werewolf?"

Larry made a sour face. "It's all bunkum, of course. Surviving the bite of a werewolf is supposed to turn you into one. You can even be born a werewolf, some say, if one or both of your parents is a lycanthrope. How did you get me talking about this, anyway? This crazy guy of yours isn't a real werewolf. He needs to be locked up."

I shrugged. "I just wondered if I could use his delusions against him. That's all."

"Thinking that you are a werewolf isn't just a delusion. It's full out wacky-crazy." Larry finished his beer and let out a small burp.

I stayed the night on Larry's sofa. I didn't want to go back out into the night and Uncle Larry was more than happy for me to stay. I could tell he was suspicious about all my werewolf talk, but he refrained from asking too many questions. Before I fell asleep, I thought of Shawn and how much I wanted to talk to him. I knew I wasn't going to be leaving the city anytime soon. I couldn't. I couldn't just walk away from Shawn. My feelings had already grown too strong. No, Levon or no Levon, I was staying.

Over the next several days, Shawn and I spent a lot of time together. Mostly we dined out or went to the movies, but finally I insisted that we go out to the bar where I'd originally met him. I'd noticed that all of our dates were on my turf, not his.

"Aren't you afraid of running into Levon?" he asked.

"I want to show him that I'm not afraid of him," I said. "Has he said anything to you?"

Shawn chuckled. "Nothing that you'd want to hear. I've warned him that if anything happens to you that he'd have me to deal with, but I'm not sure that's going to stop him. Levon is quite the zealot when it comes to any of our clan mixing with humans."

We ended up spending most of that evening at the bar. We sat at a small table near the back. Levon was there with several of his cronies. He made sure that he shot me evil looks whenever possible. Shawn and I ignored him.

Shawn finished his second beer and looked at me carefully. "Weren't you only supposed to be in town for a few days to visit with your uncle?"

"It's been stretched a few days."

"Because of me?"

I nodded.

Shawn was silent for several minutes, gazing down at his empty beer bottle in deep thought. Finally he looked up with a sly smile. "Would you like to see my place?"

"I'd love to."

His apartment, it turned out, was close by. We walked the

short distance hand in hand. When we reached his place and he opened the front door for me, I wasn't sure what I was expecting. His apartment wasn't large, but nicely furnished. There was a bit of old world charm about it, which shouldn't have surprised me since it fit his personality perfectly. He fixed us each a drink and we went out onto his tiny little balcony to enjoy the night air.

Shawn leaned casually against the iron railing and gazed at me. "You know, I don't even know what you do for a living. Is there a job that you need to get back to?"

"I'm a writer," I told him. "The job sort of goes where I go."

He shook his head with a chuckle. "That's a bad thing. Writers like to tell the truth. Life here is a truth that can't be told."

"Truth isn't an absolute," I said. "It should be, but it isn't. Truth can be distorted and twisted. Like Levon. He thinks his view is the way things should be. That's his truth, and I don't think we're going to change his mind about that."

"God knows I've tried," Shawn said.

"Another truth is how I feel about you."

His face instantly became serious. "And how is that?"

"I think I'm falling in love with you."

Neither of us spoke for a few minutes. Finally he took the glass from my hand and set it down on a small wooden table. "Let's go into the bedroom," he said softly.

Making love with Shawn was in turn wild and rough then soft and tender and then back to wild. At one point he forgot himself and his claws came out, piercing the skin on my back. I can't complain, though. In the heat of passion I also dug my fingernails into his flesh. We came at the same time, grunting and crying out in ecstasy. It was the most intense lovemaking I could recall.

Two days of apartment hunting had finally yielded at least one possibility. It wasn't a large place, but it was close to Uncle Larry and had several interesting shops nearby. The next day I went out again, but still couldn't find anything I liked as much, so I went back and signed a year's lease. I called Shawn to tell him the good news and suggested we meet for a celebratory drink.

"I'll meet you tonight in the bar where we met."

"Sure you can find it?" he asked me teasingly.

I knew I could. It may have been the result of a wrong turn the first time around, but I now looked at my getting lost as a wonderful piece of serendipity.

To be honest, I did set out for the bar a little early, just in case I had trouble finding it. I didn't. The place hadn't really started filling up yet, so I settled at the bar and ordered a gin and tonic while I waited for Shawn. The same bartender, Carol, was working. She still had her wild hair and the sardonic, world-weary attitude but she managed to favor me with a smile as she set the drink before me.

"Lost again?" she asked.

I smiled back. "Not this time."

She peered into my eyes as if trying to read my thoughts. Finally she nodded, "Yeah, I'd say you've actually found what you're looking for."

The door to the bar opened noisily. I shifted, expecting to see Shawn coming in. Instead I saw Levon and several of his cohorts. They were laughing and talking until Levon caught sight of me. Suddenly the laughter stopped as he shot me a withering glance. I turned back to my drink. Out of the corner of my eye I saw the group settle into a booth off to the side. The laughter resumed, a little louder than before.

Carol ran a rag over the top of the bar and rolled her eyes. "Children," she muttered. "You'd think they'd grow up after a while."

It struck me as odd, hearing her refer to Levon and his cronies as children. The bartender wasn't all that much older but had obviously been through a lot. She exuded wisdom, so I could see where Levon came off, to her, as a child. I nodded and sipped my drink. Out of the corner of my eye I saw someone rise from Levon's booth and approach the bar. I prayed it wasn't Levon himself. I didn't feel like a confrontation with him.

It was Levon. He jostled my shoulder as he came up to the bar and asked for a pitcher of beer. As she was pouring he turned to me with a sneer.

"Aren't you on the wrong side of town?"

I took a large swallow of gin and tonic. "I'm meeting Shawn here, not that it's any business of yours."

He leaned in close enough for me to smell his sour breath. "It is my business, that's the whole point."

Carol intervened, telling him, "If you'll go back and sit down, I'll bring your pitcher over in a moment."

Reluctantly he returned to his buddies. As Carol prepared a tray with the pitcher of beer and some glasses she said to me, "He's just a bully."

"A dangerous one," I agreed.

She shrugged. "True. But still, he's just a bully. If you continue to stand up to him, eventually he'll move on to easier pickings."

I chuckled. "You've changed. The first night I was here you basically told me to drink up and get out."

Another shrug. "Shawn likes you. I like Shawn. Therefore I like you." She hoisted the tray and made her way around the bar to Levon's table.

Ah, if only it worked that way with everyone.

Shawn arrived minutes later. When he approached, I kissed him long and hard on the lips. I could feel his bemused smile as we pressed together. When we came up for air, Shawn's eyes were twinkling. "Nice kiss," he said.

"Just marking my territory," I said with a laugh.

Shawn nodded towards Levon and company. "Any trouble from him while you were waiting?"

I shook my head. "I can handle Levon," I said.

I just hoped that was true.

Uncle Larry stood in the middle of what was to be my new living room and spun around. "I guess I've just taken the tour," he said.

"I know it's small," I replied, "but I can afford it."

He waved a disparaging hand. "Who cares about small? All you need is a place for your bed, a kitchen area and somewhere for a good sized television. Everything else is just window dressing." He pulled a long, thin package out of his jacket and handed it to me. "A housewarming present," he said.

I opened the box to find a short, silver dagger. "A knife? You gave me a knife for a housewarming gift?"

Uncle Larry snorted. "It's a letter opener, you ass. You still get mail, don't you? Or is it all emails and Internet crap?"

"I get junk mail, pretty much the same as everyone else."

I could see he was disappointed in my response, so I thanked him profusely for the gift. "I love it. It will have a place of honor on my writing desk. As soon as I arrange to have my writing desk and everything else shipped here."

He moved to the window and rested his butt on the sill. It was the closest thing to a seat in the empty room. "It seems awfully sudden, this desire of yours to move here."

"It wasn't that sudden."

"It couldn't have anything to do with this guy you've met, could it?"

Shrugging, I admitted, "Maybe a little." I figured there was no harm in Larry assuming that he was partly the reason for the move.

Once my things had arrived and I'd officially moved in, Shawn and I celebrated by making love in my new–albeit small–bedroom. I found myself hoping that the walls of my new place were thick.

When I laughingly suggested that we try to keep things down, Shawn took it as a challenge and attempted to get me to scream louder. He was quickly learning my g-spots and knew that nibbling on my neck or earlobe drove me crazy.

We made love a second time, giggling like kids.

Afterwards, I drove him home. As I turned onto the Magic Bridge, he reached over and grabbed my hand.

"I love you, Kevin Thomas," he said.

I pulled his hand up to my lips and kissed it. His skin was unnaturally warm, which he'd told me always happened days before the full moon. "I love you, too, Shawn Jameson," I said.

I followed him up to his apartment, although I didn't go in. We did spend way too much time outside his door smooching, though. Finally I extricated myself. "I've got to finish unpacking tomorrow. I really need to get some sleep."

"Call me?" he said, making the universal hand gesture of the invisible phone up to his ear.

Nothing could keep me from it and he knew it.

Back at my car–now actually mine, not a rental–I felt like singing. I didn't know where our relationship was headed, but we'd said the word. Love. There was no going back now.

I thought the car handled oddly when I pulled away from the curb, but I was on such a high that it didn't really worry me. It wasn't until I'd turned at the end of Shawn's street that I could tell there was something wrong with the left front tire. I pulled over and got out to find it was flat.

I couldn't help but think Levon and his claws had something to do with it. The tire was in good condition and I was fairly sure I hadn't run over anything that would cause a puncture. I looked around. The area I was in was mostly apartment buildings. Down the street was a hamburger joint, but it had closed for the night. On the opposite side of the road was a small park, complete with children's swings and slides. I could see shadows moving, darting between trees. Wolves. One was a pale wolf. They were rapidly moving towards me. Levon and his cronies.

I jumped back into the car, cursing myself for forgetting my cell phone. I turned the key in the ignition, thinking that–flat tire or not–I would have to make a dash for it. No sooner did the engine start, however, than the car shook violently. The wolves had converged.

One had leaped onto the hood and was snarling at me through the glass. At least one other was on the roof, which sounded as if it was going to crash down on me at any moment. The pale wolf was at the driver's side door. One swipe of his huge claw and the window shattered.

I'm pretty sure I screamed. If I didn't, I should have. I figured I had just seconds before his razor-sharp claws would be pulling me out of my car and ripping me to shreds. Somehow I reached into my jacket pocket and pulled out the letter opener Larry had given me. I'd kept it on me, thinking that it might be an effective weapon. Seeing the ferocious animals rocking my car, I knew how foolish that thought was. I had no chance fending off werewolves with a cheap letter opener.

As Levon reached in I jabbed the point of the opener into his arm. He yelped loudly and retreated several steps, but I could see by the fury in his eyes that I'd made a mistake. I may have hurt him, but that only pissed him off more. If his intent had been only to scare me, that was gone now. There was murder in his eyes.

He threw himself against the door, rocking the car. I heard more glass breaking. I gripped the letter opener tighter.

The pale wolf reached in to grab me. I shrank back just as a large shape hit the pale wolf in the side. There were howls from the other wolves as two figures fought on the sidewalk.

Shawn must have been watching from his window and had noticed that my tire was flat. Whatever the reason, he'd come back out to check on me. Now his dark wolf was biting and snarling, wrestling with the pale wolf.

The battle was short but furious. The dark wolf bit into the side of the pale wolf's face, drawing out a howl of pain. The pale wolf broke free and ran towards the park. The dark wolf then turned his attention to the others. He leaped up onto the hood of my car, swatting the wolf there savagely across the face. That was all it took. The remaining wolves all turned tail, running off to join Levon.

The dark wolf–I still had a hard time thinking of it as Shawn–looked up at the moon and let out a triumphant howl. It was a magnificent creature, for sure.

The next time I met Shawn at the bar it was obvious that the story had made the rounds. Shawn had gone to the restroom when Carol set my drink in front of me. She favored me with a smile.

"On the house," she said when I tried to pay for the drink. "A sort of welcome to the fold."

"Thank you," I said, unsure of her exact meaning.

"Shawn's made it known that messing with you is messing with him. I doubt if you'll have any more trouble from Levon."

I'd actually run into Levon once since the incident. He had avoided looking at me, but I couldn't help but see that he sported a new scar running down his cheek.

Shawn returned, kissing me on the forehead before resuming his seat. He looked from me to Carol and then back to me.

"Isn't he something?" he said, grabbing my hand.

The wild-haired bartender nodded. "He must be," she replied. "He's put up with this lot," she indicated the patrons of the bar, "and yet he's still here. So, yes, he must be something special."

Shawn beamed and kissed me on the lips. I drank in his essence, his scent. I could feel his passion.

I still wasn't sure just what sort of life I was getting myself into, but I knew that I loved Shawn.

I was even beginning to love the wolf within.

LEADER OF THE PACK

Robert Saldarini

"*The leader of the pack–now he's gone...*"
The Shangri-las (1964)

The room is full of shadows in the early morning light. Only the sound of the hand-wound alarm clock edges into the dawn's silence. By today's high-tech standards the ticking would be ill-received by most people; however, the men in this townhouse enjoy their personal old ways of life. Using the tips of his fingers, Adolfo gently brushes back the hair from Raul's forehead. This tender touch makes his new lover stir in his sleep, causing him to snuggle closer; a gentle whimper escapes his lips. Adolfo raises his head to see the clock's hands point to 6:35. He can feel the aftermath of Raul's night run throbbing against his thigh. The drowsy sleep that overcomes this new recruit is no match for the adrenaline which still pumps through his body. Raul's raging erection stands testament to his male sexuality and lust for aggression.

Adolfo slides his right hand over Raul's shoulder, stopping momentarily to inspect some serious scratches he received during the nocturnal brawl. Raul winces as Adolfo's thumbnail examines the extent of the injury. Satisfied that the damage is minor, and knowing the wounds will heal fast enough, Adolfo slowly scrapes the tips of his meticulously manicured nails down Raul's back. He moves slowly over his ass and cradles the man's hairy scrotum in the palm of his right hand. As the tip of Adolfo's thumb circles the perineum, Raul's chestnut brown eyes flutter open. He smiles affectionately. He succumbs to Adolfo's advances by silently rolling on his belly and positioning himself on all-fours. Adolfo mounts quickly, immediately penetrating his young mate. This abruptness elicits a low yelp. Raul's body is neither prepared nor fully lubricated for the massive intrusion. Adolfo bites deeply into Raul's shoulder in a passion's grip where he applies enough pressure to exhibit power, however, not to break the hide. His long deep trusts induce a sexual frenzy, causing Raul to ejaculate with immense force; a natural instinct associated with a male marking his territory. The muscular contractions that accompany Raul's orgasm bring Adolfo over the edge. He again surges his hot Canis lupus DNA into his newest beta-male.

A full night of activity and the early morning sex take their toll on Raul. He slowly relaxes and falls back to sleep. Adolfo slips out of bed and into his boxer briefs, adjusts his package, and leisurely crosses the room. The morning sun has changed from timid to bold as it pummels the Venetian blinds searching earnestly for any hairline fracture that would allow it to illuminate the darkness. A thin halo of light frames the perimeter of both windows. Adolfo stops and looks in the mirror so he can scrutinize his body for telltale marks from last night's adventures. He runs his hands over his furry pecs and removes a small twig that had entangled itself in his hair. Once satisfied, he steps through the bedroom door and slowly closes it behind him.

Adolfo enters the kitchen. Sitting at the table eating breakfast is a member of his pack; a man with the body of a linebacker, one who would make the fiercest opponent nervous at a line of scrimmage. "Good morning, Yeller, you are up early after a night-run."

Yeller replies, "Some of us have to work." He looks up from his cereal bowl with a shit-eating grin.

On the way toward the coffee maker, Adolfo ruffles his housemate's thick head of blond hair. Leaning against the counter with a mug in hand, he takes in the beauty of Yeller's form. Dressed for his construction job, the man's white t-shirt fits his body like a layer of skin. His back is solid and defined. When the boys are running through a moonlit park, Yeller is always easy to locate. His blond pelt gives him a unique identity as well as his name. Within the pack, only Adolfo knows that Yeller's German birth name is Ralph.

The ability to regenerate tissue and ward off disease not only makes men of their kind immortal in a natural environment, it allows them to age virtually only minutes in a year's time. It is their lycanthropic metabolism which prevents them from growing old. By cultural standards, an onlooker may think the men in Adolfo's pack are in their early-to-mid twenties. Yet, failure to age promotes occupational hazards for werewolves. Employment usually centers on hard-labor jobs which do not raise the credentialing issues white collar positions demand. No mortal would believe that Adolfo graduated from the University of Vienna in 1932.

Adolfo refills his cup and takes a seat across from his old friend, "It was a good run last night. The air was clear and the moon bright."

Yeller pushes back his empty bowl. "Yes, it was. Your new boy is having one hell of a good time. He's a feisty son-of-a-bitch."

"Come on man, cut him some slack. Raul is new to our way of life. I think this was his third transition. Have you forgotten how it was at the beginning?"

Yeller smiles, "I remember the first time very well, it scared the shit out of me. Cravings that overwhelm you like the pangs of starvation. Then follows the contortion of both your muscles and bones which puts you at the razor's edge of total ecstasy and pure pain."

"The process is not always pleasant, but the result is euphoric."

"That it is, Adolfo. Hey, I don't know if it is me, but your new pup, there is something about his eyes that reminds me of Conán. And, after his transition is complete, his pelt is the same color as our creator."

Adolfo nods his head in agreement. "You know, the night I saw Raul in the Blue Light Lounge, I thought the same thing. For a moment when he was standing there among his friends, I had to look twice because at first glance I thought it was Conán. How foolish the mind can be, I mean after all it's been what, fifty years since Nazi Germany?"

"Try over sixty years. He made me in 1938."

"Yes, I recall, he made me only months prior. What a horny cur he was."

Both men laugh heartedly at the remembrance of their

distant past. Memory is powerful and can sweep away decades to a time where mortal lives and immortal lives are matched in both time and place. It was snowing in Berlin that December night.

Adolfo and Conán are sitting at a corner table within *Spiegelsaal* at the *Ballhaus Mitte*. Through the door, with fresh snow on his hat and shoulders, enters an incredibly handsome and fit SS-officer in full uniform. Apprehension fills the room. The scantily clad cabaret singer continues unaffected by her audience's mood swing. Lately, she experiences many moments like this.

'Ladies' in their finery avoid any eye contact with the young officer, given that the once sexually free Germany that followed World War I has grown exceptionally conservative. Tensions begin to ease when this man of authority makes his way through the crowd to get to the bar.

Conán sits perfectly still watching the officer's every move. Adolfo knows the hunter's silent and deadly stare. He tries to garner his attention, "Don't you think it is strange that an SS-officer would be in here while in uniform?"

Conán replies, "I want to make him, you make it happen."

Adolfo is taken aback by his comment. Until now they were partnered, only the two of them roam side-by-side as both men and beasts. When they met in the Viennese café, Adolfo was captivated by Conán's charm and rugged beauty. He was a tourist who claimed to be visiting from Ireland. From the start, Conán showered Adolfo with attention. Then one night while walking in Donaupark along the Danau it happened: the astonishing transformation, the attempt to run, the tackle, the tearing of fabric, the mount, all this culminated with a fierce bite that shattered Adolfo's shoulder bone at the moment of the wolf's orgasm.

In the weeks that followed, Adolfo fell deeply in love with his creator. Conán explained and detailed the aspects of the new lifestyle often leaving Adolfo in amazement. It turned out that Conán was never bitten by a brother, he was created by sorcery. He shared that when in Ireland, he'd had an affair with the husband of a Celtic sorceress. Using her power, she'd given an ordinary townsman the beauty of Michelangelo's David in return for his undying fidelity. When she discovered their sexual indiscretion, she'd deformed her poor husband and turned Conán into a werewolf.

A sorcerer's creation is a lone wolf; one destined to roam as no existing pack will accept him. In addition, his life is riddled with hardships.

Conán grows impatient. "Go and find out about him."

Adolfo carefully watches the dynamics at the bar. From the time when the officer ordered his drink, the well dressed man with the pencil mustache standing alongside of him has moved about two-meters away. Therefore, there is now an approachable runway. A glance at Conán shows him still in killer stance. He sighs knowing that he will get no plan of attack from his partner.

Adolfo walks up to the bar and positions himself next to the SS-officer. At six-feet-four-inches tall and boasting crystal-blue eyes, there is no doubt why this man is Hitler's ideal male. Noticing the bartender is exceptionally busy with other customers, Adolfo calls to the pudgy-faced worker for two glasses of brandy. An exasperated look from the harried man reassures Adolfo that there would be enough wait-time to enable him to accomplish his mission. The officer, unmoved by his surroundings, drinks from his glass looking forward into space.

Adolfo plunges into the situation. Leaning toward Conán's prey he says, "You can grow old here waiting for your drink. The service is so poor."

"I found it to be fine, the barkeep fetched me bourbon immediately."

"Well, with all due respect sir, the uniform demands prompt service. It is rare to see one of Hitler's finest in a place like this."

Once the brandy transaction is complete, the officer and Adolfo return to the table where Conán smiles a welcome.

"Conán, this is Ralph Harzer, *SS-Hauptscharführer* of the 7th Company of the *Leibstandarte SS 'Adolf Hitler'*."

Conán stands, "I am honored, sir, that you would join us for a drink. It is not often that we are in the company of someone as powerful as you."

Ralph removes his hat and hastily combs back his thick

blond hair attempting to resurrect the required neatness of his academy cut. "*Nein*, we are all men here, right? Sharing a drink? I left any power outside this door."

Adolfo gestures, "Please join us, have a seat."

Ralph pulls up a chair, placing its back to the table and straddles the seat, "*Danke sehr.*"

The night slips by as quickly as does the drinks and good cigars. Around 3:30 A.M. Ralph stands and stretches, "Well gentlemen, I best be on my way."

Conán responds in kind, "Yes, we should be leaving also. Ralph, do you have a car?"

"*Nein*, I'll take a taxi."

"No, by all means, let us drive you back to your flat."

Adolfo glances at Conán, wondering about his plan seeing as neither of them have a car. As they exit, Conán and Ralph walk side-by-side as Adolfo follows behind. The snow has stopped and the night is dry and crisp. Adolfo walks about six paces back barely being able to make out the conversation ahead of him due to the crunch of snow beneath his feet. Ralph, in his slightly intoxicated state follows blindly thinking the destination will lead to a car ride home.

A few city blocks away from the Club, Conán says, "Fuck, it is cold, let's cut through this side alley to save some ground."

Adolfo knows not to follow when the two men turn into the darkness. Instead, he leans against the old brick building pulling his coat tightly to his body for warmth. From the alley he hears a low guttural growl followed immediately by the stammer of a man who is simultaneously shocked and scared for his life. Seconds later, there are the sounds of an aggressive attack. Adolfo closes his eyes in recent memory of his experience; one, which was initially horrifying, yet faded quickly into ardor. He rests the back of his head against the cold brick. Adolfo surrenders to an overwhelming sense of melancholy. The evening that started off with the promise of forever with Conán, ultimately ended in a new sense of competition. Maybe this is the sorceress' curse, or maybe this is how men of his kind behave, there are so many unanswered questions. A tear streams down Adolfo's right cheek when the silence of the night is filled with the proud howl of conquest.

After the second run, Conán gives Ralph the nickname "Yeller." Adolfo and Conán continue to live together while Yeller attempts to balance his life between prominent SS-Officer and wolf. There is little passion between Conán and Yeller. Yeller maintains a cautious distance from his creator. Adolfo cannot put his finger on it, but there is a reason for his behavior, one that Yeller refuses to share.

On the night of the full moon, January 5, 1939, Adolfo and Yeller run for their lives. The night is freezing cold as both Conán and Adolfo, on all fours, cautiously make their way from the alley of their apartment building. These two powerful wolves silently wander through the shadows outside Berlin's populated district. The air is thick with German superiority and the winds of war. The light tap of paws on the frozen ground brings a third and golden wolf to their side. The tree-line gives way to a large field which needs to be crossed. With ears straight-up, all three listen carefully; the terrain appears to be isolated. The leader of the pack lowers into a crouch position for a run. The two beta-males crouch in response.

Conán leaps into the snow covered grass and bolts forward in a full dash. Simultaneously, Adolfo hears the hard empty snap of Yeller's teeth. He offers him a curious look. It is in this hesitation that Yeller swiftly grabs Adolfo by the throat. A rifle shot echoes across the field and Conán drops. Yeller releases his grip and both wolves bring their bellies down to the cold earth watching in earnest.

The murmur of German begins filling the night air as both Adolfo and Yeller see SS-officers trotting across the frozen ground. One man cups his hands around his mouth and bellows to his colleagues, "The silver bullet will not kill him, you must use the silver knife to destroy his heart and then we must decapitate the beast to make sure he can never return."

Adolfo holds back his desire to whine as his heart is breaking at the sight which is unfolding in front of him. Yeller nudges him with his snout in a silent attempt to tell him they must leave. Realizing there is nothing to be done here, Adolfo takes his advice. The boys turn, remain low, and bolt through the underbrush.

The journey takes them miles from the city, whereby, they cross frozen fields and slip over ice-laden streams. The pads beneath Adolfo and Yeller's paws crack causing fur to become blood-soaked. This exhausting escape ends short of dawn when they happen upon a bombed-out village. There is no sign of life; the silhouettes of partial buildings outline the horizon. A farmer's path brings the wolves to an abandoned barn; one which somehow has been able to avoid the shells of an advancing attack.

As the morning light filters through the hastily shut barn doors, Adolfo awakens. He lay resting his head on the golden hair of Yeller's firm chest. Adolfo realizes he has nothing, not even a pair of socks for his aching feet. Nevertheless, scavenging the deserted village will yield what they need. But that is all for later, for now, he drifts back to sleep.

"Adolfo!" Yeller snaps his fingers quickly. "I said, I have to head off to work."

Adolfo realizing he was lost in his past responds, "What? Oh, I'm sorry. I was so deep in thought. I didn't hear you."

Yeller has one foot on the kitchen chair as he tightens the laces of his work boot. "I said, I need to get to the job site. What the hell are you thinking about?"

"I was remembering when we first met in Berlin."

"Geez man, what brought that on?"

"I guess it was our discussion about Conán that did it."

Yeller grabs the chair, turns it around and straddles the seat. His actions elicit a crooked smile from Adolfo, since times may change but the behavior of men does not.

"Listen, my friend, I try not to go back there."

"I know, me too, but there are times–"

Yeller cuts him off mid-sentence.

"Well, maybe it's time to come clean with you."

"What?"

"Do you remember the night we met in *Ballhaus Mitte*?"

"Yes, of course I do, it was at *Spiegelsaal*."

"Well, I didn't just happen to stop in there for a drink. It was part of my mission."

"Mission? What the hell are you talking about–mission?"

"You see, I was part of a secret Special Forces team of the SS which reported directly to *Der Führer*. Jews, homosexuals, and gypsies where not the only targeted groups, men like us, werewolves, were also to be purged. However, the concentration camps' gas chambers would not exterminate us, so we needed to be taken out one-by-one."

"So, Yeller, are you saying that you came to the Club to kill us?"

"In a way yes, but the immortality factor and given the fact there were two of you, this mission could not be so easily done. I was on a suicide mission."

"A suicide mission?"

"Yes, my orders were to go to the Club and be bitten, and then ultimately I would be terminated. I was to lead both you and Conán to the pasture on the next full moon for assassination. The records indicated that there were eight werewolves in German territory. It was hoped that after we exterminated the two of you that I would be transported to other regions. Due to my blond hair and rank I was selected so the SS would be able to discriminate between me and the target. Once all the werewolves where eradicated I was to be killed. During the briefing, it was abundantly clear that this needed to be done for the good of *Deutschland*." Adolfo lowers his head, "And for all these years, I thought on that night your bite was in response to seeing or smelling the men. I believed you were saving my life. I never thought that it was a trap."

"But Adolfo, I did save your life. I was abandoning my mission. My natural preservation instinct and loyalty to the pack had worn down my old values to the German cause. At the edge of the field I realized we needed to get away; yet Conán was too quick or my decision was too late. I went for his haunches, my nose felt the tips of his fur, but my teeth did not make contact. That was then when I turned my attention to save you."

"A setup?" These were the only words that Adolfo could say. For decades he had wondered how the SS could have possibly known the path of Conán's night run. He had deliberated on how they could have organized an assault with silver so quickly if they had only been seen on the advance.

"Trust me, if I could have saved Conán, even at the cost of my own life, I would have. The German brainwashing was so powerful and I have lived with this demon since that very night. I think about the letter and key that you mailed to your friend, Hans Müller, explaining that Conán was dead and that there could be no return. I've pondered on how hard it must have been for you to invite Hans to take anything from your flat if indeed anything was left by the time he received your correspondence. Do you think I have not held the shame and guilt of my actions deep in my dark soul?"

Adolfo looks into Yeller's blue eyes and sees the veracity of his words and torn emotions. "I do trust you, you have been at my side since that night, loyal and devoted. I hold no animosity or resentment. You are my brother."

Feeling exceptionally awkward, Yeller rises from his chair, "Well, enough of this, I am going to be late for work."

Adolfo stands also, taking two steps to embrace his old companion by wrapping himself around his friend's powerful back. Yeller licks his ear. The men walk to the front door, and after a final goodbye, Yeller double-times down the outside steps to the sidewalk. Adolfo quietly enters his bedroom where Raul is still fast asleep.

On his desk sits a steel-framed vintage print. The photo is the only thing that remains from those years. It was sent in a letter by Hans Müller around 1951, during the rebuilding of Germany. Müller explained that when he got to the flat it had been ransacked. This particular photo managed to slip under a dresser. Adolfo lifts the photo and tilts it toward the filtered light.

The faded black and white photography shows two well dressed men. The younger man is seated while the other stands behind him with his hand on his partner's shoulder. The image looks like one taken at an amusement park in an old-time photo gallery, since the man in the chair has not aged.

Adolfo never responded to Hans Müller's letter. How could he explain? He wonders if Müller is still alive and if so he would be in his nineties. So many wish for immortality without ever thinking about the cost of what is taken away. Adolfo touches the image of his maker with the tip of his index finger.

Behind him Raul stirs in his sleep.

WAR OF THE WOLVES

Charles Long

The first time I went through the transformation, I was shocked by how easy and painless it was. I expected it to be accompanied by the sound of bones cracking and the excruciating ache of muscles tearing. Instead, there was euphoric ecstasy akin to sex. Within the span of sixty seconds, I had transformed from human into sleek wolf. I was seventeen when I accepted the offer of a lesbian named Desdemona and became a werewolf.

That was two years ago.

Tonight the pack has gathered on the roof of the building where we all reside. Jackson–an easy-going jokester–sheds his clothes, briefly naked in the moonlight before transforming into a red wolf. He approaches the cinnamon and white Lothario and licks his muzzle. They have been a couple since before I arrived.

Looking up at the waxing moon, I feel the overwhelming urge to shift, pull my linen shirt over my head, and kick off my shoes and jeans. The cool September air sends a chill through my body, but I'm suddenly warmed when I spot several of my pack mates admiring my muscular frame. Unable to resist the change any longer, I allow my body to flow into wolf.

A slender, graceful creature named Medea approaches and rolls onto her back. I rub my muzzle against her neck and then lay across her supine body. She is intersexual as a human and as a wolf, but presents herself as female. There are no other transgendered werewolves in our pack, but I've heard that Desdemona may visit one in Arizona soon to invite her to our merry band of misfits.

It is how I joined the queer pack.

With life unbearable and no one to turn to, I'd called a gay teen help line. A woman with a husky voice became my friend for an hour and a half. Her words were a balm. A week later, a beautiful woman with long raven hair and bright green eyes approached me as I was leaving school. She said she'd heard about my problems and had a solution. There was no mistaking her voice.

I don't know what I expected her to say, but she described a place where I could be myself. It sounded like a dream. She told me to meet her in the park at sunset.

That afternoon I couldn't concentrate. My parents asked if I was on drugs. When twilight finally descended, I headed to the park and found her waiting for me.

"Hunter, I'm going to show you what you can become," she said. She slipped the cotton sleeves of her dress off her shoulders letting it fall to the ground. I wondered for a split second if she had been sent by my parents to seduce me.

"Hunter, do not be afraid." She held out her arms. "Promise you'll be brave."

I nodded.

"No harm will come to you."

Then Desdemona's eyes flared and darkened as her nose elongated. At first I thought it was a trick of the moonlight. As she fell forward, her arms and legs transformed and her body grew dark fur. The shift was drastic and wild, almost violent but I never thought to run, I was transfixed. Within moments it was complete, before me a coal black wolf with Desdemona's eyes and a small shock of white beneath her throat.

"You're beautiful." My voice seemed not my own. I spoke to the animal like it was human, because I understood it was.

The wolf approached and opened her jaws, revealing her very sharp teeth. Yet I was calm. The jaws closed and the wolf licked my hand with her smooth, warm tongue. Looking up at me with intelligent eyes, she seemed to want me to understand that everything would be okay. Maybe it is what I wanted to believe.

Then Desdemona lay on the ground.

Without thinking I knelt beside her and stroked the thick black coat. As I pushed my fingers into fur, I felt the steady beat of her wolf heart and was overcome with emotion. I actually fell forward, sobbing.

I didn't see Desdemona resume her human form, but after a few minutes, I felt her hand on my back. Felt a maternal concern. With my head in her lap, she stroked my hair.

When she offered to make me a werewolf, I readily agreed, but it was nothing like I expected.

I wondered if she would turn back into the sleek black wolf and bite me. Instead she caressed my hand and opened a small case containing a hypodermic needle.

"This will sting. You'll feel it almost instantly, as if power is coursing through your veins, and you will feel a need to shift. The best thing to do, Hunter, is to close your eyes, breathe steadily, and focus on your senses. You will hear more than ever before. You will smell the most delicate scents. You will see in a different way."

I nodded.

A slight prick of the needle and my life was forever changed.

"You will never again feel alone or threatened. You are free, Hunter." Desdemona told me. "Free to be who you are. My pack is now yours. Now be the beautiful creature I know you can be."

Then, simply, it happened.

My body convulsed and I felt it shifting. I writhed about and when the transformation was done, I felt strong and powerful and majestic. It was the first time I had felt any of these things. I howled with delight.

Desdemona knelt before me, stroking my coat, "Now you are one of my children, Hunter. I will protect you just as I protect all my family, my pack."

The night I accepted Desdemona's gift seems a lifetime ago. It changed me forever. Tonight rubbing noses with my fellow pack mates, I am free as she promised.

Jackson, Lothario and I face each other; our scents comforting. Lothario rolls onto his back, kicks his legs in the air. I playfully bite the thick fur around his neck. Jackson bows his muzzle and brushes a cool nose tenderly through Lothario's ruff and I leave them to their intimate play.

Our entire pack, thirteen in all, is either gay, lesbian or transgendered.

I spot Garm, who has scars on his arms from self-mutilation where, in wolf form, hair doesn't grow. Garm, who named himself for a Hell-hound, is the size of a petite girl and barely speaks above a whisper. He is Asian and was rejected by his entire community.

Most of the members of our group have taken new names and left behind their human ones. Jackson and I are the only exceptions.

Besides Desdemona, Garm, Jackson, Lothario, Medea and me, the pack consists of seven others. Two lesbians, Artemis and Freya–the former quite butch while the latter is not. Both have been known to share Desdemona's bed but never each other's.

Romulus, the alpha male of our pack, is a stocky man and a formidable wolf. I've heard that he saved Desdemona from her maker. Though he is dominant, and can be quite aggressive, Romulus is a surprisingly tender lover. He has bed many of the males in the pack, including me.

Then there are the fair haired twins, Hati and Skoll, who are named after wolves that chase the moon and sun.

Cerberus, named after the three-headed dog that guarded Hades, is in fact a quixotic, hot-tempered Italian-American who is easy on the eyes in both human and wolf form. I've had a crush on him since he arrived six months ago, but I waited too long and he found himself a beautiful mortal lover named Ben.

Anubis is a twenty-three year old man the color of dark tea. Transformed, he actually looks more svelte than the average wolf and Desdemona named him for the jackal-god of Egypt.

We are all there when Desdemona arrives. Naked as Venus rising from the foam, she walks among us. We all, save Romulus, bow our heads in supplication.

She approaches me, kneels and scratches behind my ears.

"Hunter, someone needs our help and I want you to go. I know you're ready. Will you do this for me?" I lick her hand and rub my cheek against her bare thigh. "You spoke with him a couple days ago. His name is Jared."

I can smell that she's in heat and I know she'll take a mate this evening. Artemis and Freya are already drawn to her, circling closer.

"He reminds me of you," she says. "He's surrounded by those who would do him harm just for being himself. Will you leave tonight and go to him?"

The alpha female is mother to us all. She is loving and nurturing, protective by nature, but this evening she seems anxious. It compels me to morph back into human form.

"I will do as you ask."

Her black hair mingles with mine as she leans forward and hugs me. I'm confused because I sense fear. Nothing makes Desdemona afraid, so I worry there's more than she's telling me.

"There's a late flight tonight. You will find him at school. Ask if he wants our aid."

"Just as you did, when you came for me." The memory brings a smile to my lips.

"Yes, Hunter," she said. "I cannot go. I trust you. Remember: Do not force him to choose our way. Simply ask what he needs. If the situation warrants, you may offer him the gift."

"I know what to do. I'll make you proud."

She kisses my cheek. Turns away and into her lupine form; then howls at the distant moon.

"Homo."

The pejorative hangs in the air.

I watch the Bryndyll Coyotes finish their practice. It has been tainted with numerous homophobic epithets and violence directed toward one player, Jared Lucas. Watching in lupine form, I've been able to overhear comments that my human ears would not have picked up.

When the football practice ends, I resume human form and dress before I slip into the locker room. Jared is easy to spot: blond hair, blue eyes, a massive frame. What I thought was kohl underneath his eyes is not. Jared actually has a black eye.

Two half-naked men—one tall and dark, the other freckled with a shock of orange hair—stroll toward the showers. As Jared pulls his gear over his head, they grab him and slam him hard into his locker. Everyone laughs. In my mind's eye I transform into wolf, raining down carnage on them, but I know Desdemona expects better of me.

"Excuse me." My voice is clear and strong; certain.

Two years ago I would have shrunk from the scene. Not now, after the gift, after the strength my pack has taught me.

The brunette and redhead turn to face me.

"Who are you?" the brunette asks.

"I think you owe him an apology."

The entire locker room is silent. The coach sits in his office and I can see he watches the proceedings without any intention of interceding. I glare at him with cold eyes before my attention is drawn away.

"Fuck you," he says.

"Is that what you'd like?"

His reaction is vitriolic and instant. As he draws back, I will my lupine form to rise; my senses on the cusp of lupine and human. As he punches at me, I dodge then I yank his towel and leave him standing naked. To his credit, he's built like a warrior; however, the chill in the air hasn't been kind, so it's my turn to snicker.

The redhead puffs up like a gorilla but I give him no time before I utter an animalistic growl. The room grows deathly silent. It's a cheap parlor trick, but it stops the homophobe in his place.

I turn toward my mark and speak.

"Jared, I'd like to talk to you. Shall we meet outside?"

I exit the locker room, and a few minutes later, Jared walks out alone. Despite everything, he finds it in himself to smile and I feel a compelling desire to kiss him.

Controlling my urges, I say, "Jared Lucas, my name is Hunter. I've come to help you."

He runs his hand through his mop of blond locks. I can see he doesn't understand.

"You called the hotline where I work."

"Holy shit! And they sent you?"

"We were concerned about you." I spot the brunette, his red-haired sidekick at his back, in the doorway watching us. "Can we go somewhere to talk?"

At his recommendation, we drive to a secluded place at the edge of a ravine. When we arrive, twilight is near.

"The black eye?" I ask when the engine dies and we sit in silence.

"One of the assholes you met."

"They did it because you are gay?"

"I wasn't going to tell anyone but they found a magazine in

my book bag. Then the shit hit the fan."

I know he's trying to sound tough.

We get out of the car and sit on the hood. Far below, at the bottom of the ravine there's the glitter of a small creek. The embankment is heavily wooded and I can sense the wildlife.

"Your parents?" I ask after it is clear that Jared is waiting for me to speak.

"They don't understand or don't want to." He hangs his head and I know he's holding back tears.

I take his hand in mine, and I realize how large they are.

"I want to offer you protection, if you need it."

"They'll win," he says flatly.

"They won't, Jared. I'm here to help." His bright eyes rise to meet mine. When he had called the hotline, he had told me that he'd never even kissed a man. Now it seems he might, head bending to mine, but before our lips touch, I feel a pellet hit my right shoulder.

I slide forward and turn; another pellet hits me in the chest. It seems as if the whole football team descends on us and I worry that I have failed Jared. That I have failed Desdemona. Yet they are only six...six boys, not yet even men.

"So you really are a homo?" It's the brunette. Beside him the redhead holds the offending pellet gun. I want to snarl.

"Jealous?" I really shouldn't provoke them.

"Fuck you. I don't know who you are, but we're gonna make sure you don't come around again."

There is only one thing I can think to do. I turn to Jared and say *sotto voce*, "You'll be okay. I promise. Just try not to panic, no matter what happens."

Of course, he knows nothing of my plan, so he responds with a confused gaze. I have no time to explain.

I jump down the ragged slope of the ravine and disappear into the edges of the woods. I know Jared thinks I've already abandoned him; my chest tightens, I know his pain. Hastily throwing off my clothes, I shift. Darkness has come and I am in my element. I throw back my head and howl.

Without the slightest effort at stealth, I cross to where it will be easiest to climb and double back to Jared and his tormentors. Muscles strain on the ascent and then the grass is soft beneath my feet and sings my passage in a voice lost to human ears. I see Jared on the ground and even afar I can smell the blood on his lips.

I lunge forward and leap, toppling the brunette and wanting to tear at the tender throat but only snap and snarl. His terror tastes sweet and I leap for the next, clamp my teeth into the pants leg of another tormentor, dragging him to the ground. Tearing the fabric with savage abandon, I play the monster and draw a little blood before leaping onto the car and loosing a bloodcurdling howl. Two pairs dart off.

Redhead–with more courage than I'd thought–takes aim with the pellet gun, but I leap and lock his arm in my jaws. The sound of breaking bone is punctuated by his cry of pain.

I can smell urine and fear. I release him, circling the one I sense is their leader; the brunette. He hasn't had time to rise. I place a paw on his chest and breathe into his face–all menacing teeth. His eyes grow wide and I touch my cool nose to his. He trembles so violently that I think he might crumble into pieces. I lick my tongue across his lips before I back away. His red-haired friend pulls him away one armed, holding his broken right arm close to his chest. I wonder if he'll grow into a better man. Brunette finds his feet, scrambling up and then they are gone, their voices quickly fading.

In the distance I hear a car.

Jared is frozen in place, and I move slowly, tentatively so as not to startle him. To my delight, he does not flee, rather he watches as I lower my head and whimper. I hope that he'll approach me, but that proves too much to ask. After a short pause, I stride toward him and sniff the air. Edging my muzzle delicately toward his hand, I finally make contact and nestle my jowl in his palm. A frisson travels my wolf spine as he responds with a caress. It is time to do what I must: resume human form.

When I rise and face him, his eyes are soft and kind and a hint of a smile creases the corner of his mouth. There's still blood on his lips; I want to wipe it away but hold back afraid he won't let me.

"I don't want to see you suffer anymore for who you are."

The silence is too long and then he asks, "Is that what I can be?"

I smile, relieved. "It's your decision. We just want to offer you our help. You'll always be welcome among my family."

Jared shocks me more than anyone ever has when he walks boldly up to me, grabs the back of my head and kisses me fully on the lips. There's a sharp tang of blood, but I don't mind. For someone who has never known the affections of another man, he finds expressing his gratitude easy enough.

That night, in my hotel room, Jared tells me about his life. It's all familiar and heartbreaking.

"I've known for a long time that I'm gay." His intensity is sudden: "But I just want to know what it's like."

The sentence confuses me. "What do you mean?"

"I want to know what it's like to be with a man."

As the implications dawn, a coy smile creases my lips.

What would Desdemona think if I allowed him to seduce me? I have a conversation with her in my head and she answers; it has to be his choice.

And it is.

He kisses me. He undresses me. He carries me to bed.

Afterwards I offer him the gift and he eagerly accepts.

The next day, we return to my city late in the evening. Oddly, I haven't heard from Desdemona, so I hail a cab to take us home. Jared holds my hand the entire way and I try to tell myself that my feelings are simply sexual attraction. Instead, ridiculous as it sounds–even to me–I feel as if Jared is my destiny.

The night air is cool and damp. City traffic is unusually sparse. The cabbie turns up the radio to listen to a news report about attacks by stray dogs and ice runs through my veins.

Jared gives me a quizzical look and I simply shake my head.

As soon as we arrive, I throw money at the cabbie, grab our luggage, and rush into the building. My panic makes Jared uneasy.

"I'm sorry." I sling the bags into a corner in the empty lobby. "Something's just not right. I should have heard from Desdemona and these attacks sound like werewolves."

Jared looks around. "Where are they?"

It's a big building but I know. "They're on the roof. We gather there at night." I grab his arm.

When we burst through the rooftop door, I'm relieved to see my pack, twelve wolves in the moonlight. Next to me, Jared utters, "Wow." Then I notice that they are all facing outward, like buffalo protecting their young.

"Strip," I command and begin to do the same.

Jared follows my lead. I kiss him passionately, smile and then shift. Without hesitation or awkwardness, Jared transforms. Though I can't take any credit, I still feel immense pride at his deftness.

Stepping away from the alcove of the doorway, I see the danger and my heart races. A rogue pack of wolves stand on the edges of neighboring buildings.

As though she had been waiting for my arrival, Desdemona transforms to human, at her side a storm cloud grey timber wolf, Romulus. A large tawny wolf on the building opposite shifts to parley.

"You're a pack of freaks, an abomination." His voice is gravelly, accented. I know he wants us to break without a fight, to hide in shame. I swallow my snarl.

"Leave our city and we won't harm you." Desdemona's voice is cool, but her words only make the interloper laugh.

"It's not my pack that's going to get hurt. It's yours."

She doesn't flinch, takes two steps forward and Romulus shadows her.

"We will tear you apart if you try to harm any of our pack," her anger is flint hard, I feel it.

Again, the interloper laughs. He steps onto the ledge, a pointing finger targeting us all. "Make no mistake. Every one of you will die today."

Then he leaps through the air and lands, transformed, three feet in front of the alphas of my pack. Leaping in eerie silence, his entire pack follows his lead.

Desdemona shifts into her dark wolf. The rival alpha lunges and Romulus does the same. The two engage mid-air. Guttural growls accompany the violence as they tear and snap at each. Two grey enemy wolves leap onto Desdemona's back. Then the rest of the interlopers engage.

As I rush forward from the sidelines, I tackle a white and black male. His back paw catches me in the rib cage, drawing blood, but that only spurs me on. Grabbing him by the muzzle, I bite hard and refuse to let go. He almost catches my eye with his flailing forepaw and I release him to save my eye. As I bob to the right, I sink my teeth into his flank eliciting a yelp. I see movement in the periphery. The two fighting alpha males are tumbling–snarling and ripping–our way, but it's too late to leap out of their path. The four of us crash into a heap.

Romulus is first to his feet, grabbing my opponent and snapping his neck with a fierce shake of his head. The tawny alpha leaps onto him and I use my muzzle to push him over before he has an opportunity to clamp teeth into my alpha.

I see Desdemona charge a young, bulky silver male and lift him off the ground with a sweep of her powerful head. As he jumps to escape her, she shoves him over the side of the building.

Even a werewolf can't survive a twelve story drop.

Then she whips around and confronts a rusty colored female. I don't have a chance to witness their battle; someone grabs my tail in their jaws and draws me back into the fray. Hati and Skoll are bloody; twin flashes across my line of sight.

A memory of bright blue eyes distracts me and I search for Jared, between snaps and snarls. I don't see him and I grow fearful, but the wolf at my side gives me no time to search for him. He has my throat in his jaws, but my thick mane protects me. Distractions are thrust aside and with one desperate leap, I break free. Then swiftly follow Romulus's example and grab the wolf's spine just above his shoulder blades.

I have never killed.

When it's done, I'm shocked and stunned. The dead wolf shifts back into a young man with a tribal tattoo around each bicep. His hair is not quite red enough, but still I imagine a resemblance and bile is in my throat.

Desdemona claws at the soft underbelly of the rust-hued female, slashes again exposing the creature's heart. It transforms into a statuesque blond who breathes her last labored breath.

An unearthly growl arises from the far side of the roof and I turn in time to see Romulus tear out the throat of the alpha male.

Two more wolves are driven over the side of the building, and then the last of them break and flee. Their fear suffuses the air.

When it is clear the danger has passed, I rush toward the rooftop door and find Jared, bloody but safe. I lick his muzzle gazing into warm and bright blue eyes.

Needing my voice, I shift back to human form. "Are you okay?"

Jared shifts, still on all fours beside me. I can see a shallow gash in his side.

"I'm fine." He grabs my bicep and squeezes. "I thought you promised I'd be safe with your pack."

"I'm so sorry. I didn't know." I choke.

"Hey. I'm just kidding. I'm fine. Is it like this all the time?" I remember his smile the day we met; even in here on a battleground Jared can smile and because of it, so can I.

For a moment there is silence and then I hear the voice of Desdemona.

"Romulus, are you hurt?"

"No. That sonofabitch thought he had me." His voice is steady, strong.

"He's dead now." Desdemona is cruel in victory; a mother satisfied her children are now safe.

I look over my shoulder and see Desdemona approach Romulus, offer him her hand. Battle-worn and bloody, they're still beautiful. Together they gaze at us, their pack. Every eye I imagine can't but be drawn to them.

"You did well," Romulus tells us all. "After hearing of our victory, no wolf will ever try to usurp our territory. This is our city."

Cries of triumph rise.

Desdemona says, "I'm proud of you all."

She and Romulus disengage as they move in different directions. She draws near and turns to Jared and me. "What have we here? Jared Lucas, I presume."

Their eyes lock as they appraise one another; emeralds and sapphires.

I think of his reticence by the ravine but Jared surprises me and speaks first.

"Thank you for sending Hunter." His hand clenches tight

round my arm.

Desdemona leans in and kisses his cheek; then mine. "You come at an interesting time," she says.

"You're part of our pack now," Romulus says joining us, with Garm and Anubis at his side.

As my pack mates approach our new member, one voice cries out. When I look up, search it out, I see Jackson cradling Lothario's body.

We have not all made it through the confrontation with the rogue pack.

Desdemona flies to his side, tears already in her eyes. "Jackson." She clutches him tightly; holds them both.

Our voices turn to howls.

Later, Jared comes to my room. The dawn breaking colors him in blood and there's an awkward silence between us. I can't find the words to break it, but again he surprises me and finds them first.

"I'll hold you while you sleep, if that'll help," he says.

I say nothing and he leans forward, clambers onto the bed to join me. He stretches out beside me, smelling like power and passion and sex.

"Hunter." His breath tickles my neck. "Thank you, thank you for sharing your gift with me." I know he means more than the hypodermic filled with wolf.

"I'm glad you accepted." I tell him. "Glad you're here."

"We'll always..." He reaches his arms over me, embraces me. "...always protect each other."

There's nothing left to say as I close my eyes and wait for sleep in the arms of my werewolf lover.

FLIP CITY

Lucas Johnson

They said the park was dangerous at night, but Ryan went anyway. *How bad could it be?* He thought the walk would help clear his mind.

The cold night air sent shivers through his body and he wrapped his scarf tighter as he passed streets that were only sporadically lit after the last power surge. Somehow the street lamps seemed weak against the night.

In the park, trees muffled the sounds of the city. He shivered again and left the footpath seeking solitude in the darkness of the trees. The blackness of the woods was complete. Even the moonlight failed to filter through the canopy.

He was alone without her.

A twig snapped and brought Ryan out of his thoughts. He stopped, held his breath, but there was only silence. He was about to relax when he heard a nearby growl.

A wild animal or some rabid dog roaming the park, he thought. The animal howled into the night and he panicked and turned to run, but it was already at his heels. Pain shot up his leg as the animal bit into his calf. He let out a yell and stumbled forward, falling onto the hard paved footpath. He rolled, holding up his hands and tensing for an attack.

None came. He looked back the way he'd come and saw dark eyes watching him from the shadows of the trees.

Ryan could make out the animal in the shadows, darkness against deeper darkness. It was clearly a wolf, panting softly. He expected it to lunge out at him, but it only slunk back into the darkness, leaving Ryan alone on the path.

He lay motionless for minutes, expecting it to return. When it was clear it was gone, he struggled to his feet, favoring his injured leg. He briefly wondered where the wolf had come from, but stranger things were happening in the city.

The wound was superficial but messy. Blood seeped through his ripped jeans. He wound his scarf tight around it and fumbled for his cell.

The hospital was crowded. He was told he would have to wait. He sat in the waiting room, pain like a sheen of drugs clouding his mind. His thoughts wandered back to that afternoon. What the hell had happened?

Lily had been livid when she walked out. Her lips curled back in a demonic snarl, throwing him a last glance over her shoulder. One minute they had plans for dinner–a nice little restaurant downtown where they folded the napkins into swans on the table–and the next she was gone. What had he said?

The duty nurse called out a name and he glanced up. There were people with electrical burns, with scratches and bites scattered among the pale and sickly faces. One had an intricate pattern cut into his cheek, clotted blood obscuring the design. Ryan shuddered, looked away. *What was happening to the city?* There'd been three power surges since the new power plant had been connected to the city grid. Homicides were up, people were found dead in the alleys covered in strange wounds. The paper ran editorials of police inaction, political corruption, terrorism–but Ryan thought there was something they weren't saying. And now there were wolves in the park.

Wine. He'd mentioned wine. He'd suggested pasta to her, and a nice merlot. Lily flew into a rage.

Ryan couldn't figure out what had gone wrong. They'd saved the money for this dinner for weeks, scraped it together from their dead-end jobs. He wondered if she was already back waiting for him, to explain and to apologize.

Her reaction was the kind of crazy he'd seen on the news–a professor at the university attacking a student, a woman murdering her husband in his sleep. No pattern in the crimes, no motivation.

When a doctor finally stitched Ryan up and gave him a rabies shot, he just shook his head.

"Third animal attack tonight," the duty nurse explained. There were dark rings beneath her eyes.

She gave him an appointment slip for more rabies shots before turning to the next patient. Everyone in the hospital looked tired.

Ryan slept late. He guessed it was the pain meds the doctor had given him. His leg ached, but the bandage was clean. He gave it no further thought.

He searched the apartment for signs that Lily had been there, but found none, until a knock at the door gave him brief hope. It wasn't Lily. A man stood in the hallway. He looked a couple years younger than Ryan, eighteen, shaggy hair tousled like he hadn't bothered to comb it. His leather jacket was too small.

"Hi," he said.

"Who the hell are you?"

"Danny." He was awkward, shy.

"What do you want?"

"I saw you in the park last night."

Ryan scowled. "And you followed me home?" He felt a surge of anger and it made him think of Lily; the snarl on her lips.

"You doing okay?"

"I'm fine. Fuck off."

"Wait!" Danny said. "You're going to need help tonight."

"What the hell are you talking about?"

"It's not safe for you to stay around here. You should come with me."

Ryan snorted. "Yeah, that's going to happen."

He slammed the door.

He was restless all day.

The news had stories about missing children, warehouse fires, religious cults, neighbor turning on neighbor. The police had their hands full, petty crimes were being ignored. By late afternoon, he couldn't stand being cooped up anymore.

The sun was already setting. Shadows stretched across the park and Ryan found it empty–abandoned–people having already left for safer areas of the city. He thought of the wolf, briefly, but he stayed anyway.

He was alone, surrounded by trees, when the sun went down.

He heard a rustle in the undergrowth, smelled fresh meat, and remembered nothing else that night.

He woke to the cold morning air. Wrapping his arms around himself instinctively, he realized he was stark naked.

Ryan scrambled to his feet, looking for his clothes, but instead found another body lying on the leaves.

It was Danny, peacefully asleep, curled among the leaves in a fetal position. In a moment of complete surprise, Ryan's eyes drifted over tight legs, a nearly hairless torso, and a firm backside, before he remembered himself and wrenched his eyes away.

What the hell happened last night?

Danny woke.

"Good morning," he said. His eyes slid unashamedly over Ryan's body.

"What the hell is going on?" Ryan demanded.

"You were bitten the other night," Danny said, like it explained everything. "That means you were infected. Sorry."

Ryan frowned. "What the hell are you talking about? We didn't–I mean, I would never–"

"It was your first night, it takes awhile to learn to control yourself, so I followed you, made sure you didn't hurt anyone." He added, "Nothing happened."

"I don't know what the fuck you're talking about," Ryan said.

Danny sighed, pulled a pile of clothes from under the leaves and tossed them to Ryan. "I bit you the other night–I'm sorry, it's hardest to control at the full moon."

"I was bitten by a wolf, not some–" Ryan stopped. "No fucking way. You're fucking crazy."

"Strange things are happening in the city," Danny replied. "I was infected over a month ago, before most of the shit even started."

The clothes were unfamiliar. They fit, but the shirt was too tight and the jeans hung low. He wondered what had become of his own clothes as he dressed.

"You want me to believe there are werewolves in the city?" he scoffed.

Danny shrugged. Ryan looked away as Danny began to pull on his pants.

"Well, yeah. After all, you are one now."

"Bullshit."

After a moment of uncomfortable silence, Ryan shivered. "I'm going home."

"Wait," Danny said, struggling with a t-shirt. "You're going to feel more aggressive, you're going to want meat. Be careful–the last thing you want to do is hurt someone, right?"

Ryan just kept walking.

His apartment was empty.

She hadn't returned since the fight. All he had in the fridge was beer. He stared at the six-pack for a moment, then–*morning be damned*–grabbed two cans. He opened the first, sat down in front of his computer.

He searched online for news of the city.

There were more links than he had expected. He skimmed the headlines, snippets of blogs and editorials that caught his attention. *Unexplained attacks...people acting strangely...priests claiming demonic possession...doomsayers claim the end is nigh.*

He reached for the second beer.

Police impotent to help...no answers...Sergeant Darian Torres spearheading investigations of unexplained crimes...string of murders...serial killer...no answers.

With the third beer in his hand, he grew bold enough to dial Lily's cell number. It rang–but there was no answer.

The fourth beer and he couldn't remember opening it. He tried her number again. When she didn't answer he threw the phone across room. He grabbed his coat.

Standing in the hallway, he sniffed the air. A rush of scents overwhelmed him; the old man who lived in the apartment next door; gingersnap cookies baking; a musky scent he uneasily recognized as Danny; and Lily.

Her scent lingered in the hallway. Somehow, from the way the scent hung in the air, he could tell that she hadn't been to the apartment since the night she stormed out. He could follow it. He could find her.

He took the elevator. In the lobby he caught the scent trail again and followed it out the back door. Down the alley and away from the apartment building, then a right turn, a left. The scent was weak but still there. A sudden right and he lost it. He felt a brief panic, a throb of burning frustration but then there it was again, heading west. She'd avoided the main streets, her path following the darkest back roads.

It took him an hour, sniffing his way along side streets like a lost dog. People avoided him, crossed to the other side of the road, but all he cared about was reaching the end of the trail. She didn't stay anywhere long and where her scent lingered, he smelled blood.

He didn't know what he would do when he finally found her and hadn't decided when he stumbled upon her suddenly, in a back alley, the air thick with the smell of blood.

Lily was speaking quietly with a stranger. The air danced with their scents–Lily; a masculine musk from the stranger; sweat and fear and blood.

A sudden fury grew within Ryan. To him, the stranger was the enemy, the one who had changed her, taken her from him. When he saw Lily move closer to the man, he charged. They didn't even notice him at first. Then, they heard him and she leapt away, the stranger drew a knife. Ryan, ignoring it, jumped at him. He knocked the man to the ground, a growl in his throat.

"Ryan?" Lily's voice drew his attention.

He saw her eyes–and they were dead, emotionless. He turned back to the stranger, nose bloodied, terrified. He was overcome with the smell of blood. He snarled and grabbed the knife from the stranger's hands.

Instinct took him over. He stabbed the blade into the man's throat.

Lily screamed, and it sounded like anger, not fear. Ryan staggered back. Another snarl grew in his throat, he felt the beast within him, felt the wolf taking him over. He smelled the blood on which the stranger choked. He turned and ran.

"I knew you'd be back," Danny said.

He hadn't left the park. Ryan found him sitting on a bench,

throwing stale bread to the pigeons. His eyes never left the birds, a predatory set to his features.

Ryan shivered. "I need help," he said, sitting down beside Danny.

"I know."

They sat in silence for a moment. Danny tossed the last of his bread. Ryan shifted uncomfortably.

"So...will you help me?"

"Yeah. I'll help," Danny said, standing. "Come with me."

Ryan hesitated. "Where to?"

Danny sighed. "Not very trusting, are you? We're going to my place."

"Why?"

Danny shrugged, "It's easier...once we get further away from people."

"Fine," Ryan said, rising. "But I have some questions while we walk. You said something before about controlling it. How do you do that?"

"That's something you have to learn. Practice. It takes time."

"Yeah, but I mean, what is it you can control? Doesn't the full moon make you transform, end of story?"

Danny shrugged. "It's not that simple...the full moon–and the nights before and after–force a change. It takes you over; you become an animal with a taste for human flesh. It's maddening and you have no control. You can't even remember at first."

"Like last night." And the hunger was still in him, bubbling at the surface. He tried not to think of it, but images of the stranger came to mind, blood flooding from his throat.

"Yeah." Danny was nodding. "But with practice, you can keep control when you change. It's hardest under the full moon–even my control slipped the night I bit you."

"Your control slipped? Your control slips for a second, and I'm stuck with this–this curse." He let Danny be the target of his fury; it drove away the guilt.

Danny looked away. "I know. I'm sorry. I–I'm trying."

Shame filled Danny's voice, and Ryan forced himself to calm down. He needed Danny's help now.

"Anyway," Ryan said. "So you can control the change."

"Yeah. I can even make myself change voluntarily, and stay

in control."

They emerged from the trees into a small clearing. An aging maintenance shack stood amongst piles of rotting leaves. An old sign that sat in the mostly-dark window read Beware of Dog. Ryan snorted.

Inside, it had been converted into a simple living space. A cot in one corner, an old couch against a wall and cookware stacked on makeshift shelves beside a portable oven.

"Cozy." Ryan said and couldn't keep the sarcasm from his voice.

"I can't stand the city any more, the people. It's hardly ideal, but it's home." Danny paused. "You can stay here if you want."

"I have a place."

"I know. You might find it more comfortable here."

"With you? Unlikely. Are you going to help me or not?"

"Yeah. It'll take time though. We can't be around people for too long. It's dangerous."

Ryan snorted. "For us or them?"

It took a lot of convincing to get Ryan to agree to spend the night at the shack. Ryan argued. He said that he'd be fine. That he didn't need to live like a bum.

Secretly though, he'd been convinced immediately. He didn't want to go home. He didn't trust himself around people. There was blood on his mind and he was afraid he'd hurt someone else.

"The first thing you'll have to learn is to control your urges," Danny said the next morning, frying some bacon on the portable stove. The smell of cooking fat made Ryan's pulse quicken. "The animal inside has a taste for flesh that rises even to the human surface."

"Sounds like you've done research."

Danny shrugged. "I had no one else. I needed to be sure about what I was. You have to practice your control around people. Learn to be among them without attacking."

"How will we do that?"

"We'll take a walk."

They wandered through the park. When they passed someone Ryan's nerves would go on edge, their scent would make him salivate, his heart would pound in his chest. His eyes drifting to flesh–meat–tender throats to be torn out with sharp teeth. He had to wrench his eyes away, think of something else. Then they would pass another and the battle would begin all over again.

After half an hour, he was exhausted. They retreated to the shack.

"You did well," Danny said. "Didn't kill anyone." He winked.

Ryan looked away. "I don't know how long I can do that."

"You get used to it. It's hardest when you're first infected."

"I can't trust myself to be alone. I'll hurt someone."

"It's okay. Stay here as long as it takes."

A few days later Danny decided that they would leave the park to buy supplies. Ryan kept his eyes on the ground and made it to the store without incident, but when they were stocking up, surrounded by other shoppers, he was overwhelmed. Anxiety struck him, the crowds of people smelling of food, the open meat counter, assailed his nose, blood pounded in his ears. Danny pulled Ryan close, staring into his eyes. The intensity shocked Ryan. He found himself registering the rich colors of Danny's irises and the warmth of his breath and the fact that he definitely did not smell like lunch.

"Breathe through the mouth." Danny told him.

"I need to get out of here."

"We're almost done. Just take deep breaths through the mouth. Think of something else."

They managed to get everything on Danny's shopping list but by the time they left the store, Ryan was sweating heavily.

Back at the shack, Ryan flipped through a discarded newspaper he'd grabbed while Danny made hamburger.

Jack the Ripper in the City? the headline read. There was a serial killer hunting the side streets and alleys of the city, with an MO that mirrored the legendary Jack the Ripper. But there were still several murders unconnected with this killer–the police didn't attribute the latest one to him. They had a quote from the main investigating police officer, Sergeant Darian Torres, who seemed to be one of the only cops even trying to deal with the crazy things that were happening to the city. 'The victim was stabbed in the throat with a pocket knife. There is no reason to link this incident to any other case we're currently investigating.'

Ryan thought of the stranger in the alley, the blade in his throat, blood washing over his hands. He flipped the page.

"Anything interesting?" Danny asked, sitting down beside him.

"Another power surge, a gang fight downtown, a string of murders...all of them sounding like front page headlines, only they're appearing on almost every page now."

Danny nodded, silent.

"More reports of animal attacks; electronics exploding...what's happening to the city?"

"The stuff of nightmares," Danny said quietly.

"What do you mean?"

"Think about it. There were never werewolves in the city before. Now there are. Gremlins jinxing the electronics; animals attacking; people possessed by dark forces... Demons have come to the city."

Ryan wanted to scoff, but Lily came into his mind. Her sudden anger, leaving their apartment and never coming back, the inexplicable pilgrimage she'd made through the alleyways. The emptiness of her eyes. Could a demon be doing that?

"Demons," he echoed.

"Everything's changing."

Ryan suddenly wondered what life Danny had had to leave behind. He looked at him; saw the sorrow in his eyes.

He didn't plan it and couldn't say why he did it–maybe some animal instinct he couldn't control, maybe Lily's absence, maybe the compassion that Danny was willing to show him–whatever it was, he leaned into Danny and their lips came together. At first the kiss was soft and then, suddenly, hard and demanding. Their bodies pressed together, Ryan curling his fingers into Danny's unruly hair. His pulse quickened, he felt the animal inside, hungry for more.

With a gasp, he pushed himself away.

"What–?" Danny looked concerned.

But Ryan was on his feet and out the door.

He was sitting on the park bench beside the pond when Danny found him.

"Screw off." Ryan didn't look up.

"You okay?"

"I said screw off."

Danny was silent.

"It's the animal inside," Ryan said. "I can't control it, that's all."

"Okay."

"I'm not gay."

"I said okay. Anyway, it's just a label. Gay, bi, queer, straight, they don't really mean anything. Love is love, right?"

"I'm not!"

"I'm just saying."

They were silent for a long time.

Finally Danny asked, "What now?"

"I can't go back to the city, I can't control this. Just keep your hands off me."

"Okay." Danny didn't argue, didn't mention that Ryan had been the one to kiss him.

Ryan stood and they walked back to the shack in silence.

Things in the city got worse and Ryan saw more evidence of what he began to label 'the nightmares' everywhere: people missing for days only to turn up with no memory; evidence of ritual sacrifice–animal at first and then more; a burning man walking slowly through a police station, leaking flame like blood. Often there would be some quote from Sergeant Torres. *Did he know?* Ryan wondered if he was investigating the nightmares themselves or was just another cop doing his job. He always seemed to show up where the nightmares struck. Did this cop realize what was happening to the city?

Despite his interest, he watched from a distance. He didn't live in the city anymore. He lived with Danny, in the park. Danny who was a friend and a mentor and the family Ryan had never had. So what that Danny was gay? Ryan could look past that.

And yet, more and more he felt something different when he was with Danny.

He ignored it.

And Danny still tried to teach him control.

"Full moon's coming. You don't want to hurt anyone."

They stood in a small clearing in the woods, far away from the path.

"Think like an animal." Danny said unhelpfully. "Feel yourself inside the body of a wolf, smell the air with your snout, grip the ground with your paws, balance yourself with your tail."

"I don't remember anything from the one time I was a wolf, how can I feel those?"

"Use your imagination. Stretch out your senses."

"This is fucked up."

"Just concentrate."

The cold air was biting. Ryan tried imagining a fur coat keeping him warm. He listened to the wind, breathed in the decay of leaves, the early winter smells and caught a whiff of Danny's musk. Ryan, remembering how he'd followed Lily through the side streets of the city, focused on Danny's scent. He breathed deep again, felt his animal senses take it all in.

Then, he was on all fours and running toward Danny. His eyes told him Danny was a man; his nose told him Danny was a wolf. Playfully, instinctively, he closed his teeth around Danny's ankle. Danny fell, held out his hands to ward off the attack.

With an effort, Ryan latched onto his consciousness and was suddenly human again. He was naked on top of Danny, his clothing in tatters where he had stood moments ago.

Adrenaline rushed through Ryan's body, animal instincts fought for control. He was drunk on it, he reveled in the feeling.

Maybe it was that rush, maybe it was animal nature taking over; maybe he just wouldn't admit that it was what he wanted. Whatever the reason he kissed Danny.

This time Ryan's tongue boldly slipped through Danny's parted lips. He rubbed up against Danny; the lithe body felt familiar and comfortable. He entwined his legs into Danny's, forgot the frigid air around him. Cold hands sought warmth, ran up the slim waist on both sides, slid under Danny's coat, under his shirt, to warm against the tight muscles. He felt arousal move through his body to his loins.

Danny struggled free of his coat, wrapped himself in Ryan's embrace. Ryan felt Danny's hesitant hands close over his back, and when Ryan didn't protest his hold became tighter, harder. He could trace Danny's left hand as it slid lower, grabbed his ass.

Ryan broke the kiss, rose and pulled off Danny's shirt, closed in again with renewed vigor. Danny's hand shifted from the ass to slide between their bodies and find Ryan now fully erect. Letting out a gasp, Ryan worked at releasing Danny's belt. A moment of struggle, then it was open and Danny was sliding his pants off.

Ryan found Danny hard against his tight briefs. He watched his own hand travel up a solid thigh and slide beneath the material; reach for the erection, caress it with tentative fingers and then grab hold of it. The underwear quickly became constricting and Ryan tore it off. Then they were pressed together again, lips and tongue meeting, hands exploring, massaging, stroking.

Danny wrapped his legs around Ryan's body, moved him lower. Ryan explored his way with his hands and slowly, carefully–exquisite pleasure roiling through his body–entered Danny. Danny moaned and Ryan pushed further. They locked together, moved together, one inside the other. They were one, one being, one creature, one animal.

They didn't speak afterwards. Ryan rolled off, shivering, suddenly cold. Danny reached out to him, but Ryan abruptly stood. They went back to the shack in silence. Ryan dressed awkwardly in fresh clothes and avoided Danny's eyes. They slept–at least, Danny slept. Ryan lay awake for hours, his back turned to Danny. Then when his restless mind drove him to it, he snuck out of the shack.

He wandered aimlessly, his mind too full of jumbled thoughts to string anything together. He left the park, heading down back streets until he found himself in a dark alley somewhere. It was early; the sky was still dark and the street lamps failed to reach their fingers of light into the alley, but he could see well enough.

It reminded him too much of the alley where he had found Lily. He turned to leave, but two figures had come up behind him. He'd been too lost in thought to notice. He didn't know how long they had trailed him through the dark streets.

"We'll have your wallet," one said.

"I don't have one."

"Well ain't that too bad." The man pulled out a knife.

Instinct kicked in. In an instant, he was a wolf. He snarled, lashed out with his teeth, ripped through the man's arm. One of the men tried to stab him, but his hide turned away the steel blade. He tore at flesh and above the yells he heard the other man turn and run.

Warm blood flowed around his teeth and he released the man too late. He backed away from the body; the second man he'd killed.

He became aware that he was not alone in the alley. A familiar wolf stood opposite him, Danny. They both transformed in the same moment; Danny stared, in disbelief.

"What–what did you do?"

Adrenaline still pumped through Ryan's veins. He burned with lust, ran forward, pushed Danny against a graffitied wall, closed in on lips with his mouth, groped with his hands.

At first Danny resisted, confused, repulsed. As Ryan's mind balked at forcing himself on Danny, Danny relented; kissed back, let himself be taken. Forcefully, Ryan hoisted Danny's legs up, pinned him to the wall, entered with ferocity, unbridled lust. Danny wrapped his legs tight around Ryan's body, pulled him in.

The next morning, Ryan woke alone in the shack that had unexpectedly become his home. Stepping outside, he sniffed the air for Danny's scent and careful not to transform, followed the trail through the trees.

Danny sat at the foot of a tree in the clearing where Ryan had first transformed. Ryan sat down beside him.

Danny was hugging his knees against his chest.

"You killed that guy."

Ryan shifted uncomfortably. "He attacked me."

"It shouldn't have happened. You shouldn't have been there."

"What do you mean?"

"You shouldn't be this, Ryan. *I* made you this. I let my control slip and I made you this."

Ryan's eyes softened, he reached out a hand awkwardly.

"Hey. You can't blame yourself. You didn't want this."

"I did want this," Danny said. "I couldn't control it but I was so happy when it happened. I was alone, struggling with this...this insanity. You made it bearable. But now *this*...it's my fault."

Ryan said nothing. He pulled Danny close, wrapped arms around him. They sat in silence, curled together under the trees.

Days passed. With Danny, Ryan found himself high on life. He had never felt so good, so right.

The city grew worse and Ryan grew better.

His first full moon arrived too soon. Ryan knew it was coming, but the changes it wrought were sudden, painful. Sun set and he was a beast. He barely clung onto his mind; instincts ruled him and he ran off into the trees while Danny was still transforming.

He found her quite by accident.

"You have something I need." The voice was feminine, cool and familiar. Ryan stopped, listened.

"I do?" Male and scared.

He inched closer, looked towards the figures wreathed in shadows. A pale young man; nervous and gangly. And opposite him, a caricature of her smile on her lips, Lily.

He growled, low in his throat, but they didn't hear.

He caught a glimpse of Lily's eyes. They flickered like embers in the dark, with the anticipation of something dreadful. Then a light burnt through the darkness, followed by a shout. Two police officers ran out of the night, one holding a flashlight, both holding guns. Ryan recognized Sergeant Torres from his photographs in the papers. The pale man squealed, panicked, turned to run, but the second cop was too fast. He tackled the figure to the ground.

Lily used the distraction and made a move. Unnatural speed lent to her by whatever had taken up residence inside her skin. Torres didn't notice, didn't see the flash of the blade she drew.

Ryan saw and without thinking he leapt. Barreling out of the darkness, he caught them all off guard. Torres spun in alarm and fired his gun. The shot found its mark–pain sliced through Ryan's leg, but he was intent on his target. He sunk teeth into her arm, Lily screamed and the blade somersaulted from her hand. The force of his impact knocked her to the ground and he held her there.

His instincts told him to run; he could almost smell the danger and Torres had already shot him once. Still, he couldn't release Lily.

Sergeant Torres inched forward.

Torres who had been at every major disturbance wherever the nightmares had seeped into the city, who would surely know that Lily was not what she seemed and that neither was Ryan. *He must know.*

Torres slipped a hand into a pocket. It emerged holding an amulet, cut with a strange runic design. He held it towards them, spoke a strange word, and Lily gasped, her body froze.

Ryan hesitated, refused to release his hold on her.

"She's immobilized," Torres said and Ryan wondered if he spoke to his partner or to him. He wanted to release Lily, but the animal he had become wanted to close its jaws on Lily's throat, drawn by the taste of blood in his mouth.

He closed his eyes, thought of Danny, thought of his human body, thought of human hands and feet, felt the memory of Danny's body under his own. When he opened his eyes, he was human. He was naked and his leg was bleeding.

"You're not what I've come to expect," Sergeant Torres said, holstering his gun. "You're the first of these nightmares that's saved my life." He bent to examine Lily's blade.

"So you do know." Ryan struggled to a sitting position and examined the wound. Weren't werewolves supposed to be immune to bullets?

Torres grimaced. "They're silver," he said, mirroring Ryan's thoughts. It's all that can hurt some of the things in the city these days."

Ryan glanced at Lily. "What did you do to her?"

"Used a cultic ritual to paralyze the demon within her."

"You were tracking her?"

Torres nodded. "Just one of the city's nightmares.

"So it *is* unnatural...the city, the nightmares?"

"Says the werewolf," Torres said dryly. "There are a few of us who are open to the truth."

"What will you do with..." Ryan threw a glance in Lily's direction.

"She was possessed," Torres said. "We'll have to exorcise the demon."

"What about...*her*?"

"She hasn't been herself, but once we get the demon out, she'll recover." He paused. "Do you know her?"

Ryan looked at Lily. Torres had confirmed it. She'd been possessed, hadn't been herself. They could be together again.

He shook his head, "No. I don't. Will you take care of her?" he asked. "When you're in a nightmare, you need a light in the darkness."

Torres studied him. Nodded.

"Good luck," Ryan said.

"You too."

Ryan released his control, let the moon take him and limped back into the trees. He went back to Danny, away from her, from the cops. Away from the city that had gone crazy, back to a light in the darkness.

NIGHT SWIMMING

RJ Bradshaw

I prefer swimming in my human form. The sensation of cool water streaming across my naked skin excites me, while water in my wolf fur is heavy. Night swimming is a solitary pastime for me and something I do regularly around 1:00 A.M. throughout the spring and summer. Beside the city's river at the end of 27th Street there are grey stones outlining what was once a small factory, now only ruins. Daisies peek out from behind crumbling walls and trees have sprouted up all around it to obstruct the city lights. The once great structure is always uninhabited at this late hour. It's here that I shed my clothes, stepping each night into the current of the river. My movements are slow as I revel in the water's touch, creeping up from my ankles to my cock, eventually reaching my smooth chest and the chestnut curls atop my head.

On that particular night, my peaceful swim was disturbed by some movement in the ruins. My sense of smell is always overwhelmed by the smoking paper mill upriver, but I could see the silhouette of a large dog sniffing about in the dark where my clothes lay, wagging its tail in glee.

Dogs are wary and often frightened of a werewolf's scent, but they have always shown fondness for me. I'm a dog groomer and even refer to some of them as friends. I think the odor of a straight male werewolf is more threatening to them than that of a gay one.

It was not the dog that concerned me. My concern lay with the owner or owners of the dog that would inevitably be trailing behind. Most humans do not share a lycanthrope's innate need for nakedness. I strained my water-logged ears in search of voices or snapping branches, but heard nothing besides the lapping of the river on the shore and the distant hum of city streets. Eventually the dog ran off and I assumed I was left again to swim in peace.

Such was not the case.

The stranger walked out from behind a crumbling grey wall on silent feet. When he stepped into the moonlight I could see he wore no clothing, his human nakedness both alarming and alluring. His slender body was dirty and much hairier than my own, a dark coat of fur covering his chest and belly. I suspected that he was a street person about to take a bath with no idea that I was there.

"Nice night," I said aloud to alert him of my presence, raising my dripping hand to wave, splashing the water as I let it fall.

He looked at me but did not respond, seemingly unembarrassed and unashamed of his nakedness. It became increasingly obvious as he stepped closer to the river that he had no intention of bathing elsewhere. My private reaction to this was somewhere between annoyance and anticipation.

"Was that your dog that I saw a little while ago?" I asked, suddenly very interested in hearing the man's voice. I looked at him while treading water, waiting for his response.

Once again he said nothing. Though I didn't get the impression he was trying to be rude. His posture was very relaxed, a little hunched even and I was certain he posed no threat. His movements suggested complete indifference, yet I could see in the dim light that he was looking at me inquisitively.

The features of his face and muscled body became clear as he reached the river to test the water and I decided my initial impression of him was wrong. He was far too healthy to be living on the streets of the city. Beneath his dirty exterior he was Caucasian, probably in his early twenties. His shoulder length hair and beard were very dark, perhaps black, and his cheekbones were higher than most humans. I guessed his eyes were dark as well, wondering if he'd swim over so I could get a closer look at them.

He scanned his surroundings and my eyes were drawn to his flaccid penis. It was uncut and not large, proportionate to his lean figure. I understood fully why his nudity did not embarrass him. The stranger was as beautiful and sculpted as any werewolf I have seen in human form and we take certain pride in our appearances. I do not usually find humans appealing, but my cock began to harden as I gazed upon him, thankful my excitement was hidden in murky water. If I could have smelled him above the stench of the paper mill, I was sure my feelings would be different.

When he finally waded deeper into the river, his steps were nearly as slow as my own. An expression of pleasure danced across the stranger's face as the water climbed up his legs to his waist and he smiled over at me before diving beneath the waves. I continued to tread water, wondering where he would surface and why he chose to swim here despite the lack of privacy.

He reappeared only a few feet to my left, glancing in my direction with a sly smile. The scent that leapt from his washed skin filled my nostrils and suddenly I understood.

"You're a werewolf!" I exclaimed. "The dog..."

"Y-yes," he said with a quiet grin. "And so-o are you."

The words were stumbled over as though he hadn't spoken for a long time. His voice was deep and satisfying.

"But, how...?"

"Y-yes?"

"How is it that I haven't seen you before?"

My astonishment came from the fact that the lycanthropes of this city are tightly knit. I knew all of them by sight and most of them by name. We tend to keep to our own. Several urban werewolves are business owners who employ other werewolves like me. The packs here do not compete as they once would have before the city was built. We even have our own employment agency.

Though humans are aware that lycanthropes live amongst them, there are still those who would gladly see us dead. We are accustomed to keeping our nature hidden.

I had never met a werewolf that was not part of my community and the stranger did not have the scent of any of the werewolf packs I knew.

"I just came to the city," he responded.

His resonant speech was increasingly more confident and so was his smile. His eyes–as I had guessed–were rich and dark, but twinkled also with mischief.

He motioned to dive, filling my nostrils again with his scent before disappearing beneath the water and again I gasped in amazement. The stranger bore not only the aroma of a werewolf, but distinctly that of a gay werewolf. Queer werewolves are a rarity in my community.

All lycanthropes accept homosexuality without reservation, our unique odor revealing our sexuality at a young age. Despite our preference for the same gender, gay werewolves remain obligated to mate in order to strengthen our numbers. A queer male is often coupled with a queer female for a short time until conception is achieved, then are free to go their separate ways. I had already mated.

My thoughts were interrupted by the stranger's splashing, reminding me of my bulging manhood. He was farther away when he surfaced, close enough to the shore to stand up and display his black-furred chest, droplets trickling down his face and torso. I was blushing furiously.

"I'm Todd," he said with a delicious smirk.

"Joseph," I responded, quieter than intended.

I realized that our names would have carried little importance had we first met in wolf form. The conversational habits of wolves are far different from that of humans.

"Would you like to go for a run Joseph?"

"Su-ure."

The word had caught in my mouth and it had become me who stammered. My absent-minded agreement to run with Todd puzzled me, as did his invitation.

Turning from me, he splashed his way toward the shore. I tried not to stare at his muscled ass as he emerged from the river and vanished behind a broken wall. I knew that he was changing into a wolf and hurried from the water so I too could change without him witnessing the impression he had made. However, what takes me several minutes took him mere seconds, the black wolf bounding around the corner before I could go into hiding. He stopped abruptly, unabashedly gawking at my erection. He wore an impossible wolfish grin and I hastily vanished behind a wall to make the change.

The change is always done in private, even between lycanthropes of the same pack. I was glad that the black wolf respected this unspoken law.

Knowing that the dampness would transfer to my fur, I wished there had been time to dry my dripping body. As my hands and feet morphed into paws, I pondered Todd's transformation.

Changing between animal and human is painless and requires little time, yet I had never known a werewolf to accomplish it so quickly.

He was wagging his tail when I rounded the crumbling stones, studying my wolf form with apparent approval. His black fur was long and badly matted in spots, his dark eyes more human than lupine, and his scent a mixture of eagerness and lust. He was magnificent.

Keen to run, he leapt passed me into the trees, I vaulting after him. We made our way along the river, its treed shores undisturbed by city development, the perfumes of wildflowers overpowering the stench of the paper mill. The black wolf's body communicated his elation, speech unnecessary. The wind dried me as it whipped through my chestnut fur and I realized I hadn't been running with another werewolf for many months. The black wolf was larger than me and much faster, stopping often to allow me to catch up. On one of these occasions, I pounced on him playfully and we wrestled, his scent dizzying me.

Nearly two hours had passed when we returned to the ruins, exhilarated and panting, acquainted with each other in a way that human interaction would never have allowed. We snuggled in each other's fur for a long while, the black wolf nibbling at my left ear affectionately, my tongue softly licking his muzzle. His warmth was soothing and there was no hesitation in our closeness.

An hour before the sun rose, the black wolf stood up, scurrying to the other side of the wall. His change took longer than before and I could hear faint murmurs of struggle. When he returned nearly ten minutes later in human form, he held several daisies in his right hand. I wagged my tail, gazing up at him with speculation as he scratched the curly fur on the back of my neck. Being touched by human hands in my wolf form was new for me and oddly pleasurable. It was with reluctance that I rounded the grey stones to make the change.

Once more I questioned Todd's transformation. His shift into wolf form had been astoundingly quick, his conversion into human form far slower than my own.

When I came out of hiding, Todd's eyes moved up and down my body hungrily and I felt my cock again begin to quiver, curiosity diverted.

"Are those for me?" I asked sheepishly, pointing at the daisies he held at his side.

"Nah, they're for my mom."

"Oh."

"Of course they're for you!" He laughed.

Todd handed them to me and I thanked him shyly. I neglected to mention that daisies were my favorite flower, one of the reasons I frequent the old factory. During the years I had been going there I had always been alone. Though Todd's presence had been unexpected, I was enjoying sharing that part of my life with him.

I had an idea then. "Grab your clothes," I said. "There's somewhere I want to take you."

The keys for the dog parlor were in my pants pocket and I had an overwhelming urge to introduce him to the dogs that we had boarded there overnight. Most werewolves detest canines, but I am very content in my profession. Many dogs display remarkable intelligence and I have learned some phrases of their simple dialect. I was sure Todd would appreciate their personalities as I do.

"I don't have any clothes," he answered.

"Where did you leave them?" I questioned.

"No, I mean I don't have any. I spend most of my time in wolf form."

"What about your job? You must have clothes for work."

"I don't have a job," he responded with satisfaction.

I didn't really comprehend what he was saying and I chuckled. "Well, what do you do then?"

His response held a hint of growling annoyance. "I hunt, I provide for my pack."

"But..."

My parents had told me stories about werewolves that still live in the wild, but I hadn't considered the possibility that I might one day meet one. My pack had never left the city. The city is our territory.

"Don't go getting all city-dweller on me," he said heavily. "I know how werewolves in the city live. I know that you work for survival and wear fancy clothes and drink cocktails and watch television in your houses. I spent part of my childhood in a city to learn how to read and write and speak in human tongue. I was given a choice and I chose to live with my pack in a den, hunting for survival. We run freely in forests and open fields and I won't apologize for that."

It became clear why Todd's shift into a wolf had been so rapid and why he had strained when returning to his human shape.

"I'm sorry," I said quietly. "I wasn't trying to offend you. It's just, I've never met anyone like you." I paused for a moment. "But if you don't like the city, why are you here?"

"Isn't that obvious?" he muttered.

"No, not really," I answered honestly.

"I came here looking for you."

"Me?"

"A companion, Joseph. Someone I can spend my life with." His eyes met mine and there was longing in their darkness.

"But I live here," I stammered.

"I want you to live with me," he stated simply.

"I don't know how to hunt."

As a youngster, my friends and I would clumsily stalk birds and squirrels in parks, but there was no necessity for hunting in the city. Urban packs had largely abandoned their wilder instincts, choosing to purchase meat at food markets.

"Every werewolf can hunt," he countered. "I'll teach you."

"But I live here!"

I didn't know what else to say. My mind was fumbling with the possibilities, the idea of leaving my territory and pack terrifying me.

"What if I lived in the city for half the year?" he asked.

He spoke the words with a self-assured smile as though he sensed my defenses were crumbling like the stones that surrounded us.

"You would do that?" I replied.

"Of course," he said calmly, "but we'll have to spend the cold season with my pack. Game is scarce in the winter. They'll need me."

"We've only just met, Todd."

He laughed then, an infectious laugh that I wanted to hear again and again.

"It's not funny," I said without conviction.

"Use your sniffer, Joseph!" he howled blissfully. "I knew you were my life mate as soon as I smelled your clothes and you knew the same thing when I swam out to you. Don't try to deny it."

"Maybe."

"I saw the evidence, remember?"

"How could I forget?" My response was bashful.

I knew he was right. I had been through werewolf dating rituals with several males from the urban lycanthrope community. A couple of months earlier I had been on a date with Robbie, a werewolf from one of the city's most influential packs. He and his family own nearly half of the lycanthrope companies, including the dog grooming business that I work for. We met at a restaurant frequented by queer humans, intentionally avoiding werewolf dens to prevent gossip in case our ritual was fruitless. Dinner was pleasant and he invited me to run with him in the park afterwards. Running together is a common practice shared by werewolf couples, gay and straight alike.

Robbie had smelled of panic, indicating that he was desperate to find his match, an emotion I understood all too clearly. I knew as well that I was not the mate he sought. The more time I spent with him, the more unattractive his scent was to me, as mine was to him. I could not ignore my instincts as he did. I accompanied him to the park but left him to run alone.

Todd's scent, however, was enticing and inspired unruly desire. If I were never to smell his skin again, I realized I would be empty. When I had agreed to run with Todd, I had in truth given myself to him completely. As I examined his naked body, mischievous eyes and bearded grin, I had no choice but to love him.

"You'll have to get a job," I told him matter-of-factly.

He nodded his agreement. "Where do you work?"

"I'm a dog groomer," I responded with obvious pride.

"Okay, I'll do that then."

I laughed at that, pleased with his reaction. "I think I'll need to groom *you* before you can work anywhere."

"Sounds fun," he retorted with a wink.

"And where will you live?"

"With you of course."

As an urban werewolf, I am expected to live with my pack, providing for them financially until I am paired. Two of my sisters had already left, but I remained in my parent's home along with my youngest sibling.

"I live with my parents and sister," I told him.

"Can't wait to meet them!" he replied triumphantly. "We'll live with them until we have our own place."

I wondered what my mother and father would think of that.

"And I have a son and daughter," I added. "They live with their mother, but I visit them all the time."

He quieted for a time then and I deduced that his pack's customs differed from my own. His silence was worrisome.

Finally he spoke. "They'll have to visit us when we winter with my pack. It's not all that far."

I couldn't believe how carefree he was about everything.

"I'm glad we got that settled," he said with finality.

"Well no, not real-"

He kissed me swiftly before I could finish, and any skepticism I had was lost.

Our first kiss was flawless, his tongue sliding effortlessly between my lips. His muscled arms embraced me, flesh tingling as his fingers caressed my lower back. I soon felt his warm erection pressed against me, my breath quickening as his teeth bit gently into my lower lip. My hands released the daisies and I fondled his ass, pulling his naked body tightly to my own, wanting him wholly, but knowing we must leave.

"We have to go," I sighed unhappily, pulling my lips from his.

The sun was newly rising, glinting on the river's surface. Before long, joggers would be taking to the scenic trails that followed its banks.

"Damn city," he grumbled, his eyes alight with lust. "We wouldn't have this problem where I live."

"You live here now, remember?" I retorted with a giggle, my hands still stroking his backside.

His tone became serious. "I want to take you there before the cold season," he said, looking into my eyes. "We don't have to stay, but I would like you to meet my pack."

"I know," I said with a smile. "I was going to suggest the same thing."

"I'm glad."

Todd's transition into city life would be very difficult for him, perhaps more difficult than I could imagine. His willingness to stay with me strengthening the newfound love and respect I felt for him. I was sure my learning to live in the wild would be equally challenging, but recognized with alarming clarity that Todd and I would endure those hardships.

"I guess I should get you some clothes," I remarked.

"I don't want any. Not yet at least."

"I like you naked too," I chuckled, "but I'm not sure what the rest of the city will think."

"I'll change into my wolf form," he replied. "I'll be your dog."

"You might pass for a dog in the dark, Todd, but not now."

"I'll be an exotic breed," he chortled.

"What will I use for a leash?" I asked grinning. "I can't just let a wild wolf roam the city without a leash."

"Use your belt," he said with a smirk, unwrapping his arms from my body.

"That's ridiculous."

"I think it sounds kind of kinky. You might like it," he commented impishly. "I know I will."

Before I had the chance to respond, Todd crouched onto the ground and my eyes widened in disbelief.

"What are you doing!?" I yelped.

The transformation was almost instantaneous. Todd's pale bare skin retreated into the black fur of the wolf with ease. Despite the taboo, I could not bring myself to look away as his feet and hands shifted into paws, his face elongating. When the change was complete, I gaped at him in astonishment. His ears were pulled back, eyes searching my expression for approval.

I slowly lifted a shaky hand and rested it atop his head.

"Thank you," I said, the black wolf wagging his tail happily.

By allowing me to watch him change, Todd had revealed his most intimate self. I had, of course, never seen a werewolf shift and could not have known that it is visually as beautiful and natural as it feels. I hoped someday to summon the courage to overlook that part of my upbringing and return his generosity.

The black wolf scampered around me while I dressed, snorting his excitement. I buttoned my pants and removed my belt, looping it loosely around his neck with a grin. Stroking his fur gently, I gazed once more at the river, already anticipating our next swim together.

"Ready?" I asked turning to gather up the daisies he had picked.

He nodded his furred head. Side by side we walked through the trees toward 27th Street, enveloped in the smells and sounds of the city that wakened.

QUEER WOLF

IN THE SEEONEE HILLS

Erica Hildebrand

My name is Claire.

Four months ago Jules told me she was a werewolf. We were already sleeping together. She should have known better, but I should have been more careful.

Lycanthropy, unless you're born with it, is debilitating. Contracting it is easier than you think, even when you're just experimenting with some very rough play in the bedroom.

It's all in the bite.

I went to the clinic–not just any clinic, *the* clinic, if you're connected enough to find it–to get tested. The clinic's only open at night, catering to the sensitivities of the bulk of their clientele.

The test was just a smokescreen, my way of trying to cross paths with the Seeonee Pack.

I sat by myself, reading a pamphlet on lycanthropy. Jules had sworn to me it wasn't a disease, but she'd been born with it. She could control it. I couldn't. So, every full moon, her pack pumped me full of sedatives and muscle relaxants to keep me from changing. Good stuff, too; the Rothschild Pack ran a pharmaceutical company.

The clinic's pamphlet talked about smells and instincts, about tapping into the primitive brain of the human psyche, all neatly arranged in bullet point factoids.

A nasty, mechanical smell drifted from where the vampires sat, reeking of preservatives and rotten fruit.

I closed my eyes and focused on smells coming from the other side of the clinic instead, smells that reminded me of childhood trips to my grandparents' farm: muddy creekwater and cedar wood shavings. Comforting and familiar. The smells of a pack.

A clean, earthy smell came closer. Cinnamon, woodsmoke, and a November breeze. The plastic cushions of the bench shifted as someone sat beside me.

I opened my eyes and flinched when I saw how close she'd

sat. She was early twenties, same as me. Her auburn hair had that short, tousled, bedhead look that I was pretty sure had taken an hour to style. Her amber eyes reminded me of white wine. Moon earrings jingled from her lobes, matching the long necklaces that draped over the cleavage her spaghetti-strap top displayed.

Her face dimpled with a devil-may-care smile and I instantly felt small and pathetic by comparison. She was gorgeous and I realized I was staring. My face heated with a blush and I instinctively looked away.

"Hi, I'm Ginny Donnelly. You're all alone; would you like to come sit with us?" She gestured to the group from whom the earthy smells emanated.

"Please," I said, and introduced myself.

"We're the Seeonee," she said. "Named so for the Jungle Book."

"Never read it," I said. I hoped I didn't show reaction, even though my heart skipped a beat. I'd found them.

She tilted her head to one side, hair and earrings tumbling in the appropriate direction. "Really? You should. It's one of my favorites."

Her pack stood as we approached, and they all pressed in around me, touching my shoulders, shaking hands. Ginny pressed me forward to the only packmember still sitting, an extremely pregnant woman of about fifty, golden trinkets interwoven in her salt-and-pepper hair.

"Mae is our pack leader," Ginny explained. "Her obstetrician works here."

She turned to Mae. "Mom, this is Claire."

"A new friend, Geneva?" I detected a note of criticism, but Mae reached her hand out and pulled me down next to her on the seat. "I smell you're new to the wolf magic. Thankfully you don't look harmed."

Catching lycanthropy was normally a violent act, like getting pregnant by way of rape, the pamphlet in my hand had told me.

"N-no, nothing like that," I said. "It was an accident." Should I be so nervous? What happened to a lone wolf when she encroached on a pack's territory? The Rothschilds had kept me intentionally in the dark.

"Who infected you?" Ginny asked, sitting down on my other side.

Jules had instructed me to be honest with them. About anything except the plan. "My girlfriend."

There was a subtle shift in Ginny's posture. "What's her name? We might know her."

"Um," I said, "Julia Straus."

Mae and Geneva didn't know her, but they asked the others. A boy with spiked hair nodded. "Yeah," he said, "I've heard of her. She's with the Rothschild Pack."

Mae grumbled beside me. "Oh, them."

I looked at Ginny, feigning ignorance.

"They're a territorial rival of ours," she explained. "They've started encroaching on Seeonee hunting ground."

I absently watched the vampires across the room, not wanting to betray that I already knew all of that. My ears and nose, however, were busy sifting out the individuals of the Seeonee beyond Ginny's clean autumnal scent.

"Does that make me a Rothschild?"

"Nah," Ginny said, patting me on the back. I roused at the touch but stayed quiet. "You're free to do as you want."

Was I crazy? Why had I agreed to do this?

I was only dimly aware of a gothed-up vampire hissing at me from across the room.

"Never mind them," Mae said quietly. "We don't associate with that kind."

I didn't lower my gaze from the vampire staring back at me; a cold oily feeling poured down my spine. I'd never been a confrontational person, but I didn't break eye contact with him, not until I heard the nurse call my name, crisp and clear.

When I stood, Ginny stood with me. "Can I go in with you?"

I nodded. We went into the back room where a nurse in scrubs took my height and weight, blood pressure, and a blood sample.

Ginny took out a length of looped string from her pocket and we played Cat's Cradle while we waited, sitting cross-legged on the exam bed. She wore her sleeves over her palms, the same way I did with the cuffs of my hoodie, and I liked that about her.

No, I told myself, *don't get sappy*. The Rothschilds told me these people were snobs. They hated anyone who wasn't a natural-born. I didn't know why Ginny was being nice to me, but it didn't matter. I wasn't here to make a friend.

"So, you come here often?" I asked.

She laughed. "That's your pick-up line? I'm disappointed."

I blushed furiously. "No, that's not what–"

"I know," she said, amused. "It just sounded funny. Yes, this is our one-stop shop for healthcare. We have to put up with that awful vampire smell but at least this way we can take note of which ones are in our territory. So, your mate let you go alone?"

"What?"

"Julia. She didn't come with you to the clinic," she said. Her expression turned serious.

"She's not my mate," I said, suddenly defensive.

"But you said she's your girlfriend."

"Well, yeah. Sure, I guess."

"Oh," she said and avoided my gaze. "I'm sorry, I just assumed. I guess it's a lupine thing. Sometimes I forget it's not human nature to mate for life–I mean, you have to admit, people are flakes."

"I guess," I said. She *was* a snob. I suddenly hated that she was being nice to me.

When they gave me the test results back and started explaining options and lifestyle changes, I didn't understand why it hit me so hard. Maybe I'd held out some fool's hope that this test would tell me the first had been a false-positive. That I was normal after all. I don't know. All I knew was that Jules had done it to me. By accident, but it happened all the same.

I questioned helping the Rothschilds take over the territory. They hadn't told me what I was supposed to do, exactly, except that I had to be among the Seeonee when I changed for the first time.

I had a week to get used to the idea.

My name is Geneva.
I carry in my veins the last legacy of Ireland's wolves since Oliver Cromwell's campaign of slaughter destroyed the packs all those centuries ago.

We Donnellys aren't strictly Irish, not anymore. Donnelly

blood mingled with the American timber wolf and eventually the pack changed its name from Donnelly to Seeonee. I'm third-generation. Also, my mom's Italian.

Even though a Donnelly bite can infect, we protect people who live in our territory. That includes culling the number of infected weres in the area, lest they run around spreading mayhem.

The problem started when Mae got pregnant, around the time my dad died, and her wolf magic went dormant. It only made sense that our rivals would try to murder the Seeonee's alpha in her vulnerable state. We had a choice. We could spend nine months wearing ourselves out worrying that at any moment we'd be attacked, wage fights and risk vampiric infection or death.

Or we could kill a human.

The human community would respond with all the fury of modern technology and send all of us–including our enemies–underground. I'd argued long and hard over the implications of the humans hunting us and our cousins the wolves, but I was outvoted.

Mae suggested that if we could get an outsider to do the deed, we wouldn't have to sacrifice any pack members. We had no control over vampires but we could dupe a hapless infected werewolf, serve them up to the humans and rid ourselves of a potential troublemaker all at once.

It was the will of the pack. That's why, against my better judgment, I went to the clinic in search of a patsy.

And I hated myself for finding Claire.

The clinic gave me some pills. Some sort of suppressant that was nowhere near as strong as the Rothschild sedatives... which I was no longer taking. At the next full moon, the change would hit me no matter what.

A few days later Ginny, who'd gotten my cell number at the clinic, called and asked me to meet her for lunch. We met at a sandwich stop.

"How's your appetite?" she asked.

I picked at my salami but otherwise didn't eat. "Must be nerves," I said.

"No. It's those pills they give you."

"What the hell else can I do?" I asked, suddenly irritated. "You're natural-born, I'm infected. It's different for me."

I'd been reading as much on the subject as I could get my hands on. Jules had, of course, loaned me some books, but she was a natural-born too and couldn't understand any more than Ginny could.

"I'm afraid," I said. "The nurses said it's going to hurt worse than anything I've ever felt. They say I'm not going to be able to control it at all."

With three days until the full moon, the lunar cycle was already twisting my insides like carnal PMS, making me snappish. I had no idea what I'd be like if I wasn't on the pills. Feral, maybe.

"Your hormones are all misaligned," Ginny said. "Those drugs are messing up your emotions."

"You natural-borns can control it, right? The change?"

"It's hard to explain." Ginny munched on a potato chip before continuing. "We feel the pull of the moon just as the tides do. But we don't go mad. And aside from the moon, we can change whenever we want." She shrugged. "It's easier if you've got other wolves around. A pack to submit to."

"I'm afraid," I said again and hell if I didn't mean it.

She reached over the table and took my hand in hers, offering a little smile. "I already talked to my pack and they agreed to help for your first change. We'll go into the woods, somewhere private, don't worry."

I shrank back and the wolf behind my eyes flattened its ears in embarrassment. I didn't want a bunch of calm, collected werewolves watching me totally lose it. I'd never be able to look them in the eye. But then I remembered, this was what Jules had asked me to do.

Ginny arched her eyebrow. "Do you trust me?"

I don't even know you, I thought. But the wolf inside me wanted to say yes, trust her. Could instinct tell me if I was going to get hurt? Could instinct protect me?

"Fine," I said with a sigh. "Let's do it."

"Good. You couldn't be safer, I promise you that. Here, I brought you something. It helps take my mind off things whenever I'm nervous." She took something out of her satchel and put it on the table between us. A trade paperback of Rudyard Kipling.

On the bus ride home, I read about the wolves of the Seeonee hills, who called themselves the Free People and protected the jungle's laws. I imagined Ginny's family was the same. Whatever the Rothschild Pack had planned, if it was supposed to hurt these people, I couldn't do it. I didn't want this.

Jules *hurt* me. She *gave* me this, put this on *my* shoulders. I didn't want anything from her. I didn't want to contribute to her plans, either.

So I called her that night and backed out.

When I tried to sleep, later, I heard distant howls with my increasingly sensitive ears. They sounded so sad.

Behind my eyes, the wolf responded to the terrible yearning brought on by the sounds. I wanted to empty my lungs and cry out yes, I want to join you. The wolf wondered if one such howl belonged to Geneva Donnelly.

Outside my window, the moon waxed.

I sent Claire a text the next morning letting her know where to meet me. Then I spent the day arguing with Mae, asserting that we couldn't use Claire for our scheme. But my mom had already found us a victim, currently bound and gagged in her garage.

The plan was to take Claire and the victim into the woods, let Claire change and then ravage him. As an infected she wouldn't remember the event, and we could make up whatever story we liked.

But she wasn't just a nameless werewolf to me, not anymore. She was alone and frightened. One more victim of a pack that didn't take care of their own.

I'd started hating myself for even considering the plan. Of course I wanted to protect my mom, but the more I thought about it, the less I wanted to kill anyone. And I didn't want to do it at Claire's expense.

I hung up with Mae just before dinnertime, when Claire was due to arrive at my place. I had invited Claire to spend the night with me, afraid that she might change early. The first change had a general twenty-four hour window, but any more specific than that was a guessing game and I could tell she didn't want to be alone.

I didn't share any of this with Mae, who wanted me to keep an eye on her and bring her to the Seeonee meeting at tomorrow's full moon.

I'd baked a ziti dish but I was too conflicted to have much of an appetite. Claire only poked at hers, too. She wore her dark shoulder-length hair down and it had been brushed to the point of silk. Her dress flattered her figure and she pulled off a casual, girl-next-door charm even when she was obviously nervous about the full moon.

I couldn't put her in harm's way.

We sat on my balcony after dinner and sipped coffee, looking out at the hedgerow and the patch of woods beyond.

"I can open a bottle of wine," I offered.

Claire shook her head. "I already feel strange. I don't want to risk lowering my guard or anything."

I nodded and we sat in silence for a time, swaying idly in the wooden porch swing I'd hung from the supports of the upstairs neighbor's balcony.

"I don't think I should be around the Seeonee when I change," she said in a quiet voice. She bit her bottom lip and I couldn't help but stare at her mouth, the softness of her skin.

"That's a good idea," I said, mildly distracted. We could avoid the Seeonee. They could just kill Mae's victim themselves and leave us out of it.

She gave me a sidelong glance, her dark eyes suspicious. "Why do you think so?"

I sipped my coffee. If I told her the truth she'd disappear on me. "I just think it's prudent. Why do you?"

Claire hesitated before answering. "I don't want anyone to get hurt."

It dawned on me then that there was a chance she'd be able to harm me. The Rothschild Pack carried the blood of the red Eurasian wolves. She might be a bit smaller than me, but we would be on par as predators. It was too much to hope for her to remain conscious through the ordeal.

"I don't see how I can live with this," she said, picking at a loose thread on my sleeve. I was very aware of her proximity.

"This is what you are now."

"But I've got some sort of sickness, isn't that what you think? That I'm going to be one of those monsters like the kind that terrorize London in the movies?"

I bit my tongue. It *was* close to what I thought.

"I don't see how you can be so hypocritical," she said. "Natural-borns are the ones who give people this sickness in the first place."

A growl threatened to rise in my throat. I realized I felt the moon's pull, too. "So you're just going to go through life believing you're a victim?"

"I wasn't *born* this way."

"*I* was. I've been one all my life. That isn't my fault." I took a deep breath, and my nostrils flared as I inhaled the natural perfume of her skin. "It's just who I am."

Instead of answering, Claire leaned towards me and pressed those soft, pretty lips against mine. Desire fluttered deep within me. I wanted to touch her, to taste her. But I couldn't do this, not until I was sure I could protect her.

Abruptly I stood and went in through the open patio door, putting some distance between us, and set my cup down on the kitchen island. I turned the faucet on.

"If you have kids," I called over my shoulder, desperately wanting to change the subject, "they'll be natural-borns like me. That isn't so bad."

I plunged my hands into the cold water and splashed my face and neck until my roiling blood calmed. My breath came shallow. The water only momentarily cooled the heat of my skin.

I toweled off, waited a moment, took a deep breath and when I heard no response I returned to the balcony. "Claire, listen. I'm sorry. I–"

Claire was doubled over in pain, clutching her stomach with both arms. I rushed to her and put my hand on her back; the muscles beneath her thin dress shivered and I cursed under my breath.

It was starting.

"Come on," I said, and pulled her to her feet. She needed to be in the natural world for this. I took her through the apartment, hoping I could get her down the stairs and out into the hedgerow. Halfway out the door I thought to grab my digital camera. Claire cried and moved slowly from the pain. I dragged her across the lawn, sparing a quick glance to make sure no one saw us, then pulled her into the forest. At the first clearing I dropped everything and started stripping off her clothes, thinking she'd not want to ruin them.

Her skin rippled with spasms.

As I yanked her dress off she cried and two sickening pops of bone and tendon signaled the forcible shift of her shoulder joints.

"It's all right," I said, stroked her hair and backed away.

She writhed on the ground, crying and begging me to make the pain stop. My heart tripped; I wanted to comfort her, but I couldn't. Not now. I set the camera to start recording, checked the angle of the shot and balanced it on a low maple branch. She'd need to see this. Through the viewfinder I saw her snout elongate and the fur grow. I stripped off my own clothes.

Her pheromones filled my nose with wafts of pine boughes and pumpkin seeds and something else, something I hadn't noticed before when her human scent masked it, something that triggered when she changed.

Some sort of drug.

The change came easy to me so close to the full moon. My shoulders dislocated and rolled forward, my nose popped, my insides burned with the familiar fire. It hurt, but I was used to it and I knew I had control. Claire didn't. The wolf magic consumed me as my vision blurred and diminished, focus going to my ears and nose. Claire's transformation was nearly complete; she was not quite a common wolf. Her fur was thicker, richer, and ruddy.

I put my big paws on the leafy ground beneath me and stood straight and tall. I was a daughter of alphas, and the wolf magic raged within me as I watched Claire, my instincts howling: *Infected. Dangerous. Stranger.* I moved forward, intending to press her into submission. She was smaller than me and I smelled fear and anger and insanity brought on by the drug. Still beneath the drug she smelled, to my utter surprise, natural.

Once she shook off the pain, Claire focused on me with fangs bared and lunged for my throat. She only caught ruff and as I recoiled she caught my leg in her teeth and a lightning bolt of agony ran up my foreleg. I lashed out in reflex and latched on the sensitive flesh of her neck, forcing her to the ground.

Despite her fury, she was disoriented and confused, though her snarls could have woken hell itself.

I held her there for what seemed like hours.

As she metabolized the drug and eventually grew docile, I wondered whether my family had engineered this unnatural aggression in her.

She whined and I finally let her be.

We sniffed each other, as is the way of wolf introduction, and she bent her head and nuzzled my injured leg by way of apology.

I watched the video recording of my change for the third time. I didn't remember any of it.

I sat curled up on the floor of Ginny's bedroom in a borrowed robe, fresh from a much-needed bath, my back against her bed. I winced at our ruthlessness, and rubbed my throat with a shaky hand.

My body ached everywhere. The wolf behind my eyes was thankfully silent.

"How long were we like this?" I asked, my voice hoarse.

"Just the night," Ginny said, sitting across from me with her back against a wall, hair disheveled from her shower. She'd bandaged her arm in gauze.

"I don't know what to say. Your arm–"

"Will heal," she said and glanced at the clock on the nightstand. The sky outside glowed pink with the coming dawn. "I have to get you out of here before tonight. The Seeonee will be angry."

She'd told me about the drug she'd smelled that had sent me into a rage. She'd also told me about her pack's plans to make me murder a human.

"Ginny," I said, but I turned my head and buried my face against her comforter. I wanted to tell her the truth. She'd already had the chance to kill me, and to trick me, and she hadn't done either.

I heard her come closer, felt a hand on my arm and when I

lifted my head she sat beside me. Wordlessly she pulled me against her and I laid my head on her shoulder.

And I talked.

I told her about my infection, about Jules, about the Rothschilds' plan to overthrow the Seeonee, about my role in it. I guessed they'd administered the drugs when they sedated me at full moons, testing on me, planning all along to make me go insane and hurt someone. I opened up to her about my fears of dealing with it alone, about what a mistake I'd made in agreeing to help the Rothschilds and how horrible I felt.

"If you hate me," I said, "I understand."

After a moment of tense silence, Ginny said, "Likewise."

Then she stiffened against me.

"My mother," she said. "That's who they wanted you to attack. That's why they feralized you with drugs."

"Well," I said, sitting up straight, "I won't be there to do it. You told me the drugs got flushed out of my system."

She nodded. "You smelled clean, after."

I touched her bandaged hand. "I didn't...didn't *give* you anything, did I?"

At that, she looked at me with her chardonnay eyes and flashed her dimpled smile. "No." She assumed an Irish brogue. "If anything, I pray you swallowed some honest Donnelly blood and put your spirit to rights."

I laughed with the relief of broken tension.

She laughed, too.

And then she kissed me.

The moment froze in tableau as that soft mouth claimed mine. Ginny hesitated, as if unsure. After my surprise subsided, I nudged my lips against hers, seeking. Accepting that as permission, she kissed with renewed fervor, parted my lips with her tongue and drew me into her lap.

I ran my hands through her disheveled wet hair and traced the features of her face with my lips, moving towards her neck. She opened my robe and slid her hands in, cool against my warm skin, sending electric shudders along my flesh.

I pulled back long enough to peel off her t-shirt. Straddling her, I slid my hands down her breasts and brushed their nipples with my palms, drawn to her body warmth. Her hands caressed my ribs. I shivered as her hands slid lower, tracing my hips. Her own thigh pressed up between my legs and I let out a little gasp of pleasure.

Ginny rolled me and laid me down on my back, parted the robe and pressed her breasts and stomach down against mine. She nudged my head to the side and wrapped her lips around my earlobe as her hand slipped between my thighs, her hair spilling across my face, our heartbeats pressed against each other.

"Oh, yes," I panted, clinging to her shoulders, "yes."

Her breath trembled against my ear and then she was inside me, eclipsing all other sensation. Moaning against her shoulder, I wrapped my legs around her waist as her careful rhythm built a slow mounting pressure within me.

I arched my back and drew her hand in, deeply, her body radiating warmth against mine. The sensation crested, then faltered, lingering.

"Claire," she whispered. "Oh, Claire."

Listening to her voice, so genuine, I surrendered to her. Ecstasy blossomed and exploded within me. The world fell away.

When it passed, she held me, fingertips exploring the contours of my body. I'd never dreamed I would feel so safe at the hands of a wolf.

After a moment, I took a deep breath and said, "Now let me touch you."

She smiled, nipped at my throat. "What's your hurry?" She pulled back to gaze in my eyes. "Think I'm letting you go anytime soon?"

My heart swelled. I answered with a kiss, long and slow.

I laid my ear against the spot between Claire's breasts and listened to her heartbeat, letting it lull me. She dozed on the carpet, her fingers tangled in my hair.

I recognized then and there, watching her sleeping, that I wanted her as my mate. There wasn't a doubt in my mind. I didn't care that she wasn't a natural-born; she had smelled perfectly natural to me.

Before long I couldn't lie still any more and in the afternoon I returned to idle stroking along her skin, warm against my own. She eventually squirmed and made little half-asleep noises. I set my mouth to work rousing her as pleasantly as I could, her legs parting as she realized what I was up to.

Suddenly alert, her nails dug into my shoulderblade.

"What time is it?"

"Who cares?"

Claire opened her dark eyes to look at me, but they slid closed again as I pressed a palm to her cheek and she turned her head to kiss my fingers.

Then she started to sit up. "The full moon," she said.

I rested my hand on her chest. "You changed last night. Don't worry, it won't happen again so soon."

"But the Seeonee think I'm going to be there," she said. "And the Rothschild Pack knows I won't."

I froze. "You told them you weren't going?"

Her expression turned worrisome and I reminded myself she wasn't to blame for this.

She said, "I told them I wasn't working with them anymore. But what if they send someone else?"

"What are their plans?"

"I don't know. They kept me in the dark."

I started to disentangle myself from the blankets.

"I should get to them," I said, glancing at my clock on the nightstand. We'd been here all day, I thought ruefully. Evening approached.

Claire sat upright, wearing a pained expression. She was still sore from her change. "I'm going with you."

"You shouldn't," I said, pulling on my underwear. "I haven't talked to the Seeonee yet. They think you're coming to play their scapegoat."

"I'm not going to let you face this alone," she said.

I opened my mouth to speak but flinched at a loud crash. Someone kicked in my front door and just as quickly, footsteps sounded in the living room. I pushed Claire to the floor behind me, but as soon as the shadows appeared in the bedroom doorway something stung my thigh and I looked down at a tranquilizer dart.

The dart, the room, and the advancing figures spun out of focus as the ground rushed up to meet me.

They'd found me. I didn't expect them to come after me, but they had. Ginny landed beside where I lay, unconscious, and I threw myself over her to shield her from the red wolves that stalked into the room on their hind legs. Peter stood in the doorway. Peter, alpha of the Rothschilds, a tranquilizer gun in his hand.

Even worse, Jules was there, too. I recognized her instantly: curly dirty-blonde hair, firm little figure. She was only a few inches higher than five feet and, even so, she was strong. She'd had to quit rugby after she'd broken the clavicle of a girl twice her size.

The wolves came towards me. I didn't know what to do. I didn't have the instinct for this sort of thing. They grabbed my arms with their padded hands, hauling me to my feet. Naked, I shivered.

Lamplight glinted off Peter's glasses as he scanned the room. He stroked a hand along his short grey beard and motioned to the wolves.

They pulled me along after him. One of them stooped and lifted Ginny, throwing her over its shoulder. Peter rummaged through Ginny's satchel until he found her cell phone.

"What are you doing?" I demanded.

"Breaking up your little love nest," Jules said, arms crossed. "Is this who you left me for?"

My nostrils flared. "I left you because you used me," I said.

Jules jabbed a finger at my unconscious lover. "Like *she* isn't? You're just an infected to her." She stepped forward and pain registered on her face. "I'm sorry. I never should have let Peter talk you into this. But once this is over, we'll talk."

"Once *what* is over?" A chill crept up my spine as I watched the other wolf carry Ginny out the door. I struggled but the wolves manhandled me to a less mobile position. "What are you doing to her?"

"As much as I'd like to, I'm not doing anything. But, one way or another, we take the Seeonee territory tonight." She sniffed at me. "You've already changed."

"If you hurt her, I'll—"

"You'll what?" Jules raised her eyebrows and spread her arms, inviting me to explain. "You'll what, Claire? Kill us all?" She stepped forward and touched my chin with her fingertips. "Don't you see how they planned to use you?"

I did. Ginny had come clean with me about that. But there was no way Jules could know. "You're lying," I said.

"Why would I lie to you?" Her hand moved from my chin and stroked my cheek.

I turned my head away from her reach. "I don't know what you're talking about."

"Then you're a bigger fool than Peter thought," she said and took a step back. "The Seeonee were going to use you for murder and let the community kill you for it."

I blanched. She *did* know. But how?

I didn't have time to think about it. Jules pulled a hypodermic out of her pocket and removed its plastic sleeve. The wolves tightened their grip on my arms and one grabbed a fistful of my hair. Another held out my wrist.

The wolf inside my head snarled. "What is that?"

"Another cocktail, better than the last batch," she said.

She came at me with the needle but I struggled. The claws in my hair tightened and pain lanced up the back of my spine. Jules grabbed my face and brandished the needle in my field of vision.

"You can hold still and let me administer this," she said with an undercurrent of a lupine growl, "or you can keep up the shenanigans and I'll jam it straight into your tear duct. Which will it be?"

Terrified, I held still. She grabbed my wrist, tapped the veins there with the back of her fingernail, and administered the sharp prick. The fluid filled me like ice water.

Tingling followed the numbness and the wolf howled inside my head, trying to claw its way out. I started to black out, but shook my head violently to clear my vision. The change was coming again, this time spurred by the drug. "Why are you doing this!"

Jules waggled the empty syringe at me. "Test subject."

My skin crawled and my shoulders already ached with the phantom pain of last night's disjointing. My legs faltered and the red wolves dragged me along as they followed Jules out of the apartment. I wanted to vomit. My head spun. Tingling spread to the rest of my limbs, my mouth watered and my vision tunneled. I couldn't think straight.

Next thing I knew, I was dropped on my knees in the gravel of the driveway. I did retch and felt a little better afterwards, except the drug made my heart race and spots clouded my vision again. I heard Jules's voice, painfully loud in my ears. "Did you make the call?"

The plastic click of a shutting cell phone was as harsh as a gunshot.

"Yeah," Peter said. "They haggled over a rendezvous spot and barked my ear off. Pretty convincing, to their credit."

Footsteps on the gravel crunched like a coffee grinder. I wanted to cover my head but my arms wouldn't move. My shoulders popped and I blacked out as they readjusted.

"They'll come right to us," Peter said. I strained through the blurry vision and saw him crouch down beside Ginny. He stuck a needle in her arm. I realized there were more red wolves in the parking lot, perhaps a dozen.

Jules walked over to me, straddled me, and draped a loop of chain around my neck. I growled a deep, horrible sound at her and it shocked me that I'd made such a noise. I looked down at my hands and instead saw black paws. The pain and rage faded.

I was *conscious*. The change had come, and I was still conscious. This wasn't the same drug as before.

Jules tightened the chain and pulled my head up, but her finger pressed against the nape, under the chain, to prevent it from choking me. She bent to my ear.

"I know you can hear me," she whispered. I couldn't see her and I tried to struggle away, but she put a knee between my shoulderblades and yanked my head higher. "I know you can, Claire. So listen to me."

A car pulled up with a blaze of headlights. The doors opened and Mae got out, along with two of the Seeonee, who dragged out a shackled fourth person. He was a scruffy man, bruised and beaten, but he wore designer jeans and a leather jacket. His eyes widened when he saw us.

I tried in vain to sniff for Ginny, but Jules' quiet, urgent voice distracted me. "I told you I wasn't lying. I knew what Mae was planning to do with you because Peter told me. Just watch."

Peter sauntered to the car and, to my astonishment, kissed Mae on the cheek. He put his hand on her swollen stomach. "How's our son?"

Mae's hand covered his. "Doing fine, sweetheart."

"Peter?"

The voice belonged to the shackled man.

"Peter, what's going on?"

"I'm sorry, David," Peter said, putting an arm around Mae's shoulders. "I don't know what you expected from our arrangement, but it wasn't meant to be."

David hesitated, realizing the danger he was in. "But you said you loved me."

Peter smirked at the man. "You didn't honestly think I'd be satisfied with a human mate all my life, did you?"

I could hear David's panicked heartbeat.

Jules rested her other hand, the one that gripped the chain, atop my head. I thrashed but she was strong enough to hold me still. "That's the man you're supposed to kill," she whispered.

Mae appraised me with a glance, then nodded and asked, "How is Geneva?"

"Ready to wake up with a bad temper," Peter said. He glanced at his wristwatch. "When's the rest of the Seeonee due?"

"Any minute."

"Good. Get your perfume ready," Peter said. He stripped out of his suit. The two Seeonee that had come with Mae did the same. One of them handed her the car keys.

"Remember," Mae told them, "these are our new packmembers. We can't have an all-out war. Attack only the dissenters. You know who they are."

"Including the Donnelly girl," Peter told them. "Do whatever's necessary to kill her when she comes after your alpha." He put his hand on Mae's stomach again. "We've already got a new heir, combining the bloodlines."

I bristled. So, that was the plan all along. Unite the packs, but destroy anyone who didn't accept it. We'd *all* been duped. I snarled and when Mae caught sight of me she flinched. She spoke to Jules. "Is she feralized?"

"Yes," Jules lied. "She'll kill David like you want, as long as he's in her path when I unleash her." At that, the smell of David's sweat soured.

"Good," Mae nodded and turned back to Peter. "Good."

Howling sounded in the woods. I felt the immediate urge to answer, but Jules tightened the chain to prevent me. Peter bent beside Ginny, injecting her again. She stirred and started spasming.

Mae stood back as Peter and the others changed. While they shifted, Jules bent and whispered quickly in my ear, "There's some of us who want the alliance, but we're not satisfied with these two liars. When I unleash you, do whatever you think is right. There's going to be a fight either way." She hesitated. "I'm sorry I exposed you to this. I'm trying to make it right."

She stroked a hand down the side of my furry neck. Then she slipped the chain off and I heard her begin her own change, clothes ripping.

I did the one useful thing that occurred to me. I filled my lungs, reeled my head back and howled.

Seeonee howls responded. Closer now. I strained to listen and I heard them brushing against undergrowth in the forest. I howled again. A dozen grey wolves charged from the hedgerow into the gravel lot and bodies of red and grey clashed in a sinister fight beneath the brightness of the full moon. I couldn't tell which were loyal to the alphas and which were loyal to the packs.

Peter, a big red wolf with a dark muzzle, watched me. His fur twitched and half a heartbeat later he bolted for David, who'd been handcuffed to a parked car and was trying desperately to get away.

A small red wolf darted past me and hopped on Peter's back, biting at his face and the pair locked in snarling melee.

I ran to Ginny, who had changed and gnashed her teeth like she'd gone mad. The grey wolf was bigger than me. Her injured foreleg was still bandaged. I nosed towards her but she snapped at me and I backpedaled and then she saw Mae in human form. I smelled something foul and swiveled my ear towards Mae, hearing the hiss of aerosol. Mae was spraying something from a small perfume bottle. I bared my teeth instinctually at the rotten smell of vampire odor, but I was able to control my predatory urge.

Ginny wasn't.

She charged Mae. I blocked her path. I didn't want to hurt her but she snapped at my throat and got a mouthful of fur as I flinched away. I caught her on the injured foreleg and bit through the bandages; she yelped in pain but kicked me loose.

She rushed for Mae again.

I jumped on her back, letting instincts lead me, and clamped down on the back of her neck with my jaws. *Please*, I silently begged. *Please, stop.*

I held her with my teeth as the battle raged around us. Wolves stalked towards us but never reached us, either blocked by another dogfight or engaged in one by Jules' supporters.

Ginny raged beneath me like a grey hurricane, but I clamped down harder and prayed that she'd snap out of it. She was stronger than me but her leg was lame now and I'd pinned her.

I had no idea how long the drug-induced rage lasted. I tried to think back to the video recording of last night. It hadn't lasted long, had it? Seemed like hours now.

My jaw ached, threatening to lock up. Ginny settled down and I must have dropped my guard because she wrenched free and spun on me, black lips peeled back from deadly fangs. I wasn't quick enough. She bit down on my throat and rolled me onto my back. Her growl vibrated against my neck.

She had me. I closed my eyes and waited for the inevitable crush of my windpipe. Or was it the jugular first? I clung to the memory of last night's tenderness. I wanted that to be my final thought in life. Joy, not pain.

The sounds of fighting faded around me, as did the sounds of Ginny's growling. I squeezed my eyes shut. I'd saved her. That was enough.

Instead of oblivion, the jaws lifted and a wet nose pressed against my face a moment later. I wasn't dead. I squinted open one eye.

The grey wolf licked it.

When I regained consciousness, I had my jaws around a red wolf's throat. Was I fighting or asserting dominance? Not knowing frightened me.

The red wolf smelled like pine boughs and pumpkin seeds. *Claire. Oh, God.* I pulled away immediately and searched for signs she was all right. She seemed to be.

I scanned the area. Were we in danger? I smelled the Seeonee, but other wolves too and blood. Lots of blood. A large black-muzzled male lay bleeding out beneath the shadow of a parked car. A human lay slumped and bleeding against the car.

In the distance I saw red tail lights and heard the screech of accelerating tires. A horrible vampire stench was fading in a whiff of car exhaust.

Claire nuzzled me and nudged me to my feet, though my foreleg threatened to give way beneath me. She sniffed at my face and I smelled a mixture of worry and relief on her. She was a wolf but...but she seemed aware. She wasn't maddened by the infection at all.

One by one, wolves–all except the dead–shifted back to human form, the moon's influence sated for another month. When I shifted back, I wobbled and sat in the dirt, my head swimming.

Claire wrapped her arms around me and squeezed so hard it almost hurt.

Almost.

I sat in the waiting room of the clinic while Ginny got dressed in the medical wing. The doctors had checked her thoroughly; she'd been so pumped full of drugs.

Jules came back from speaking with the toxicologist and sat on the plastic chair beside mine with a sigh.

"Peter's dead and hell if I know where Mae ran off to. Her life is forfeit, but ultimately that's Geneva's decision."

"She'll let the child live," I said, and I was certain about it.

"David is still alive," Jules said. "Infected. But if he wants our drugs, he's welcome to them. I doubt we'll see the human backlash Mae and Peter dreamed up."

"I think I've had enough of your drugs to last a lifetime," I said.

She nodded, not meeting my gaze. "But that's what I can offer you." She reached into the pocket of her torn jeans and pulled out a prescription bottle of pills. "If you want them."

"More sedatives?" The wolf inside me bristled.

"No," she said and balanced the bottle on the armrest of my chair. "What I gave you tonight. Clarity of the natural-born."

"Thanks," I said quietly, not sure what else to say. I watched the others–Seeonee or Rothschild, I couldn't tell in human form–filter out of the medical wing. They all wanted to shake Jules' hand.

When we were alone again, she said, "Claire, I am so, so sorry for everything." She scrubbed her face with her hand, looking exhausted.

"Jules?"

"Hm?"

"Thanks for not letting me down." I squeezed her shoulder in gratitude and stood.

I went into the back of the clinic.

Ginny walked towards me in the sterile hallway. She smiled at me, that dimpled smile, and I couldn't wait the length of the corridor. I ran to her and threw my arms around her, claiming her mouth with a kiss. She wrapped her good arm around my neck and tangled her fingers into my hair, exploring my mouth with her tongue before pulling back, her pupils dilated in the chardonnay irises.

"Wait," she said, "I need to know if there's anything else left unspoken between us."

"There *is* one thing," I said, clasping my hands at the small of her back and sneaking them underneath her shirt's hem. "Rothschild pills."

"What about them?"

"Jules is going to offer them to infected werewolves who want to keep control during the change and I...I was thinking about taking them." I quickly added, "But I won't, if you don't want me to."

She gently tugged my hair in response, biting her bottom lip in a wicked grin. "What do I look like, some kind of snob?"

I smiled at that, biting back an affirmation I had once believed to be true. She pushed me through the nearest door and then we were alone. Once inside, Ginny lowered her good hand to my hip and pulled me against her. "You don't need my permission for anything, Claire. You're free to do as you want."

"Remember you said that. I don't want any objection when I rip your clothes off in about thirty seconds."

She leaned in close. "I love it when you leer at me like that. It's absolutely wolfish."

I flicked off the fluorescent light and let our hands and noses and mouths take over in the ensuing comfort of darkness. My mate's scent bewitched me and I breathed it in: cinnamon, woodsmoke, and a November breeze.

A WOLF'S MOON

Quinn Smythwood

"To every wolf their moon..."
Traditional opening to the oral histories of the
people of wolves; the werewolves of the world.

It was not a moon night. Not one that coerced him to change. Still as he paced the room it felt like he was a wolf dressed in man clothing. It was a scent that worried him. Like teenage hormones, the scent left him on edge, uneasy and unpredictable. So the werewolf paced, unsettled by the pheromones of a stranger.

Pheromones; a primal signal that crossed the bridge between man and wolf. Survival, food, sex...a bridge which rendered both beast. The stranger, unseen, had been a male predator on the hunt. Sebastian had tasted that in the air twisted through the mediocre palette of human pheromones.

It had been plain; the wolf had been hunting man-flesh. If you were wolf the interloper's pheromones painted a sex-scented interactive tableau, setting the bedroom as openly as setting the table. Seb knew the wolf intimately, but not the man.

A frustrated growl slipped out; the werewolf had deliberately impregnated the club with invitation, then with equal care concealed himself.

Cleopatra who had been standing at his side had sensed it only second-hand, reading Sebastian. The bodyguard perhaps had been a barrier, keeping the stranger from coming forward. Sebastian regretted that Cleo's wolf was one that she might put on or take off. Had she been wolf, he wouldn't have needed to explain, she would have smelled the pheromones. For now the mystery lingered between them and Cleo, he knew, would probe at it later.

Seb moved towards the inward-looking window of his apartment and looked down into the arboretum, a verdant square of ferns and fern trees. He could glimpse movement, even from the heights of the penthouse suite; between the trees the white of Cristobella and the black of Cleo, the cursed wolf and the enchanted. There was no trace of the silver-white that would mark Hadrian, the spirit alpha of the queer wolves of the city. Hadrian, Sebastian's lover.

Now, Seb needed him. Yet Hadrian did not materialize.

Where the spirit went was Hadrian's secret.

"Every wolf has their moon." Seb's tone sketched his own history, bitter in his throat.

Hadrian, you use me, let me use you for once.

He waited by the window, tempted to open the French doors, step onto the balcony and howl at the crescent moon. He could signal a symphony from the body corporate, their throats sounding to the glass ceiling above. He resisted. Movement was a temptation to pace and Sebastian was afraid it would wear the wolf through his skin. Even though he knew it was impossible without the right moon.

At last he gave up on Hadrian slipping through his walls. With deliberate care he inched his way to the bedroom and into the cold comfort that waited there. The sleep he expected to fight for came quickly.

In his dreams the interloping wolf was a shadow beside Sebastian.

"You're older than you seem," the stranger said.

The moon above was full and pregnant with his change.

"My moon is turning, you should step back," Seb warned, "I'm a lunatic."

"The moon bound wolf." The stranger was a voice and a shadow.

"You should step back," Sebastian repeated. The moon large above him opened her silver womb and he began to change. Only in the dream he split in two and was confronted with his wolf.

"Did you let me step back?" It was Hadrian, alive and standing just ahead of them. Seb's wolf caught his scent and lunged forward.

"You killed him?" The stranger asked.

"So he claims," Sebastian replied as they passed Hadrian's

remains and stepped into the bedroom in which Seb saw himself sleeping.

"I'm dreaming."

"Of a kind," the stranger agreed and his pheromones surged over Seb. They sank onto the bed together, the stranger a dark veil over hard, muscled flesh, built like Hadrian and for a moment Seb confused the two.

"Hadrian."

"No," the stranger rebuked. His hands running across Sebastian's skin were gentle. The kiss was lips and fangs; soft and deadly. "It is your strange wolf."

"Interloper." Sebastian played a brief internal tug of war, to push or to pull as the weight of the stranger reached across his body. Sebastian succumbed, not consumed by the animal in his wolf, but by the animal in his man. They moved beyond words, found the broken language that brought things together and shattered them apart and the climax when it came was cold and wet.

Sebastian woke panting and the room was empty but for the pheromones and the sex scented tableau of the dream; sticky and too quickly cooled.

Cleo joined him for breakfast. She wore a simple green dress with gold bangles up her dark bare arms and her wolf skin was around her throat, thick and rolled tight. Wearing it like that, she had a wolf under her flesh and her eyes were amber threaded brown.

"You going to tell me what happened last night now or later?" Cleo always assumed that her way would eventually fall into place no matter what the obstacles. She picked at a pile of heated-to-warm bacon, found a lean pink rasher and rolled it between the fingers of one hand before popping it whole into her mouth.

"Perhaps later, after you've lifted Bella's curse." His reply was meant to be cutting, but Cleo shrugged it away and in the same movement snuggled into her wolf skin. Her eyes flashed like an animal's caught in bright headlights; beaten copper.

"Later then."

Sebastian scowled, stabbed at a yolk on his plate and watched the yellow spill over the pink of rare meat. He avoided glancing up at her, though as always his eyes were drawn to the wolf skin. Where Cleo had purchased it was a small curiosity, but Seb had no intention of finding his own enchanted skin. A wolf's moon hardly ever changed. He could wear Cleo's wolf skin and nothing would happen until the night of the full moon when Sebastian would go away and a wolf would take his place.

"Still on your mind though isn't it? Share the burden. I won't tell...not even Bella." For a bodyguard Cleo had a single flaw. She talked too much. Still she spent all of her free time in her wolf skin with poor cursed Cristobella who never spoke at all.

"I'll whisper it in Bella's ear then you'll have something to talk about." He heard her drawing in a deep breath before she replied and realized that she was tasting his mood.

"We talk...the wolf skin understands." Cleo's words were clipped. He had struck his mark this time and regretted it. He looked up in time to catch her running fingers through the dark fur of the wolf pelt; nails shifting between polished pearl and black talons.

"Why are you packing wolf today? Fifteen seconds not going to be enough?" He spoke to change the topic, mend the bridge between them but also for the sake of his own curiosity. It was rare to see Cleo with her precious pelt unworn, giving her just enough wolf to heighten her senses and reflexes. Cleo's heightened reflexes meant more than in your average werewolf. She already had fifteen seconds–give or take–of precognitive head start.

"Hadrian's business, Sebbie," Cleo replied, relaxing into feigned indolence and searching out another prime piece of bacon. "Don't ask because Cleo won't tell."

Hadrian came as though summoned. The air beside Cleo frosted and Hadrian gradually took form.

"Sebastian...Cleo." His voice was strong. It was clear that he'd prepared for the day; conserved his energy. Phantoms weren't exactly dime a dozen. Even among werewolves it wasn't often that one saw the departed not departing.

"Good morning, Hadrian." Cleo rose, glancing at her wristwatch. "We're cutting it rather fine today."

"This one might go long, I needed the reserve," the spirit

replied, though his ghost greyed eyes, which only hinted at the blue they had corporeally, were locked on Seb. To the werewolf's heightened senses, Hadrian was flat; the only cue was visual. The instinct was always to breathe deeper, to draw the concealed scent from him; even Cleo with her wolf running beneath her skin parted her lips, nostrils flaring briefly.

"I called for you last night." Seb laid aside his fork.

"I know." Hadrian skirted the table though he could just as easily have moved through it. "I needed my energy for today, Sebastian. It's important for us. We will talk later." The spirit reached out an insubstantial hand, brushed against Seb's cheek and the fine hairs rose in response. "Now, we need to go."

Sebastian nodded and rose. He had dressed for the role, taken a suit from Hadrian's closet, pale grey and pin-striped with a powder blue shirt. He gazed into Hadrian's eyes as they came closer, a smile half formed and played across the phantom's lips and Seb imagined they would kiss–as he pictured it every time–before the ghost slipped into his skin and Sebastian went away.

If the moon claimed him one night of every month, then her hold over him was light in comparison to the days that Hadrian took. Still, it was the moon that irked Sebastian more and as he returned from his dreamless absence his vision swam with color and his ears were flooded by the cacophony of sound.

This was all wrong.

He jerked back into a chair and someone kept him from tipping it over. He smelled Cleo before he saw her. His questioning look went unanswered and she avoided meeting his eyes. Surprised he glanced around, realizing that they were within the club and that the air was tainted with the interloper's calling card...and that it was fresh.

"Yes, he's here." Hadrian was faded; dust motes on the air neither bright nor silver-white, but worn and faded.

He looked dirty, Sebastian decided and though he couldn't smell the phantom's fear, the years of being Hadrian's avatar had woven between them a fragile psychic link. Hadrian was too weak to filter what Sebastian fished from the ether between them and the werewolf flinched at what he discovered. Hadrian spoke before he did, a frail whisper directed at Cleo. "Leave us." She moved without a word, stopping some distance away that allowed them both to pretend she couldn't hear them.

"You weren't going to tell me," Hadrian chided.

"You never told me that you'd know anyway," Seb accused, but part of him wasn't surprised. His anger was quick and it burned away as swiftly as the phantom was waning. "You have been hunting him."

"Yes." Only something other than human could have picked out the voice between the music and clubbers. "He's strong…potent." The phantom was spent, it flickered. "Come to me," Hadrian said then was gone.

Seb knew he should leave the club, but he was reluctant to walk out on a mystery that even Hadrian had not been able to solve. As he rose from his seat a girl said, "What was that smudge on the air?" Her friends steered her away into the press of bodies that shifted across the dance floor. Seb ignored them. He moved towards the crowds.

Cleo was at his side before he had taken a couple of paces.

"Well now I know," she said, "And I hope we're leaving."

"You and Hadrian cheated," Seb replied, trying to focus on the conversation, Cleo's familiar, wolf-tainted scent, the vibrant green of her dress; anything but the interloper's pheromone enchantment.

"You cheated first." Cleo leaned into him, brushed her wolf pelt against his bare skin. A flare of power, moon and wolf and magic that grounded him, Cristobella and Cleopatra's scents surrounded him. "He's too strong, Sebastian…too strong for you." She didn't move to physically drag him from the club. Again she brushed against him, seducing him with the scent of Hadrian's wolves.

"Too strong for you?" he asked.

"It's not me he's after." Cleo studied the crowd, he could sense the tension in her body. "I'm not–" she caught herself, eyes locked with his own and they were copper "…his type."

He tasted the lie and it made him open himself again to the stranger's pheromones. It could have been calling any werewolf… but it wasn't.

He wants me.

Some might have thought this obvious, but that kind of ego didn't usually fit in a room quietly and Sebastian did.

"He targets us all," Cleo said and her eyes were hard. They reflected only the death Cleo would bring to anyone, anything that threatened Hadrian or his wolves. "We have to leave, Sebastian."

He nodded, leaning into her and allowing her arm to snake around him and draw him closer still. Breathed in the scent of her wolf skin, alive still and warm; flushed away the stranger's pheromones.

"Let's get out of here."

Cleo guided them towards the exit. Her fingernails were talon sharp and cold when Seb brushed against them and he knew she intended using them if the interloper approached. A dark haired man, young and beautiful, studied them as they passed. There was fire in his eyes but he carried no wolf inside. As he brushed past the atmosphere turned electric. Sebastian recognized the thrum of something supernatural and even Cleo cast a probing gaze in the man's direction before they were out of the club.

"Who was he?" he asked.

Cleo shook her head. "Someone new, not our hunting wolf..." Her tension melted only as she pressed Sebastian into Hadrian's white limousine. Following him in, she closed the armored door behind them. She locked it as though there weren't wolves who could tear it away and scoop them out. "We'll know tomorrow."

She leaned forward and spoke to their driver, an older wolf with greying hair.

Sebastian caught him gazing into the rear view mirror, jade eyes curious as the telltale scents painted a story within the confines of the vehicle.

"I'm okay." He offered a weak smile knowing that unease would ripple out rapidly through Hadrian's wolves. Hiding things from werewolves wasn't easy, which made the secretive interloper a very dangerous opponent.

And he wants me.

Cleo's gaze seemed accusatory as she settled back into her seat beside him and the vehicle began to move. She dug her fingers into her wolf skin, her jawbone flickering like poorly edited stop action photography. A garish fanged beauty, she looked out into the streets illuminated by neon rainbows and the growl that had waited in her throat all night stole out.

Hadrian hated being this weak. Drained of everything it was difficult even to perceive the world of flesh and blood. Around him glared the seductive light of an abyss that threatened to separate him from everything he cherished. Hadrian tried to focus on the circle that kept him from falling into the waiting light.

It seemed frail and fragile; a sliver of silver set into a marble floor. He dared not even reach to his wolves, to Sebastian, to borrow strength and know that they were safe.

You cannot have him.

Hadrian suppressed the anger he dare not give form, knowing it would rob him of precious strength. The strange wolf threatened everything, but had fixed on the one thing Hadrian would not stand to lose.

You shall not have him.

He focused on Seb, picturing the dark, sombre eyes.

Don't give in Sebastian.

Powerless, trapped in the silver ring, Hadrian could only wait for the strength to enter the world again.

Seb stepped from the elevator alone. Upon arriving at the apartment building Cleo had flung aside her green dress, bangles and shoes before the wolf skin swallowed her naked form. In silence she'd gazed at him as the metal doors closed, the elevator taking Sebastian up to his apartment.

He crossed the corridor, wishing that he still had Cleo's pelt to rub against and breathe in her wolf. Even the scent of their chauffeur, coiled pheromones of wolves and men–despite the insistent lingering sex–was more welcome than the naked air which invited his senses to revisit the potent summons of the interloper.

Entering the bare hallway of the apartment, Sebastian closed the door, leaning against it. His body did not shudder, but beneath the flesh his wolf was seduced by a dangerous yearning.

"Hadrian...where are you?" He didn't expect an answer. He forced himself further into the empty apartment, removing Hadrian's clothes as he did.

Hadrian?

He stretched out mentally for the burning star of his lover and it seemed a flickering candle just beyond the horizon of his senses.

The last of Hadrian's clothing slipped from his skin. Sebastian headed for the bathroom.

Under the hard, hot stream of water he tried to wash away the interloper's invasive presence. Sebastian owed everything to the werewolves that had gathered under Hadrian's banner. His moon left him at the mercy of his transformation. It had cost Hadrian his life and without the watchful, protective pack to guide his dangerous wolf, Seb would surely have followed. Hunted down; slain for the crimes of his wolf that knew nothing of guile. Or taken in vengeance by the angry progeny he left cursed in his wake.

Sometimes, in his dreams, he hunted the predator that had stolen his life and given him a cruel moon.

It didn't matter what a wolf's moon; their bite quickened in the blood a changeable heritage. It wasn't about the wolf that bit you, or people like Cleopatra wouldn't need to find enchanted wolf skins, they'd simply bare their throats. Still some people were willing to gamble and thought they could beat the odds. Others, like Sebastian, never were given the chance to make a choice.

Out of the shower, he left the steam for a cooler room.

Sebastian dried himself, still dirty from the desire embedded in the queer call of the strange wolf. It felt like a betrayal of Hadrian and his pack to stand at the window looking out into the city.

Isn't it more dangerous, not knowing the face of the interloper?

The question was valid, reasonable even, but for the lust still heating his blood.

He won't be lured out, Hadrian already tried.

He wondered if the interloper had noted a difference between them. Hadrian, broad and powerful, had the poise of a warrior. The spirit's strength—more than merely physical—radiated. Did Seb's more slender build exude a different, confident strength when it moved to Hadrian's will?

"What are you under the mask?" In the dark mirror of glass and night, Sebastian pictured the shadow of his dreams and recalled how he'd mistaken the interloper for Hadrian. The feel of him was revisited, hardening the fever that waited beneath Sebastian's skin.

He wondered if Cleo had joined Bella yet in the arboretum.

The trickle of energy became a small stream that gradually grew into a river. Hadrian drank from it though it was a tainted font, filled with the poison of unease. His wolves were on edge. It fed Hadrian, but the energy was unpalatable. He felt it as a storm that swirled round his essence, but at least he had power enough to seal himself away from the abyss. The silver circle burned.

He hung in the air, the fission of his own spectral light spreading an absinthe glow. Only the silver ring was untainted. Though the energy was brutal, bringing the spirit the closest he'd ever been to feeling ill since his death, it had restored his reserves. He reached for Sebastian and his essence followed.

It was not with the silver-white radiance of the moon that Hadrian rose within the apartment as Seb contemplated returning to the club; the light he threw speckled the walls emerald. Startled, Sebastian whirled round to discover the specter etched with a swollen green nimbus.

"Hadrian, what..." he trailed off.

Does the spirit grow ill...is this his suit of envy?

"You're here." Hadrian's voice was staccato but the relief was evident. The softening of his features as fears were quelled lessened the stark effect of the jealous halo.

Knowing that it would seep through his mind when Hadrian again wore his body, Seb hesitated, bit his lower lip. "I almost wasn't," he admitted. "Too dangerous, Hadrian to leave this as an unknown; I–we need to know what...who we're facing."

"And tempted, Sebastian?" Hadrian couldn't conceal the hurt, it seeped through his voice.

"There is a chemical..." romance was on Seb's lips but he swallowed it and fished for an alternative, "...persuasion. It is not as if my heart were in the pheromones."

Hadrian studied him, nodded slowly but there were doubts still cast in the high brow. Sebastian's breath caught in his throat and it took him a moment to realize that he had doubted the spirit's affections for him.

He felt guilt like his own betrayal had been consummated with the interloper.

"Hadrian..." He struggled to shape his words; reached out a hand seeking a contact that the spirit could not yet give. The fingers trailed chilled air, as he traced the defined cheekbones, imagined the hard-soft texture of the fine, trimmed silvering beard. "I could never turn from you." He felt it in that moment, the bond between them. Something almost forgotten, almost buried.

Hadrian flexed spirit muscles. He was beginning that alchemy towards an all too brief corporeality.

"I have been distant," he confessed. "I looked back at the weeks, the months, the years; I saw how little I've given." A wave of chilled air breathed out from him. "You wouldn't know...don't know that I could stand losing everything." The green light faded; white skin drawing into focus. "It wouldn't matter, Sebastian, but if I lost you...then, only then, is everything truly lost."

The admission twisted through Seb like wildfire. He moved closer to Hadrian, his own skin reacting to the chill with goose bumps. There was a resistance in the air where Hadrian's spirit was distinctly congealing.

"You're my ghost, Hadrian." Assertive, strong, unlike himself, his voice sounded forceful to his ears. "I don't stay for the empty apartment, for the moments when I'm the one who almost isn't there. You wouldn't imagine anyone would stay for that, not without reason?" The cold was plateauing, beneath Sebastian's fingers the spirit was hardening to flesh; the sharp definition of Hadrian's muscled form. "In the beginning...it was only you and I, Hadrian and Sebastian," he murmured, "I miss that, but I don't expect us to turn back to simpler times."

What do I want?

The interloper flashed only briefly through his mind; what he recalled was only that the strange wolf had felt like Hadrian in the dream. "Just, build up a little energy to spend on me..." *once in a while?* The knots of unmet need, every energetic copulation without the afterglow of a tender embrace, demanded more; "... every moment you can."

"I died for you," Hadrian said. Suddenly solid–a shockwave of icy air–he drew his arms around Sebastian; body beginning to warm. A moment only his touch was glacial, like ice running over Seb's skin. Their bodies pressed together. The energy that had been drained in building Hadrian's pristine, pale flesh had temporarily cooled the ardor.

In that pause, Seb considered Hadrian's statement. It had only been spoken aloud between them once, he realized. Sebastian had never asked how, but he'd dreamed it every night at first, now intermittently.

I didn't want to know, too afraid of the blood and the pain.

Still, he had questioned Hadrian about his past, something his spirit lover had refused to divulge. He was Hadrian, was all he'd say and he was Sebastian's.

My ghost, my lover, my alpha.

Heat was seeping between them; Hadrian's body now generating the same serpent energy that coiled up Seb's groin.

"Was it for my sins?" He thought of the wolf that waited for the moon; bound beneath his skin.

Iron was supple in Hadrian, his arms were gentle for all the strength within the thick corded muscles. Encircled by these arms, Sebastian rested his head against the man's chest and breathed the washed out pheromones of his lover.

Hands, large enough to swallow many things in their firm grip, lifted Sebastian's chin gently.

"You have no sins that I could ever see," Hadrian whispered. Sebastian's response was smothered by the heat of Hadrian's lips and tongue. The embers of desire blew incandescent; flesh pressed together. The air grew thick with the mutual scent of their need; tongues darting.

Their maleness between them, hard cocks mimicking the play of lips and tongues, painted a gentle wetness that promised a flood. Sex was a wave that crashed over them; their bodies spilled across the floor and they made love.

In the afterglow, bodies slick with sweat, saliva and seed, Hadrian slowly melted in Sebastian's embrace. They lay silent, eyes locked, Hadrian's hand laid across his lover's chest.

In the final moment, the air sighed as it filled the vacuum, the spirit's hand clasped his flesh unwilling to let go. Ice, the touch lingered even as Hadrian vanished; a dream lover spent.

Drained himself, Sebastian would not have stirred till morning but the floor was hard and cold without Hadrian to glamour it. He rose and forced himself back into the bathroom to fire heat into his chilled body. Under the steaming water he felt better than a corpse. The interloper rose now like a dagger at his throat, a threat that made his wolf-granted hackles rise.

"Enough...it's enough now," he said and knew he would have to go. It was time he protected Hadrian.

"Dalton. Lucien Dalton." His hair was dark and curling. Eyes blue, but not like Hadrian's which were rich and royal. These were pale. They fixed on Sebastian, cerulean waves that washed over the bound wolf. The stranger, he sensed, held tightly onto that ethereal metaphysical tide. There was none of the chemical lust and romance in the air of the club that Sebastian had experienced earlier. He'd thought the interloper gone until the young seeming werewolf had appeared at his side.

"I wish you hadn't come," Dalton said.

Seb tasted relief. Still it puzzled him that the interloper would retract his invitation now, revealing himself so casually. Avoiding the mesmerizing gaze, he considered the wolf. The interloper wore black, tight against his skin, like the lace in Sebastian's dream. The cut of his body was overly familiar and Seb looked away, face flushing.

In that moment he spotted her, Cleo, back in her green dress, watching them from the bar with a hard set jaw and eyes large and brazen. Their yellow irises seemed more wolf than human, but the emotions that gathered there were not what you would ever see in an animal. She turned her angry gaze away from him and he felt like an outcast. Cleo had washed her hands of him, but if he did this right he knew he could win her back.

He forced his attention away from the enchanted wolf.

"I came to find you and tell you the same thing," he said. He wanted to know the reason behind the sudden change of heart, but to ask might give Dalton another impression.

I'm not interested in him. I just need him to leave us all alone.

A metaphysical storm had been brewing when he left the apartment, the entire building charged with tension. It had frightened him. Cleo was merely a touchstone of what moved through Hadrian's wolves. The storm would be devastating.

"I'd have left you standing alone." Lucien Dalton ignored his words, scanning the club.

What kind of wolf are you? Sebastian wondered.

"But you've already been noticed and he would never let you simply leave. I'm sorry." Once again the pale blue of his gaze fixed on Sebastian and the younger wolf felt caught in headlights.

"What are you?" The question slipped unbidden past his lips, while his mind still struggled to comprehend the meaning of Dalton's words.

Dalton's lips twisted into a sad smile.

"Forever wolf," said a new voice, the scent of honey and flesh and more; the hairs on Sebastian's arms rose as he turned to the voice. "A rare moon, it's not every day you meet an immortal wolf." It was the bronzed beauty that Sebastian and Cleo had picked out of the crowds when leaving the club earlier and Seb recalled the interest he had shown in them. The electric charge in the air deepened.

"Alistar." Dalton's voice was a warning growl.

"Alistar Sawl," the newcomer introduced himself, ignoring Dalton. "I was hoping to get a chance to speak with you alone, but... beggars can't be choosers." The air was suffused with Alistar Sawl's presence.

Nothing like a lover's quarrel. Sebastian recognized the taste of jealousy seeping through Alistar's pores; a spice that he could not hide from a wolf. He forced back the nausea of the energies that the man commanded and shook his head.

"I'm not the one you need to talk to."

"You are. I know Lucien and you are." Alistar's smile was sardonic, the sensual lips not so provocative amidst dark stubble.

"Alistar–" Dalton began and his voice choked off as the electric atmosphere rose an ampere higher. The air hardened like every atom was a pearl swallowed.

"Have you even thought about me, Lucien?" His voice was vibrant; it left nothing unaffected in its wake. Sebastian at last identified the font at Alistar's core; human and mortal bathed in the twilight energies that had been harnessed by his sorcery.

He's just a man with a whole lot of power.

"It doesn't matter...I've thought for the both of us." Alistar threw his arms around them, drew them together like a small coterie. His supernatural strength falling across their shoulders, a weight far heavier than his arms and neither bound wolf, nor forever wolf could deny him as he led them through the crowds towards the exit of the club. "Now it's time we restored things to how they should be."

Sebastian glanced back towards the bar, the effort a strain against the dark eddies of the sorcerer's power. An effort in vain; Cleo had slipped away and he was alone.

Alistar had a car waiting. There was something unnatural about their driver. With the sorcery thick in the air, making every breath a burden, Seb couldn't tell more. They drove a while, bricks and stone drawing them deep into the twilight edge of the city; the buildings became similarly burdened by twilight energies, impossibly ancient, impossibly solid. Then, they left the car and were drawn up stairs and into a grey building that prickled the senses like a cathedral, dust motes flickering the air. Alistar's strength was unyielding.

The heart of the building was empty. Death had cohabitated the space with the honey and flesh scent of Alistar Sawl, as well as the twilight electricity that still webbed the air and the ground. Seb could feel his heart lurch to a different beat, a rhythm that unsettled him and set his wolf to wildly gnawing at his insides; slashes of sharp agony that felt like the onset of a transformation. The echoes of their footfalls across the tiled floor were swallowed.

As they were led towards the pool of moonlight that spilled across Alistar's altar, a rude thing of inelegant metal, Sebastian forced himself to reach beyond the twilight electricity. His senses felt the strain, resisted against the abuse but the scents sharpened, at a cost. It felt like a blow to his nose. He could tell that Alistar had not held the abandoned building long despite the pervasiveness of his presence. The darker scent, the death that shrouded the air, was no ordinary perfume. It was unnatural and Sebastian could only wonder at what the sorcerer had brought here.

The altar, as they closed on it, was coldly familiar; an operating table.

"Here is where I leave you, Lucien." Alistar pointed to a place on the moonlight's edge and Seb made out a dark circle etched into the floor; a binding circle.

Dalton resisted; his muscles bunching beneath the skin; chest straining as though he struggled against a monster. It was only the truth Seb realized, even if the struggle was internal. For a moment, the air was solid and neither of them could breathe. Dalton, driven by the sorcerer's will, stepped into the circle and the war was lost.

"Don't worry, Lucien. It's not forever." Alistar drew Seb into the moonlight and his wolf gave a silent howl that nevertheless reverberated through his core. If only the moon above had been full, but then Sebastian wasn't sure that would give him any greater leverage. Alistar forced him onto the steel operating table. His hands brushed over channels where blood might soon be flowing, his blood. There was a whimper in his throat and a growl, but neither could emerge with Alistar's twilight airs smothering them.

Lucien Dalton's pale blue eyes, bright in the half shadows, watched as Alistar completed securing Sebastian to the table. The sorcerer used straps of leather which told Sebastian that he had the measure of his wolf, knew that it could not emerge.

In his binding circle, Dalton trembled and his hands grew

talons. He tried for a full transformation but all that happened was that the chamber reverberated with the breaking and re-knitting of bone and Alistar pursed his lips in displeasure.

"There'll be plenty of noise soon enough," the sorcerer said. "Until then we can either talk, Lucien, or you can howl uselessly at the walls."

Dalton's talons remained. His features were hard, but could not conceal from Seb the scent of his despair.

The irony that lay in the binding circle mocked both prisoners; take only a small step and one was free...but the circle forbade such a move. Without help Lucien Dalton and all his supernatural power was like a battery connected to a void. Sebastian could barely move, the weight of sorcery laid across him made it difficult even to breathe. Black motes swam before his vision.

The last leather strap was buckled tightly into place, pinching Seb's left wrist in a vice-like grip. The sorcerer examined his handiwork before the air softened, as he withdrew power. He stood a little taller and Seb felt a small sliver of hope; Alistar had limits.

Still, his power had proven enough. Sebastian barely had the strength to test the leather straps.

"It's the third one, Lucien. You can't deny it begins to look like a collection." Alistar was calm, despite his jealous fever. Seb strained against his bonds until weakness seeped through his muscles. He began to wonder if the last thing he saw would be the sorcerer above him or the interloper wrapped in shadow and bound in an invisible cage.

"And what is it you think you're collecting, Alistar?" Dalton asked.

"I'm not–" Alistar began then paused. A hint of irritation swept away, control so swiftly restored. "Our collection if you want, Lucien. The hearts you've claimed, I've only gathered. You do like beautiful things." Alistar looked down at his captive. He trailed a finger down Seb's forehead, across the bridge of his nose and the softness of his lips down the exposed throat and chest; breaking buttons with energies not exerted by the delicate path of his finger. Once more Seb's skin goose fleshed, but there was no erotic aftermath; just fear that lodged in his throat.

"Young and beautiful." Alistar stopped his finger inches before Sebastian's crotch then brushed aside the silk of the shirt. The buttons fell like cannon balls to the floor. Sebastian and Dalton flinched at their impact.

"Really, I'm sparing him the moment you cast the aged husk aside."

"I never cast anyone aside, Alistar." Dalton's voice was soft.

"That is not true. I aged and you left, Lucien. You can't deny that." The anger was there in scent, tangled with honey and flesh. Yet the voice was cool and the sorcerer's smooth hands caressing Seb's chest were not trembling. Above all, this control frightened Sebastian. "A discarded husk you thought me, but…things that are lost I discovered could be regained."

"I never left you. You left, Alistar. Jealous of my youth, afraid of your age, you turned away. You stole the first heart from me, Alistar, just as you stole the second." Hurt wafted from the trapped wolf and Sebastian wished that Alistar Sawl had wolf senses to taste it. Lucien Dalton had loved unconditionally…once.

A silence, the sorcerer affected for the first time by Dalton's words and Sebastian dared hope.

"You moved on, Lucien. I knew you would, it was what you wanted…you wanted me to leave, take away the faded beauty that no longer matched the happy photographs." Alistar stepped towards Dalton. "Look at me, I found it again…the beauty of my youth." His body and pheromones said more; he had expected Dalton to wait for him. He had expected Dalton to be beguiled once more by beauty. Sebastian's hope flickered away; Alistar would not turn his course. In his twisted view of the world, value was skin deep.

"No, Alistar." Dalton locked eyes with Sebastian briefly, the power wrapped within him made contact with the bound wolf. Seb's wolf howled. It tore at flesh but they both knew that every wolf's moon was set. Still, it seemed Dalton had tried to change it and as a result, Sebastian could only clench his teeth, his body under assault from within. So, while Dalton's voice was clear, the words were difficult for Seb to understand. "You lost your beauty. It never lay in your youth."

The failed transformation waned, the wolf subsided and Seb drew in a small breath of relief; released it in a sigh.

Alistar stood frozen, but this time Sebastian could spare no hope. Logic was not something the sorcerer was open to. There was a madness there, not yet fully revealed.

"Listen, Lucien. Listen to my heart." Alistar's voice was a command, it coerced and both werewolves could only comply. They listened and slowly discerned it. Two hearts beating as one, Alistar Sawl's small but growing collection.

Dalton howled.

"You can't turn away from all my hearts, Lucien," Alistar said. He withdrew from Seb's line of sight and reappeared at his side. Again that soft, gentle touch was on Seb's chest; seeking out the now frantic beating of his heart. "How many hearts will I need before you'll love me forever?"

Hadrian! Hadrian! Sebastian howled. The sorcerer was monstrous; even the werewolf within quailed.

"What have you become, Alistar?" Dalton's hands–human and powerless–were fists, white with the force of his exertion. He tried to buy time.

"Beautiful, young," Alistar replied. "It didn't have to be hearts to regain that youth, but it was poetic. Now, I'm eternally young." He paused, smiled like a wolf with lips parted. "And perfect for you, Lucien." His hand lay above Sebastian's heart, the fingers rapping along to the beat. "You know it's what you've wanted and sought, for so very long." It was clear Alistar Sawl was certain he had the key that could break through any armor that stood between him and the forever wolf.

Sebastian, able to taste the truth in both men, knew that on some level the sorcerer was right. Dalton, however, still railed against the naked, ugly truth.

"I could never, Alistar. Never. Never. Please, Alistar...please." His eyes darted between victim and predator.

A sound, so faint that were it not for his wolf hearing, Sebastian would have missed it, drew his attention to the dark. It was unmistakable, a door had opened.

Hadrian?

"You can, Lucien," Alistar was saying, oblivious to the event.

Sebastian. A whisper in Seb's mind, a frail thread; Hadrian was powerless even to manifest. *Sebastian.* The despair was palpable in the voice that seeped through his mind. It was not Hadrian that had breached the sorcerer's fortress.

"You will." Alistar's fingers pressed into flesh. Pain shot through Sebastian's chest; the twilight energies rose up, snapped and crackled; raised the hairs on his body. The pressure around his heart grew and black motes danced like approaching angels come for him.

Sebastian! Hadrian's howl was stronger; Seb could almost feel him reaping the black storm that had brewed around the apartment building; feel it infecting the spirit wolf.

"Alistar, stop!" Dalton's voice was filled with his own cerulean power. The fingers paused, but the sorcerous energies did not dissipate.

"You cannot change this, Lucien." Alistar loomed large across Sebastian's vision, leaning forward to gaze at the forever wolf. "What was it you said? Every wolf has their moon...and every sorcerer has their path."

Seb heard the click of talons on the tiled floor and the muted slap of naked skin. His vision clouded by darkening angels, he perceived at first only shadows and the copper flash of wolven eyes.

Cleo?

Perhaps the angel-motes drew back, or Sebastian's mind simply colored the missing pieces; his vision cleared a little and the dark skin of Cleopatra glowed in the shadowed hall. Naked, she moved towards him, her wolf skin in her hands and the white of Cristobella at her side. Already Cleo was drawing her skin about her, the enchantment spilling across her mocha skin.

Alistar's fingers sank into Sebastian's chest. Cristobella leapt. She crashed into Dalton and the binding spell broke.

Cleopatra flowed into her black wolf, her voice loosed in a howl that filled the chamber. Sebastian felt the fingers retreat.

Dalton, freed, gave a cry of victory; his gaze locking with Seb's, the cerulean went violet as he unstoppered his moon. The wolf that emerged was golden, his clothes shredding like black confetti.

Three wolves closed on Alistar Sawl.

"You can't stop the inevitable; you can't keep me away forever,

Lucien." Faced by three werewolves, Alistar's calm remained unbroken. Sebastian twisted–gasping at the pain–to face the sorcerer. The twilight energies pulsed out, a wall of force that reached out to hold back the advance of the wolves. Christobella's growl came soft, grew strong and was joined first by Cleo and then by Dalton. Alistar's eyes narrowed. A jeweled bead trickled down his face as the exertion proved too great. His energies collapsed and a black wolf leap over Sebastian as Cleo, snarling, went for Alistar's throat. Bella was a white streak, dashing forward beneath the steel surgery table. The coppery scent of blood curdled the air, but Alistar Sawl did not scream; his scent only grew stronger and honey mingled with raw power. The wolves were flung back, their bodies–ebony and ivory–targeted to the leaping gold of Lucien Dalton.

Alistar, bloodied and pale stood as though the attack had been ineffectual; his eyes darkening, his body twisting; transforming. Wings grey and ribbed with black burst from his back.

"There are many things one can do with a heart, Lucien," Alistar said as a black nimbus enveloped him. The wounds on his arms from the werewolves' bites closed. "Especially when one has the heart of something not quite human."

Sebastian wondered at the nature of the second heart within Alistar Sawl's chest.

The wings beat, a gust of wind carried the scent of honey and flesh through the air. Then talons, dark and thick grew from Alistar's fingers and grey fur sprouted across his arms. Before his jaws twisted into a muzzle and deformed his beautiful face, Sebastian read the confusion that bloomed there.

"Werewolf bite..." His voice was weak. He did not know what a bite from Cleo's wolf would bring, her nature was in enchantments and the wolf skin, but Bella's bite was certain to carry the moon's curse. What Alistar would become was now beyond the control of either of his hearts.

His clothing tore, peeled from his body like shedding skin as the corruption of wolf and other blazed through him. Alistar Sawl was shaped and reshaped. He found his voice and it broke between screams and howls, until the bones stopped breaking and mending. He rose; a grey gryphonesque creature neither wolf, nor human, nor other.

The three wolves inched toward him, hackles raised and teeth bared.

You spare him but hours and days. The thought struck out, cut through them all as Alistar Sawl snapped his grey and black wings; the jaws of his wolf unclenched, loosed an off key growl. The sorcerer lifted from the floor, hovered above Sebastian; cool gusts of wind oozing honey and the ripe scent of flesh. *Lucien, I have forever, but this bound wolf has only what I give him.*

A talon lashed down and clashed in the air against a dark black fist. Hadrian, the storm enfleshed, was there. He was dark, Nubian, a death god and his head was wolf and snarling.

You haven't saved him either. Alistar beat his wings; gave a sharp, high shriek that shattered the skylight above.

Hadrian flung himself across Sebastian as the rain of glass cut the air. When Hadrian rose, the sky was empty.

Alistar Sawl was gone.

Hadrian, skin still dark but head no longer that of a wolf, unstrapped Sebastian as Cleo and Dalton shifted back from their own furred forms.

"It was foolish to leave, Sebastian," Hadrian said, his eyes still deep, rich blue against the black polished marble of his skin. "We have to get you home."

Cleopatra joined them, her wolf skin wrapped round her throat as though she were not naked. "What about him?" She threw a dark glance in Dalton's direction.

"He'll be coming with us," Hadrian replied. There was a moment's pause as he studied the forever wolf. Then his eyes dropped back to Sebastian and love glimmered there.

"The car is out front," Cleo murmured.

"Alistar's driver?" Sebastian asked, recalling the shado-wed figure that had not spoken, not even glanced back during their journey in the car.

"The sorcerer's chauffeur did not linger once you were escorted from the car, Sebbie," Cleo said. "I don't know where he went...but we'll find out." She touched his forehead, her brow crinkled in concern before she turned away, towards Lucien Dalton. "Don't give me a reason," she told him, voice clipped. Bella growled softly.

"I won't. You're taking me where I want to go."

"Make no mistake, we're not welcoming you as a friend," Hadrian said. "We have some questions for you."

Lifting Sebastian from the table, Hadrian held him to his chest. It felt warm and safe and the scent that was Hadrian lay faint beneath the honey and blood and violence of Alistar's temple. Seb breathed it in.

From the corner of his vision, Dalton was gestured forward by Cleo; Cristobella falling into place so that between them, Hadrian's wolves had the interloper hedged in. Dalton caught his gaze.

"I meant what I said." Sebastian's voice was hoarse. "I wish you hadn't come. I don't want you. I don't need you." He leaned into Hadrian's arms, rested his head against a strong shoulder.

The forever wolf smiled.

"I won't give up so easily," Dalton replied. His eyes flicked between Seb and Hadrian, studying them both.

Hadrian glanced up at the broken skylight. "You're not the one we're worried about."

He carried Sebastian away. Lucien Dalton, Cleo and Bella came after.

BIOGRAPHY

Queer Wolf Contributors

Naomi Clark lives in Cambridge, UK, and has been writing stories ever since she learned to write. Although werewolf fiction is her true love, she also dabbles with angels, demons, and the occasional vampire. You can find out more at http://violetcorona.blogspot.com

Laramie Dean is a recent transplant to Denver, Colorado, after finishing his PhD in Playwriting with a focus on Queer Theatre. He originally hails from the plains and mountains of Montana. When he was in 2nd grade Stephen King sent him an autographed copy of 'Cycle of the Werewolf' and he's been hooked on lycanthropes since.

Michael Itig is a pseudonym for Mike Laycock. He has lived in London and Stockholm, and has written for various publications including *The Pink Paper* and *Immunotherapeutics Quarterly*.

Ginn Hale lives at the foot of a young volcano, with two old cats and a perfectly aged wife. Her publications include '*Feral Machines*', (Tangle anthology), '*Touching Sparks*', (Hell Cop anthology) and '*Wicked Gentlemen*', which won a Spectrum Award for best novel.

Anel Viz a native New Yorker, now teaches at a small liberal arts college in the Midwest. His published works include a volume of prose poems, '*Lux Carnis and Our Acreage*', several short stories and '*Val*', a novella-length vampire story in '*Night Moves, vol 2*'. He is currently revising his first novel.

Cari Z is a Colorado girl who loves snow and sunshine. When she isn't writing, Cari is enjoying the great outdoors, wishing she'd brought a book and trying to remember to finish her to-do list.

Jerome Stueart is a science fiction and fantasy writer living in the Yukon Territory. His work has been published in Strange Horizons, Fantasy Magazine, two Tesseracts anthologies, and other magazines. As a teenager he wanted to meet up with a werewolf, get turned into one, and then have a wild hairy buddy to run around with.

ANDI LEE is a fantasy fiction writer from England. She has a BA in Creative Writing, and an MA in Research. She enjoys exploring sexuality in the realms of a fantastic setting; where limitations from the real world need not apply. She currently edits for webzines, writes her own newsletter and continues to write 'The Novel'.

CHARLIE COCHRANE is constantly amazed that she's a published author and can often be found looking at Amazon with an inane grin. She usually writes historical gay mysteries/romances–her Cambridge Fellows Mystery series began with '*Lessons in Love*'–so she's been delighted to spread into pastures new with '*Wolves of the West*'.

MOONDANCER DRAKE is a Cherokee author of paranormal lesbian romance. She's also a vocal advocate for civil rights and the responsibility of all people to take better care of Mother Earth. If you want to know more about Moondancer and her writing you can visit her at her website.
www.moondancerdrake.com.

STEPHEN OSBORNE is the author of '*South Bend Ghosts and Other Northern Indiana Haunts*'. He has also had stories published in such anthologies as '*Ultimate Gay Erotica 2008*', '*Hard Hats*', '*Best Date Ever*', '*Best Gay Love Stories*': '*Summer Flings*', '*Unmasked*', and many others. He lives in Indianapolis, where he can often be found trailing along behind Jadzia, the Wonder Dog.

ROBERT SALDARINI is a college professor, author, and consultant. His latest novel is a mystery entitled, '*For the Least of My Brothers*'. Saldarini has been a diversity and inclusion trainer for fifteen years with a primary focus on the sociality of minority cultures.

CHARLES ALAN LONG works full-time and spends much of his free time writing. He's had a dozen stories–ranging from sports erotica to superhero stories–published in a variety of anthologies, and one of his detective stories was awarded an honorable mention in a competition. He's working hard to publish his first novel and lives by himself in Ohio.

Lucas Johnson is a creative writing student at the University of British Columbia. A long-time fantasy fan and writer, he's pleased for this opportunity to indulge other fantasies. This is his first published story.

RJ Bradshaw was raised and educated in Trenton, Ontario. He currently resides in Saskatoon, Saskatchewan, where he founded a romantic greeting card company to showcase his poetry. 'Night Swimming' is his first published work of short fiction

Erica Hildebrand lives in Pennsylvania, where she writes speculative fiction and draws comics. She is a graduate of the Odyssey Writing Workshop, and seeks out bad movies for their camp value. Find out more on the web at www.ericahildebrand.com.

Quinn Smythwood would like his toast buttered on both sides, but until then makes ends meet working by day and writing by night, even on full moon nights. With his head set firmly in the clouds, speculative fiction is the only playground his imagination indulges in.

edited by
James EM Rasmussen edits dry financial, medical and legal material for a living, he's working on changing that. Creatively he was a founding editor of the well received 'Electric Wine' ezine which ran for two years.

Dr. Phillip A Bernhardt-House has the dubious distinction of being an expert on queer werewolves, with one of the only published academic essays on this topic (in *Queering the Non/Human*, ed. Giffney and Hird, 2008), and will soon have a book out that sprang from doctoral research, detailing at painstaking lengths the characteristics of dogs, wolves, dog-heads and werewolves in Celtic cultures (forthcoming late 2009).

QUEER WOLF

QUEEREDFICTION
Visit the website at
www.queeredfiction.com

Find out about our latest releases and read all about our forthcoming anthologies and titles. Find excerpts, release dates and how you can order these exciting novels from:

QUEEREDFICTION
out between the pages